Glo...

five Book S...

Surrender(4)

"Refreshing, unique, classic. . . . Assured narratives, deft characterizations and fast-moving plots are givens. Graham does it better than anyone!"
—*Publishers Weekly*

"Wonderful characters . . . brilliant!"
—Harriet Klausner for *Painted Rock*

Rebel(3)

"Magnificent . . . enthralls you with scorching sensuality . . . skillfully combines a captive/captor romance with a powerful historical novel . . . sizzles with action that never stops."
—*Romantic Times*

"Successful, sensuous romance."
—*Publishers Weekly*

continued . . .

Captive (2)

Runaway (1)

A Magical Christmas

"Heather Graham [is] the Judith Krantz of holiday fiction. Her story glides along with enormous authority."   —*New York Times Book Review*

"A wonderful ghostly holiday fable. An enchanting and heartwarming story . . . a perfect gift for the season."   —*Romantic Times*

And don't miss Heather Graham's newest contemporary novel of romantic suspense . . .

Drop Dead Gorgeous

from Onyx

Glory

Heather Graham

A TOPAZ BOOK

TOPAZ
Published by the Penguin Group
Penguin Putnam Inc., 375 Hudson Street,
New York, New York 10014, U.S.A.
Penguin Books Ltd, 27 Wrights Lane,
London W8 5TZ, England
Penguin Books Australia Ltd,
Ringwood, Victoria, Australia
Penguin Books Canada Ltd, 10 Alcorn Avenue,
Toronto, Ontario, Canada M4V 3B2
Penguin Books (N.Z.) Ltd, 182–190 Wairau Road,
Auckland 10, New Zealand

Penguin Books Ltd, Registered Offices:
Harmondsworth, Middlesex, England

First published by Topaz, an imprint of Dutton NAL,
a member of Penguin Putnam Inc.

First Printing, February, 1999
10 9 8 7 6 5 4 3 2 1

To Leland Burbank and Leslie Metcalf, two of my favorite people, with lots of love and best wishes on their engagement. Cheers! A lifetime of happiness to two wonderful people.

And to some of the folks at Penguin Putnam.

First, to my editor, Audrey LaFehr. Thanks for being supportive and critical, demanding and giving, all the things an editor should be—and thanks especially for pointing out my mistakes, frailties, and weaknesses—yet always having the faith to let me rework my own manuscripts.

To Marianne Patala—thanks for always being there, and for so many things.

To Genny Ostertag for all the little details.

And to Louise Burke, publisher, thanks for all the incredible support, honesty, and encouragement.

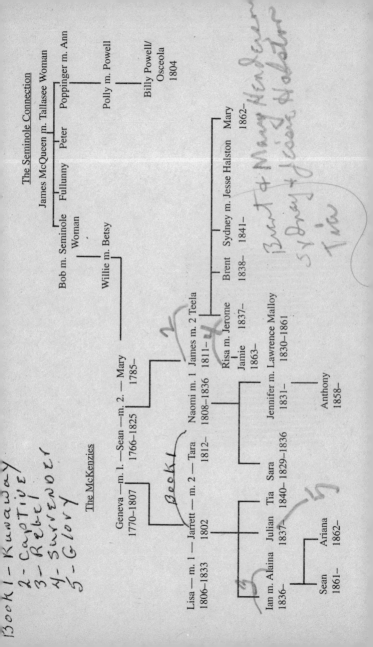

Book1 – Runaway
2 – Captive
3 – Rebel
4 – Surrender
5 – Glory

The Seminole Connection

James McQueen m. Tallasee Woman

Fullunny   Peter   Poppinger m. Ann

Bob m. Seminole Woman   Polly m. Powell

Willie m. Betsy   Billy Powell/Osceola 1804

The McKenzies

Geneva — m. 1. —Sean —m. 2. — Mary
1770–1807   1766–1825   1785–

Jarrett — m. 2 — Tara
1802   1812–

Naomi m. 1   James m. 2 Teela
1808–1836   1811–

Brent   Sydney m. Jesse Halston   Mary
1838–   1841–   1862–

Risa m. Jerome   1837–
Jamie 1863–

Lisa — m. 1 — Sean — m. 2 — Tara
1806–1833

Book 1

Jennifer m. Lawrence Malloy
1831–   1830–1861

Anthony
1858–

Ian m. Alaina   Julian   Tia   Sara
1836–   1837–   1840– 1829–1836

Sean   Ariana
1861– 1862–

Brent + Mary Henderson
Sydney + Jesse Halston
Tia

Prologue

〜

Dreams . . .

She knew that she was apart from the battle, she knew that she dreamed. What haunted her was that she had dreamed the dream before, that it had come, and it had gone, and it was coming again.

She was apart from the battle, and yet she could see the carnage, breathe the black powder on the air, hear the cries of the men. She saw it all as if she stood on a distant hill. She could feel the heat beating down upon her, the slightest brush of a breeze lifting her hair. She could see the battlefield so clearly.

Once, there had been cornfields. Great sheaves of green and gold, bending and bowing to a summer's day. Now those sheaves were shorn, stripped down by gunfire as men fought, struggled, bled and died. Brothers, neighbors, fathers, sons, honoring the same God; speaking the same language. Blue and Gray mingled in death; no color remained for the fallen except for the black of eternity.

She wanted to call to the men, to stop them from dying, and yet she could not.

She saw a long dirt road where troops struggled to hold a line. Upon a hill stood a tiny church. Men were coming forward to defend it. An officer wearing a captain's insignia was leading them. His blond hair was streaked with mud and sweat. He called out, his voice strong and powerful, beckoning, as he marched out first into the field of battle. Bullets flew; the men sought the cover of a farmer's stone wall. The captain, his back still to her, managed to take his troops into the field, despite the hail of bullets. The air was so thick with black powder that she could not see his face at first, even when he turned, looking back to a man who had fallen. An injured man, calling to him.

She knew the captain, even if she denied in her heart that it could be him. She felt the pain all over again.

She heard him shout to the others. And then he went back.

She tried to cry out; she tried to stop him. And for a moment, the briefest moment, he gave pause. As if he heard her, distantly, somewhere in his heart. Yet, it didn't matter. If he had known that death was a certainty, it wouldn't have mattered. All of his life, he had learned to live one way. Courage and compassion were virtues under God; he could not leave an injured man to die. There was no life without honor and mercy.

Ducking low, he hurried back across the field of battle, closer, closer, closer still to the injured man.

Then the bullet struck him. Dead on, at the back of the neck, near the base of the skull. Perhaps it was merciful.

It was a mortal hit.

For a moment, he was frozen in time, *life* caught within his eyes. Regret, pain, the things that he would never see, never touch again.

He mouthed her name. He saw the sky, the crimson, setting sun. The field, the bodies merging in his fading vision with the earth. What he saw was green and sweet and good, and what he smelled was the redolence of the earth, the summer's harvest. . . .

He fell forward. And the light within his eyes, like the light of that day, was gone. Forever gone . . .

She struggled to awaken. She had dreamed this dream before; she had lived the reality and the pain of it, and in her sleep she fought it, wondering why it should come to haunt her and again when it was past. But as life faded from his eyes, so light faded from the sky. Then it came back brightly; the dream began anew.

She stood on a different hill. And watched different men.

They marched in great, sweeping waves. Again, the field was alive with smoke, with powder, with the thunder of cannon and shot. A cry could be heard on the air, a challenging cry, a sound of pride and determination and a defiance of death. A Rebel yell. Despite it, she thought, the South was dying here.

She was confused, aware a new dream mingled with the old. She saw Richard, her husband. Again, he was dying . . . but then he rolled, and turned, and it wasn't Richard anymore.

This soldier's hair was dark. He lay upon the ground, unhorsed by cannon fire, thrown far from his mount. Then he rose, calling out to those who had followed him, ordering help for the dead and dying men. He ducked the black hail and dirt rain of the explosions still coming, raced through the barrage of fire all around him. He tied a tourniquet on one man, ordered another dragged back—announced another dead. There were so many injured!

He was too close to the battle lines, and suddenly bullets were flying as well. The clash of steel could be heard as the foot soldiers who had survived the barrage as they charged the enemy lines met in hand-to-hand combat with the defenders.

And that's when he was hit. . . .

She saw it, as she had seen it before. Saw the bullet strike, saw the look in his eyes. His own mortality registered instantly, for he was a physician, and he knew, and he started to fall. . . .

The field was suddenly alight with a burst of color against the black powder of cannon and rifle fire. Streaks of sunlight, gold and hazy, mauve, crimson, color like that of a setting sun, a dying day . . . life perhaps, was like a day, sunset bursting like a last glory, fading to black. . . .

She awoke with a start. The sun was no longer setting upon rolling hills and fields bathed in blood. It was just rising in the eastern sky, yet its gentle morning streaks touched the white sheets of her camp bed, nightdress, and canvas tent with a haunting shade of palest red. . . .

Like an echo of blood.

She had dreamed death once before, and it had happened. Richard had died. Death would come again. If she didn't stop it.

How? How could she stop this great, deadly tide of war? She couldn't, she couldn't, she didn't have the power. . . .

She had to stop *his* death. Perhaps she could warn him. Stop him. Julian? With his pride, loyalty, determination—

pigheadedness? *She had to! She could not bear this agony again.*

She rose quickly, washed, dressed, and emerged from her tent in the medical sector of the Yankee camp. Corporal Watkins, the orderly standing guard duty, was just pouring coffee. "Why, Miz Rhiannon, you're up way too early. It will still be several hours before the firing commences again, I'll wager." He handed her the coffee he had poured, shaking his head. "This must be mighty hard for you, and other folk, I imagine. I mean, to some Northern boys, the only good Reb is a dead Reb, but then you folks from the South who were against secession, why you know they're some good folks in Rebel butternut and gray. And cannonballs, ma'am, they just don't know the difference between a good man and a bad, now, do they?"

She took the coffee he had offered her. Her fingers were shaking. "I have to see General Magee, Corporal Watkins."

"Why, he'll be busy, ma'am, planning strategy—"

"Now, Corporal. Tell him I have to see him. And he'll see me. I know that he will."

Yes, General Magee believed in her, he would see her. What then? Once she'd baited, tricked, and betrayed Julian McKenzie?

He'd loathe her. But he'd be alive to do so. And one day perhaps, far in the future, a child would have a father.

Julian had been lying awake a long time.

He hadn't gone to bed until he'd been ready to drop. There were so many injured. And still, so early, he'd awakened. Morning was still in the future, yet the very first rays of dawn were just beginning to touch the heavens. Awake, he'd come to sit out in the open, aware that he had to rest, if not sleep, before entering into surgery again. He was glad of the night's touch of coolness against the summer's heat. The air was clean tonight, good, sweet. He needed its freshness. War was indeed terrible. He could not operate fast enough, he could not heal, he could not cure, he could only cut and saw, move as quickly as his limbs would manage. He dared not feel, not think, not wonder, nor worry. . . .

Yet he could not help but worry, and think about Rhiannon in his few precious moments of peace. Damn her, but he could not forget her. From the moment he had first seen her, standing upon the stairway, she had somehow slipped beneath his skin, and into his soul. Ah, but he was the enemy. She was a witch. Haughty, stubborn, far too proud, ridiculously argumentative. And yet . . .

God, how he wished she were with him.

No one had such a touch. She was magic. She healed. She haunted. And he was afraid, because she was with the Yanks now, as she wanted to be. Not in relative safety where he'd sent her, but near, perhaps, on this battlefield, eager to save the lives of her own countrymen.

"Captain! Captain McKenzie!"

Startled by the urgent call, he pushed away from the tree he leaned against and rose quickly. Dabney Crane, one of the civilian scouts, rode toward him, dismounting quickly.

"What is it, Dabney?" he asked, frowning.

"A message from the Yankee lines, sir. I was approached by one of their riders."

By day, battle raged. But when the fighting fell silent for the night, messages often passed between the lines. No one stopped them; every man was aware that the time might come when their own kin tried to reach them, and far too often, for one last time.

"My brother—" Julian began, a terrible lump in his throat. Was Ian across the lines? He never knew where his brother might be.

"No, sir, there's no bad news about your Yankee soldier kin. This has to do with a lady."

"My sister, my cousin—"

"No, sir, a different lady. A Mrs. Tremaine. She's serving with their medical corps, sir. The rider, a man I've met with now and then regarding other personal exchanges between troops, gave me an envelope, and I was given strict instructions that I was to give it to you, and no one else, and that I keep this all in strictest confidence. But I'm to summon you, now, quick, before the day's fighting can commence. She has to see you, sir, at the old Episcopal church down the pike."

"She has to see me?" he inquired, his stomach tightening. She had some warning for him. Or some trick. He started to hand the envelope back, unopened. "Tell her I can't come," he told Dabney.

"She says the matter is urgent, you must come, sir."

"Why would this lady think I would be willing to see her, now, when I am so sorely needed elsewhere?"

"Sir, I can't say. Perhaps you should open the envelope."

He didn't want to do so. He gritted his teeth, looking down at the cream parchment. He opened the envelope, and read the words.

"Captain McKenzie, I know how unwilling you must be to answer any missive of mine, but I must see you. I am relying upon the fact that you were raised a gentleman, and as such, with death on every horizon, you would not leave me to lead a life of shame, nor cast an innocent into the ignomy of a tainted future. Therefore, sir, I beg of you, meet me. There is a small Episcopal church down on the pike. I'll not keep you from your war long."

Dabney Crane didn't say anything. He studied Julian with intense curiosity.

Julian stared back at Dabney, determined to betray nothing but disinterest. Yet his heart was suddenly hammering with a fierce beat as he wondered just what was truth here. Had she finally ceased to deny what had come between them?

"Captain?" Dabney said anxiously.

"I can spare but a few minutes. Men are dying."

Dabney shook his head sadly. "That they are, sir. I can't begin to imagine those who will awaken this morning to die by nightfall. But I do suggest, sir, that if you have a mind to see this lady at all, you take your few spare minutes now. Colonel Joe Clinton from Georgia had agreed to meet his nephew, Captain Zach Clinton of Maine, at the river last night. Captain Zach showed, but Colonel Joe had been killed."

Every muscle within him seemed to tighten. What if he refused to meet her, and he died? And what if she were expecting his child, would she raise it with another man's heritage, another man's name?

Pride, he taunted himself. What it could do to a man was terrible.

"Sir?"

"I need my horse—"

"Take old Ben, sir. He's a healthy mount, and as fast as the wind. You must go now. Before the troops begin to waken."

And before it's determined I'm a deserter, he thought wryly.

"Sir," Dabney reminded him, "time is of the essence."

Julian hesitated. He didn't trust Rhiannon. But if it was a trick, he decided grimly, no matter—she was going to get what she had asked for. "I'm going immediately," he told Dabney. "Go quickly now and waken Father Vickery. Send him behind me, quickly."

"Yessir." Dabney smiled, delighted that he seemed to have brought off an intimate liaison.

Julian accepted Dabney Crane's offer of the use of his horse. Riding past Rebel pickets, he identified himself, and crossed the Rebel line into the no-man's-land between the Rebs and the Yanks. Approaching the church, he slowed his mount, and waited on a ridge where the trees still stood, remnants of a small forest all but destroyed by cannon fire. He watched, carefully surveying the area.

The church itself was on a spit of open ground, with much of the foliage and many of the fields around it mown down by the fighting. If there were Yanks surrounding the church, he should have seen them. Dismounting from his horse by the trees, he watched cautiously a moment longer, then hunched low to the ground, inching his way across the open expanse before the small church. Reaching the doorway, he pressed it partially open, and slipped inside.

She was there. She stood before the altar, her back to him, her head bowed. She still wore black. Black was the color typically worn for a full year of mourning—and God knew, she mourned her Richard! But for her wedding to another man? Yet, even if she was sincere in this endeavor, it still meant nothing more than words and respectability to her. She wore black inside, around her heart, and he hadn't the power to lighten that shade.

Still, it appeared that she had come alone. He took his time, watching, waiting, wary of her. Wanting to appear casual, he leaned back comfortably against the doorway, arms crossed over his chest.

"You summoned me?" he said quietly at last, and she

spun around, startled, alarmed, her hand flying to her throat.

For a moment, just for a moment, in the soft, flickering candlelight of the small church, he thought he saw a flash of emotion in the depths of her bewitching green eyes. Then she regained control, hiding whatever feelings had plagued her.

"You've come!" she said.

He shrugged, keeping his distance from her. It was amazing, but nothing seemed to mar her. Her mourning clothing was simple, as befitted her work in the Union field hospitals. She was slim, worn, weary, and still regal, stately, and very beautiful. Her hair was neatly pulled back, netted into a bun at her nape, yet its rich darkness seemed to shimmer blue-black with the slightest touch of the candlelight. Her throat was long and elegant; her fingers cast against it were the same.

"I repeat, you've summoned me."

She nodded, looking down then. "I didn't hear you come," she murmured. "Have you been there long?"

"Long enough. Are you communing with God? Or with Richard?"

She raised her head; her eyes caught his. There was fire within them at his caustic tone. "This is extremely awkward for me," she told him, her voice sincerely pained.

"I can imagine. You have gone from thinking you could convince me that nothing had happened to demanding that I do the gentlemanly thing."

"I believe . . . that it's necessary!" she whispered.

"And Richard has been dead just a little too long?"

"How dare you mock him!"

"I'm not mocking the dead, Rhiannon, just calculating the facts."

"How rude!"

"This is war, Rhiannon. I'm afraid some of the niceties of life have slipped away. You summoned me because you want something out of me. So please, talk to me."

"What do you want out of me?" she demanded fiercely.

"Well, an admission that something happened."

She gritted her teeth and her eyes touched his with a glitter of anger. "Oh, my God, don't you understand? I didn't want anything to happen, I still can't believe that I . . . that I . . ."

"Mistook a flesh-and-blood man for Richard's ghost."

They still stood the length of the aisle apart. He thought that she would have slapped him had they not. Perhaps he deserved it. It was simply hard to have been used as a substitute, then summoned as a social convenience. But if there was a child . . .

He waved a hand in the air. "Never mind. As you pointed out in your letter, it's a deadly war. I want my child born with my name—it is my child, right? You haven't been seducing other men in the midst of drug-induced illusions, have you?"

She stared at him with regal disdain, then started down the aisle to pass him by. "You never mind. Whatever comes in the future will have to come. Nothing could be so wretched as you—"

He didn't allow her past him. He caught her arm, and forced her eyes to his. "Where's the priest, Rhiannon?"

"What?"

"You summoned me to marry you. Where's the priest?"

Her eyes widened. "He's—he's on his way. I—I needed time to talk with you, to ask you first, naturally, to—"

"To set me up?" he accused softly.

"No! I—I—" she stuttered. Her lashes fell again. "Damn you! I need you to marry me." She stared at him again, fire in her gaze once again. "Do you wish to do it or not?"

He hesitated, smiling slowly.

"If you've just come to torment me, let go—"

"Marry you? Of course, with the greatest pleasure. How could I possibly refuse such a heartfelt request?"

A sound at the door sent him spinning around. Damn her! She so easily taunted him from the care he usually took. But it was Father Vickery who had come, the young Georgian Episcopal priest.

"I'm sorry I've taken so long," he apologized, nervously stroking his chin as he hurried in. "I wanted to make sure that I properly record the marriage, assure that it's legal."

"Of course!" Rhiannon said softly. "You were sent here, to help us, of course?" she queried.

Julian watched her. Had she been expecting a priest? Or

was she assuming Vickery had been sent by her Yankee cohorts?

Vickery cleared his throat. "We needed witnesses as well," he said, opening the door a few inches farther. "I really moved as quickly as I could, recruiting these ladies!"

Two young women had accompanied them. They both smiled.

"This is so romantic!" said the rounder of the pair. "I'm Emma Darrow, this is my sister, Lucy."

"Lovely, just lovely!" Lucy agreed.

"Thank you," Rhiannon murmured.

"Charmed!" Emma supplied, and giggled.

"So lovely!" Lucy said again.

"We must hurry and get back. The dawn is beginning to break in earnest, and God knows what horrors today will bring!" Father Vickery said. He caught Rhiannon's hand, hurrying down the aisle with her. "You stand there. I'll give you into marriage myself—you are the lady in question, right?"

"Yes, she is, Father," Julian supplied dryly, since she was the only other female present. If the whole thing weren't so sad, it would be amusing.

But Father Vickery, though nervous, suddenly seemed to have his wits about him. He began the rite of marriage, speaking very quickly, but clearly. When it came time for Rhiannon to give her vows, she stared at Julian in white silence.

He squeezed her hand so tightly she eked out a cry, but then, choking over the words, she spoke them. Clearly. Loudly. Keeping her hand tight in his, Julian gave his promise to love, honor, and cherish her, as long as they both should live. He used his family signet ring for a wedding band.

"I now pronounce you man and wife. Kiss your bride, and get back to camp!" Father Vickery said. He hurriedly started down the aisle to exit the church. "Emma, Lucy, come along, come along. Julian, you must hurry! Kiss the lady, be done with it!" It was a final warning. Father Vickery fled, but still, Julian didn't touch his bride.

"This is what you wanted, isn't it?" he asked. She looked as if she were about to expire.

"Well, one way or the other, it is done," he said briefly.

"But you'll forgive me; I really can't linger. Yet, I warn you. I pray to God you'll have the sense to keep safe. I may be in enemy territory, but I do have ways to make sure that you don't risk a child's life the way you do your own."

He turned away from her. "Wait!" she cried.

He turned back.

"Stay, just a minute. . . ." she whispered.

He shook his head. "I can't stay."

Quite suddenly, she threw herself at him. She came into his arms smelling seductively like roses. Her fingers twined into the hair at his nape, she came upon her toes, and found his lips. Her tongue teased for entry. Stunned, he found himself enfolding her to him, weeks of abstinence tearing into his system, and giving him a hunger for her that seemed to tear into his heart and mind. He kissed her passionately in return, holding her close, tasting her, savoring each second. . . .

Then vaguely, he became aware of the sounds beyond the church. She broke away from him at last.

Her words were whispered with lips not an inch from his own, still damp from the passion of their kiss.

"I'm sorry, Julian. But, you see, you would have died."

The passion? The *trickery*. He'd been right all along. He'd been the biggest fool in the world. She had lured him here, careful of the timing, keeping the Yankees away at first, knowing full well he would be watching for a trap. But now, they had arrived. Discreetly. Quietly. They were outside the church, ready to break in, to seize him should he become too enamored of his bride.

He wore a Colt in a holster at his side, and at times, he wore a dress sword as well. Not tonight, and not that it mattered. He was a surgeon, a medical man, not a strategist, and not the usual Yankee prey. And many Yanks would just as soon die as face a Rebel surgeon. But many more were probably willing to bear his touch if it meant that their lives be spared, or if a limb might be saved.

Bitterness swept through him. He wasn't going to pull the Colt, kill the men sent to seize him, and go down in a blaze of glory himself. They'd shoot him down from the front door. And he intended to live. Besides, there might be a chance to escape later without being shot down, if he kept his wits about him.

He pulled away from her, staring into her eyes. The truth was there. Every bit of it. She had planned this, so that he might be captured. She had thrown the kiss in at the last minute so that he would not leave too quickly. "You bitch!" he accused her softly.

"I said I was sorry!"

He caught her about the waist once again, jaw taut, ice seeming to fill his veins. He held her with such a force that she was crushed against him, her back arched, her chin high. "Dear wife," he promised her, "trust me, I will see to it that you are very, very sorry, indeed."

She shook her head, angry now at the way he held her—and that she hadn't the power to escape his arms. "You persist in being a foolish Rebel. I'm not your wife, and you will not make me sorry! That priest was no more real than my story."

So it had all been a ruse. But she was mistaken.

He laughed softly. "I beg to differ, my dear. That was Father Vickery, out of Atlanta, devoted to his Georgian boys. Georgians, being Florida neighbors, try to help us out and the good Father Vickery just happened to be the closest clergy when I was getting ready to ride out. You may not be expecting my child. But I'm afraid that you are my wife."

Disbelief touched her eyes.

The door to the church burst open. "Captain McKenzie! Julian!"

He knew the voice, and he wasn't surprised, other than the fact that a general could be spared at this hour to take part in a capture. He had saved General Angus Magee's foot when the fellow had nearly pushed it to a point when only amputation would have saved his life.

"General Magee, sir!" he returned pleasantly, still staring at Rhiannon.

"Julian, step away from Mrs. Tremaine and drop your weapon, sir!"

He stepped away from her, his eyes pinned upon hers. He smiled slowly, reached for the Colt, tossed it down. His stare didn't alter or flinch as he heard the men rushing into the room to take him. Yet, as they reached him, they didn't touch him, they hovered awkwardly around him.

At last he drew his gaze from her green eyes. "Good

evening, gentlemen. No, I'm afraid it's morning. Where does the time go? It seems to fly when so many are about to die, doesn't it?"

One of the men cleared his throat and started toward him. Julian shook his head, smiling. "There's no need for force or manhandling, my good fellow. Point me where I am to go, and I shall proceed."

"Just come along, Julian," General Magee said. His still striking, if aging, face, lined with pride and character, seemed to sag that night. He stood just in the entry of the small church.

"Aye, sir, as you wish," Julian said politely. "Tell me, since we have this happenstance to meet, sir, do you know if my brother is well?"

"Yes, Julian. Ian is well. But he isn't a part of this; he knows nothing about it—"

"No, sir. My brother wouldn't be a part of such naked treachery."

Magee stiffened. "Mrs. Tremaine?" he said softly, ready to defend and protect Rhiannon.

Julian had reached the general at the door, but he knew she walked behind him. He stepped out to the clearing. Yankee horsemen were aligned thirty feet from him. He turned back. Magee had exited the church, Rhiannon at his side.

He smiled, addressing them both. "By the way, your pardon, General Magee, but she is Mrs. McKenzie now. I'm afraid you and your men were a little late," he said, his tone apologetic.

Magee stared at Rhiannon. "My dear girl, is it true?"

"No!" she said, her whispered word alarmed.

"General, I swear to you that it is. Father Vickery will tell you so, before God. The lady is over twenty-one. So am I. The marriage is legal and binding. With witnesses. Ah! And in private, sir!" he said, lowering his voice so that only the general and Rhiannon could hear his words. "As I did the right, proper, and most gentlemanly thing, coming here at the lady's summons—and since I have become your prisoner—I ask you to do me a service. As an officer, and a gentleman. Rhiannon is in your medical service," he said softly, "be kind enough to keep an eye on her. She has a tendency to believe herself dreaming of her dear departed

Richard—then turning to the nearest living, breathing body—"

She stepped forward and slapped him. It was a hard, stinging strike. Hard enough to make him feel the blow straight to his jaw.

He lifted his hand to his face, then bowed deeply to her. He turned around and started for the horse that the Yankee's held for his use. He swung atop the animal. It was sleek. In excellent condition. He saw the opportunity he'd been waiting for. A gap in the Yankee line. Lying against the horse's neck, he moved his heels against its flanks. It leapt to life, bolting straight for the gap.

"Stop him!" Magee commanded. "What, will we be the laughingstock of the battle, losing a lone surgeon?"

"Men—" Magee began.

Two cavalrymen managed to fill the gap. It didn't matter. Julian needed only spin his mount and ride hard straight back and to the left. But when he swung his mount around and started pell-mell back, *she* was there, in his path, eyes on his. Tall, straight, as still as a statue, challenging him.

Not much of a challenge. She knew he would stop.

He reined in his mount. Instantly, the soldiers were on him, dragging him from the horse. One of the men swung at him with the butt of his rifle. A good, solid blow. Julian's head rang. The whack had been strong enough to cause a fracture, pray God, no.

He started to fall, the world going black. But he saw her. Saw her beautiful green eyes upon his. He reached out. She screamed, but he had caught her hand. And with what strength he had left, he pulled her to him.

And she came down with him. The world continued to fade. No matter. He smiled at her. Tried to mouth words. "I swear, dear *wife,* you will be sorry."

Indeed. Brave, bold words, especially when the world was fading to a total black. . . .

"He's unconscious, ma'am, if you'll take my hand. . . ." one of the young horsemen offered.

Rhiannon looked up. Nodded. She looked down at Julian again. His eyes were closed, a long lock of dark hair had fallen over his forehead. "You'll just never know, never believe, that I did this . . . because I love you," she whispered, knowing that neither he, nor anyone else, could hear her.

Cannon fire suddenly exploded far too close to them. "Get the prisoner up and to the field hospital!" Magee commanded. "The day's work has commenced, and gentlemen, may I remind you, the fate of a nation may rest here today!"

The fate of a nation. What of the fate of *people*? Did she have the power to change fate? She'd been willing to risk anything to change her dream. She'd tricked him, betrayed him.

He'd tricked her. And now, if he'd told the truth, they were evermore entangled in a hopeless web. . . .

Fate. Had it all been destined, from that first night when he had ridden through the foliage to the isolation of her house, and into her life?

Chapter 1

*P*addy MacDougall was dying.

Julian McKenzie carried his stalwart old friend before him on the scrawny gray nag with a show of courage and a sinking heart. If he didn't get the sergeant to some decent shelter soon, get the bullet out of his leg, and stanch the flow of blood, the man would almost certainly perish. Their ragtag troop of skirmishers, eleven in all including him, a surgeon, ostensibly a noncombatant, had ridden hard, zigzagging a good distance from their camp to avoid discovery by the Yanks in pursuit, and now, though it seemed they had eluded the enemy, they were far from home.

"There, sir, up there!" Private Jim Jones called out, pointing through the trees. "A house!"

The sun had begun to set several minutes ago and that, combined with a light billowing of summer's fog, gave a surreal appearance to the pine forest surrounding them—and the pathway to the plantation house ahead. In classical Greek style, the house boasted a large porch with six massive white columns. Its last coat of paint had most probably been white, but time and the elements had faded its pristine color to a dull gray that all but matched the dusk and fog. The forests and foliage surrounding the house had grown wild, and the place appeared to be abandoned.

"Thank God!" Julian breathed, blue eyes sharp on the facade before him. "Let's get Paddy to shelter, men. The place looks empty, but hopefully we'll find a place where I can make Paddy comfortable and get to work."

"Wait, sir! Colonel, sir!"

Julian paused, looking back. Liam Murphy, just eighteen—if he was telling the truth at that, and the newest

recruit among their troops—was anxiously calling to him.
Julian realized unhappily that all the men were looking at
him as if he were a military man, trained for strategy. His
older brother—the Yankee, he thought with dry amusement—was the one who'd gone to West Point. He'd gone
to medical school.

Steady nerves under fire and an ability to assume command when field officers had lain dead around him had
recently brought him a battlefield promotion to colonel of
their small militia unit, which frequently made him the officer in command. Due to the strange conditions under
which they fought—too few fighting men in a state that had
been stripped of the majority of her troops—he found himself in combat situations despite his oath to save lives.

Guilt often plagued him by night; survival instincts kept
him returning fire by day.

"I don't think we should go there, sir," Liam told him.
He was a skinny youth with earnest eyes as green as the
fields of County Cork, from where his family hailed. His
father had died at the second Manassas, his mother of fever
or a broken heart, and his three young sisters were now
scattered to relatives about the South. He wasn't bitter, and
he wasn't determined to fight for revenge, but justice. For
a youth he had a good head on his shoulders, and Julian
arched a brow, ready to hear what he had to say.

"Private Murphy, I have a dying man here," Julian said.

"I don't think that the place is empty, sir."

"You know this house?" Julian asked.

Liam nudged his mount, an old gelding that looked as
if it would fall over in a heavy breeze, urging it closer
to Julian.

"I've heard tell of the place, sir. It's said the folks there
were Unionists—we might be riding into danger."

Julian stared at the house. It didn't much matter who
had owned the place if it was deserted. And if it wasn't,
well, at worst, someone's old mother and maybe a mammy
were left behind. As small as their band of soldiers was,
they could surely hold their own against a few women.

"Private Murphy, I acknowledge your concern. But I've
got to find shelter where I can work."

"Colonel, we've got to have a few minutes rest as well,"
Corporal Henry Lyle told him, nudging his own mount for-

ward. "Liam, boy, we'll take care, but we were on the road two days solid searching out that Yankee depot, and now we've been running night and day." Lyle, a grizzled old codger of indeterminate age, solid and steady as rock, looked at Julian over Liam's head. They were exhausted and beaten, and shelter lay ahead.

"There's more," Liam said stubbornly.

"Oh?" Julian queried.

"A witch lives there. Or she did."

Henry Lyle broke into laughter, along with the rest of the men, Kyle Waverly from Palatka, Keith and Daniel Anderson out of Jacksonville, River Montdale from Tampa, and the Henly cousins, Thad and Benjamin, out of Tallahassee.

"Liam, if there's a witch in there, we'll burn her," Thad said, riding by Liam to ruffle the boy's hair. "God a'mighty! If there's a witch anywhere near, I'm praying she can conjure up a chicken or a hog. I'm hungrier than a bear."

"Don't count on any hogs," his cousin Ben said, riding on by him to reach Julian. "Maybe we can scavenge up some roots or old canned food. Doc—Colonel, sir—what do you say?"

Julian looked at the house, then at Liam, who was as red as a beet but who was still looking at him steadily. He shook his head at Liam. "Boy, I haven't got any choice. If there are any witches up there, we're just going to have to deal with them. Paddy's dying. I can feel his blood seeping through my fingers."

"And hell, if there are Yank sympathizers in there, it won't matter much, anyway. We don't have any real uniforms," Kyle Waverly, a young schoolteacher before the war, a graying philosopher now after two years of constant skirmishing, reminded them. He hiked a brow at Julian, scratching his bearded chin. "If there are any Yanks, we can just say we're heading on in to join up with the Unionists at St. Augustine. Who would ever know the difference?"

He was right. As one of the few militia units left to attempt guarding the state, they had started off in Florida colors of their own making. Time had worn away any attempt at uniforms. Mostly in the heat of summer, they wore cotton shirts and breeches, threadbare at that, and whatever footwear they could get their hands on.

"We'll move in. I'll talk when necessary," Julian told them. He nudged his horse forward.

They rode down the overgrown trail to the house. There, Julian dismounted, pulling the Colt he carried before hefting Paddy's unconscious body from the haunches of his horse to his shoulder. He motioned for Jim, the Henlys, and the Andersons to circle around the back of the house and for the other men to follow him. Carefully, he walked up the steps to the broad porch. A swing sat upon it, caught by the breeze, and it was easy to imagine better times, when moonlight had played down upon the nearby magnolias, casting a glow upon the dripping moss while soft breezes whispered by. The swing still moved gently in the breeze, but the foliage was overgrown and the columns were linked by spiderwebs.

He strode across the porch to the door, anxious to work on Paddy's injured thigh. To his surprise, the double mahogany doors at the entrance were locked. He backed away, then threw his shoulder against the left door. The wood shuddered. He kicked the door, and the wood splintered at the lock. A second kick opened the door, and he stepped into the entry.

To his astonishment, candles gleamed from polished tables in an elegant breezeway.

Like many an old plantation home, the house was symmetrical, with wings expanding off a large central main hall. As Julian stepped in, his Colt at the ready, Paddy over his shoulder, he came to a dead halt, surveying the place warily. The hardwood floor gleamed. Richly upholstered chairs were angled against the wall, along with a hall tree and occasional tables and two tall cherrywood hutches, all polished to a fine gleam. An Oriental runner lay in the center of the breezeway flooring, the midnight blue within the design matched by the carpeting up the staircase that led to the second floor.

A woman stood upon the stairway.

She was dressed in black—mourning black. She stood so still, unruffled and elegant, that she might have been a witch, a very striking witch. She was tall, very straight, dignified—hauntingly beautiful. Despite the somber apparel her lithe—yet richly curved figure—seemed all the more enhanced. Her hair, wrapped in a chignon at her nape, was an even deeper shade than the ebony of her gown, shining almost blue-black in the glow of candlelight and kerosene lamps. Her complexion was pure ivory; her features were classic. She stared down at him with bright vivid green eyes.

How long they stared he did not know. He forgot time and place, and even the two-hundred pound man he carried over his shoulder. When he spoke at last, he managed only an acknowledgment that she was there.

"Madam."

"Sir," she said, and her lip curled with cool contempt as she evenly suggested, "you might have knocked."

He had been raised in polite Southern society, and though he had spent several years under terrible circumstances, he felt his cheeks redden beneath her disdainful scrutiny.

"Sir?"

He heard Liam behind him, and he gave himself a mental shake, breaking the strange spell she had cast upon him. No spell, he told himself. He had simply been taken by surprise.

"My apologies, madam. You will excuse us. My—my friend here needs care, and we thought your place empty."

She arched a brow, looking at the human burden he carried. For a moment some dark emotion touched her eyes and passed through her face, but it was a fleeting shadow and it was quickly gone.

"My house is not empty, as you can see."

"Then, madam, we need your hospitality."

"For a drunkard?" she inquired quietly.

Julian gritted his teeth together. "No, madam, he is injured." He lost patience. "Ma'am, I'm afraid you can offer hospitality, or we simply must take it."

"And what else will you take?" she asked wryly. "The cattle are gone, as are the cotton and other livestock. And the silver."

"Ma'am!" Kyle Waverly stepped into the hallway to Julian's side. "We're on our way to join up at St. Augustine. Paddy here shot himself cleaning his rifle. Dumber than hell, but he's a dear fellow, I swear it, and Julian—he's a doctor—is just trying to save his life. Please."

"Rhiannon! It's all right—they *are* Yanks!" someone whispered.

Julian looked upward along the stairway. At the second-floor landing stood a second woman, this one a few years younger than their elegant hostess, perhaps sixteen or so to Rhiannon's twenty . . . plus? Yes, he judged, their unwilling hostess had to be in her early twenties. She was composed, regal, and serene.

Rhiannon. Something stirred in Julian's memory from ancient tales of Britain. Rhiannon . . . it was Welsh in origin, a masculine name when given to several princes of the old realm, feminine when it was given to a beautiful sea witch from folklore. It somehow seemed fitting for their unwilling hostess.

"My friend is bleeding on your very handsome runner, ma'am," he said pointedly. "I need somewhere to tend to him."

"There's a downstairs bedroom; you needn't bring him up," the woman, Rhiannon, said, and at last she moved, gliding down the steps with smooth elegance.

She noted Kyle, River Montdale, and Liam all standing behind Julian and his burden and nodded to them in acknowledgment. Then she swept by Julian, heading down the hallway and leaving behind a soft, subtle scent of roses. He followed her, glancing back to see that the girl who had stood on the second floor was hurrying along behind them as well. "Thank God you're Yanks!" she said anxiously. "My Lord, I've been so frightened. There are so many desperate folk here, you know. People who think Richard deserved to die, fighting for the North, when he was just doing what he saw as right. And have you heard what some of the Reb soldiers do to Yank women when they find them alone? Why, sirs, it's just terrifying!"

"Rachel!" the older woman snapped. She spun around and stared at the young girl, her eyes as sharp as saber points.

"But, Rhiannon—"

"Rachel, go to the kitchen and start some water boiling," Rhiannon said firmly. She met Julian's eyes, aware that he was watching her.

"I'll get the water. And don't worry, Rhiannon knows more about medicine than most doctors. Oh, sorry, I don't mean to offend you, sir; I'm certain you're a very good doctor, but—"

She broke off. Rhiannon was staring at her again, and she exhaled guiltily. "I'll get the water."

Rhiannon took a lamp from a table and opened the last door on the right side of the great hallway. They entered a sparsely furnished but impeccably clean bedroom. The bed was covered with a quilt, which she quickly stripped away, baring clean white sheets.

Julian slid Paddy from his shoulder to the bed and tossed off his plumed hat. Paddy remained unconscious, and Julian quickly assured himself that his friend retained breath and a pulse.

"Liam, my bag," he called. "And quickly, scissors, we've got to get—"

He started to turn, ready for one of the men to assist. But she was there, scissors in her hand, ready to cut away the makeshift bandaging Julian had managed before they had been forced to flee.

He didn't know what her training was or where her knowledge and experience came from, but the younger girl, Rachel, was right—she was certainly competent, more so than some doctors Julian had had the ill fortune to work with. She didn't blink or blanch at the horrible sight of poor Paddy's ravaged leg; she quickly cut away the bandaging and the remnants of Paddy's pants. Before she was done, Rachel returned with steaming water, excusing herself as she made her way through the rest of the men who milled awkwardly in the doorway.

"Men, see to the horses and our situation here," Julian said, watching the top of Rhiannon's dark head as she finished her task. "How many others are in the house—or on the property?" he asked her.

She looked up at him, her green eyes unfathomable. "Mammy Nor and Angus, that's all," she said.

"And they are . . . ?"

"Our servants," she said simply, looking back to Paddy.

Servants, Julian thought. She didn't say darkees, Negroes, or slaves. Servants. It was definitely a Yank household. He should know. Florida was a sadly split state. The third to secede from the Union, she was still peopled by many who were loyal to the old government. His father was one; his brother was another. They had many Negroes working at Cimarron, his family's plantation outside Tampa. But they weren't slaves; they too were *servants*. Free men and women, paid for their labor. His father had always been adamantly antislavery. Julian didn't believe in the institution of slavery himself—it didn't seem possible that a human being, with a soul, could belong to another—but he was also aware that an entire economy was based upon slave labor. Of course, the matter of economy didn't make the institution of slavery right, but suddenly freeing men and women to starve didn't seem the right answer either.

"Sir!" Liam said, returning, setting Julian's surgical bag on the bedside table.

"Thank you," he murmured, opening his bag, then turning to tend to the washing of Paddy's wound.

But Rhiannon was busy already. "Soldier," she told Liam, "take his shoes and hose. I'll tend to the cleaning."

Liam did as told, and with the younger girl at her side, Rhiannon began cleaning the wound. Julian hadn't managed to get the bullet as yet; he hadn't dared withdraw the minié ball without first being certain he wouldn't start a hemorrhage. Better to leave it than cause Paddy to bleed to death as they escaped.

But now . . .

He turned with his forceps to see that she had bathed the wound and doused it liberally with the contents of a bottle of whiskey. He stared at her, arching a brow. "Keeps infections at bay," she said.

"I know," he murmured wryly.

She was staring at his medical bag, seeing how devoid it was of critical supplies.

But he had sutures—made of horse hair these days but very serviceable nonetheless. And his bullet extractors were fine—a gift from his father when he had graduated from medical school. He found his best position and carefully felt the wound with his fingers, seeking the blood vessels to assure himself that removing the bullet wouldn't cause greater harm. He found where the bullet lay.

She was at his side, soaking up blood the moment it obscured his field of vision.

He found the bullet. Within a matter of minutes he had it removed, thankfully without damaging any major blood vessels. Paddy was a fierce old coot of an Irishman—he'd not want to lose a leg.

Julian threaded his surgical needle, noting while he did so that she was using her whiskey to cleanse the wound once again. He set to his task of sewing torn flesh. As he did so, Paddy began to come to, swearing and moaning, even those sounds accented by his native land. "Holy Mary, Mother of God, Colonel, but it hurts like all that's blessed—"

"Sip some of this," Rhiannon said, bringing the whiskey bottle around to Paddy's head. "It won't hurt so bad."

"Ah, but you're an angel, lass, a true angel," Paddy said. He gulped down the whiskey, staring at her. "Not that I know who in the world ye are . . . Lord! Colonel!" he shrieked, swigging hard from the bottle once again. "Will I lose me leg, Colonel?" Paddy demanded.

"No, I don't think so," Julian said.

"Bless you."

"But I can make no guarantees," he warned quietly. Wounds like this were never good. When infection set in, it was usually lose the limb or lose the life.

And sometimes it was both.

"Bless you, but it hurts . . ." Paddy said.

"Drink more," Rhiannon said, watching Paddy. She was almost smiling, and with the softness touching her features, she was even more stunning. "Later, I've laudanum—"

"Laudanum?" Julian said, staring at her. It was a supply he was sadly lacking.

"I grow poppies," she said.

"Who is this angel, Colonel?" Paddy demanded.

"A kindly Yankee widow who has taken pity on our small band of recruits," Julian said firmly, wishing Paddy had remained unconscious.

But Paddy was no fool. "Ah, and grateful we are, ma'am," he said passionately. "Still, have you a name, angel?"

"Rhiannon," Julian said, snapping his suture with his teeth, and staring across the bed at her.

"Angel!" Rachel suddenly piped in from behind her. "That's nice. They've been prone to call her a witch hereabouts!"

"Rachel," Rhiannon murmured.

"Witch?" Julian inquired politely, hiding a smile.

She shrugged. "I told you, I grow poppies and other medicinal plants. To some that makes me a witch."

"Ah," he said.

"Angel," Paddy protested.

"It's all in the eyes of the beholder, isn't it?" Julian queried lightly.

She didn't reply. She smoothed Paddy's forehead, then took the basin of bloodied water and left the room, Rachel at her heels.

"You're sewn, Paddy, but you lost a lot of blood, and you're very weak."

"I'll make it, Colonel. You got me here, you patched me up. I'll make it," Paddy said cheerfully. Then he winced and sucked on the whiskey bottle once again. "An angel. Must be an Irish angel—she's an angel with whiskey!"

"Get some rest," Julian said, patting his shoulder. "We'll stay until daybreak. Then, I'm afraid, we'll have to get on the road again. There's no help for it, Paddy. We're cut off from the rest of our own troops."

"The lady thinks we're Yanks?"

"An expedient lie Kyle told," Julian said briefly.

"Ah, then. I'll get some rest and not be such a burden when we ride come the daylight," Paddy said.

Julian patted his shoulder.

"I'll stay with him," Liam offered.

Julian nodded, retrieved his hat, and exited the room. He could hear conversation and followed the sound of it. Corporal Lyle and Keith and Daniel Anderson were seated at the dining room table, eating bread, cheese, and cold meat. Lyle saw him and quickly stood. "Sir! Jim, Kyle, Thad, River, and Ben are on guard. They've eaten, so now these boys and I are—"

"Having some supper, of course," Julian said. The meat was cold, but the smell of it was still tantalizing. He sliced a piece; it was smoked beef. Delicious. He sliced another, wolfing it down. He looked up.

Rhiannon stood in the hallway, looking in. He felt the atrociousness of his manners, then felt anger, because she couldn't possibly understand what it was to fight and never having enough to eat.

He cut off another piece of meat, knowing she was

watching him. He wolfed it down as well. "Ma'am," he said, "we do thank you for your hospitality."

She turned away, starting down the hall. He got up and followed her, but she had disappeared. He walked along the great hall and discovered that she had stepped out the breezeway door to the porch beyond. She stood with her back to him, beneath the moonlight, and he was taken again with her grace, her serenity—and her chilly disdain for her uninvited company.

She didn't turn around.

"What is it—Colonel?" she demanded, her back to him.

"We do thank you for your hospitality."

She still didn't turn, and so he walked around her until he faced her.

She stared at him, rebellion flaring in her eyes. Then she smiled coolly. "Colonel, sir," she said, and the words had never sounded so mocking, "don't you recall informing me that if I didn't offer my hospitality, you would simply take it?"

"All for the war effort," he replied smoothly.

She studied him, her mocking smile deepening. "Ah! Yes, all for the war effort."

"I'm sorry. I'm assuming you lost your—father? Husband?" he said, indicating her attire.

"Husband."

"Where?"

"Antietam."

"Last year . . . I'm sorry."

"Yes, so am I."

"Were you . . ." he began, then paused, wondering why he was questioning her. "War is brutal on us all. Were you able to see him before he died?"

"No, I—" she hesitated, biting her lower lip, obviously in pain. Then she shook her head, and her guard slipped just a little. "No, I hadn't seen him in months. Not until . . ."

"Until?"

"Until he died." She said it strangely. As if she had seen him slaughtered on the battlefield.

"I'm very sorry."

"Yes, you've said so, I'm sure you are. Now, is there anything else you want to know, Colonel?" she demanded.

He crossed his arms over his chest, irritated that she was so impatient to dismiss him. He was suddenly very aware that he was unshaven and covered in dust and blood and mud. He was a tall man, broad shouldered and powerfully built, if a little underfed.

Well, it was war, not a social, and she was a widow. A Yankee widow who he was certain would happily slice his throat if she knew he was a Reb. Yet she was very beautiful. And her scent was sweet. For the life of him, he could not help but be attracted and aroused.

Then he recalled, once upon a time, he had received a proper Southern upbringing.

He bowed deeply to her. "No, ma'am, I did not intend to waylay you."

"Then," she said politely, "I will not allow you to do so."

She stepped by him, and as she did so, he turned, his eyes following her. "Actually," he said firmly, "I would like to know about your garden."

She paused, shoulders squaring. For a moment she refused to face him again. Then she turned and asked pleasantly, "And why is that?"

"Why?" he repeated, frowning. "I'd like to see what you're growing, how you're managing it. You said that you're growing poppies, that you have laudanum—"

"Ah, but, sir! To what use will any knowledge of *my* garden be to you? Will you be near enough to pillage my herbs?"

"Pillage?"

She hesitated. "North or South, sir, troops do nothing but steal from the civilians in the name of whatever cause they choose to honor."

"I don't *pillage*, ma'am." He walked to her, circling around her once again. "Rape, steal, rob, murder, plunder, or pillage."

"Then what do you do, Colonel?" she inquired, eyes glittering as she watched him.

"Survive," he said simply. And this time he was determined to have the last word.

Only one way to do so. He turned and walked determinedly into the house once again.

So much for Paddy's angel.

She was, he assured himself, as he'd heard, a witch.

Strangely, a chill swept along his spine with that thought. He was just tired. Bone tired. The ride, the skirmish, carrying Paddy from the field of battle, riding hard with the weight of another man. He wanted rest, needed rest, and damn it, he was going to have some rest.

And yet . . .

He could feel her eyes, see her in his mind's eye.

Rhiannon.

A witch, a sea witch, with the power to heal?

And very definitely, the power to haunt.

Chapter 2

~⌒~

Rhiannon Tremaine watched as the man re-entered her house, oddly torn by the emotions that assailed her.

He was a liar. She had known that from the start, and she wasn't sure that it was anything special about her senses that assured her it was so or not. He was a soldier, certainly, but he was no Yankee. He was a tall man, handsome despite his unkempt, threadbare appearance. Powerful, strong, and probably far too capable, she thought, again, despite the fact that he appeared lean and lanky, given his height.

Charming, wary, even as he lied.

And he was definitely a liar. His gaunt cheeks gave him away. He moved about with an alarming, effortless, fluid speed, but he moved like a man accustomed to desperate measures, a man who moved with soldiers forced to strike and retreat quickly. He would always be watching.

He'd been enduring hardships lately, and though the war itself was damned hard on everyone, she was certain he had to be a Reb. And his friend had been injured fighting Yanks. He'd shot himself, indeed! They might even be Rebs returned from the fighting to the North.

She lowered her head, thinking that they would be an unlikely troop happening upon her house as they had if they'd been with the fighting in the North. Yet they were Rebs, and they had guessed that she was a Union sympathizer, so they had lied.

She wondered if they were dangerous.

Naturally, they were dangerous. All weary, war-torn, hurt, and starving men were dangerous. And despite the high-minded ideals of so many of the men on both sides, there were those who had lost all thought of morals or honor. She'd heard numerous horror stories about deserters breaking in on defenseless plantations, stealing, destroying property, and assaulting women. Even before Richard's death, she'd allowed nature to take back the front lawn, and she'd done her best in every way to make the house look abandoned.

She frowned. If someone were to come and put a bullet through her heart, she wasn't terribly sure she'd care. She'd known for a fact long before the official letter had come from Richard's colonel that her husband had been killed. And now she alternated between numbness and pain that cut like a knife. She didn't want to be a coward, but sometimes the pain was so bad that she thought death might be a welcome relief. But she was responsible for Rachel, her husband's cousin, and for Mammy Nor and Angus. Though many of her neighbors did consider her a witch, she was still fascinated enough by herbs and medicinal plants and the simple power of nature that it didn't matter—they could call her witch. Most said the word with simple gratitude. She enjoyed healing those who were sick.

In body, and soul, she told herself dryly. It didn't hurt, she thought, that opium was one of those healing drugs with which she was quite adept at making.

"Miz Rhiannon!"

She spun around. Angus, her husband's manservant, now her right-hand man in all things, had come around the back to speak with her.

"Angus! I need to speak with you."

"That's what I thought, Miz Rhiannon. Now Miss Rachel has gone around giving all those soldiers places to sleep—she's got that colonel upstairs in the guest room. Mammy Nor done seen to it that plenty of food is been set out for the soldiers. I think they're well, fine, and proper cared for, I do."

She nodded. "Good. Now we have to report them."

"What?" Angus was a big man, tall and built like a bull. Startled, hands on his hips, he looked ferocious. She smiled. She liked ferocious very much—when ferocious was on her side.

"Angus, these fellows are liars. Rebs. When the colonel has gone to bed, I want you to set out for St. Augustine.

Find a Captain Cline. He's an old friend. Tell him I think that I might have some notorious Rebs here."

Angus widened his eyes. "Rebs! Here, in this house! Why, those boys has been polite, courteous, downright decent."

"Angus, you don't have to be rude to be a Rebel. Trust me, I know what these men are."

"I trust you. I knows enough to trust you! But are you sure you want me to report them?"

Rhiannon hesitated, startled by the thought that she didn't particularly want her guests to come to harm. But she was pretty sure that she was harboring men who continually harassed the troops around St. Augustine, men taking a toll on Union lives.

"Miss Rachel said the colonel was a fine doctor . . ." Angus began, shaking his head.

"A fine doctor, but he carries a Colt repeater as well, Angus." She bit her lower lip, disturbed to realize she was uncertain. She was someone with what they called "second sight," but it felt as if the colonel saw far too much when he looked at her. Maybe it was just that he made her feel . . . something. Conflict, maybe. She hadn't felt much of anything in so long that . . .

She swallowed hard, lowering her head for a moment. She was filled with turmoil. She found him to be a very disturbing man. Naturally, she told herself. She was playing a game of wits with him because he was a lying Reb. But there was something in his voice, in the eyes, in the way he looked at her . . . He made her feel tremors of unease deep within herself.

He needed to be in a prison camp, she assured herself. She didn't want him dead. She wanted him captured because of the harm his troops caused. For his own safety, and certainly that of others.

She felt dizzy suddenly. She closed her eyes, bracing herself. The image came anyway. She could see Richard again, see him as the bullet impacted, see his eyes, hear him call her name . . .

Then Richard was gone, and she saw the Rebel colonel. Saw him calling out an order, staggering as he ran to his horse with his wounded friend over his shoulder. Saw him aiming his Colt as Union troops came in pursuit . . .

Her eyes flew open.

She looked at Angus.

"They have to be reported."

The colonel taunting her now was a Rebel, plain and simple. "Angus, it's important that you go to Captain Cline. He's a good friend, and he'll be careful. I don't want men killed in my house or because of any action of mine. The Rebs have to be taken as prisoners."

Angus scratched his head. "Miz Rhiannon, we're still living in a Southern state—"

"This was my father's house, Angus. He built it. He left it to me. And it's my state, just the same as it's their state. I happen to think that the state should return to the Union, and they want it to be part of their Confederacy."

"Still, the state did leave the Union!" Angus persisted in warning.

Angus had never been a slave. Born in Vermont like Richard, he'd had several years of schooling, and Richard had liked to argue issues with him to see matters from a different perspective.

Richard was gone, but Angus still liked to argue.

"Angus, please. I've heard that most of the people in St. Augustine opened their arms willingly to Union troops— they couldn't live without Yankee dollars. There are many other Unionists in Florida, I assure you. Now, please! You will see to the welfare of our guests, and then you will ride out to inform Captain Cline that they are here."

"It don't feel right," Angus said.

She hesitated. It *didn't* feel right. She waited, hoping some thought or insight would come to her. But she felt the night's breeze and nothing more.

"Angus—"

"Yes, ma'am, it is your home," Angus said, "I just hope they don't burn it!" he told her firmly.

"They—they won't burn my home."

"Other Unionists have been dragged out of their houses and forced to watch as they burned."

"Those incidents are rare, Angus."

"Rare, perhaps, but passions do run high when it comes to this war, Miz Rhiannon."

"They won't burn me out, Angus," she murmured with a dry assurance. "Too many people think I'm a witch."

He shook his head. "You'll have these fellows in your house, and it will take me so long to get Captain Cline in St. Augustine, and so long for soldiers to get back."

"We'll treat these soldiers decently, Angus. They'll never know what we're up to until it's come about."

"It could be morning before the Union soldiers arrive." She swallowed hard.

She was suddenly . . . afraid. The feeling was strange. She hadn't cared about her own welfare in a very long time. . . .

"Do it, Angus, please," she said firmly.

He nodded and left her.

She watched him go. After a moment she looked down and saw that her hands were clenched. She stretched them before her. They were shaking.

She needed a drink. Not a ladylike concept at all, but she needed a drink. Badly.

No, she needed more. Much more. She needed to slip away to her room, away from these soldiers. She didn't want to see them. Angus would go for help; she just needed to lock herself in . . .

And escape. These men, the war, the past. Her own way.

Julian had thought that his unwilling hostess might have followed him—just to argue with him. But she hadn't.

He returned to the dining room, where River Montdale and Thad and Ben Henly were hungrily consuming their suppers. He joined them, this time helping himself to the bread and cheese and some homemade wine.

"You looked around out back, boys?" he asked the men.

Before the war the Henlys had made their living off the land, trapping and fishing. If he would trust anyone to know the woods, it was the two of them.

Ben, a cocky and handsome dark-haired youth with dimples, grinned.

"Colonel, this place is about as remote as you can get."

His cousin Thad, a little older, agreed. "We searched the barn, the stables, the smokehouse, servants' quarters, everywhere. If this is a trap, it's a damned good one."

"Still, we'll keep guard—"

"Keith, Daniel, and Corporal Lyle are patrolling the grounds. We'd figured we should spell each other in groups of three every two hours until morning, sir," River Montdale told him. Montdale, twenty-three years old with dark eyes and long dark hair, was part Seminole, as good a man in the wild as the Henlys.

"Sounds a good plan to me. I'll take a turn at guard duty before dawn—"

"Sir, the way I see it," River protested, "we've got it covered. Liam keeps an eye on Paddy, and you get some sleep, because you've stayed awake too damned long and ridden too hard while trying to keep Paddy alive. And," he said with a smile and a shrug, "you're the ranking officer."

Julian grinned in return. "I am damned tired."

"And Paddy may need you in the night," Ben said.

"True," Julian said. "But I doubt it. He'll sleep well."

"Sir, if you'll excuse us . . ." Thad said.

"Get some rest," he told them.

The three left him. When they were gone, a regally tall, slim black woman came into the room bearing a silver carafe and a wine glass. She appeared ageless, a handsome woman with deep, dark eyes, almond skin, and a mysterious smile.

"You're the colonel?" she said.

He nodded, watching her. She was lithe, sinuous, completely at ease. Her face was a fascinating one, unlined yet filled with a character that usually came with age. She was very proud, and afraid of no man, he thought.

"You're Mammy Nor?"

"I am, sir. Angus runs the grounds for Miz Rhiannon; I run the house. This is my special berry wine. I brought it out only for you. It's potent, sir. Rich and potent. It will warm your blood. If you want your blood warmed."

"Well, you know, my blood has run very cold lately. I think I'd like your wine very much."

"Can you handle it, sir? You know, there are those who claim the mistress to be a witch."

"*Is* she an evil witch?

"Not evil."

"But a witch?"

"Who's to say? My folks hailed from down N'awleans way. They tell stories about voodoo priests and priestesses, good magic, bad magic. Then there's the old way, the ancient *white* way, the folk who studied wicca and the like. Earth people. The real magic is in the earth, you know, sir.

The Indians know this, the African people have always known it. Mostly, these days the white men have lost all memory of everything that the earth can give. You're a doctor. You should know. You don't need to be a witch to make magic. The mistress can create magic."

"With her potions?" he inquired.

"Lord, what the earth does give!" Mammy Nor exclaimed.

"Good and bad. Did you poison the wine?" Julian inquired politely.

She cast back her head and laughed. "Lord, no! Why, Colonel, if I was to kill a man, I'd put a bullet between his eyes."

"Indeed," he said, smiling, certain that Mammy Nor would do so. "I believe you would."

"You know that the wine is not poisoned because I have said so?"

"Yes," he told her.

"I like you," Mammy Nor said, studying him seriously. "But so, since I like you, I warn you, you'll sleep well. Or . . . you won't sleep. The wine is warm, it's good. It eases the little pains in the body, and plays with the mind, perhaps just a little bit. Maybe you'll sleep and it will give you dreams. But these days, eh, sir, the dreams are better than the truth in daylight. So, you sleep well, you dream sweet dreams. The wine's potent, that's all I say. Take a sip."

He did so. It was an excellent full-bodied wine, almost a port. It was dry without being bitter, fruity without being too sweet.

"Well, Colonel?"

"You make wonderful wine, Mammy Nor."

"You don't know just how wonderful yet, Colonel!"

"I'll be careful."

"Have a good night, sir. Sleep well. Dream sweetly."

"Thank you."

With a knowing wink and a slow turn, she left him alone. He couldn't help thinking that it was a strange household.

The wine was good. It seemed to flow through his limbs, and, as she had said, it eased all the little aches and pains. Though he was certain it wasn't poisoned, he still sipped it carefully. The earth witch who owned the place was a Yankee, which meant he had to be careful. But the lulling heat that filled his veins was addictive. A second glass seemed in order. God, yes, it was potent, and very good. Besides, he'd always been able to drink his share of bourbon. He could surely handle a couple glasses of wine.

As he sat there, just finishing it, Rachel came in to the room.

"Oh, sir, there you are!" she said happily.

"Hello, Rachel."

"Have you eaten?" she asked him.

She was young, charming, effusive, and sincere. He smiled in return, suddenly wishing he weren't living out a lie for the evening, since she was so pleased to have them.

"Yes, I've eaten."

"Good. Then come on up."

"Up? Where?"

"I've made arrangements for everyone, sir, but since you're the ranking man—" She broke off suddenly, frowning. "You are, aren't you?"

"Uh—yes, at the moment."

"You've a private room, upstairs. The other fellows will share, though they say they have to take turns on guard. Is that right?"

"I'm afraid so."

"Ah, well, follow me."

"All right. Just let me look in on my patient."

He did so. Paddy was sleeping peacefully. So peacefully that he paused, listening for Paddy's heartbeat and his slow, deep breathing.

"Don't worry," Rachel said, tugging on his arm. "Rhiannon gave him some laudanum. He'll sleep like a baby. That wound must have hurt blue blazes."

He didn't object to an injured man being given a pain-killing drug—just to the fact that Rhiannon had chosen to do so without asking him. But then again, it was the common household cure for every little ache and pain, quite popular among the ladies—young and old, North and South.

"Perhaps I should speak with Rhiannon," he said.

"She's gone to bed for the night," Rachel told him.

"You'll have to speak with her in the morning. Don't yell at her."

"I can hardly yell at our hostess."

"She meant well."

"Did she?"

"Of course. She wouldn't do anything bad to anyone. I told you—she's better than most doctors. She was in Washington for a while, petitioning to follow Richard's regiment as a medic, but she couldn't get permission, so she worked in a hospital there. She's magic."

Magic again. "Is she?" he inquired skeptically.

"Honestly. And she sees, you know."

"Sees what?"

"More than most."

He lowered his head, hiding a skeptical grin. "She's a prophet?"

"Oh, no, and she'd be furious if she thought I told you such a thing. Sometimes she just . . . knows things. When they happen, right before they happen. And she can find things and people and . . . she's just magic, that's all."

"And what is Rhiannon to you? Are you related? Do you see things as well?"

Rachel laughed. "No, I'm afraid that I can't see things right before my eyes most of the time. Richard—her husband—was my cousin. Rhiannon watches out for me . . . Come on now, sir. You do look haggard."

He arched a brow.

"Oh, I am so sorry. I didn't mean to be rude—you don't look *bad*. You're a very handsome man. Oh, dear, I guess it's quite forward for me to say such a thing . . ."

He started to laugh. "I'm not offended, but rather, Miss Rachel, I am deeply flattered. And I am tired, and I'm sure, quite haggard. Thank you for your kindness. Lead away."

She brought him upstairs to a large pleasant room with a big bed, French doors leading to a balcony, and something even more inviting—a hip tub filled with steaming water.

"Like it?" she asked him, delighted by his expression.

He caught her hand and gallantly kissed it. "This might be the nicest gift I've received in years."

She blushed. "I'll get out of your way, then. There are towels on the chair, there, and some soap. We still have

decent soap, by the way. From France. But it's not per-
fumed or anything—it just isn't that awful lye everyone
seems to be using these days. I promise, you won't smell
funny tomorrow or anything."

"Good. It's terrible when your men think you smell too
pretty," he told her gravely.

She laughed. "I'll see you in the morning, Colonel."

"It's a wonderful room. Thank you."

She shrugged. "I think it was a nursery once, attached
to the master's chambers. I'm not really sure. Rhiannon
inherited this property from her parents, so there haven't
been any little children around for a long time. Sleep well,
sir. I'll see you in the morning."

She left him, and when she did so, he couldn't get his
clothes off fast enough. A bath and a change of clothing
had gotten to be a luxury. At his base camp they were, in
one way, lucky. The river ran cool, fresh, and beautiful
quite near them, and due to the constant heat, men were
drawn to the river. It wasn't that often that he went without bathing.

He plunged into the tub, feeling a deep comfort as the
steaming water soaked into him. Then, before lethargy
could steal over him, he grabbed the soap—heedless of
what it smelled like—and scrubbed himself energetically
from head to toe. He'd already had lice twice during the
war and he washed furiously at every opportunity. Thor-
oughly scrubbed, he leaned his head back and relaxed.

God, but the hot water felt good. And the wine had been
potent—just as Mammy Nor had warned. It seemed to steal
through his body, warming him, relaxing him. He felt lazy,
redolent, good. Pictures of the sick and injured—soldiers
writing in pain from fever, gunshot, knife wounds, and am-
putations—which so often slipped into his mind, faded. He
felt as if he had gone back in time. He might have been
home, at Cimarron, listening to the night, feeling the air.
A breeze against the heat could be so wonderful. And tonight there was a soft, cool breeze. While he lounged there,
he could just hear leaves rustling, brushing against the
house. It was all lulling. He hadn't felt so relaxed in a very
long time.

After a while he began to hear more than the whisper

of the night. He heard a soft, muffled sobbing sound. Quiet, so wrenching that it tugged upon the heart.

He was in the old nursery, next to the master's chambers. That meant his hostess's room was next to his own.

It was terrible to listen to her grief. In the course of war he'd seen many men die. He'd never accustomed himself to death. He had learned, though, that he had to keep moving, steel himself to continue working mechanically, even when it went against the very fiber of his being to see a young life fade on the operating table beneath his very hands. He knew that for every man he lost, a widow grieved, a mother sobbed, or a child was left fatherless. War was brutal and cruel. He knew that. He knew the pain. He lived with it, fought it, day after day.

And still . . .

The soft, muffled sobbing seemed to steal into him. He tried not to listen, to respect the privacy of her grief. But then, in the midst of it, he heard a sudden exclamation.

"No, no, noooo!"

He heard something slam and he jumped up, dripping. For a moment he felt as if he were weaving—a reaction from the alcohol content in the wine. Swearing, he reached for his towel and wrapped it around him. He staggered from the tub and steadied himself. He found his Colt on the chair where he had set it when he'd stripped. Colt in one hand, towel in the other, he was about to bound out into the hall and find out who or what had assaulted his hostess when he realized that there was a connecting door between the two rooms.

He strode pell-mell to it, tried the knob, and found it locked. Afraid that she was in real danger, he rammed the door with his shoulder.

A far flimsier door than the main one below, it gave readily—the lock simply breaking from the hinge. His impetus took him, towel around his waist, gun in hand, into the center of her room.

There was no one there. Not in the room.

Rhiannon sat in a whitewashed wooden swing out on her balcony. If not for the moonlight, he wouldn't have seen her. Barefoot, in a long cotton gown, she sat, knees curled into her chest, rocking. Her ebony hair was loosed from its coil and streamed down her back like a silk shawl. She looked very young, a lost waif, a magical creature indeed, caught by the pale glow of the soft moonlight.

She should have heard her door break open, but it appeared that she hadn't even noticed his arrival.

Stunned, he started walking toward her. He stopped suddenly as he stepped in liquid. Looking down, he realized that he had just missed stepping on the remnants of a shattered glass. A small pool of wine lay next to it.

He stepped around the glass and walked toward the balcony. When he had nearly reached her, she heard him at last. She leapt to her feet, spinning around to face him, startled and afraid.

"How dare you sneak up on me!"

"I hardly snuck up on you, considering the fact that I broke a door apart to reach you."

"What in God's name are you doing in here?"

"Trying to rescue you."

"Rescue me?"

Her eyes skidded over his body, taking in the towel and the gun. Her eyes widened.

"Rescue me—you're aiming a gun at me!" she said indignantly. Then some emotion passed through her eyes. "Are you going to shoot me?" she inquired a little breathlessly.

As if there might be a reason he would consider shooting her.

"Why would I shoot you?" he inquired.

"Because—" she began, and broke off. "You're—carrying a gun. It's aimed at me."

"I thought you were being attacked. And I'm not aiming at you."

"Attacked? By whom? Your men?" she queried.

He gritted his teeth, growing impatient and feeling very much a fool. His head was still swimming. He was standing in her room with a towel and a gun. "You were crying—then you screamed," he explained.

"Don't be absurd. I didn't scream."

"You did." Damn her. He hadn't drunk *that* much wine.

Suddenly her gaze slipped from his. Her words and tone faltered. "I'm—I'm sorry. I must have been dreaming, it was a . . . nightmare, perhaps . . ."

And then he knew.

There was something not quite right about her. Her eyes,

when they met his again, were widely dilated. She held one hand behind her back, like a child hiding a forbidden toy. He frowned, stepping forward. "What have you got?"

"Nothing." She backed away from him in such a way that he was determined to persist. He cast his Colt to the foot of her bed and reached for her, drawing her to him. She stiffened at his touch, her body trembling. She struggled to free herself, but he caught her wrist, wondering what it was she was so determined to hide. A gun? A knife? Had she been planning on entering his room and murdering him while he slept?

"Give it to me!" he commanded harshly. He slid his left arm around her waist, forcing her hard against the length of his body. He squeezed her wrist and forced her to drop what she held.

"Let me be!" she pleaded, for she hadn't the strength to stop him from forcing her clenched fist open. What she held fell to the floor, and as he stopped to retrieve it, he looked quickly back up at her, startled. It was a small, corked vial. Laudanum? Or a truer form of the drug, pure opium.

He understood the look in her eyes as he rose to his feet, staring at her.

"Laudanum or pure opium?"

"None of your business!"

"You're an addict."

"No!" she protested. "Give it back, no . . . I'm not addicted, I just . . . sometimes . . . please . . . I need it!"

He gritted his teeth. God, yes, laudanum, a legal drug. In times of peace so plentiful! It cured headaches and women's ills, and yes, of course, it was good for pain.

And for forgetfulness.

It could be essential in an operating theater; he knew that because so often he didn't have any. If not for his cousin Jerome being a blockade runner, he might never have the drugs he needed, especially since the serious fighting took place so far away. He could surely use more of the drug.

Yet laudanum was also easy to abuse. He'd never forget one of the first corpses he'd worked on in medical school. In life she had been a beautiful young woman with golden blond hair and bright blue eyes. In death, she had lain ashen and gray, naked, displayed for dissection, the victim of her need. She'd been found in a field, and no one had known who she was or where to find her kin. And so she had come to the medical school. It was later discovered that she was the child of a wealthy and prominent family, but she had run away from home after acquiring an irresistible hunger for the drug that had killed her.

"Colonel, please . . ."

Her voice was husky, low, pleading. He shook his head.

He was furious. There was so much death and horror in this war! That she could be so careless with something so precious as life . . . !

He gripped her by the shoulders and shook her. She was taking the drug and drinking wine. A potent combination indeed.

"What is the matter with you?"

She stiffened against his touch. "You don't understand—"

"But I do."

"Let me go. I must—" she began to insist angrily.

"You don't need this."

"I do. Just tonight."

"I'm telling you, you don't."

"God damn you! Who are you to tell me anything?"

She wrenched free from him, backing away, her eyes meeting his with a challenging fire.

"So you're free from me," he said very softly. "You don't think that I can stop you if I choose?"

She was alarmed at his determination. "What is it to you what I choose to do with my life?"

"You won't have a life!" he assured her.

"Don't be absurd, I know what I'm doing—"

"Do you? You're fooling yourself. Opium and wine. In large quantities. You don't think there's enough death and misery in the world?"

"This isn't your affair! Now, please give it to me—"

"You've already had too much."

She was dead still for a moment, realizing he knew she'd already been taking the drug. Then she tilted up her chin and stared at him with a cool disinterest. "No, Colonel, I never have enough. And this is not your affair."

He took the two steps that brought them back together

and reached for her. She cried out in alarm, but he drew her close to him again, determined to get his point across. "I'm a physician, and I can tell you that this is dangerous. Listen to me—"

"Go to hell! Leave me alone! I repeat—just who do you think you are to come in here and tell me what to do?" she demanded heatedly. Her body was stiff; she struggled again to free herself from his hold. When he refused to grant the least quarter, she brought her fists up between them and slammed them hard against his naked chest.

He didn't stop her assault, but stepped closer to her, forcing her against him so that her blows had no impetus. "Oh, do you think that you can hurt me?" he asked. "You're drugged, weak, and pathetic."

"Pathetic! Oh! I will hurt you—" she cried, redoubling her efforts.

He caught her wrists. She flung back her head, staring at him.

"Fight me!" he taunted. "Go on, fight me. Try it."

She tried to wrench away, realized quickly that she could not.

He jerked her back. Her eyes blazed upon his with loathing.

"You don't need it," he told her. "You are going to listen to me. You can die abusing opium. You know that, don't you? Are you trying to die? Are you really such a coward?"

She inhaled sharply, and he knew that he had at last touched the core deep within her. "I'm not a coward."

"The worst kind," he told her.

"You *really* don't understand. It hurts. I saw him. I saw him die. I heard him call my name. I saw the blood, I saw his eyes. I can't forget. I can't get it out of my mind. I lie alone at night, and I hear him call my name. Over and over and over again until I can't bear it—"

"You can't hear him."

"I saw it!"

"You weren't on the battlefield."

She shook her head, eyes meeting his searchingly as if she sought some kind of understanding. She then lowered her head, as if she were too exhausted to fight him further.

And he was sorry. He wanted very much to take her into his arms and hold her and comfort her.

She didn't want such comfort from a stranger. All he could do was try to make her realize what she was doing.

"Don't," he told her softly. "Don't do this to yourself."

"Just let me go!" she pleaded, her voice feminine, sweet, weary.

"I won't let you do this," he said firmly.

She wasn't so exhausted. Her chin rose, her eyes touched his like daggers, and she went into a frenzy of struggling once again, trying to scratch, bite, hit, and kick. She knew where to aim her blows, and he realized he was struggling to keep her from hurting him. Her foot connected with his towel; it was suddenly disengaged. Swearing, trying to maintain the towel while keeping her from blackening his eye, he lifted her and carried her across the room, slamming her down on the bed and leaping down atop her, using his weight to pin her. For several seconds she continued to struggle against him—then she went dead still. She stared up at him, barely breathing, her fingers still wound around his upper arms. It was only then that he realized he'd lost the towel completely and her cotton nightgown was wound nearly to her waist.

"You are hardly behaving as a Southern gentleman," she told him, her face rigid as her green eyes met his.

"I'm joining up with the Yanks, remember?"

Her eyes closed momentarily, then met his, and she shook her head. "The accent, sir, is Southern. There are smart Florida boys with the Union. Southern men are bred to courtesy."

"Northerners aren't?" he inquired.

"Of course. But not with quite the same enthusiasm. Since your place of origin has been established, I think it would be in good keeping if you would behave with honor and chivalry and get up and leave me to my own choices."

He thought about it for a moment, then shook his head. "No, I don't think so."

"Damn you, where are your manners? What was your mama doing while you grew up?" she queried, determined to shame him.

He eased back, grimly amused by her efforts. "Well, now, ma'am, my mother did teach me to be respectful to proper ladies. But I went to medical school. And there we were taught simply to take drug addicts into hand before they hurt themselves or someone else."

She flared. "I'm not a drug addict!"

"I wish that were true."

"I'm not addicted. I just—" she broke off and closed her eyes, weary of the fight. "Would you just leave me be? What can this matter to you?"

The fire had left her; the last was close to a desperate plea.

He touched her cheek softly. Her eyes flew to his. "I'm a doctor," he told her quietly. "I can't let you destroy yourself." He hesitated a moment. "And I'm a simple man as well, who can't bear the thought of such youth and beauty perishing in the pursuit of a moment's solace."

He felt her slender frame begin to tremble beneath him. Her brows furrowed. "I think—I think I need it."

"No."

"I can't face the night; I can't sleep."

"I'll lie here with you."

She shook her head. "No, no . . . men think that widows, that . . . you don't understand. I loved my husband."

"I do understand. I've seen far too many men die."

"He called my name!" she whispered.

"He loved you, too."

She fell silent, her lashes fluttering over her eyes. He stared down at her for a long moment. She didn't speak; she didn't struggle. He eased himself from her, lying at her side, smoothing her gown down the length of her body. His towel was at the foot of the bed. He reached for it, drawing it about himself. He wondered if she had fallen asleep. She suddenly inhaled with a deep shudder. He reached out, hesitated, then smoothed back a lock of her dark hair. Her features were fine and fragile, her skin flawless.

She curled toward him suddenly. Trustingly. He continued to stroke her hair. She needed sleep. Simple sleep, without drugs.

He was barely breathing, aware of the way her hair teased his naked chest, the soft feathering of her breath against his flesh, the delicate touch of her fingers where they brushed his side. Her scent was intoxicating. And he was not blind. Flickering gold candlelight played over the

white cotton gown, creating shadow and light, falling over
the fullness of her breasts, the shadowed scoop of her belly,
the rise of her hip. He touched her hair, and she came even
closer to him, sleeping now as peacefully and trustingly as
a kitten. She'd best not move too far, he thought, or she'd
brush against a piece of him so ready that she'd leap away
like a bird taking flight.

She sighed tremulously in her sleep. Her knuckles moved
down his breast plate. He gritted his teeth, determined that
he must move. Anything overt on his part would be taking
advantage of her pain and drugged state.

She moved even closer to him, as if she melted against
him. Touching him. Sleeping. Resting so peacefully, so se-
cure. She had been taking an opiate, he reminded himself.
How much, of course, he didn't know. A lot. She'd known
what she'd been doing; she'd meant to do more. She'd
meant to knock herself out.

Maybe she was taking advantage of him.

He started to ease away.

Instinctively, she moved closer again.

Where was the potency of that wine he had drunk?
Shouldn't that make him able to sleep as well? He was
desperate for rest; tomorrow they had to ride again, and
he didn't know what Yankee patrols they might encounter.

He couldn't lie here awake all night. He eased his head
down, thinking that he did have to move somehow.

Somehow.

Oh, God, he'd never sleep here as he was. He could feel
her, breathe her, sense her . . .

It felt as if the length of him were on fire. Hot. Burning.
A wickedly hard, fast pulse beat throughout his veins
drummed through his limbs; he throbbed, ached, was constricted, tight, in agony . . .

He groaned aloud. She didn't move.

He tried to ease away. She moved closer. Reached out.
Her hand lay upon his naked chest.

Again, he tried to move.

"No . . . don't leave me," she whispered.

He closed his eyes.

Where is that sleep you promised me, Mammy Nor? he
wondered. Had he lost the feeling of warmth and comfort
from the wine, could he bring it back? Breathe deep, feel

the heat in his veins, feel it ease the tightness in his limbs . . .

He needed to feel the breezes again, remember a time before the war, remember peace . . .

He prayed for sleep.

Chapter 3

〜

She'd been in love with Richard Tremaine as long as she could remember. He hailed from Virginia, very near Washington, D.C. She had been born and raised in north Florida. But their fathers had known one another forever—they had both come from a small town in Wales. Richard's father had become involved in American journalism, and hers had found Florida, salt production and plantation life. But the men had remained friends, despite the changing climate of the country. It helped that Rhiannon's father had remained an ardent Unionist, totally against secession, no matter what the outside pressure set against him. In 1860, while the threat of war had billowed around them, she had blissfully wed Richard in a small ceremony in Washington. The first night of their marriage, she had awakened screaming, the remnants of a terrible dream haunting her. She had seen a battlefield strewn with the dead, and all around them, men calling out with haunting taunts.

We can whomp those Yanks in a matter of weeks . . .

Those Rebs will be sorry they started this after we give them one good lickin' . . .

So many bodies, mangled, burned, bloodied, eyes opened, staring.

She hadn't wanted to tell Richard, but he knew about her dreams, and that she often simply knew things, and so he had listened to her, and he had soothed her. She had been afraid, and so he had told her that he could take her mind off of her nightmares, and he did, making love to her, sitting up with her, sharing wine, making her laugh, making love again . . .

But she had seen a glimpse of the war to come, and when

*Richard had received his commission, she'd had the dream
again. She had begged him not to fight, but he had told her
that he didn't have a choice. And when Florida had rushed
to secede from the Union, she had been numb.*

*Dreams. She prayed that they would not haunt her so.
Richard had always said that she had to think about the
good, and forget, block out, what she found to be painful.
What frightened her. Sometimes dreams were warnings, perhaps, of things she could stop from happening . . .*

Richard.

Beside her now.

*She knew, of course, that he couldn't be beside her now.
He had perished. She had seen it. In a dream. But dreams,
perhaps, were deceiving, because she could touch him, feel
flesh, feel heat, warmth, the wonderful, electric feel of life
beside her in the shadows of the night . . .*

*Remember the good, he had always told her, and he had
been the good. Dreams could bring happiness as well as
pain, he had assured her. She'd dreamed about his death,
but he was with her now, and so, perhaps, the dream had
been a warning, and she could keep him now, stop him from
going into battle, make him stay, with her . . .*

*She touched him, feeling the muscles ripple within his
chest, the sleekness of his flesh. The quickening movements
in him as the brush of her fingers teased and aroused his
heated flesh . . .*

She could keep him. Make him stay.

*She pressed her lips against his shoulder, his throat, lower,
her fingers upon his flesh all the while, stroking, teasing,
arousing . . .*

He was so still. Still as death . . .

No . . .

*He groaned, in the night, in the darkness, in the sweetness
and life of the dream.*

*And he touched her face, cupping her cheek with his palm,
brushing her lips with his thumb. She felt an instant stirring
deep within her, a hunger, an aching, deeper, more desperate, than she had ever known before. Perhaps, because it
was a dream, each sensation intensified, the pad of his thumb
upon her mouth, the fever heat of his body, brushing against
hers, the extent of his arousal . . .*

He kissed her. Lips barely touching hers at first, then

forming upon them, devouring them. She felt his tongue in her mouth, tasted him, wanted him. She returned the kiss with sweet, manic passion, wanting more and more. His hand moved from her cheek, molding over her breast, his palm erotic as he rotated it over the cotton of her gown. Desire—a white hot flash of sunlight—seared straight through her, and she ran her hand down the smooth, lean length of his body, finding the hard protrusion of his sex and stroking. The sharp intake of his breath against her lips assured her that she touched with magic—or witch's spell— and she trembled with both need and pleasure when his hand slipped beneath her gown and slid between her thighs. How strange . . . she'd been so uncertain on their wedding night, fearful of showing what she felt when he touched her, when they made love. But he'd taught her that love created its own boundaries, and he wanted all that she brought to his bed, witch, angel, enchantress . . . laughter, passion, lust . . . all belonged between them, and he wanted a wife who wanted him. She hadn't known how much she missed this . . . hadn't thought . . . hadn't . . . since . . .

Oh, God. He pressed within her . . . touched, withdrew, rotated his thumb . . . withdrew just slightly, creating a rhythm that increased in tempo, teased and beckoned, aroused until she was arching, writhing for more and more. His lips were against hers again, against her throat, her collarbone. Her gown was thrust up, and his mouth flowered over her breasts, her abdomen, lower, lathing, soaking, teasing, tormenting . . .

She was in a frenzy, digging into his shoulders, tearing into his hair. And he rose above her, liquid, lithe, powerful, in the moonlight, thrust himself within until she was filled and shuddering, writhing once again, eager, famished, dying. He moved fully in her slowly, again and again, and when she thought she would go mad, he suddenly increased his pulse, and he was with her like the wind, like thunder, a force of nature, thrusting so deeply, again and again, sweeping into her, and causing her to soar . . . to fly against fear, and nightmares, and haunting visions of . . .

Battlefields.

And death . . .

Blurred images started to form in her mind. She fought

them. She felt him. His touch. His movement. His stroke within her . . .

So hard now, starved, passionate, demanding.

So good.

"Oh!" A cry left her lips. There was nothing but sensation, blinding sensation.

No visions could touch her when she was held with such volatile passion within his arms. No pain . . . just this sweet sublimity, breaking upon her, spilling like cascades of hon-eyed water, seeping between them . . .

He fell against her.

"Richard," she whispered.

Blissfully weary and replete, she was unaware that he stiffened.

And gave no reply.

The fervent pounding on the guest room door, accompa-nied by an urgent "Colonel!" drew Julian from an embar-rassingly deep sleep. The wine, he thought. Potent, indeed. He'd slept like the dead, dreamed . . .

"Colonel!"

He tried to rouse quickly, but it was as if he were coming from a deep, entrenching fog, uncomfortably lost and disconcerted . . .

He usually awoke at the whisper of the wind.

He bolted up and became aware he lay beside his hostess in a plantation house somewhere north and not far west of St. Augustine. The pounding began again.

Dreams. Mammy Nor had warned him that his dreams would be sweet indeed. Yet . . .

He had to cast off the sluggish sensation that still seemed to grip him. He bolted to his feet, reaching for the towel he had worn to the room. He hurried the distance between the two rooms, closing the door with the broken bolt be-hind him.

"Colonel!"

No time with the call so urgent to reach for his breeches; he hurried to the door to his room and threw it open. Corporal Lyle was there, anxiously waiting for him. "Horses, sir, riders, about fifteen of them, coming down the eastern road."

"Yanks?"

"Yes, sir."

"Coming directly for the house?" he inquired sharply.

"Yes, sir, I'm afraid they are."

She had known. Witch—or simply an intuitive woman—she had known that they were Rebs. Though, grudgingly, she had given them hospitality, in her manner, and perhaps had intended to make them think themselves safe.

While she had reported them.

"How much time do we have?"

"Ten, fifteen minutes, I reckon. Then them Yanks will be at the door."

"How's our patient?" he asked, quickly regarding Paddy.

"Doing fine, sir."

"I'll see to him quickly."

He dropped the towel, reaching for his breeches, and stepped into them. Shoeless, shirtless, he sped down the stairs and into the room where he had treated Paddy.

Paddy was up. He had been given a fresh white shirt and a torn pair of clean breeches to wear. Rachel was busy re-bandaging his thigh.

"I'll take a quick look," he said gruffly.

Rachel stepped back. The wound was clean, there was no bleeding. His stitches were small and tight. Paddy would do all right; he was going to have to.

"I can ride like the wind, and you know that's true, sir," Paddy said.

"You'll have to take care—"

"I will. And River can help patch me with his Seminole magic if there's bleeding again."

"Get to camp, and for God's sake, get to bed and stay there," Julian ordered, working deftly to pack the wound so that the stitches wouldn't split.

"Aye, sir,"

"I'll finish the bandaging, doctor, sir," Rachel said. "He's healing fine. You sew better than a seamstress."

"Thank you, Rachel," Julian said. "This is very kind. You know that we're—"

"Rebs. Yes, sir. You'd best get moving."

Corporal Lyle was behind him. He turned, giving orders quickly. "Tell River, Thad, and Ben to get Paddy and move inland before heading south. River will know the old Seminole trails, and I'm willing to bet the Yanks coming after us are from Ohio or Michigan or some such place. The rest of us will take a southeastward trail, keep them following us, and give you a better chance to escape more slowly with Paddy."

"Yessir."

"Get moving, then."

He left the room, hurrying back upstairs and looking out the large bay window above the breezeway hall to ascertain the position of the Yankees. They had ten minutes at best. He hurried on to the bedroom to finish dressing. Once there, he snatched up the rest of his clothing. As he slipped into his shirt, he stared at the doorway between the two rooms. His Colt remained in her room, dropped at the foot of her bed where he had left it last night. He stumbled into his boots then strode quickly to the door. With the bolt gone, a touch of his palm threw the door quietly open. Maybe he wouldn't even awaken her, and then he wouldn't be so tempted to throttle her.

But she wasn't sleeping. She had just risen, awakened, perhaps, by the sound of the riders. Tall, lithe, her hair a wild, tousled ebony cloak, she appeared ethereal, and still so breathtakingly beautiful that he paused. She stood near the bed, ashen, confused, far more disoriented than he, he realized—yet staring down at his Colt where he had cast it the night before and trying to determine her chances of reaching it.

And using it?

It suddenly infuriated him anew that she should be so careless with her life. She'd reported them—casting herself into danger should battle erupt in her house, and yet she had been so certain that they would be easily swept away that she had dared douse herself with drugs and wine.

And now, it seemed she was so determined on their capture that she would draw his own gun against him. He had no desire to discover just how ardent a Yank she was. He walked quickly across the room. She saw him, saw his face, and suddenly made a dive for his weapon. She reached out, fingers grasping, but he was there too quickly, catching her by the length of her hair. She cried out, jerked back, but he loosed her instantly. He reached for his Colt, sliding it into his holster.

"A Colt-carrying doctor!" she exclaimed. "What a wondrous physician, so concerned with life!"

"I am concerned with life. At the moment I'm concerned with my own."

"No one intends to kill you—"

"Then what did you intend with my Colt?"

"To—waylay you."

"Why? Because troops are on the way to capture us?"

She was motionless for a moment, very straight, as she tried to regain her dignity. She was still wearing her cotton nightgown, her long dark hair was free and streaming down her back in wild disarray, and she seemed completely distressed and unnerved, as if the past hours were a complete blur to her.

Did she remember what happened? he wondered.

Her vivid green eyes touched his. "If you were a good Yank, sir, as you proclaimed, it would be your countrymen coming to your aid."

"I never actually proclaimed myself a Yank, ma'am," he said politely. "Naturally, whatever I am, I do thank you for your hospitality. However, we will be taking our leave."

She stared at him, lifting her chin. "They'll catch you, you know."

"Well, that was your intent. But I doubt it. I'm from here—they're not. I know where I'm going, they don't. But I thank you for your concern."

Her eyes flickered downward. He turned, striding for the hallway door, and was startled when she called him back.

"Colonel?"

He stopped, turning to look at her. God, how she wanted to be cool and aloof and watch him walk away without a further word! But she didn't seem to be able to do so. "You did sleep in your own room?" she inquired. It was a whisper so soft that he could barely make out the words.

He hesitated, watching her. The wine had been potent. He had been exhausted. Had he dreamed . . . awakened within a dream only to continue in a deeper sleep? The night seemed so fleeting. He could be the perfect gentleman, tell her what she wanted to hear.

He could, but . . .

Why on earth would he want to?

"My own room? Ma'am, my own room is far away, south and across the breadth of the state."

She was very pale. "I don't . . . I don't remember much. I mean . . . I remember you coming in here, taking the—the opium from me . . . and nothing more."

"Nothing more? Well, you didn't need the opium. Another dose and you might not have awakened."

"Sometimes it's easier to sleep."

"Ma'am, that is definitely the coward's way. You don't need opium. Thousands of dying soldiers out there do."

"Colonel, why can't you understand, my life is none of your concern."

"I'm leaving."

"But I—I need you to tell me. I mean, I don't know . . . I'm afraid I was very lost . . ."

"Fine. Be specific. Just exactly what is it you want to know?" He wasn't going to give her anything. Even as he stood there, knowing full well he needed to run, he wanted to stay.

No, he couldn't abide a wasted life.

Certainly not hers! He needed to stay, to be with her, to make her see the addiction . . .

He couldn't; nor could he stand guard over her and keep her from the dangers she presented to herself. He had to be harsh, cruel. And perhaps she would learn a bitter lesson. He smiled politely. "Are you still trying to delay me from leaving, ma'am, in the hopes that your Yankee friends will catch me?"

"No . . . yes . . . no, I—"

"You didn't send for them?"

"Yes, of course—"

"Because you knew we were Rebs."

"Yes."

His smile broadened. "But you don't know what did—or didn't—happen last night?" he inquired politely.

Her color went from ashen to crimson. "Nothing happened last night, Colonel—"

"As you say. Good day, ma'am." He swept his hat from his head, bowed, and determinedly left her bedroom.

Rachel was standing in the breezeway as he hurried down the stairs. He looked at her and apologized. "I'm sorry. I'm honestly sorry that we're not who you'd like us to be."

"Paddy has already gone with the men as you ordered. The others are waiting for you just outside. The Yanks are nearly at the house."

"Thank you," he told her gruffly.

He strode for the door.

"Colonel, wait, sir. Please—"

"You know I can't wait."

"Yes, I do know, but I want you to know that you should come back. If you need to. Come back if you need . . . herbs. It doesn't really matter what side you're fighting for, you'd rather heal men, I can see that in you," she said.

He stopped, turned back. Young and earnest, she was watching him, pale but steady, her eyes, touching his, were very sincere.

"Thank you."

"God be with you, sir, even if you are a Reb."

"God be with you, Rachel."

He walked back to her, cupped her face, and lowered her head, planting a brief kiss on the top of her head. He turned and strode quickly out.

Liam Murphy held his horse's reins. Corporal Lyle, Kyle, Keith, Daniel, and Jim awaited him. He mounted quickly, nodding in acknowledgment to Liam's silent warning that the Yanks were almost upon them. He indicated a side trail out of the yard, nudged his horse forward, and heard the others fall in behind him. He entered the cover of a pine forest to the immediate east of the property, and when the others had followed him to a safe distance, he reined in quickly. "Corporal Lyle, keep everyone moving back toward camp, straight toward camp, no engagements!"

"And you, sir?"

"I'll see what I can of the Yankee position. And if I'm able, I'm going to double back for some of Mrs. Tremaine's medicines. I won't be more than a few hours behind you at best."

"Aye, sir!"

Corporal Lyle spun his horse around and indicated to Liam to lead the others forward.

Julian watched them disappear into the brush and pines, then doubled back.

Keeping within the cover of the trees, he saw that the Yankee party had converged on the house. The men were dismounting. A tall dark-haired colonel was in command of the small group—strange, Julian thought, for a Union colonel to have been sent out in charge of such a small party.

"Colonel, should we give chase?" a man queried.

The colonel walked toward the steps, then turned back, observing the overgrown foliage that surrounded the house and the woods beyond. He shook his head. "These Rebs know the terrain, Shelby. You could give chase from now till doomsday, and they'd still be a step ahead."

Julian was suddenly certain that the Yank colonel was staring straight at him.

He stared back from under cover. *Maybe not the others, but you could give chase, and possibly catch us,* he thought. He ducked back behind the trees.

Rhiannon doused her face again and again in the icy water. Her head was drumming, and worse. She couldn't shake the dreams that had haunted her through the night, and for once in her life she was very afraid.

He had come in from his room—fully dressed! He had left her. She had passed out, and he had left her, and her dreams had been just dreams, but oh, God, how vivid, and yet she couldn't have, she just couldn't have . . .

The little vial of opium she'd been about to imbibe was on her bedside table. She stared at it, feeling ill. How much had she taken? Enough. Too much. And then she'd had the wine, and . . .

She'd sat outside, feeling sorry for herself. *His* fault. She was all right day by day when she was alone. But she'd seen him, and known that he was a lying Reb, and still, there had been that empathy in his eyes, beautiful eyes, and the texture of his voice, his touch, even watching the movement of his hands as he'd extracted the bullet. She had loved Richard. She missed Richard with all her heart. The pain probably would be with her all her life. But loving him, missing him, had made her somehow very vulnerable.

This was all his fault. The Reb's fault.

No, not really. She'd taken laudanum before—and pure opium. In fact, she was aware that she'd gotten into taking it far too often. Just a touch, she'd told herself over and over again, but it had gotten to where she'd had that "touch" on a daily basis.

She'd known better.

And last night . . .

She'd taken too much. When she shouldn't have touched anything, when she should have been careful, awake, aware. What if the Yanks had come earlier? What if there had been shooting? She'd thought that she would be in her room, locked away, safe, but what about Rachel? Oh, God, how could she have been so careless, so irresponsible?

It was him; he had somehow made her feel more afraid, more alone, more lost . . . she had thought that her little "touch" of the drug would calm her, but then she'd taken more than a touch.

Then?

She couldn't remember, didn't know. She was so very afraid that . . .

Her dreams had been sweet. Time had swept away. And she'd been with Richard again.

But Richard was dead.

And this had been so real . . .

Mammy Nor's wine. Of course, Mammy Nor's wine. Added to fantasy and relief gained from her field of poppies . . .

She spun around and looked at her bed. The pillows were bunched, the sheets were in disarray, but then, she did have a tendency to twist and turn at night. She hugged her arms around herself, shaking. She still wore her gown, yet the very air around her seemed to carry a hint of . . .

His scent. The Reb's scent.

A masculine scent, so subtle, maybe not even real, and yet it made it seem that his presence remained, touched her, permeated her . . .

She groaned aloud just as Rachel banged on the door and called out her name.

"Rhiannon!"

"I'm coming."

"The Yanks are here," Rachel said reproachfully. Rachel knew that she had sent for the Yank scouting party—to capture the Rebs. She also knew their guests of the night before hadn't been Unionists. She simply didn't care.

"I'll be right there."

Rachel went away. Rhiannon stripped off her gown and took a hasty sponge bath. Her flesh seemed tender. Her imagination, surely. Oh, God, the night seemed a total haze, like a dream in a field of clouds, and yet there were moments she recalled so vividly, as if Richard had returned, as if he had been with her . . .

She dressed hastily, wishing that there weren't quite so many tiny buttons in her black bodice. Every move she made seemed difficult, as if she had lost all sense of coordination. She could see, yes, she could see all manner of things she didn't want to see: it was true, it was horrible, and yet it seemed that now she had been blinded . . .

Don't think about it! she commanded herself.

The Yankee patrol she had sent for was downstairs. It had taken them long enough, certainly, and she wasn't at all sure why they weren't in pursuit of the Rebels. They couldn't be far.

She started from the room, then paused, seeing again the small vial of opium he had kept her from taking. A strange tremor shot through her veins. Just how much had she taken last night along with the wine? How much more might have killed her, eased away all pain? Permanently. Shaking, she suddenly realized that she didn't want to die. She hated it that Richard was dead, but she didn't want to die.

Nor did she ever, _ever_ want to face another morning like this one, wondering what had been fact and what had been fantasy. Surely . . .

"Never again!" she vowed silently. She picked up the vial of opium. "Never again, I swear it."

She was about to toss the vial into the fireplace when she remembered how desperately medicines were needed throughout the South. She might want the Union to win the war, and she might even be bitter. But she'd seen enough to know that she didn't want any shattered man to lie in agony beneath a surgeon's knife when this much of an opiate could ease his pain.

She set the vial down. She would touch no more of her own medications. Nor would she destroy what others might desperately need.

She started from the room once again. She was dizzy and

miserable. Rachel was waiting for her on the landing. Rachel had never seen her like this. She tried to smile, although she was aware that Rachel was angry with her, though God alone knew why. Rachel had been born and bred in the North. The Rebs had lied to her as well. Rachel had adored her cousin Richard. But she was angry about the Rebs, nonetheless.

"Rachel, you might have seen to the Union men, helped Angus and Mammy Nor see to their thirst."

"Oh, I've greeted the Union men," Rachel told her solemnly. "I was just curious . . ."

"About?"

Rachel smiled innocently. "Your reaction to them."

Rhiannon sighed. "Rachel, I knew the men last night were the enemy, and yes, I sent for this patrol. Are you forgetting that Richard died fighting for the North? Rebels killed him, Rachel."

"The war killed him. He was probably shot by some poor fool just trying to survive the same," Rachel said.

"But Rachel, don't be mad at me because I sent for a Yankee patrol."

"I'm not mad at you."

"Then—?"

Rachel shrugged. "Come meet the soldiers. You'll see."

Rhiannon sighed and lifted her hands. Even that seemed an effort. She was so shaky. Her head continued to pound. The world waved in front of her, as if the air were like the ocean, and undulated with an unseen current.

"Are you all right, Rhiannon? You look ghastly," Rachel told her.

"Thank you."

"You're entirely white," Rachel said, studying her with real concern

"I'm tired. It was a bad night."

She felt sick. She hoped that she was walking down the stairs in a normal manner.

Yet as she neared the ground floor, her heart began to hammer in an alarming manner. A wave of eerie fear swept over her. There was only one soldier in the hallway.

Him.

He had returned.

Tall, dark-haired, with his piercing blue eyes, he stood in

her hallway now in a crisp, clean Yankee cavalry uniform. He awaited her, his plumed hat in his hand, his eyes searching as he stared up at her, waiting.

She was seeing things.

No, he was back.

He was everywhere. He had come to haunt her life, to taunt her forever, to make her feel again, when she had learned that she could find oblivion . . .

She looked at him, feeling the world begin to spin around her in a most disturbing manner. She tried to open her mouth. She wanted to speak.

"Ah, Mrs. Tremaine, I'm so sorry to disturb you, but I needed to ask you questions about your recently departed guests, if you'd seen—"

The ground was swept from beneath her feet. She didn't have vapors—not even little ladylike flutters—and she'd never fainted in her life.

But suddenly the world was cold and dark, and she was slipping to the floor.

"My brother, Mrs. Tremaine."

Rhiannon was dimly aware of the Yankee colonel's words, but they came too late.

She continued her slide into darkness.

Chapter 4

$\backsim\!\!\!\!\!\!\!\sim$

"Mrs. Tremaine."

She opened her eyes. She was lying on the sofa in her parlor. He was still there. Sitting by her side, studying her with concern. He was the spitting image of the Rebel doctor who had stormed into her life.

"Brother," she croaked.

He smiled, nodding. "Are you all right, then? I'm Colonel Ian McKenzie, U.S. Cavalry, and I'm terribly sorry to have startled you so. When your man arrived in St. Augustine, I was anxious to ride with the troops—I had planned on coming out here during my visit before your messenger arrived."

She tried to sit up, pressing her temples.

"Mrs. Tremaine?"

His voice was even like the doctor's, with a deep timbre and soft hint of the South.

"I'm all right," she said quickly. "Twins?"

"No, not twins, though I have been told we look quite a bit alike," he added politely, watching her face. "I admit, I've never had quite such a reaction from an acquaintance of Julian's, but . . ."

"You look just like him," she murmured. "Same eyes, hair, the shape of your face—"

"No," Ian McKenzie interrupted with a subtle smile. "He looks just like me. I'm older. By a year."

"And of course . . . you're in a legitimate uniform, and not nearly as gaunt—"

"I'm on the side that eats more frequently," Ian McKenzie said dryly. "And don't worry about Julian—nor should he be underestimated. He may be lean, ma'am. But he's lean muscle, and knows enough to look after himself."

"I wasn't worrying about him," she murmured.

"Yes, of course not, he's a Rebel, the enemy," Ian McKenzie said, yet she thought that he looked at her strangely, and she felt her cheeks redden; what was he seeing in her?

"McKenzie . . ." she said, then shook her head. "Oh, my God, yes, my father used to speak about your family! You have a home near Tampa Bay. Your father settled there even before my father came here."

"We're indeed long time residents. And you were invited to Cimarron many times, Mrs. Tremaine, but you and your father had a tendency to be North on business."

"Yes, I suppose we traveled frequently," she said, suddenly feeling like a fool. She'd seen him and passed out. She smoothed back her hair. "So . . . sir, you and your men missed the Rebel troops?"

"By a matter of minutes, I'm afraid," he told her. "Are you sure you're all right? You still look quite pale."

"She had a difficult night."

The words, which seemed to carry the hint of a taunt, came from Rachel, and Rhiannon realized that her young ward had been there, standing behind the Yankee colonel all the time.

"I sent Angus to Captain Cline. Was the captain unavailable?"

"The captain was wounded in a skirmish."

"My God, is he—"

"No, not dead. Healing nicely."

"Thank God."

"Yes. I came in his stead. And we were late. My apologies. We rode as quickly as we could once word had reached us. Again, I apologize for causing such distress. Perhaps I should get you some brandy, a glass of wine—" Ian suggested.

"No!" she protested sharply, then realized how rude she sounded. "I—I would love some water, please." Rachel was staring at her as if she deserved to be wretchedly sick.

Ian McKenzie brought her a glass of water from the sideboard. She pushed herself up and accepted the water, drinking it in a single long swallow. She did feel somewhat better. She managed to sit with some dignity.

"Rachel, will you ask Mammy Nor if we might have coffee served here?"

"Certainly," Rachel said.

Rhiannon smoothed her skirts, trying to control her trembling, her eyes downcast as Rachel left the room. The colonel continued to stand near her, watching her.

"Are your men out giving chase?" she asked him.

"No."

She looked up at him, startled. "But—"

"They could run in circles for hours. They could be ambushed. Slaughtered. It would be futile."

"How can you be so certain?"

"Because I know my brother. He knows the landscape, the roads, the pine forests, the rivers. His men are Florida boys. They're gone, and we'd need more than a few green fellows out of Michigan to find them."

She stared straight at him. "In all honesty, since it just happens that you were at the base in St. Augustine, and happened to lead these troops, did you try to miss your brother, Colonel McKenzie?"

He shook his head. "No, Mrs. Tremaine, I did not."

She frowned, remembering that he had said he had intended to come to see her before.

"Colonel McKenzie, you said that you already were coming to see me. Why?"

He hesitated a moment, then reached into the pocket of his uniform jacket, handing her a letter. "This has taken some time getting here, since your husband's commanding officer was determined to give it only to someone who could hand it to you directly."

She stared at the envelope in his hand, feeling a wave of pain sweep over her, like the tide upon the beach.

"I don't understand. Richard's body was returned to me by rail almost immediately after the battle. I was told that I was very lucky . . . that not many bodies were actually returned to their loved ones," she said.

"The army tries, Mrs. Tremaine—"

"It's just that there are so many corpses, right?" she inquired on a whisper.

"Your husband's body was identified and sent home right

after the battle, ma'am. This letter was found in his personal effects after. He was highly respected, Mrs. Tremaine, and as I said, his commanding officer was anxious that this letter, addressed to you in his own hand, reach you."

"And since your home was Florida . . ."

"It is still my home, Mrs. Tremaine. My home is a beautiful place just outside Tampa, my folks are there, my brother and sister remain in the state—very near here. It's my ardent belief that the country will one day be reunited, and I will live here again. I maintain my ties here. My wife, children, and a cousin-in-law and her baby reside in St. Augustine."

"I see," she said.

She moistened her lips. She wanted to wrench the envelope out of his hands, and then again, she didn't want it at all—she was afraid of it. She looked up at him again. "So your wife is here, your family, your extended family."

"Yes."

He had just said that, she realized. But she couldn't seem to stop. "Your children. Nephews and nieces?"

"Not yet. Neither my brother nor my sister has children as yet."

"Soon enough, I imagine."

She was talking away idly. Repeating herself, making little sense. Prying. Anything to keep from taking the envelope that she wanted so much.

"Well, I believe one of them will want to marry first," he murmured.

"Not married," she said.

He walked over to her and came down on a knee, offering her the envelope. "I didn't mean to cause you pain. I thought you would want this," he told her. He was strikingly handsome, charming, kind. The empathy in his eyes was almost more than she could bear.

"I do want it," she whispered. "Desperately." Already, tears were stinging her eyes. She blinked them back furiously and reached out with shaking hands to take the letter.

"I'll leave you alone and return presently," he said quietly.

He left the room. Rhiannon opened the envelope, amazed that it could have remained so clean and white throughout the long journey home.

Tears flooded her eyes.

Dearest Wife,

If you should receive this, it will mean that I have perished in this great struggle of ours for the freedom of all men and the preservation of the Union. God knows that we are right, and so I am not afraid to die, and my only regret is to leave you, when it seems you were a part of my life forever, and yet, our time together was so brief. I don't write to sadden you, to burden you to a greater degree, but to tell you that you were always the joy of my life, determined, adventuresome, so very brave, and so full of love for life. (All right, my darling, pigheaded, willful, and so on, as well!) But through these very traits, you will survive this great agony which has rended a nation, and God grant, my lady, I will watch you from heaven and pray for your happiness. In my memory, I do beg you to live life for all that it is worth, and to seek happiness, for the greatest crime, I see, when life is so fragile, is to refuse to accept its beauty. Remember me always; cease to mourn me. With love into eternity, your devoted husband, Richard.

The last words swam before her eyes. She started to cry, great, wretched sobs that threatened to tear her apart. The letter drifted to the floor, and she leaned against the arm of the sofa, shaking and wondering anew just what wretched betrayal she might have practiced against so fine a man.

Julian kept his distance, watching the house. He saw his brother ride out, commanding the Yanks to post guard.

Certain that his brother rode alone, he moved deeper into the pine woods, coming to a copse where he dismounted and waited once again. Soon enough, he heard his brother's horse moving slowly and carefully through the forest. Ian would never be taken by an ambush; he'd learned far too much, not just from the military, but from their father and their uncle, James. James, half Seminole, had learned bitter lessons about hiding.

"Over here, big brother," he called dryly.

Ian turned in the blink of an eye; even hearing his brother's voice, he took no chances. The barrel of his Colt, identical to Julian's own—was aimed at his heart.

"I'm alone."

"So I see."

Ian holstered his weapon and dismounted from his horse. He approached, and Julian grinned, greeting his brother with a heartfelt embrace. Moments when they met now were rare.

He drew away from Ian, searching out his eyes. "Is there something wrong? Why are you here? Shouldn't you be busy in a Northern campaign somewhere? Last I heard, you'd been assigned running intelligence from Lincoln himself to whichever general was trying to lead an eastern campaign against Lee."

"Someone had to bring orders to St. Augustine, and I requested the assignment."

"It's convenient that your superiors allow you to visit your wife," Julian commented.

Ian arched a brow. "I've been assigned here several times, and not for the convenience of my family life, but because it's assumed I'm far more likely to be effective against Rebels like you."

"I'm a medical man, Ian."

"I've heard you've been involved in some shooting."

"People shoot at me, I shoot back."

"You'll become fair game. The enemy will be justified in shooting you. Doctors have been killed in this war, Julian—"

"Civilians have been killed in this war, Ian. What would you have me do—stand there and take a shot?"

"No. It was just good to think that you and Brent might have survived this war, that's all," Ian said.

"We've all got to survive it," Julian said tensely. He suddenly felt weary. The war was bitter, frightening, better not to think about. All of their lives, they'd been a close-knit family—not just Ian, he, and their sister, Tia, but their cousins Jennifer, Jerome, Brent, and Sydney as well. For the most part, the McKenzies fought for the South.

No matter how he tried to look at the situation, to their uncle, James McKenzie, the Federal government had done nothing but bring pain, suffering, exile, and death to his mother's people, the Seminoles. Therefore, he was a Confederate. Jerome, James's older son, had chosen to fight for his state, and Brent, James's younger son, was a surgeon with the Army of Northern Virginia. Jennifer had tried spying for the South for a while after her husband had been killed, but she'd nearly been killed. Sydney had worked in Southern hospitals, and was now in Washington working for prisoner exchanges.

Ian had chosen the North, knowing that he'd become an outcast from his own family, but though Julian had chosen the Florida militia and Tia worked with Julian, their father, Jarrett McKenzie, remained a Unionist as well. The family was sadly split, with Jerome's wife being the daughter of a Northern general while Ian's remained, at heart, an ardent Confederate. Both women had taken up residence in St. Augustine, passing the time by working with a surgeon there, and they had all crossed battle lines before, determined to help one another out during times of danger, no matter what the cost. Blood could indeed be thick—thicker than any loyalty, despite the passion of their convictions and disagreements. Julian was able to see Jerome every few months—his cousin was a blockade runner who did his best to supply Julian with drugs and medicine. It was more difficult to see his only brother.

They fought on opposite sides.

"How are Alaina, Risa, and the children?" Julian asked huskily.

Julian thought that his brother hesitated, but only briefly. "They're all very well, thank you. Have you seen Mother and Father?"

"Not in months, I'm afraid, but Tia was home a few weeks ago and said they were fine."

"I miss them," Ian said. He swept off his cavalry hat and dusted the trail dirt from it, gazing toward the west. "I miss going home. I miss our conversations, and our arguments, and I miss Cimarron."

"Think it will ever end?" Julian asked.

Ian looked at him steadily. "It will end. Eventually, Northern manpower and supply will strangle the Confederacy."

"Maybe." Julian looked back at him just as steadily. "But perhaps Europe will step in and recognize the Confederacy and put enough pressure against the Union that the Federal government will think good riddance at last and let the South go. With elections coming up, maybe the antiwar candidate will win."

Ian leaned against an oak tree, crossing his arms over his chest, and grinning. "Too bad we can't just settle the argument here and now."

"Fight it out, like when we were kids? Because you think you can take me?"

"I'm still older."

"I think I am a little taller."

"I'm in better shape."

"I resent that."

"I've got at least twenty pounds on you right now."

"Careful, you well-fed Yanks will run right to fat."

Ian laughed, setting his hat back on his head. "I imagine you did well enough last night. Mrs. Tremaine seems to be managing a well-working household."

"Oh, yes. Entertain the Rebs and summon the Yanks!" He frowned. "How did you happen to be the one to ride out here, Ian?"

"Well, I was hoping to see you. I thought you might be in on this, and if we were going to capture some ragtag militia that might be taken as spies, I wanted to make sure someone was in charge who was in a mood to take prisoners—and not so bitter he'd want them all shot."

"That was good of you, big brother. As you can see, though, the ragtag band has gone."

"I've always given these troops credit, Julian. So do the powers that be. People know that your men are quick, disciplined, and able to wreak chaos, which makes them dangerous, no matter how small their numbers."

Julian nodded. "We've got to do our best, Ian. You know that. I know that you feel you have to fight for the North; you know these boys feel they have to fight for their land."

"I also had a message for Rhiannon Tremaine. I needed to deliver a letter found with her husband's effects. He was with Colonel Egan at Antietam. Egan is a friend of mine and wanted the envelope hand-delivered. Which I was pleased to do, being curious to meet the lady."

"Oh?" Julian inquired.

Ian shrugged. "She's supposed to be a witch, you know."

"I believe it," Julian said blandly.

Ian arched a brow. "An interesting witch, a white witch,

so goes rumor. She can make poultices to cure the deepest wounds, forecast the weather, and find lost children."

"Rare talents indeed," Julian murmured.

"Do you believe in them?" Ian queried him.

Julian lifted his hand in a vague motion. "I've known her only briefly. How could I judge?"

"You're a doctor, she's supposed to be a healer. Aunt Teela always had a talent with all our scrapes, cuts, bruises, and illnesses. Perhaps this Rhiannon is the same."

"She's quite competent in a medical situation," Julian said noncommittally.

"So she helped patch up a Reb!" Ian said.

"She'd been told he was a Yank."

"Ah, but she knew that you were a pack of liars, didn't she?" Ian mused with a touch of humor. "That is, if she does have special sight. And since she sent word to the troops at St. Augustine . . ."

"She knew we were lying, and she played along. What else could she do?" Julian asked, irritated that his brother seemed so curious and probing. Ian knew him too well.

"She does seem an extraordinary woman. You mean that you weren't impressed?"

"You're married, Ian."

"Indeed. I am. You're not. Well?"

"Yes, extraordinary," Julian said impatiently. "And foolish."

"How so?"

"The use of laudanum and other opiates—on herself."

Ian studied his brother, lifting a brow. "She's grieving. I was sorry I had the letter, but I had no choice but to give it to her. I'm afraid that it will cause her greater pain."

"Other women have lost their husbands. Mothers have lost their sons. Our cousin Jennifer lost her husband—"

"And became a spy, grew careless in her bitterness, and nearly hanged for her actions," Ian reminded him. "We tend to forget, it is also a woman's war, and often the waiting is the worst of it, and then the knowing, and the living on, day after day, when all seems lost."

"That's quite a speech."

"Alaina gave it to me," Ian said and grinned. He shrugged. "I've too often been in Washington when the lists of the dead have arrived after a battle. I've seen the eager waiting, the hope, the dismay, the desolation, and the tears. She is in pain. Time will help heal her loss, but she's not had enough time as yet to begin to mend. This war will leave a sea of widows, and many will grieve until their dying days."

"Her dying day is going to be soon if she doesn't take care," Julian said.

"A pity. She's enchanting."

"So is your wife," Julian reminded him.

Ian flashed him a quick smile. "No one ever needs remind me of that. Alaina is enchanting and gracious. I think that I should try to talk Mrs. Tremaine into moving into St. Augustine, where she will be safe from you Rebel rabble. There are those who believe she can be useful."

"She can be useful."

"I wish she would agree to come with me, but I doubt it. Perhaps she might be put into greater danger, since the army would surely want to explore her 'sight.' She is remarkably talented, I believe. And, of course, a Yankee."

"Meaning?"

"Who knows when her very unique talents might be required?" Ian said.

Did she have a strange kind of prophetic sight? If so, the Rebs could definitely use her more. But she would never aid the Rebel troops, and Julian found himself telling his brother, "Make her come with you. Pressure her. She should not remain in that house."

"I'll certainly try." Ian shook his head, and his voice held a tremor. "God, but it's good to see you, little brother. I've got to talk quickly, though. I'll be missed soon, I'm afraid. Can't have the troops know I'm fraternizing with the enemy. Nor do I dare let the lady know the truth of the matter. She thinks that I managed to miss capturing you on purpose."

"Did you?"

Ian hesitated. "No," he said.

Julian smiled, certain that Ian was lying. "Thank you, brother."

"I still think you've saved more lives than you've cost," Ian said. "Still . . ."

"You're the one who takes too many risks, Ian," Julian said huskily. He shook his head. "You shouldn't do that."

"I always calculate my risks, you know that," Ian told

him. "And as I said, I was hoping to see you—without us having to shoot at one another, of course. I wasn't expecting Mrs. Tremaine to be so astute—or so alarmed at the sight of me. Meeting her was an interesting experience."

"Why, what are you talking about?"

"I walked in, and she passed out."

"What?"

"Took one look at my face and apparently thought that you had come back into her life."

"She thought you resembled me so closely?"

Ian sighed with mock impatience. "Julian, I'm older. You resemble me."

"I met her first, therefore you resembled me."

"That's still not the way it works, but no matter. Tell me, whatever did you do, little brother, to cause the widow such distress?"

"I kept her from killing herself."

"Oh? She didn't appear to be contemplating suicide."

"I took her drugs away."

"No more than that?"

Julian hesitated. "I took them away rather forcefully," he said after a moment. "We argued the point, and she was a bit under the influence at the time."

"You used to have more patience, little brother."

"I used to have more time away from torn and dying men to have patience with those who have given up, big brother. And then again—" he began, but broke off with a shrug.

"Then again—?"

"She angers me. Because she is a witch perhaps, a spellbinder, far too knowing for her own good."

"Maybe she needs to be doing more than she is. She'd make an excellent nurse."

"By all means."

"I'll make the suggestion to her."

"Yes, do that," he murmured, surprised that it should disturb him that Ian might give her such a suggestion. Ian could possibly entice the widow away.

Still, Julian realized, it was what she needed, to become involved with others again, to become passionate in the fight to save lives, to see that others still lived and needed help.

"I have to get back, Julian. But I had wanted to see you as well on a separate matter, and one very important to us both, at that."

"Is something wrong?" Julian demanded.

"Wrong?" Ian said dryly. "Yeah. Even more than the simple fact of war, and the fact that we are enemies in that war."

"What's happened?" Julian asked.

"Two things. First—" he began, then hesitated, and Julian realized that although his brother's tone was light, he was very worried. "First, I've heard that Jerome was attacked running the Yankee gunboats just off the coast here. He eluded capture, and the Yanks believe that he put into a cove somewhere south of here. They think he sustained an injury. If so . . . they'll be bringing him to you."

Julian let out a long breath. His cousin Jerome was known to take chances. He was a man Lee would have loved to have in the Army of Northern Virginia because he made quick decisions and moved with the speed of lightning.

"How badly injured?"

"Standing all the while, so say the sailors from the Yankee sloop. I've kept Risa from knowing as yet, but she'll find out soon enough."

"Jerome will reach me. His men know my position well enough."

"I imagine they'll be able to reach your camp sometime tomorrow, though you know as well that the Yanks will be looking for Jerome, and his men may have to move slowly."

"I'll be ready for him. Don't worry, Ian. You know that I'll do anything in my power for Jerome."

"I do know that. I know you're the best there is, and I know Jerome is as tough as a gator. But I also know that wounds fester, and that men die far too easily from infection. I'm just scared as all hell. And I hope he does reach you by tomorrow or the next day."

"Why?"

"Well, that's the second thing I wanted to tell you. I've heard rumors that they'll be pulling more boys out of the militia, sending them north to fight the major campaigns. There's a lot of talk about you, both sides of the line. You did save U.S. General Magee's foot, you recall. The general has maintained a keen interest in you, and he let me know that he's heard there's been talk on the Southern side of pulling you out of militia and giving you a regular army commission."

Julian stared at him, his heart sinking.

Leave? There was barely anyone left here to fight, barely anyone left to heal the ones who were fighting, and they wanted to strip down the state even more.

"Thought you should know," Ian said quietly.

Julian nodded, then grimaced. "Funny, isn't it? My Yankee brother comes to tell me what the South is doing."

"Told you," Ian said, "we're going to win this thing."

They were both afraid, he knew.

They both just wanted it to end.

"Your Michigan or Ohio young'uns are waiting for you, Ian. Tell me, do these fellows speak English? Or have you got another group of immigrants fresh off the boats from Europe?"

Ian grinned, shaking his head as he turned and walked to his horse. "These fellows speak English," he called over his shoulder.

"That's right." Julian said, following him. "Why give the foreigners the restful duty in Florida? Send those fellows right into the fray! Kill them before they get too fond of the country they're dying for."

Ian mounted his horse. "I'm not running the war, Julian."

"Yeah, I know," Julian said, patting the head of his brother's roan. The animal was well fed, with sleek fur. He looked over at the gray mare he was riding. His horse showed more rib than flesh. Maybe he and the gray belonged together. He looked up and offered Ian his hand. "Thanks, brother. It was damned good seeing you. Take care."

"Stay out of the line of fire, Julian, for the love of God." He hesitated. "When Jerome reaches you, get word to Risa somehow. She'll want to be with him."

"Naturally, I'll get word to his wife—and to you, through Alaina. You keep your head down, Ian."

Ian nodded. He turned his roan and started back toward the house in the pines.

Julian leaned against the oak tree and watched his brother go. Then he turned toward the plantation house set deep in the overgrown foliage.

Maybe Rhiannon Tremaine would manage to rouse herself enough to accompany Ian and set her talents to the healing of wounded Union soldiers.

And maybe not.

She was stubborn. Pigheaded.

She might turn Ian down, determined that she was going to stay at her home.

Perhaps she really was a witch, a white witch, with the power to heal. Maybe she had the gifts of a true natural healer.

He leaned against the tree, watching the house for a long, long while . . .

Maybe . . .

Maybe he needed her himself. Well, fate was in her hands right now. She could go with Ian, or . . .

He'd damned well go back for her himself.

Chapter Five

~~~~~~~~~~~

By the time Ian McKenzie returned to the house, Rhiannon had regained her composure. She was also prepared for his resemblance to her earlier Rebel visitor, though she still found it uncanny and unnerving.

Coffee and food were served, and she sat in the dining room with Colonel Ian McKenzie, listening to his suggestion that she either come into St. Augustine for the duration of the war, or find work with one of the hospitals.

"I tried to become a nurse when Richard was first given his commission," she told Ian. "They wouldn't allow me in."

Ian grimaced. "Yes, I know, at the beginning nurses were only accepted if they were old and homely. But I assure you, things have changed. The sheer load of casualties in this war has forced changes. If you decide you want work in a hospital—even in the field, I'm sure I can arrange it."

She nodded, watching him. "If Rachel is willing, I think I would love to work with the soldiers."

"It's hard work, grueling work. But sometimes a soldier makes it because enough care is given."

"And that is surely worth the effort. To save just one life would be . . . gratifying," Rhiannon mused.

"So . . . will you come back with me to St. Augustine today?"

"I . . ." she faltered. She wasn't quite ready yet. "I need a little time."

"Time . . . time to what?" Ian inquired politely.

"Oh, well . . ." she said, and waved a hand in the air, then shrugged. "To pack, for one. To give instructions to

Angus and Mammy Nor. To see to it that my home is secured the best I can leave it in my absence.

"That sounds reasonable. But you will come?" he persisted.

"I believe so."

"I'll return in a few days," he told her. "You really must come with me then. I think that leaving this house—for now—is your only course of action. Think on this—it might be dangerous for you to remain here."

"Why?"

"The Rebels will consider you a traitor."

"They were not—vicious men."

"No—but others might return."

Rhiannon nodded after a moment. She could be in danger. She had known that before she had betrayed the Rebels.

"I'll give the matter deep thought, sir," she assured him. "And I will probably accompany you when you return for me. I agree that it makes sense."

"I wish that you would come with me now."

She smiled and said, "Honestly, I do need time. That's all. And . . . thank you."

The Yanks departed soon after their conversation. Rhiannon watched them ride away, then fled to her room, reading Richard's letter over and over.

She couldn't simply have left that day.

Absolutely not. Not when he had brought her such touching words from Richard.

She had needed this time. Yet as she read, she looked around her room and felt again a great distress at not knowing what she had done in the night.

She had to do something. She couldn't stay on here, the way she had been going. If she was now allowed to be a nurse in a Union hospital, she wanted to be one. If she could help save a soldier's life, spare anyone this agony, it would make life itself . . .

Worthwhile once again.

She set the letter on her mantel and launched into a flurry of activity. It was a good afternoon for cleaning.

She stripped her bed, telling herself that the sheets needed a good washing. The sheets, herself, her nightgown, her mourning clothing . . .

Everything needed to be fresh.
She was going to start over.
After tonight.

Julian proceeded carefully, moving closer to the house but keeping a certain distance. He watched the Yankees depart, his brother riding in the lead, then watched a while longer, to make certain that the enemy had all ridden away.

Rhiannon Tremaine had not ridden with them.

He watched as Angus rolled a tub out into the back, and the household prepared for an afternoon of laundry—mainly sheets, some clothing. He wondered if she had made an agreement to leave with the Yanks at a later time.

He didn't intend to approach the house himself until dark. He didn't want to steal from anyone, but he needed the poppies she had grown and many of the potions she had created. And he was equally determined that he needed her. Forcing her to accompany him wouldn't really be an act of abduction—she was simply too valuable to be left to her own devices. But old Angus was one big son of a gun, and he wanted to be careful moving around her property. He had no intention of being captured.

He spent the latter part of the afternoon resting beneath the shade of a large pine. He closed his eyes for a brief moment, and was alarmed when he awoke, realizing he had dozed when he sensed someone near him. A noise had awakened him; her man, Angus, was preparing to chop wood not fifty feet from where he rested.

Julian rose quickly, scolding himself for his carelessness. He was damned lucky he hadn't been captured.

When the tall, heavily muscled black man turned and saw him, he was standing. He hadn't pulled his gun, having no intention of shooting the man.

Angus, staring at him, froze. "You gonna shoot me, Reb?" he asked quietly.

"Are you planning on killing me?"

Angus slowly grinned and shook his head. "So what are you doing back here, Doctor, sir?"

"I need some healing potions," he said, staring straight into Angus's black eyes. "And a healer."

Angus looked back at him steadily. "Oh?"

"What do you think?"

Angus leaned back, watching him carefully. "I think Miz Rhiannon has been in some powerful poor way as of late. She set such a store by her man, she did."

"I thought she might leave with the Yanks. Did she say anything about doing so?"

Angus shook his head. "No, sir."

"With all the washing, I thought she might be getting ready for a long trip.

Angus shook his head once again. "Sheets, sheets, more sheets, her clothing, her room, herself. She was even scrubbing the bedroom walls before she tucked into a hot tub herself for a good hour or so."

"Angus, I know you think I'm wrong in this war, but I need to take her with me. I won't let any harm come to her, I give you my word. When she's helped out with my wounded cousin, I swear I'll give her safe passage into St. Augustine."

Angus stared at him for so long that he wondered if he was going to have to give up his quest and ride away—or shoot and kill an innocent man to achieve his purpose.

"What do you want me to do?" Angus asked him after a minute.

Julian hadn't know that he was holding his breath until he expelled it at Angus's reply. "I want to ride out of here in darkness, but before it grows too late so that I can cover some fair territory before morning."

"I'll see that you're all set." Angus set his hands upon his hips then. "But you'll have some mean convincing to do, Doctor."

"I can persuade her."

"If you can't talk her into going?"

"I'll carry her."

She'd whirred through the afternoon with a burst of action. By early evening the bedding they had washed was sun-dried and back in place, her clothing and undergarments were washed and pressed, her hair was shampooed, and she smelled faintly of roses herself.

With new resolve, she picked up Richard's letter one more time. She was going to get her life back in order. She would learn to live with Richard's loss in a more responsible and mature way, no matter how painful.

No more drugs. Ever.

She left her room quickly, anxious to be alone for a few hours.

Richard was buried in the small family plot across the lawn and just up the very small roll of a Florida hill. She did love the state, and she would be loath to leave it for any length of time. So much to the far south was flat swampland, but here the land did roll—just slightly, and there were some wonderful acres of pine forest, and acres of rich red clay. Despite the summer, it was cooler here than in other places in the deep South. But home wasn't a place to hide. It was a place to love and to cherish, and she would always do so now . . . no matter what the war brought.

The sun was setting as she left the house and walked the distance to the graveyard with its wrought iron gate and fencing. Golden rays of the dying light streaked through the leaves of the oaks and pines scattered throughout the burial ground, casting a soft haze upon the dying day and giving just enough illumination so that she could clearly read the markers. Her parents were to the left, with handsome granite markers ordered from Philadelphia, along with a baby brother who had died at birth. Her father's cousin, Hampton, was a few feet from her folks, and behind him lay a number of the men who had been employed at the salt works, and Jimmy Lake, the traveling teacher who had been killed at Shiloh. Richard was to the right of a great oak.

She drew his letter from the pocket of her skirt, and again felt tears sting her eyes. She knelt on the ground before his marker. The breeze picked up, strangely cool for summer, touching her face, her hair. Rain, she thought distractedly. It didn't matter. She reached out and ran her fingers over the engraving of his name. She could almost see his face, his smile, hear his voice. When contemplating dying, he had thought of her, had wanted nothing but life for her.

She leaned forward, her face in her hands.

The wind whipped up higher. Darkness and rain were on their way. It seemed only fitting.

A strange unease suddenly ripped through her. She

raised her head, wiped her eyes, and looked around anxiously. Then she froze.

He was back. Colonel McKenzie. Not the Yankee colonel—the Rebel one.

He leaned against the nearby sprawling old oak, arms crossed over his chest as if he had stood there a while. He watched her with cool blue eyes that were both disdainful and dispassionate. Tremors washed through her, and she gritted her teeth, staring back at him. She thought that she had washed away all dreams, fears, and memories. Yet had she been dreaming about Richard?

What had she done last night?

"What are you doing back here, Colonel?"

"You didn't leave with the Yanks," he said.

"No. Was I supposed to have done so?"

"Yes."

"Why?" she inquired. Then she remembered Ian McKenzie's persistence that she come with him, and she thought that she'd been a fool to think otherwise—the McKenzies had met that day, no matter what lies they told her or their troops. She also remembered Ian's warning that the Rebs might want retribution against her.

"Have you come back to burn down my house?" she asked.

He arched a brow, gazing past her to the house. "It's a fine structure, handsome, sound. Why would I want to burn it down?"

"Because this is a Confederate state, and I'm a traitor to it. Isn't that the way you see it?"

"Yes, but I haven't come to burn down your house."

"Then why are you back?"

"You, Mrs. Tremaine. I have come for you," he told her lightly.

"Me!" she repeated, startled. She stared at him, certain he was taunting her.

"Yes, Mrs. Tremaine. You should have gone with the Yankees. Now you'll have to come with me."

She shook her head, eyeing him warily. Carefully, she came to her feet. Was he so angry that she had summoned the Yanks? Did he mean her serious harm for what he saw as betrayal?

"I'm not coming with you anywhere!" she whispered.

"But you are." He took a step toward her.

She turned and ran.

He might look weary and gaunt, but he was faster than a cheetah and upon her in a matter of seconds. He caught her by the shoulders and she spun around, tripping over a root. She fell, and he was caught up with her motion, and they crashed down to the ground together.

With the air knocked from her lungs, she gasped for breath. He was far quicker to recover, rolling her over, pinning her down as he straddled her.

"Oh, come now, Mrs. Tremaine, I cannot believe that you're so afraid of me. After what happened last night—"

"Nothing happened last night!" she cried.

"Deny what you will. That's not the point here."

"The point, sir? There is no point! You're a Rebel, I'm not. You invaded my house. You weren't welcome, but I helped you keep your friend alive. There is nothing else, I owe you nothing. Last night you broke down my door— after having invaded my house!—and you rudely took my medicine away from me."

"Medicine!"

"Medicine kills pain, doesn't it?"

He stared down at her. "I took your opiate away, yes. And yet, if I did it so rudely, what a pity that you can't really remember the rest of the night."

"I . . . fell asleep."

"You did do that, yes."

"And I sent for the Yankees. I can't be sorry for that! Well, is that it then? I'm a traitor, under arrest, to be punished, is that what it is? I still won't go with you. Hang me, shoot me, here and now!"

"You'd like that, wouldn't you? An easy out! The wretched Rebs killed your Richard and turned around and executed you as well. You'd die damned happy, wouldn't you?"

"Don't be ridiculous—"

"You wouldn't have to kill yourself then."

"I've not tried to kill myself!" she flared furiously.

"Fine. Then you can summon something called courage and help other people."

"What?"

"We're going to have a little stroll through your personal

pharmacy, Mrs. Tremaine. Through your garden. Then you're coming with me."

"You can steal every plant, shrub, vial, and potion on the place, Colonel McKenzie," she told him. "But I won't be coming with you anywhere."

"Because you want to stay here and prostrate yourself on Richard's grave daily?" he demanded sharply.

She inhaled a long breath, staring at him, feeling the rigor of the muscles in his thighs where they clenched around her and feeling the angry heat and power within his eyes.

"If that's what I choose to do—"

He leaned toward her, blue eyes as cutting as an ice fire. "Richard is dead, Mrs. Tremaine. Dead and buried and, as some believe, in a far better place. Others are still here. Still fighting, still bleeding. People who need you. I can swear to you, I have done surgery on both Yanks and Rebs. If you are blinded to the fact that you can help heal those who are desperate, then I will open your eyes."

"You can't make me come with you—"

"How strange. I believe that I can."

"You cannot mean to force me!" she said contemptuously.

"That I do."

She stared at him, astonished. "That's kidnapping."

"I don't give a damn what it is."

"You—you can't do any such thing!" she stuttered. "Where were you raised? Southern gentlemen do not behave this way. I will not allow you to behave this way—"

"Oh, what will you do—shoot me yourself? Find your Southern virtue so compromised that you'll kill yourself—with an overdose of drugs and wine?"

His features were as hard and implacable as his words. Chills seized her and then, deep, hot frightening tremors. She wanted to twist away. She was so afraid . . .

He'd called her a coward already. She wouldn't let him know that she was afraid of him. Afraid of herself, afraid of the void of a night that had passed.

She raised her chin, surveying him coolly. "I wasn't trying to kill myself! Colonel McKenzie, who do you think you are? I don't have to go anywhere with you. You are the one in danger, the one who had best do as I say. Angus will shoot you if I tell him to."

"I don't think so."

"You underestimate Angus."

"I've seen Angus. He doesn't look like a cold-blooded killer to me."

"He'd kill you instantly if he thought you were threatening my life."

"But I'm willing to bet he knows I'm trying to save it."

"Will you stop that! I am not suicidal—"

"Only accidentally suicidal."

She gritted down hard on her teeth, staring at him. She remembered him standing in the middle of her bedroom. She had been—on the balcony? He'd been wearing a towel and a gun, no more. What then? He'd tried to take the vial from her, and they'd argued, and she thought she remembered losing the argument, crying . . . And then?

Sleeping.

Dreaming.

"I'm telling you, I am not taking any opiates—"

"Good. I need you in control of all your faculties."

She narrowed her eyes. "Understand me. I'm not coming with you—"

"You are."

"To assist in surgery on more Rebs—"

"Yes, as a matter of fact. One Reb in particular. A blockade runner. A man who has provided a desperate people with life-saving supplies."

"You're the great physician. You save his life."

"I'm a physician—good enough to know that all my skill in surgery means little against a flaming infection."

"What makes you think I can make a difference?"

"Rumor has it," he said dryly. "I watched you with Paddy."

"I competently ripped his trousers."

"You know how to clean a wound, salve it, bandage it."

"So do many people."

"Not nearly so well."

"I'm not saving any more Rebs—" she began in a stubborn whisper.

"You're saving this one."

"Why? Because he bests his Northern enemies with such skill and talent?"

She was startled when he stared down at her a long while before answering.

"No," he said after a moment. "Because he's my flesh and blood. He's my cousin."

She fell silent and after a moment he rose, reaching a hand down to her.

She stared at his hand, and back to his eyes, shaking her head.

"I—can't come with you."

"I insist."

"And if I don't . . . ?"

"I cart you off, screaming and hollering."

She smiled. "I'd be worthless—your superior officers would make you let me go."

He leaned down toward her. "Mrs. Tremaine, I very often am the superior officer in these parts. You should have gone with my brother, Ian. But you didn't. So now, you can come with me."

"I was going to go with your brother. In fact, he's coming back, and I have every intention—"

"That lie will not serve you now."

"Will you listen to me! I'm telling you the truth. I really intended to go—in a few days' time. I had some things here that I had to do—"

"Cry a few more buckets over Richard's grave."

Jumping up, she backed away from him. "How dare you! How dare you even speak his name! You didn't know him, you didn't know what he was like, the kind of courage he showed, the way he was willing to die for others—"

"The way he would want you spending your life dying over his grave now?" he queried.

"I was saying good-bye."

"Good, because I'm ready to go."

"Then go!"

"You're coming with me. And we've work to do before we leave."

She was poised to run away from him once again, certain he meant to reach out, grab her arm, and drag her along with him.

But he walked on past her, and she realized that he was

heading for the house, and that he meant to go through her store of supplies without her.

"Wait!" she cried, coming after him. "You have your nerve! You told me that you didn't rob, rape, pillage, or the like, and here you are, *stealing*—"

"I'm not stealing anything. You're giving me what I need. You're supplying the sons of your state with the medicines they need to live."

He was walking very quickly, and she was surprised to find herself hurrying along beside him. "Oh, you are a wretched, sorry bastard, McKenzie. Doctor, indeed! You will twist anything, you are a manipulator, a—"

She broke off, suddenly realizing that she was indeed being manipulated.

She stood still, smiling. "Fine, sir, you want to pillage my garden and my supplies? You are carrying a gun—I'm not. I can't stop you. So go ahead, help yourself."

She spun around, hurrying back toward the cemetery. A dense pine forest began just a few feet beyond the graveyard, and she could disappear within it and hide until he'd been forced to take his leave.

She didn't hear him—or sense him. He came up behind her so quickly that she let out a stunned gasp when he swept her into his arms, doing another about-face to return to the house.

She slammed a fist against his chest. "Would you let me down?"

"No."

"Damn you, let me go—"

"I'll be delighted to do so. Extremely delighted to do so. Just as soon as I can hog-tie you and find a muzzle," he said.

"Don't you understand?" she demanded, struggling against his hold. "You're a Reb. I despise you."

"Interesting. You didn't despise me last night," he remarked casually.

She sucked in her breath, startled by his subtle attack. "I did, I do, I despise all Rebs, and I can't bear you holding me, touching me."

"Again, you were not so delicate last night."

"I fought with you last night."

"And ripped off my towel."

She gasped and started pummeling him in fury once again. "I did not! I wouldn't."

He shrugged. "Maybe not on purpose, but you did!" He was taunting her; there was a mocking light in his eyes as he stared down at her.

"There was nothing!" she cried, her voice rising desperately. "Nothing happened last night."

He was silent, walking along with his long strides, heedless of her pummeling fists and struggles.

He reached the rear entrance to the house and brought them through the back door. "Angus!" she cried in frustration.

But there was no one in the main house. No one was there to answer her cries. Where they had gone she didn't know, but she could feel the emptiness.

Yet just when she thought that she would explode with the velocity of a cannon, he set her down in the center of the small rear hall, between the pantry and the kitchen.

"Your potions, Mrs. Tremaine?"

She glared at him, fists clenched as her sides. "When he comes back," she said, "Angus will shoot you."

"Angus is saddling your horse, Mrs. Tremaine," he told her.

Stunned, she stared at him. "I don't believe you. Angus is from Vermont. He's a free man. A friend as well as a servant. He is appalled and sickened by slavery—"

"I don't own any slaves, Mrs. Tremaine. If you wish, you can go upstairs for more clothing and a few personal effects. I can see your jars and vials. I'll take care of packing these things."

She stared at him. He was already assessing her stores of ointments, salves, poultices, and opiates. He knew exactly what he wanted, what he would take.

She backed away, still disbelieving that he could so calmly demand that she accompany him, and sped up the stairs. She burst into Rachel's room, seeking help, but there was no help to be found. The girl wasn't there. Stunned and angry, she walked back into her own room.

She began swearing softly, wanting to know where everyone had suddenly gone, and what in God's name was happening.

She realized, as she ranted, that she was packing a small

canvas bag, as if she did, indeed, intend to be away several nights.

If he was going to force her to come with him, she'd have some of her own things, at the very least.

She opened the wardrobe, reaching for her cloak. It was summer and the heat could be intense, but rains came at night, and they could be cool.

The wardrobe was filled with Richard's civilian clothing. *How could she have forgotten?* For a moment, standing there, she was so struck with fresh pain that she couldn't move. Then the numbness and reality began to set in. Richard was gone. And as horrible as it might be, the Reb doctor's face was a far clearer picture in her mind right now.

Far clearer than she wanted it to be. Haunting her, making her so afraid . . .

Don't think. Don't be afraid. Be down to earth, cold, simple, factual.

Fact. The Reb doctor's clothing was in sad repair. With shaking hands she took out a shirt and a pair of breeches. She gritted her teeth, feeling the onslaught of a headache and wishing she could take some laudanum.

She spun around, feeling an uneasy sensation.

He was there, standing in her doorway. Blue eyes sharp, hard, relentless as he watched her. Handsome face hard, mocking, as if he could too easily read her mind. "You're ready?" he inquired.

She didn't answer him, but indicated the clothing she held in her hands. "Your things are badly frayed."

"And those are Richard's?"

"Yes."

"No, thanks."

She wanted to slap him. She was making a supreme sacrifice, offering him Richard's clothing. "Don't be ridiculous," she told him angrily. "Your clothing is worn, in danger of falling apart."

"I don't want to remind you of Richard," he said flatly. "I don't want you to think of me as him, and I don't want you calling me by his name."

She shook her head. "You're nothing like Richard. He was kind and courteous."

"And a Yankee," he said dryly. "Good St. Richard. I'm sure I'm nothing like him."

"You can take his clothing. I'd never mistake you for my husband."

"Oh?" He arched a brow, and she felt a flush of heat and apprehension as he walked across the room, taking the clothing from her.

"So you've never mistaken me for Richard. Really?"

He stood directly in front of her. She could see the pulse ticking at his throat, the strange look in his eyes. Her breath seemed to be ripped away, and she suddenly felt her heart slamming against her chest.

"Colonel, sir, I pray that you cease being so rudely insinuative—"

"I'm not being insinuative at all. I'm trying to establish facts."

"McKenzie, you bastard—"

He turned away from her, walking over to her rosewood secretary and picking up one of her journals. "I've taken clippings, seeds, and some roots," he said, thumbing through her inventory of plants. "You keep good records," he told her, sliding one of her books on flowers and herbs and their properties from the secretary. He flipped through it. "This is better than a number of the medical journals I've read."

He sat down at the chair in front of the secretary, reading.

"You can use Richard's clothing," she said stubbornly.

"No, thank you." He said politely, firmly. He didn't look up.

"Fine, then you can get out of my room."

At that, he looked up at her. She was uneasy again as his blue gaze slid slowly and curiously over the length of her. He shrugged, crossing his arms over his chest. "Do you recall at all that you weren't so eager to be rid of me last night?"

"You burst in here."

"Yes, I did. So you do remember that. What else?"

"There was nothing else!" she insisted.

He stared at her a moment longer, then looked back to the book he had been reading.

She hurried over before him, planting her hands on the

secretary to stare furiously into his eyes. "You stopped me from taking the opium. I do remember."

He looked up at her politely.

"Don't, don't, please, don't!" she whispered desperately.

"I'm not doing anything," he told her.

"You are! You are implying—you are saying things— you are insinuating—"

"What did happen last night, Rhiannon?" he asked her. "You tell me."

"Nothing. Nothing happened."

His blue gaze met hers for a long moment. He rose. "Whatever you say is what happened, Rhiannon. Whatever you say."

He reached out suddenly, capturing her hand despite the fact that she tried to snatch it away. His eyes remained locked with hers. "You're shaking. Look at your hands! And you should see your eyes. You don't remember the night, you *refuse* to remember the night. And you told me you weren't addicted! Now here we are again! Last night was painless—until the doubts and fear set in, right? But tonight will not be so easy. It's going to be a very long, hard night for you, Mrs. Tremaine. Very long. And be warned, there won't be any giving in—I'll fight you again."

He turned away from her and walked out of her room.

Chapter 6

❧

That night, as Julian had well imagined she would be, Rhiannon was sick.

Julian had been amazed at the help he'd received from both Angus and Mammy Nor in getting Rhiannon out of her house. She'd actually packed a few belongings, and though she'd been concerned when speaking with her two remaining servants, they had not been worried. "We aren't really in any danger here, Miz Tremaine," Angus had said, winking. "You were the Yankee living in the heart of Dixie. Why, with the trees so wild and all, we'll probably go the rest of the war without a single body even passing by."

Rhiannon had run back upstairs to make sure that Rachel was nearly ready. Rachel was pleased to be leaving, even if it meant going to a Rebel camp. Angus and Mammy Nor had stood together, staring at Julian.

"You two really going to be all right?" he'd asked.

Angus had laughed. They'd be fine, he'd assured Julian. They would look after the place, they would make sure that it was kept up. And, they both swore, if troops came through from either the North or the South, they would take to the trees until the soldiers were gone.

"We'll be right as rain, young man," Mammy Nor told him. "Miz Tremaine, she needed to be out of here, and if you ain't exactly what we were counting on, I sure do know that the Lord works in a mysterious way. You see to Miz Tremaine, and you watch out for your own hide, Doctor. There are some gray clouds around you, and that's a fact. You protect yourself."

They had left with Mammy Nor and Angus waving good-bye.

Julian was even riding a new horse. A bay in far better health than the skinny but loyal old nag he'd left behind. Angus had promised to see to the horse and fatten her up.

Julian used the moonlight to travel, moving quietly along dark, overgrown, lonely trails. At first the going was easy enough. He'd spent the majority of his life in the state, and he knew more of the old Indian trails than many an old Indian.

As he rode, though, he grew bitter at the thought that he might soon be reassigned north. Half the time now he didn't know what he thought about the war. He didn't believe in slavery, but he didn't believe in the Federal government's right to dictate what his state should do. He'd heard from friends that General Robert E. Lee, head of the Confederate army, had devised a plan to free his own slaves before the war started. Lee had been adamantly against secession, but when Virginia had seceded, Lee had gone with his state. It was strange, he thought. Once the decision had been simple for him. Florida had seceded, Florida boys were hurt and dying, he was a doctor, he had to help his own. But all he could see now was the destruction of his state, of his family, his home, everything he loved.

These thoughts burdened him, but sometime during the ride he realized that he had been preoccupied for a long time, and that his female companions had quietly ridden alongside.

Julian probably would have pushed on farther, but he realized that it was around midnight. Looking back, he saw that Rachel could scarcely remain in her saddle. Rhiannon, at Rachel's side, was keeping a keen eye on her young ward. She sat straight in her saddle, but no matter how she might be trying to hide it, she was in pain. The moonlight illumined the ashen color haunting her beautiful features. She was shaking and shivering as well, clenching her teeth hard to disguise her discomfort. Withdrawal, he realized.

"We'll stop just ahead," Julian told the women. "There's a stream up there and the remnants of an old Indian village."

Rhiannon arched a brow to him as they turned down a heavily overgrown trail. Yet he knew where he was going. Down the trail and just around a crooked little path, he came to a small copse he knew well. His uncle had brought him here years before; it had been one of the camps used by the Seminoles just before General Jesup had tricked the famed Indian leader, Osceola, into capture. Though the copse hadn't been used as a settlement in years, travelers who knew of its existence came through now and then, and the thatch roofs had been somewhat kept up and the platforms were cleared often enough to make them easily dusted now for sleeping quarters. A little stream, a tributary to the St. Johns, lay just ahead of the chickees, and Julian pointed the water out to the women after helping them from their horses. He tethered the animals, taking saddlebags and blankets from them and arranging sleeping quarters for Rhiannon and Rachel high on one of the chickees. Assuring himself that they were resting in relative safety—only the one, heavily foliaged trail led to the chickees by the stream—he walked to the water himself. They had both been drinking their fill, and Rachel seemed too weary to realize just how pale and quiet Rhiannon seemed to be.

"Will we be all right, sleeping here?" Rachel asked him anxiously.

"We'll be fine."

"There are snakes, aren't there?"

"That's why the Seminoles built their houses up on platforms, Rachel."

"Why didn't they build walls?"

"Because they had to run too often to stay away from the soldiers," he told her. "Once they did built log homes. But the soldiers kept coming and burning them out. They learned how to build fast, serviceable dwellings that they could desert at will. So they built chickees. You may like it. It's nice, sleeping like this. Up from the ground . . . but still getting the night breeze."

"You've slept in these before?"

"I have an uncle and cousins who are half Seminole, down by the deep swamp. I've slept in lots of chickees. You'll be fine, honest. I'll be watching over you. Your blanket is set up over there."

She smiled at last. Rhiannon stood by the water, still and silent—and very white. Rachel kissed her on the cheek, yawning. "Actually, I think I could almost sleep standing. Good night, I'm going to crawl into my blanket."

She left them there. Julian eyed Rhiannon, then knelt by the water. It was cool, clear, delicious. He slaked his thirst, then realized she was still standing there.

He rose. "You're all set up to get some sleep next to Rachel."

She nodded, but then suddenly lurched away from him, stumbling against a tree. She reached out a hand, steadying herself; she leaned over and was sick.

"Rhiannon—"

"Stay away from me," she cried, trying to move more deeply into the foliage.

"Rhiannon, let me help you—"

"No!"

But he followed her, and when she doubled over again, retching in dry heaves, he put an arm around her for support. She pulled away and stumbled back toward the water. She fell to her knees and drenched her face, throat, and hands. She remained on her knees, not moving but shaking violently.

"I'll be right back," he told her hoarsely.

He strode to the chickee where he'd lain their blankets, hiked himself up. Rachel was asleep already. He took Rhiannon's blanket and strode back to the water. He swept it around her and lifted her up and into his arms. She didn't have the strength to stop him. He had carried her a few feet from the stream, toward the chickee, when her hand fell against his chest.

"No!"

"I'm just taking you to the chickee—"

"No, please, don't go near Rachel."

He paused, standing very still. She didn't want Rachel to see the seriousness of her addiction. He turned and walked back toward a clearing blanketed with pine needles that was but a few feet from the stream. Using a tree for leverage, he sank down with her in his arms, keeping the blanket wrapped tightly around her. It was a beautiful night, warm, not hot, the air touched with a pleasant, caressing breeze.

Her teeth were chattering, but she looked up at him, making a feeble effort to free herself from the bonds of his arms. "You need to . . . let me go," she whispered miserably.

"I'm trying to warm you."

"I'm . . . all right."

"The hell you are."

"I may be sick again."

"You may."

"I don't want you to see me . . . like this."

"I'm a doctor; your condition isn't something I haven't seen before."

"My condition—"

"Withdrawal, Rhiannon. From your opiates."

"I'm not withdrawing from anything—"

"You are. And you know it."

"Then . . ." she began, then hesitated, clenching her teeth for a moment. "Let me have something, please, just a touch of laudanum."

"No."

"I can't stand this."

"You're going to have to."

"My stomach keeps knotting. You don't have to feel responsible for me. I knew . . . I know what I'm doing."

"Oh, yeah, you know."

"Please . . . I'll wind up throwing up all over you."

"It's happened to me before."

She shivered violently. "This is awful—"

"Yes, it is. And you're going to suffer tonight. I warned you that you would. But I told you as well, I've been through it."

"Not with me!" she whispered. Her eyes touched his desperately. Such startlingly beautiful eyes. So brilliant, so vividly colored, against her ghostly pale features. She wanted so badly to escape him, but hadn't the strength of a kitten at the moment. She closed her eyes again, and he tightened his hold on her, cradling her shaking body against his.

"I can't bear this!" she whispered.

"You can."

"I'm so cold."

"I'll keep you warm."

"No, you're the enemy, please . . ."

"You're damned right. What an enemy! I'm—"

"Something, give me something, let me withdraw slowly, surely—"

"Rhiannon, one night will be bad. You'll have bad times

after as well, but this will be the worst of it. I can get you through this."

Her eyes closed. "I'm going to die."

"No, you're not. I won't let you."

"Please . . ."

He wasn't quite sure as to what her *please* referred to—if she wanted to die, or if she wanted him to stop the pain. He couldn't do that; he could only do his best to help her make it through the night.

She started shaking with greater violence. He held her more tightly. He cradled her head against his chest and kept telling her that she would make it. She could make it, she could bear it, and she would . . .

Sometime during the night she drifted to sleep. She woke in another spasm of shudders and he cradled her to his chest, talking her down again.

She lay quiet. He brushed her cheek with his knuckles. It looked as if she was regaining a bit of color. She moved in his arms. For the moment her violent shivering had ceased.

She opened her eyes and stared up at him. "Why . . . why are you doing this . . . to me?" she whispered.

"To you?"

She hesitated a long time, staring at him. "For me," she said then.

He smiled slowly, wondering why himself. She was an enemy. But she was different; a witch, with a talent. A talent that needed to be used, he thought.

And yet it was more.

He arched a brow, starting to speak, then hesitated, a slight smile curving his lips. He might have told her that she was simply too beautiful to let die, that he knew her too intimately to let her go. But he refrained. She was really suffering. It would have been too cruel at the moment.

"Why?" she whispered softly again.

He refrained from any biting comment.

"I'm a doctor," he told her. "I can't let anyone, man or woman, soldier or civilian, throw his or her life away."

"I wasn't dying—"

"Yes, you were."

Her eyes closed again. "I still hate all Rebels, you know," she said softly.

"Well, that's a sentiment shared by many, I imagine," he said, "though, frankly, at this moment . . ."

"What?"

"I just hate the war," he said.

She clenched her teeth. "It's starting again," she whispered miserably. "The shaking, the cold . . ."

"It's all right. I promise you, I'll hold you through the night. I'll keep you warm."

She closed her eyes. Tears trickled from beneath them. "I can't stand that you're seeing me so . . . I can't stand anyone seeing me so. If you could just let me have a bit of laudanum . . ."

"No."

"I can't do this."

"You have to do this."

He cradled her more closely against him. "It will be all right," he told her. "It will be all right."

When it was very late, she slept at last. At first she continued to shiver and shake in her sleep. And finally, toward the morning, she began to breathe evenly.

A touch of pink came to her cheeks.

She slept peacefully, her head against his shoulder, her fingers resting on his chest.

It wasn't over. She would have more bad episodes. But she had weathered the worst.

"Is Rhiannon all right?" a soft voice asked.

Julian awoke with a start, unnerved, feeling a spike of panic. He'd never been forced to run as his uncle had, nor was he part Seminole like his cousins, but he'd spent enough summers with them to have learned that the man on guard never allowed himself to fall into a deep sleep. He was usually good, damned good. And hell, he'd been in this war long enough to learn to awaken at the first rustle of leaves, a shift in the air. He should have been able to awake instantly at the sound of footsteps approaching them.

He hadn't. He'd been sleeping soundly, like a dead man, in a way he hadn't slept in years.

Rachel, wide-eyed with concern, was staring down at

him. He straightened, feeling Rhiannon stirring in his arms. She awoke, her eyes touched his, huge and vividly green, as she too awoke in disorientation.

"Rhiannon?" Rachel said.

"She's fine," Julian said curtly, rising, drawing Rhiannon to her feet as well. "Rhiannon had a touch of fever," he lied to Rachel. "She had a rough night. It's not all over, but the going is much easier from here on out."

She stared back at him, not disputing him, but neither did it seem she much appreciated his covering for her.

"Thank God that we're traveling with a doctor!" Rachel said lightly. "Especially since we're all used to Rhiannon curing everything . . . it's tough when she's the sick one. But are you really all right? Rhiannon, you do still look very pale."

"Yes, thank God we're traveling with a doctor," Rhiannon murmured dryly. "I'm fine, or I will be," she assured Rachel, trying to smooth back a lock of straying hair. "I need some water and . . . Rachel, we brought coffee, right? Mammy Nor sent coffee along, didn't she?"

Rachel nodded, looking at Julian and smiling happily. "Real coffee," she told him.

Coffee was getting harder and harder to come by in the South. People were brewing blackberry leaves most of the time for tea, and coffee usually meant a brew of burnt chicory.

"Real coffee. That sounds wonderful. I'll see to the horses and leave you ladies to your privacy," Julian told them.

"And breakfast!" Rachel called after him. "We'll get some breakfast made for you, too."

"Good. Thanks," he said.

"We'll get you stronger looking, just like your brother," Rachel added.

He'd been striding toward the horses; he stopped and turned back. "My brother looks stronger?" he inquired, his indignity only somewhat feigned.

Rachel covered her mouth with a hand, holding back a laugh. "I'm sorry . . . not stronger, I mean . . . he's just . . . healthier looking!"

He wagged a finger at her. "Don't be fooled, young lady. Appearances can be very deceiving!"

"That's right, Rachel," Rhiannon said quietly. "Rebs tend to be lean, hungry—and very dangerous. You seem to be forgetting that fact far too easily."

Julian met her cool gaze. "Danger comes in many guises, doesn't it?" he asked softly. Then he added to Rachel, "Whatever you've brought for breakfast, I will heartily enjoy. Real coffee is always a treat these days. Thank you."

He turned determinedly and strode out of the copse area to the spot where he'd tethered the horses. He found himself grateful for the lush grasses around them. The horses would need sustenance today.

To give the women time alone, he walked the horses some distance down a trail before turning in toward the stream again. There, standing in water that rose midway along his boots, he allowed the horses to drink their fill. As he did so, he was surprised to realize that although he was downstream, he could hear Rhiannon and Rachel talking. He should move, he thought, but then he smiled, curious despite the fact that he had been raised to have better manners.

"Don't dawdle, Rachel," Rhiannon said. "Let's get moving, let's get breakfast on—"

"My goodness!" Rachel said cheerfully. "It sounds as if you're eager to reach the Rebel camp!"

"Don't be absurd, I just don't want . . . to stay here. I'm restless, I suppose."

"You don't look well at all."

"I'm fine."

"No, you're not, you're pale, trembling, fragile—"

"Trust me, Rachel," Rhiannon said impatiently, "I am not fragile."

"It's so good that we're with a doctor."

"A Rebel doctor."

"I don't care. He's wonderful."

Julian patted the bay, grinning slightly. He'd known he'd like Rachel from the start.

"He's a Rebel, Rachel." Julian's smile faded, hearing the hard edge in her voice. "He is part of the army that killed my husband—your cousin—and thousands upon thousands of other good men."

"He has to be a decent man. Look how he has cared for

us. I am sincerely glad that he wasn't captured or injured when you summoned the Yanks to slaughter them all."

"Rachel! I didn't want anyone slaughtered! I wanted them captured—"

"He's been good to you. He took care of you last night when you were sick."

There was a long silence. "He's a doctor. He's sworn to take care of people who are sick."

"He took care of you," Rachel repeated stubbornly.

"He's the enemy."

"Everyone around us is the enemy! They consider us traitors around here, remember?"

"Just because so many others are wrong or misguided does not mean that we should be wrong as well. Slavery is wrong, owning people is wrong—"

"And many Southerners don't own slaves. I heard that General Lee had already made plans to free all of his slaves before the war began."

"To secede from the Union is wrong—"

"It will only be wrong if the South loses," Rachel countered. "Some people thought it was wrong when the Colonies broke away from Great Britain! And then, it was all a big headache for our founding fathers—thirteen clocks had to chime as one, thirteen states. Each different, each wanting the right to make its own laws, what was right for the people of that state—"

"Rachel!"

"Well, that's history—"

"And history is usually written by the winner. And in this, trust me, eventually, the Union will prevail."

"Rhiannon, you have to see things from both sides. You usually do, you're usually compassionate—"

"I'm sorry. Maybe, since Richard was killed, I'm simply out of compassion."

"Thank God, then, that your doctor isn't."

"He is a Rebel," Rhiannon said heatedly, "and if the opportunity arises again, I will summon Yanks to try to take him—dead or alive."

Julian heard a splashing sound. Rhiannon had turned away, dousing herself in more water, he thought.

"I think you're being awful and hateful!"

More splashing. Rachel had followed her.

"Rachel—"

"There's something you can't see, you won't see. He isn't horrible, he's helping you—I think you're afraid of him because he's a Rebel and you can't quite hate him. Or maybe you actually do *see* something in the future between you two, maybe you're so afraid that—"

"Rachel, I see nothing! Nothing at all except . . ."

"Except what?"

"Blood. More and more bloodshed," Rhiannon said wearily. "Now leave me alone, please. Is your coffee ready? I would dearly love a cup. And the bacon smells wonderful." She hesitated, her voice softened. "Your Reb colonel will be pleased. What a lovely meal you've made."

Julian could smell the bacon then. And it was good, causing a tightening in his stomach that was almost painful. Bacon. Of course. Delicious cooked food . . .

It wasn't the bacon. It had been the coldness in Rhiannon's tone. The promise that this was war, and it never ended.

How strange. He was a good distance away, hearing them only. But he felt as if he had seen her face as she spoke. As if he could see the ice in her beautiful eyes. What a difference day could bring. He could remember her anguish last night. The tortured look in her eyes then. The delicate, yes *fragile,* beauty of her face. Even the vulnerability, the *trust,* if only for a matter of minutes. And her voice then, so soft . . . *I don't want you to see me like this . . .*

But that had been the night. And day had come.

So she'd turn him in if given the chance.

He'd damned well see to it that she never got that chance.

Chapter 7

∽

"Captain McKenzie?"

Brent McKenzie, field surgeon with Longstreet's division of the Army of Northern Virginia, had been bent over his camp desk, examining his records of sick and injured men treated on the field, returned to duty, sent to local hospitals—or buried on site or returned in pine boxes to their families.

He looked up as his name was called.

Colonel Samuel Wager, an adjutant to Surgeon L. Guild, medical director in the field of the same troops, was standing at the A-line entrance to Brent's field canvas office and quarters. Brent started to rise, but Wager waved a hand. He entered the tent and took a seat in the folding camp chair in front of Brent's desk.

"Record keeping?" Wager asked.

"It's required," Brent said.

"As if there isn't enough to do. I read a paper you wrote recently, by the way. It was excellent."

Brent politely smiled. He couldn't remember writing any papers lately. *Letters,* yes. He wrote letters continuously.

The greatest cause of death in the army was not from bullets. Sometimes he wondered if they could even blame the Yanks. The majority of deaths stemmed from diseases. He frequently wrote to the authorities, to Congress, to Jeff Davis, the surgeon general, to anyone who might listen. They could save lives if they could just improve their rations and their water. He frequently exchanged letters with his cousin Julian, who also believed the death rate could be cut dramatically with sanitary conditions in the army camps. Julian had remained Florida militia while Brent, in

Charleston when South Carolina had originally seceded from the Union, had joined on as a surgeon with the Confederate Army.

Though cousins rather than brothers, he and Brent had been close all their lives, sharing a love for medicine from their early childhoods. Julian and he had both spent time with Seminole shamans, learning what native swamp plants made a difference in treating such diseases as malaria and dysentery, easily acquired in the swamps. Julian had never mocked or made light of a different way of treating illnesses; he hadn't thought of the Indians as savage or lacking in intelligence in any way. When something worked, he tried to learn the reason why. When he couldn't learn the reason, he still believed in results. And so, no matter how tired he often was—or how difficult it was to get mail through—Brent spent many an evening writing to his cousin, answering letters, sharing results. They'd both agreed that the appalling rations given the soldiers often caused the terrible onslaughts of diarrhea that had eventually killed so many men. They both fought to keep human and animal waste from the camps, and to urge the military leaders to stress the importance of finding clean drinking water for the men. Julian had written him about a training camp in southern Georgia where the soldiers had complained about "creatures in the water big enough so that no microscope was needed to see the varmints," and it had been after their forced reliance on such drinking water that almost half of the troops had died from dehydration caused by severe diarrhea.

Naturally, they were plagued here by other illness as well, including measles, malaria, typhoid fever, smallpox, and mumps. Practicing medicine in camp meant treating almost every malady known to man, all manner of illness, and manner of injury. Bayonet wounds were not nearly as common as those caused by bullets; again, injuries from bullets far outweighed those from shrapnel, cannonballs, and other explosives. Most treatable bullet wounds were to a soldier's arms or legs, basically because most gut-shot or chest-shot men died on the field. So many who could be saved perished, bleeding to death while battle raged on. Often, no matter how he wanted to really practice medicine, he felt he was little more than a butcher—after a major battle, he had little recourse except to cut away limbs. Limb after limb. And with each cut of his scalpel, each stroke of his surgical saw, he worried that he was cutting a man's hope and dignity along with his flesh. Sometimes, no matter how quick and expertly done the amputation, gangrene set in, and a man died anyway. The fight for life amidst so much blood was never-ending.

But then again . . .

There were those times when he knew that his expertise saved lives. Even limbs. When his patient treatments and precautions saved a company from slow death due to a fever that was quickly quarantined, rather than allowed to run rampant. As painful as it often was, he was glad to be among the men of the Army of Northern Virginia. He missed his home; missed his family, missed his native warmth in winter. But he had gotten used to artillery fire overhead when he worked in wretched conditions on a field of blood. No matter how bad conditions and the situation were, he felt he made a difference, and that made his own life, if often anguished, worthwhile, even gratifying.

Wager was watching him, he realized.

"Paper?" Brent said, sitting back, wary, and not at all sure why. "What paper?"

"Well, all right, it wasn't a paper. It was a letter, an excellent letter sent to General Lee."

"Ah," Brent said. He wasn't sure whether to be glad that his letters had been read at all—or resentful because they had been read by a man to whom they had not been addressed.

"Yes, I read quite a discourse written by you on preventing the spread of disease . . . and, also, a passage by your Florida militia relation, another Dr. McKenzie."

"Julian's theory on the use of clean sponges in the operating theater?" he inquired.

"Yes. You both keep excellent records."

"Right. As I said—required, to the best of my ability, by the surgeon general."

Sam Wager suddenly leaned forward. "You're a most impressive young man, Captain McKenzie. As is your cousin. Both with your specialties."

He arched a brow. What specialty?

Wager was looking at him strangely. "You're Indian, somewhere in your background, right, McKenzie?"

Brent wondered where this was going. Yes, he was Indian, and Wager knew it. He had his mother's green eyes, but his quarter part of Seminole blood showed in his nearly blue-black, dead straight hair. His background was revealed as well in his broad cheekbones and the golden pigment to his skin. "My father's maternal family, sir," he told Wager.

"Seminole, right?"

Brent nodded again.

Wager sat back, lifting a hand. "Well, there, maybe that's the explanation."

Brent carefully set down his pen. "Explanation for what?" He'd known Wager a long time. Wager had never commented on his background, or looked at him in such a manner—or suggested that his bloodline might account for anything.

"Your expertise with disease."

"Excuse me?" he said, eyes narrowing.

"With the things that men and women catch . . . and pass around."

"Because of my Indian blood I would know this?"

Wager smiled. "Don't go taking offense. I mean that it makes you more aware of the way that our society brings disease from place to place. It means that you've probably spent some time with people who have learned to use nature to their own purposes more than we do. Smart people. Take the fact that so many Indians, Seminoles included, always fought half naked because they were aware that bits and pieces of fabric catching in wounds always make them worse, more prone to infection. All I mean is, you're one damned decent, thinking doctor, Captain. And your background surely helped make you that way."

"Umm, maybe," he murmured. He'd been uneasy since Wager had come in. Now he was feeling downright wary. "But, sir, it doesn't seem to me to take a genius to make the connection that more sanitary conditions help to stem the flow of disease. Colonel, please, what is the point here?"

"Well," Wager said, and sat back. If Brent didn't know the fellow better, he'd think that Wager was blushing.

"We've another outbreak, sir. One demoralizing the army, destroying morale."

"What outbreak might this be, Colonel?"

"Venereal disease, Captain. Straight and simple."

Brent frowned. Sexual diseases had plagued armies from the beginning of time. Put enough homesick men and boys into a position where they were far from home and frequently facing death on a daily basis, and they were going to forget wives, mothers, sweethearts, and seek the company of the world's oldest profession. Yes, he was aware of sexually transmitted diseases. He had done his best to help men who could only be treated and not cured; he had given out medications for tortuous itching and agonizing dripping. He had talked and counseled men—young and old.

"Yes, venereal diseases are certainly a problem, Colonel."

"And you, sir, are just the man to deal with them."

"What?" Brent said incredulously.

"General Lee himself has been in a sad quandary. Why, Master Robert has the greatest respect and regard for you, sir—"

"We've barely ever talked—" Brent protested.

"You're mistaken, sir, if you don't think that the general has seen the exceptional work you've done here. You can't realize how much hope and faith he's putting into your abilities when he plans on putting you to the task of studying and repairing the situation."

Brent was out of his chair. "Wait! I've no special abilities—"

"Captain, sir, you'll be out of the field of fire for the next few months, waging a new war, a gallant fight—"

"A gallant fight—against venereal disease?"

"There you have it, Captain McKenzie, sir! Your new orders will be to head up the treatment and investigation of these devastating illnesses. There's a special community being set up—not too terribly far from Richmond—where you'll be able to treat and study a community of prostitutes—"

"Prostitutes!"

"Yes, sir, Captain McKenzie, sir, and you can't begin to imagine the service you'll be doing your fellow man!"

Wary—hell, yes, he should have been wary. But he'd never imagined anything like this.

He looked down, gripping his hands, controlling his temper. So he'd done exemplary work. His reward was a city of diseased prostitutes?

"Colonel Wager, sir, I must protest. I think that my work with the men here is far more important—"

"The surgeon general himself recommended you for this job, Captain, considering it be an honor to command such an intensive study. You are being given this command with the greatest faith and respect."

"But the men with whom I've worked—"

"We need you, sir."

"I'd rather thought I was needed here."

Wager sat back. "You're good at medicine, at surgery, McKenzie. But frankly, in the midst of battle, sometimes, sir, a butcher is as good as a surgeon. But you needn't be too dismayed. We're bringing more men into the ranks."

"From where?"

"Some of them are coming up from your own state, Florida."

Although he'd been with the Army of Northern Virginia for a long time, he felt a painful nostalgia for his home. "The Confederate army is stripping the state of Florida of its militia."

"Not stripping it. Leaving it skeletal, perhaps. The major battles are being fought to the north, and that's a simple fact."

"But the coast of Florida lies unprotected except for her own few militia men and occasional Confederate troops—"

"I don't make policy, Captain McKenzie. It's no secret now that General Lee is desperate to wage this war on Northern soil, and so we'll all move north. You won't be needing to fret about your division's men—your cousin is being commissioned into the regular service. Longstreet fought to keep you here, but the medical experts were convinced that you were needed, so we'll be bringing Colonel McKenzie up to move with our forces."

Brent just stared at him.

If that didn't just beat all.

Julian, naturally, was going to be angry. He already felt that the state of Florida had been abused by the Confederacy. She'd been stripped of food, supplies, and men. For her loyalty to the cause, she'd been abandoned. Now more men, including him, were being pulled north.

Julian would take his place.

While he was sent to deal with prostitutes.

"Maybe," he said hopefully, aware that he was offering up his cousin to the lions, but then, what the hell, Julian was going to be angry one way or the other, "my cousin should really be given the opportunity—and privilege—of commanding the study and care of the horrible outbreak of venereal disease. He's an excellent man with disease—and prostitutes."

"The orders have already come down, Captain McKenzie. I'm sure that both you and your cousin are excellent in treating disease—and prostitutes. We're counting on you, Captain. You can't begin to imagine how much. You'll be receiving paperwork from the surgeon general within the next few days. You may choose a staff to bring with you, of course."

Wager rose. Brent stood as well.

"I still must protest—"

"Indeed, do so, sir, if you wish. It's your God-given right as a Southerner to exercise freedom of speech! But it's also your duty as an officer in the Confederate States Army to serve your country where you're most desperately needed."

"I'm needed where there's the greatest danger—"

"Good evening, sir. Godspeed you in all your efforts."

Wager left the tent; Brent stared after him blankly for a long minute.

He fell rather than sat back in his chair. He lifted his hands, as if to heaven, and spoke aloud. "Blood and guts and thousands of battle-torn men just weren't enough, eh? Prostitutes!" he said, shaking his head.

He allowed his forehead to crash down on the desk before him.

Prostitutes . . .

Yes, by God, it was one hell of a war.

Decent. Nice. Dashing.

Riding behind Julian McKenzie, Rhiannon sniffed aloud. So much for Rachel's opinion of the man. He had barely spoken to her; when he had done so, he had been brusque to the point of rudeness. When he looked at her, she felt a strange trembling inside, as if she were detestable. So much for *I'll hold you, I'll keep you warm, I'll get you through the night* . . .

Maybe not. He had gotten her through the night. But she wasn't sure she felt so much better now. She remained so tired, as if her body had fought a battle even while she slept. The only difference today was that she . . . knew.

She had been addicted. She fiercely denied that she had been trying to kill herself; all she'd wanted to kill was the pain. But she had played dangerously with her homegrown drugs, and this morning she knew full well that it had been wrong. She felt terrible.

And she felt better. She would actually have thanked him if he weren't acting like such a horse's ass!

He came to a dead halt; she reined in sharply behind him, Rachel reined in behind her. He sat very still, listening. She heard nothing but the breeze, the slightest rustling of leaves. The summer's day was mercilessly hot, and she couldn't begin to think of why he would stop . . .

"Colonel?"

The word seemed to come from the sky, from the trees, from nowhere, from everywhere.

"Right, Digby, it's me."

"You alone, sir, except for the ladies?"

"That I am."

A man suddenly jumped from the trees, landing right in front of them. He was young, slim, supple, tawny-haired with a quick grin. He smiled at Rhiannon, nodding as if he would tip a hat if he were wearing one. "Heard you were coming, sir, and heard about the ladies, of course."

"I'd assumed somebody would be meeting me," Julian said. Rhiannon looked at him, frowning, but as he glanced back at her, she understood. Julian's men had returned before them to give the others fair warning that he was bringing a Yankee sympathizer into their camp.

The young man, Digby, whistled. Three other men appeared from the trees. One was older with white whiskers, the other two were middle-aged. They were all gaunt. Rhiannon bit her lip, remembering that she'd read that Florida was supplying the majority of the salt and meat to the Southern troops. It seemed the food was all leaving the state. At any rate, it didn't seem that much of it was being consumed by Florida boys.

The whiskered man stepped forward, brandishing worn scarves that still seemed clean enough. "Ladies, my apologies. I'm Lieutenant George Smith, Florida militia, and I'm afraid you must be escorted from here on in."

"Do you want us to dismount?" Rachel asked gravely. Rhiannon looked at her young charge, feeling a strange flash of anger. Rachel was enjoying herself, feeling as if she were involved in high espionage.

"Why, no, miss, that's not necessary," Digby said. "You can't lead the horse blindfolded; I'll be right up behind you anyway."

"Wait a minute," Rhiannon protested. "This really isn't necessary. What if we swore that we'd never give away any information of the location—"

"We wouldn't believe you for a minute," Julian interrupted quietly, dismounting from his horse. He took one of the scarves from the lieutenant and came to her mount. His blue eyes touched hers with just an edge of fire. She realized he meant to leap up behind her.

"On my honor," she said gratingly.

"Your honor?" Julian inquired softly.

"Ma'am, we sure like to go by honor, but in these days, well . . ." Lieutenant Smith murmured.

She felt Julian's hands on the rear of her saddle. She edged forward as he leapt easily behind her. "Close your eyes," he warned sharply.

"It really isn't necessary—"

"I've never felt it was more so." She felt the scarf fall over her eyes. Julian tied it none too gently.

"You all right?" she heard Digby asking, and by Rachel's quick assurance Rhiannon knew that Digby was seated behind her young ward. Rachel was just fine.

She didn't think that she'd ever felt more resentful, nor had she ever imagined what it would be like to ride while blinded so. It was an unnerving feeling. Being blinded, she felt more, and she understood how those who were permanently blinded learned how to rely on their other senses, for she became painfully aware of her sense of touch and hearing. Every rustle of the wind seemed loud to her; each ray of the sun seemed to touch her with warmth. She could almost feel the direction of the rays that touched her. Indeed, the warmth was coming from the west. Twilight was coming. With it the relief of coolness that only night could bring. The breeze kept lifting, a dampness touched the air.

She could smell him. Breathe his scent. The soap with which he had bathed the other night. Something subtle, a scent which was entirely his, barely discernable, evocative, masculine, unique. Not real, she told herself. The horse was moving beneath her. She felt the clop of hooves. The gentle, soft, moist kiss of the air that was sure promise of rain. She could feel the darkness coming. Taste that moisture on the air. Hear every movement. Feel . . .

Julian. His thighs against hers, his arms around her as he led their mount. The wall of his chest. He appeared lean, gaunt. But she could feel the heat and ripple of sheer muscle as he sat behind her. Blinded, she still closed her eyes, wishing that she could quit seeing the past as well, that she could erase the confusion and fear that still plagued her heart, remaining from the night they had met. What had she done? Why was this both so painful . . .

And so easy?

She wished desperately that she could ride alone. The tremors she felt now had nothing to do with addiction and everything to do with the hard, angry man behind her who had held her through the night, yet seemed so contemptuous of her.

She moistened her lips, tried to speak with no sound, then found her voice and spoke softly. "Are we almost there?"

"Almost."

"It seems as if we've been riding a very long time."

"A little more than an hour."

"It seems like more."

"It should be more."

"Because we could betray your camp. But there are endless trails here. Overgrown, bogged down, we couldn't possibly tell anyone how to get here—"

"The Yanks know we're near the river. We have to be. Any more information and they could find us. We've shifted here and there a few times, but moving a base camp with decent hospital facilities isn't easy."

"But if we're almost there—"

"You'd give us away in a heartbeat, Rhiannon." His voice was very cold, and still, somehow, his usage of her given name made the words personal as well. She felt his whisper then against her ear, and it seemed intimate. "You'll just have to suffer along with me a bit longer, won't you? But then, suffering is all relative to time, and place and mood, isn't it?"

"You can be very cruel."

"You can be two-faced."

"That's not at all true."

"For a witch with sight, you often choose to make yourself far more blind than that kerchief around your eyes could ever do."

"Perhaps, as you say," she told him smoothly, "I choose to be blind."

"But it's a dangerous world."

"My world wasn't," she said, "until you and your men came along."

"That was inevitable. Someone was destined to happen upon your place. And it might have been far worse."

"Indeed? The *enemy* might have come along?"

She felt his irritation. "Deserters might have come along. North or South. Men with no morals or scruples remaining—"

"And we might have been compromised?" she asked in a whisper.

"You might have been murdered," he said flatly.

"Murdered? Surely, you exaggerate, sir."

"I do not. This is a strange war, Rhiannon. Fought by both cavaliers and gentlemen in some of the most tremendous extremes—privates, sergeants, colonels, and generals were friends and family before the first shots were fired; the generals were the best of friends, school chums, who fought side-by-side before. We write to one another's wives, send gifts across the lines at the birth of a child. But it's also a hellish war as well, and just as you have the cream of humanity in uniform, so do you have, at times, the very dregs of society. Men who would slit your throat for your silver tea set, my dear. And then, of course, there are those Southerners who might think you a traitor—or a witch— ripe for burning."

"Then I should be grateful that you and your lying men

came upon my place, ate my food, slept in my house, and that now you are forcing me to a Rebel camp?"

"Exactly." His voice became a whisper once again. "And, of course, you should be grateful for much more."

She tensed, wondering to just what exactly he referred for which she should be so grateful.

"You knew better than to become addicted."

She exhaled on a long sigh, relaxing against him. "I'm not addicted," she lied by rote.

He didn't reply.

"Only a little," she murmured. She realized she lay back against him in her realm of darkness. The day must have gone completely to night, no streaks of a dying sun remaining, because now her blindfold seemed to leave her in a world of total blackness. She wanted to turn and look at him. She could twist around, but she couldn't see him.

"How much longer?" she asked.

"Till we reach camp? Not much."

"Till . . . the tremors stop. And the chills . . ."

"Ah. Every day will be a little bit better."

"Oh, God—"

"Last night was the worst. Seriously, don't you feel better already?"

"No."

"You're a liar."

"I feel horrible."

"But better in a way."

She was surprised to realize she was smiling. "Only in believing that it will get better. And I'm so tired."

"Then rest."

"I can't. I'm blindfolded moving through pine land and swampy marsh."

"I'm an excellent horseman," he reminded her. "Like all gallant dashing young cavalry."

She thought she heard a note of bitterness to his voice, and she wondered then if he hadn't seen more of the war than he admitted to. She was really tired. So tired. And it seemed a luxury suddenly to be riding. Breathing his scent, feeling his arms, both experiences that were becoming all too familiar . . .

What had she done?

She didn't know. Leaning against him, she felt sheltered.

He was like rock . . . steadfast. Far too blunt, rude, arrogant . . . he had known, he had seen. A most unusual doctor, as deft with a sword as he was with a scalpel. His words could cut as sharply as any knife, yet they could heal as well, as surely as his touch . . .

Did any of it matter? She could not be among the Rebels long. They would blindfold her again and send her back to the Yanks at St. Augustine. Whatever had or hadn't happened wouldn't matter. It would be over, the war would go on, and they would go their separate ways.

Chapter 8

⁓

She must have dozed, for she came awake as Julian reined in the horse. All about them, men were shouting greetings.

"Doctor Colonel, sir!" came a shout.

Then a woman's voice. "Julian!"

Julian lifted the blindfold from her eyes. She blinked furiously, trying to adjust her eyes to even the very pale light. They were in the center of a group of tents surrounded by dense pines. The area was lit by only a few campfires and an occasional torch. In the dim light the canvas tents seemed to glow with a strange red-gold color. There were a number of men grouped around them, and she realized that they'd been joined by a further escort along the way. The men were not in uniform. They were much like the ragtag band that had come her way. Here and there she saw a pair of Confederate-issue butternut trousers. Here and there a gray frock coat or even a regular issue blue, yet none of the clothing worn seemed to denote any rank. The promise of rain remained in the air, and the night was strangely cool for the season.

"Julian!"

Rhiannon heard the feminine voice again and saw a striking young woman with nearly coal black hair and eyes and cream skin so pure that it might have been marble. She was slim, of medium height, and the men were making way to allow her through. Freed from the blindfold, and acutely uncomfortable, she struggled to dismount from the horse. She couldn't do so with Julian behind her, but he was dismounting himself already, and as he came to the ground, he turned back, lifted her, and set her down just as the dark-haired woman reached him. Rhiannon saw that young

Digby had courteously set Rachel on her feet as well, and she inched toward Rachel as the girl inched toward her. They stood together as the Rebs happily greeted one another.

"Julian! Thank God, you've come at last! We were terrified—" the woman began.

Julian caught the dark-haired beauty in a fierce hug. He lifted her, spun her around, set her on her feet again.

Rhiannon felt ill, far more uneasy than she had since any of this had begun. *Who was this ebony-eyed wanton?*

"Why?" Julian demanded, smiling. "You shouldn't have been worried. The men reached camp before me, right? You knew I was on my way."

"Aye, sir, we told Miss Tia you were coming!"

It was Liam speaking, the youngest of the men who had accompanied Julian.

"I was still afraid, Julian," she said. "We heard about the skirmishing, the gunfire . . ."

"How is Paddy?" Julian asked anxiously.

"Doing well."

"I'll see him right away."

"And then, of course—" the woman continued, but she broke off, and Rhiannon found the woman staring straight at her. She smiled slowly, assessing her as an enemy. But her smile was also slightly self-mocking. "We heard you'd encountered a Yankee witch."

There was laughter among the men. Rhiannon felt her cheeks burning.

"I'd no idea you were bringing her back," the woman continued with an edge.

"Rhiannon is no witch!" Rachel said fiercely.

Rhiannon set an arm around her young ward. "Rachel, dear, I am quite capable of defending myself—against all types of ill-mannered Rebs." She cast her gaze around the camp and the laughter subsided. She was glad of her height, for at this moment it seemed to grant her some desperately needed dignity.

"Tia, where are your manners?" Julian drawled.

"I'm afraid I left them home soon after the war began," the woman replied, still studying Rhiannon with a frank appraisal. "I apologize for calling you a witch, Mrs. Tremaine—although you are called that, no malice intended.

They say that you are a witch in the nicest way. But you are a Yankee, and therefore I wonder just why my brother brought you here."

Brother. So this was the sister to whom Ian McKenzie had referred when they had talked. She felt dizzy. Just how many of these McKenzies were there running about?

"Is there a superior officer here?" Rhiannon asked.

"Well, since Julian has returned . . . Julian," Tia said with a shrug.

Rhiannon had the strangest feeling that she had just been kidnapped by Robin Hood and his Merry Men. There would be little help to be had here, that much was evident.

"That's right, I am the superior officer, and this is a base of the Florida militia, boys. Those of you at ease, get some rest, and those of you who are on duty, get back to it, please. Digby, can you make some arrangements for our guests?"

"That I can, sir. Right this way, ladies, if you will. We've an empty tent, and ragged as we may appear, we do have a few amenities to offer. Come along, please."

With little choice, Rhiannon turned to follow Digby, an arm upon Rachel as she did so.

She felt all the Rebel eyes on her back as she walked. How strange. She might have heard a pin drop in the pine forest that surrounded them, the Rebs were all so silent.

Watching her . . .

All those eyes.

And still, she was certain that she could feel Julian's stare, blue fire burning into her.

Paddy was doing well. He remained impatiently in the infirmary tent, rising on his elbows as Julian arrived.

"I'm right as rain, Doc Colonel, I do so swear it. That Yank angel has a way with her, doesn't she?"

"Umm," Julian murmured, removing the dressing on Paddy's leg, his sister assisting at his side.

"Angel?" Tia sniffed. "That's not what I've heard!"

"Why, now, Miss Tia, no woman will ever take your place in our hearts, don't you go being jealous."

Tia smiled at Paddy. "I'm not jealous, Paddy. I'm worried. Julian, Father knew her family, you know. They owned some of the richest salt works in the state. Her father was a loyal Union man, her husband was a loyal Union man—"

Julian looked up at his sister. "Our father is a loyal Union man; our brother is a Union cavalry officer!"

"I know, but we don't invite our father or our brother to our camp!" Tia exclaimed.

"He couldn't leave her, Miss Tia," Paddy said. Julian met Paddy's eyes, but Paddy continued, "There's folks up there who might find out that she tried to turn us over to the Yanks at St. Augustine. I think your brother here was afraid that an enterprising citizen might take it into his own hands to burn the lady's house down around her— or worse."

"And maybe she deserves it."

"Tia!" Julian said, startled.

"They nearly hanged our cousin Jennifer for being a Rebel spy. If Ian hadn't happened upon them . . ." She let her words trail off. They all knew what might have happened. "And they do hang men. Right and left. For spy activities!"

"She's not a spy," Julian said.

"She would have had you killed."

"Tia, can we talk about this later?" he inquired sharply.

"I'm telling you—"

"Tia?"

She gritted her teeth. "You sound just like Father. And, Julian—"

"Father isn't here. I am your older brother. And I'm also the superior officer here."

Tia fell silent. He studied Paddy's wound. It was healing remarkably well. He told Paddy to brace himself, doused the wound with a small amount of their precious whiskey supply, and rebandaged with his sister's able assistance. He bade Paddy good night and beckoned to Tia to follow him.

They walked in the moonlight a distance from the tents, to a place where a narrow feeder for the river created a bubbling brook, a charming place in peace time, quiet, shaded, pine-blanketed.

"Julian, any time we have prisoners here it's dangerous. The Yanks know we have to be near the river. One day they'll have enough man power and courage to really come after us, and then anyone who has been here will be a real hazard to us!"

Hands on his hips, he turned to her. "Tia, we're not going to be here much longer. Not in any strength."

She frowned, startled. "How do you know that?"

"I saw Ian."

"Ian?" He saw her eyes widen at the mention of their brother. "Oh, God, how is he, Julian? How did you manage to see him? Has he seen Alaina, Risa, the children—"

"Ian is fine, doing much better than any of us, looking far *stronger*, so I was told."

"Stronger—"

"Ian is very well," Julian told her. "Apparently, Mrs. Tremaine is friends with an officer at St. Augustine who was sick, and Ian happened to be there when her man Angus arrived to call for help. He made certain that he was the officer in charge of the troops sent out."

Tia smiled. "Could he have caught your men?"

"Not without a lot of people being killed. He knew it, I knew it. I waited for him; he found me."

"One day you'll both be hanged for fraternizing with the enemy."

"Do you think that Ian and I are the only enemies who meet in this war?"

"No, I suppose not. We exchange salt and tobacco for coffee and different supplies frequently enough along the river, but still, meeting the way you two do can be dangerous."

"We're careful."

"I wish I could see him," Tia said softly.

"You could go into St. Augustine, you know. I was actually invited in when General Magee needed foot surgery!"

Tia smiled. "I would love to see the children. We've a nephew and a niece and a new little first cousin and a second cousin, and I never get to see them. And I need to see them and be a doting old aunt since we're killing off all the men and I'll never get a decent husband."

Julian crossed his arms over his chest and surveyed his sister. "God knows, no man will ever want you."

She gave him a light punch in the arm. "Honestly, Julian, by the time the war is over—"

"Who knows, you may marry a Yank."

"Never. Never that!" she promised. "Even if I do have a misguided brother who is a Yank cavalry hero."

"A Yank who knows far more about Rebel movements than we do. Tia, he believes that most of us are going to be commissioned into the regular army, that the militia here is going to be even more skeletal."

"You mean . . . you'll have to leave?"

"That's what Ian has heard."

"Oh, my God."

"And there's more."

"More? What more?" she asked sharply.

"Jerome has been injured."

She sucked in her breath. He could see her pulse pounding against her throat. "Badly?"

"It's all hearsay, so I don't really know."

"He's been injured before, a slash here or there. Oh, God, I hope it's not serious. Do you think they'll bring him here," Tia asked anxiously. "Though he has a ship's physician—"

"Yes, he does. David Stewart is an excellent surgeon, and David will patch him up, but he'll want him tended by his family—if the wound is at all severe."

"If anything serious were to happen to Jerome—"

"We'd be desperate," Julian said flatly.

Tia looked at him, afraid. The infections that set in after surgery often brought about death. Tia studied him for a moment. "Well, what do you think? Is your witch really the healer they say that she is?"

He hesitated only a moment. "Yes, I think so."

"If she can help save my cousin, then she'll be a tolerable witch." She studied him curiously. "There's more behind you bringing her back here, isn't there?"

He shrugged. "She was becoming addicted to her own painkillers."

Tia arched a brow.

"Her husband was killed."

"Almost everyone has lost someone in this war."

"Our cousin Jennifer became a spy after her husband was killed. She was totally indifferent to whether she lived or died. People react differently to pain."

"Indeed, she was in so much pain, and so drugged, she

was still able to call on the Yanks to come after your reckless hide, brother dear."

"I've seen addictions before," he said softly. "They are easy to acquire and very hard to break."

"So you risked our position—for her addiction."

"She doesn't know where we are. And we've had another Yankee guest, you'll recall. Have you forgotten that Jerome's wife is the daughter of a Yankee general?"

"But she's Jerome's wife."

"But she wasn't always."

"Oh, so are you going to marry her to keep her quiet? Would it work with such a witch anyway?"

"Right now I just want to find out what the situation is with Jerome. I just want to see him alive and well and back on the seas again."

"And if your witch can keep him from a serious infection," Tia said.

"Dear sister, your claws are showing!"

"Are they?"

"Watch it—you may be in danger of becoming a nasty old maid."

"Oh! Dear brother, perhaps you should watch it, too."

"Really? Why?"

Tia smiled sweetly. "You seem to be thinking with the wrong part of your anatomy."

"Oh, do I, indeed?"

"She's quite attractive. Tall, regal. And more."

"What more?"

"Mysterious."

"Not once you know her."

"That's what you believe."

"I'm not a fool, Tia."

"I never said that. I'm merely pointing out the woman's attributes. She's not just intriguing and attractive. There's something else about her. She's graceful . . . she moves like a cat, sensual, enticing. Ah . . . just like a black widow spider."

"Black widow spiders move like cats?"

"You're missing my point, Julian. She's quite stunning, and a Yankee—and deadly. She is spinning threads you can't see to catch the unwary in her web. Have you ever seen anyone so beautiful in black?"

"Tia! She's in mourning."

"So are we all."

"Not like Mrs. Tremaine."

"Still, brother, take care!" Tia warned with mock severity. "If she is a witch—as many have claimed—she might well cast a dangerous siren's spell upon the men around her. Be warned! You hold our fate in your hands."

"I'm not so sure any man holds his own fate in his hands anymore," Julian said dryly.

"You're missing my point, a woman's view," Tia said with a sigh. She wagged a finger at him. "Be careful. Don't trust her. If he is brought here, watch her carefully with our cousin. And watch yourself. And see that she doesn't figure out how to escape the camp and reach the Yanks."

"Well, with your woman's point of view, I swear, I stand forewarned."

She smiled. "Make light of my words! You will rue the day if you do so!" With a toss of her head, she left him there.

Watching her go, he smiled as well. He was grateful that she had chosen to work with him. They'd been through a great deal together.

His smile faded, and he wondered if she was right.

Was he thinking with the wrong part of his anatomy?

He shook his head, feeling the soft breeze around him, the gentle caress of the night. Such a peaceful place in the middle of such a tempest. He could hear the movement of the water. Tonight he could hear, feel, and see again, so clearly. Everything.

No. He knew what he was doing. He knew she was the enemy. He was wary, as he had warned himself before. He had never doubted her determination to remain the enemy. His enemy.

And still . . .

He had the strangest feeling right now. He had forced her along because he had been afraid. For her.

Tia was right in a way. Rhiannon held a fascination for him. As if she had spun delicate threads and cast a strange web. No, she had simply needed help.

But he suddenly felt that he needed her as well. Needed her here. He had seen her work with Paddy. Few men or women had such a natural touch, knew so much about injuries and medicines.

Was she a witch? Now, listening to the movement of the water, feeling the lulling touch of the breeze, he felt almost as if this had somehow been destined . . .

He snorted in the darkness, mocking himself. With another shake of his head, he left the peace of the cove behind him. He needed some sleep. He was back, safe, at his own camp. He could rest here tonight.

Or could he?

He would never sleep, he thought. Unless he had seen to her first.

It might well be a long night.

Chapter 9

$\mathcal{D}$igby was a nice young man. He was obviously smitten with Rachel, and Rachel was apparently smitten in turn. So much for Union loyalty.

But they were here, in this camp. And at the moment they had little choice but to make the best of it.

Rhiannon thought that there weren't more than fifty men in the company here, some of them old as the hills, some of them still boys. Some of those who had been at her home had joined Digby in attempting to make the tent provided them into a home. Grizzled old Henry Lyle had brought her a bouquet of wildflowers; Thad and Benjamin Henly, the men from Tallahassee, had brought them a small table fashioned from palm fronds; and Kyle Waverly, the man who had once been a teacher, had brought them a watercolor of the harbor at St. Augustine, a work he had done himself. It was small, set in a pine frame, and it fit on the little table. She was surprised that these men should be so courteous, but they didn't mention what she had done. It seemed that they respected her difference of opinion.

She did find out, however, very late that night, when she had tried to wander out, that she was under guard. Old Corporal Lyle was on duty right outside her tent.

"Evening, Mrs. Tremaine," he told her politely, as if there were nothing unusual in her appearing long after midnight.

"Evening, Corporal," she returned.

"Can I help you?"

"I had just wanted some air."

"The rain is coming soon."

"I had thought it would have come by now."

"It's going to be one whipping wind when it comes, wet as a witch's tit—oh, ma'am, sorry, I haven't been around many ladies in a long time."

She smiled, lowering her head, wondering if he was worried about his reference to a tit—or to a witch.

"Well, since it hasn't started yet, I thought I'd walk a bit—"

"I'm afraid you can't, Mrs. Tremaine."

"I see."

"I'm sorry."

"You needn't be. It's war, isn't it?"

She slipped back into the tent. Rachel was sound asleep in her camp bed.

Sitting upon her own bed, Rhiannon shivered. She was tired, so tired. The best rest that she'd had in a long time was on the horse coming here when she had drifted to sleep. She rose and tore through her belongings until she found a plain cotton nightgown. With some difficulty she stripped off her black mourning gown and undergarments and slipped into the nightgown. She was more comfortable; she could sleep, she told herself, lying down.

The wind continued to whip beyond the tent. Then, she drifted.

She awoke, feeling as if an awful darkness surrounded her. She was shaking, trembling. Nausea gripped her. It was coming again . . .

No, she told herself.

She lay back on her camp bed, but in a matter of seconds she felt her stomach cramping. She curled into herself, feeling wave after wave of tremors envelop her. She sat up again, clammy with sweat, despite the breeze that stirred. She sat there, gritting her teeth, wishing that she could die.

The lights that had burned around her were gone. The rain had come, she realized, dousing the few fires that had burned. Clouds obscured the moon. The breeze continued to moan softly, like something . . . someone . . . just clinging to life.

No, no, no . . .

"Rhiannon . . ."

Had she moaned aloud herself? She wondered if she

imagined his voice in the darkness. No. He was there. He sat at her bedside, drawing her up and into his arms.

"It's all right."

"No!" She spoke aloud, and in the darkness she wondered if she had created him within her mind, summoning him to be with her because she hadn't the courage to face the night alone. No . . . she wasn't dreaming anything. He had come. After the rain he had come, suspecting that she might be lying awake. In pain.

"It's going to be all right."

Tears stung her eyes. "It's supposed to be better. You said—"

"It is better. You just don't know it yet."

"It's so dark."

"It's a dark night."

"Rachel—"

"Rachel is fine. Sleeping."

"I can't do this."

"You can, you will, it is better . . ."

He held her, rocked with her. He eased her back to the bed.

"My stomach. I'm . . . going to be sick."

"Maybe. Try breathing deeply. Very deeply."

She wasn't sick. Slowly, the churning began to settle. He smoothed her hair back from her forehead. Night settled around her; the darkness became a gentle blanket; the breeze was sweet, cooling her. She closed her eyes, started to drift.

She felt him moving. She was holding his arms, she realized. She tightened her grip. "Don't leave me!"

She didn't know if she spoke the words or imagined them. He was stiff for a moment, then eased down at her side, pulling her against him. She felt the cotton of his shirt as his arms came around her. Felt his warmth, a wonderful, vital heat.

A shiver seized her. He tightened his hold. She eased against him.

"Remember this, Yank, come morning, when you're eager to kick me in the head again."

"You just said it," she murmured.

"What?"

"Yank. I'm a Yank, sir. And come morning, you are the enemy.

"But it's night now, and all cats are alike in the dark?" he murmured.

"Am I the cat or are you?" she whispered.

"Hard to tell at times, isn't it?" he murmured in reply.

She bit her lower lip. It wasn't hard to tell at all. She was coming to know him far too well. She was coming to need him, to long to hear his voice . . .

"There is nothing but the dark," she said. Yet she wanted him there. And she was so afraid that he'd leave. He was her strength in the darkness, all that she had. Her fingers fell over his, and she pressed against them, as if she had the power to keep them there if he chose to leave.

Had her guard left her? she wondered. What had Corporal Lyle thought when McKenzie had slipped into the tent, when he remained . . .

It didn't matter. With him there she could close her eyes. It was better, as he had said. There had been those moments, really bad moments . . .

But they had come and gone. And she was closing her eyes, and drifting again, sleeping . . .

Dreaming.

There was a ship. Tossed on the seas, swept by the rains. The river had offered a certain shelter, but even there, the spring storm had buffeted the proud vessel. She saw a face, dark against the whiteness of sheets, sleek with sweat, dark-haired, head tossing, his face, Julian's face . . .

No, not Julian's . . .

Lightning slashed the sky. She could see the room, a ship's cabin. The man tried to rise from his bed; he was pressed back by the man who was tending him. His head tossed on the pillow. She saw the bandaging around his arm and saw that as he tossed, the bandage became more and more stained with the red of his blood . . .

The ship was sailing through the night.

Coming closer, and closer.

The man's eyes opened; she felt as if he could see her, see her, watching him . . .

It was all just a dream.

And the dream faded . . .

And she slept. Deeply.

* * *

She awoke slowly to the sounds of birds chirping. Sunlight danced on motes of dust before her eyes. Warmth was pervading the tent.

She tensed, sitting up with a start, looking to her side. She was alone in the camp bed. She looked across the tent. Rachel was gone. She was alone.

She arose, thinking that she'd barely be able to stand. To her amazement, she felt rested, amazingly bright and well. Anxious, feeling somewhat vulnerable in the tent, she dressed quickly. Eschewing corset and pantalettes in the promised heat, she slipped into a light cotton shift and black gown, and stepped outside.

A new man stood on guard duty, leaning on his rifle, sipping coffee. She recognized the man as one of those who had come to her house.

"Daniel Anderson, from Jacksonville?" she asked him.

He nodded, pleased. He lifted his cup to her. "Much obliged for the coffee, ma'am."

Much obliged . . .

She should have told him that Rachel and Mammy Nor were responsible for the coffee, not her. But she realized that she didn't begrudge the man the coffee. He was enjoying it far too much.

"Is there any more?" she inquired, looking around. The copse seemed very quiet.

"Of course, I'll get you some."

He strode just a few feet away to where a small cooking fire was dying out. He poured her a cup of coffee from the battered pot there and brought it to her. She thanked him. "Where is everyone?"

"Why, up and about, Mrs. Tremaine, up and about."

"My ward, Rachel?"

"I'm not sure, Mrs. Tremaine. She woke early and went on over to the brook. Then I think she went to sort out some things you brought in your saddlebags."

"Ah . . . but there is a brook, you say?"

"That way, Mrs. Tremaine."

She arched a brow. "Am I allowed to go that way?"

"Why, of course, ma'am." He hesitated, clearing his throat. "You can have it all to yourself at this time of day. It's a nice place. The soldiers love it. Lots of trees, cool water. Soothes away a lot of the heat of war, helps a man forget that he's fighting all the time. Mighty nice place. Too bad we can't meet the Yanks there. Might cool everybody's temper. Might even end the fighting for a spell."

"It's that nice, is it?" she asked, finding that she had to smile. He was simply so sincere.

"It is. And it's all yours, ma'am. I'll see to it."

"And it's really all right that I'm entirely alone?"

"Of course."

She must have looked skeptical.

He grinned. "Unless you're real familiar with the surroundings, ma'am, there's that trail before us to the brook and back. On the other side, there's nothing but pine forest, thick and dense as the night."

"Fine, thank you, you've convinced me. I'll make my way to the brook and then, Mr. Anderson, if you will, I'll thank you to help me find Dr. McKenzie."

"As you wish, ma'am."

She followed the trail to the brook, expecting a little sliver of water despite Anderson's enthusiastic description. But Anderson had not exaggerated—the brook was wide, with water splashing over rocks, deep, delicious looking water. She lowered herself to the ground at the embankment, drinking, splashing her face. It was delicious, cool and crisp. It felt wonderful against her flesh.

She hesitated. Anderson had promised that she could have the place to herself.

The water was inviting. Crisp enough to cool tempers, so Anderson had told her.

She unbuttoned her bodice, splashing the water against her throat. Then she grew impatient, looked around, and undid the rest of the tiny buttons. She pulled the gown over her head and stepped into the water wearing only her thin shift. She lay back, soaking herself, moving into the deeper section of the brook. She moved carefully, side-stepping rocks, then twisted, floating. She could feel the water sweep around her. It was cool, shaded by oaks that wept moss above it, creating patterns of shadow and light.

It was wonderful. It seemed to clear her head, to wash away the trail dust that had clung to her, the clamminess that had chilled her in the night . . .

The brook leapt over rocks here and there, but appeared

to be several feet deep in places. There was a stretch that seemed very deep, where she could actually swim, and that seemed to lead to a fork in the water, and onward to even deeper water. The brook, she realized, fed a river. If she kept swimming against the current, she'd reach the river. The water would indeed get deeper and deeper . . .

She lay on her back, drifting, then turned to dive deeply into the water.

She crashed headfirst into something hard.

A body.

Nearly shrieking with panic, she surfaced. She faced fierce blue eyes.

Julian.

His hands were on her, fingers biting into her arms.

Ah! So much for Corporal Anderson's promise that she could have the brook to herself.

"Just what were you doing, Mrs. Tremaine? Swimming to St. Augustine to alert the enemy to our presence here?"

The water was about three feet deep. She could stand. The muddy bottom oozed through her toes. The meager cotton of her shift clung to her breasts. Exposed to the air, her nipples hardened. She felt as if she were naked, as if the sun were ripping right into her . . .

"Don't be absurd!" she protested angrily, trying to wrench away. "I spent a day on the trail. I felt muddy and hot, and the water was so inviting—"

"That you swam away from the shore. Deserting Rachel, were you? Well, that wouldn't have mattered now, would it? You do know that she'd come to no harm here."

Could he be the same man who had come to her in the darkness and held her through the agonies of hell? His jaw was set in a rigid line; a pulse was ticking furiously at his throat. His eyes were colder than a winter's frost, and his voice had a deep bite. "You can't be serious—"

"Dead serious. Note your position."

She turned. She had come far from the shore, toward a twist in the water. She was indeed heading straight into the river.

"You must think I'm a very strong swimmer."

"I'd never imagined you could come so far. Then again, I should know never to underestimate you."

She moistened her lips, suddenly wondering if he was

naked. His chest was bare. He wasn't as gaunt as she had thought, she realized. Taut muscle seemed to ripple from the surface of the water and beyond . . .

No. He was in long johns, she saw. She hadn't been breathing. She inhaled. Exhaled. Met his eyes again.

"You couldn't really think that I was trying to swim to St. Augustine."

"God knows what you might try. But you didn't need to swim all the way; you merely needed to reach the opposite shore."

"If you're so worried about what I might try to do, why have you tried so hard to . . ."

"To what?" he inquired sharply as her voice trailed off.

She lifted her chin. "To keep me alive."

He took his time answering her. She felt his eyes keenly. "I've seen enough shattered lives. Bullets tear holes in the flesh. Deaths tear holes in the lives of those left behind. All loss of life is a sin."

She forced a skeptical smile to her lips. "Ah, Colonel, how valiant! Do you use such words with all the women you meet in the course of your practice?"

"No. Do you use a drug-induced amnesia to seduce all the men in yours?"

Fury swept her. She stepped forward to slap him, but he had anticipated her response, and he reached for her arm, capturing her, drawing her against him hard before she could land a blow. They were both soaking wet. His chest was bare and hers was scantily covered, and as she came against him, she became very much aware of his vitality. His warmth and strength seemed to sear her. She felt his breath, his movement; she longed to stroke the flesh on his shoulders and chest.

Richard. Except for the image of him dying, she hadn't seen him in so long. So very long. Hadn't touched him, been touched, felt his caress, the excitement, the love . . .

He held her harshly, impatiently. His eyes bore down into hers, a strange cobalt reflection of the water. Then his fingers were suddenly on her chin, lifting it. She felt his eyes burning into hers, coming closer and closer. She moistened her lips, anxious to twist her head, to move away. She wanted to cry out, because she knew what he was going to do.

She didn't twist away. He held her too tightly, she tried to tell herself.

Not a word left her lips.

His mouth formed over hers, hard, forceful. His tongue pressed entry between her lips, swept, tasted, ravaged with a sudden fierce hunger. His right hand was at the small of her back; she was pinned against him. His left fingers stroked her cheek, her throat, closed over her breast. His thumb rubbed her nipple over the all but sheer cotton, and the sudden streak of searing sensation that swept through her was staggering. It seemed to streak through her limbs, tear into her flesh, flood her veins, soar into an intimate center somewhere between her thighs while his mouth . . . his mouth continued to move over hers, ravaging, passionate, sweeping away thought and day and sunlight. The touch was evocative, exciting . . .

And no longer forced. He neither held her chin, nor her back. His lips touched hers, he cupped her breast. The knuckles of his other hand moved lightly along her body, touching low against her abdomen, her waist . . .

"Bastard!" she cried, wrenching free from him, stumbling back in the water. "What are you doing? Why? How could you, when you . . . when you know . . ."

He stood still, narrowed eyes dispassionate, arms crossed over his chest as he studied her.

"When I know what?"

She wiped his kiss, his touch, from her lips, staring at him, shaking. She was so unnerved. So frightened. Now it wasn't so much a matter of *what had she done!* It was a matter of *just what was she doing, oh, God!*

"When you know how I feel. He is dead, dead, don't you understand?"

"He may be dead, but you are very much alive," he said. He took a step toward her in the water. "Whether you want to be or not. But then, just what is it? Do you somehow think that you're supposed to want to be dead as well?"

"I am supposed to grieve. We're all supposed to grieve!"

He nodded. "Grieve, yes. Throw ourselves on funeral pyres, no."

"I've not done anything like that."

"No, you just deny every living instinct you have."

"I don't. Just because I deny you—"

"It's not a matter of denying me. But you think that you can pretend that things you've done aren't real—what happens if there are consequences?"

"God damn you, nothing happened, there are no consequences!" she cried furiously. "And what are you doing here, torturing me in the water? Don't you have wounded men to tend to somewhere?

She paused suddenly, remembering her dream of the night before. In a halting, distant voice she said, "Your cousin is coming."

"What?" he asked, startled.

"His ship is nearly here."

He stared at her, eyes narrowed. "How do you know? How do you even know he's on a ship?"

"I saw it."

"When?"

She shook her head impatiently. "In my dream. I'm telling you, your cousin is coming, and he . . ."

"He what?"

"He needs help badly."

He paused only a second longer and then moved past her. He started swimming. His strokes were hard and sure. He was an excellent swimmer. Naturally. She should have expected as much, she thought. He was like an extension of this land he loved so much. Like her, he'd grown up where the days were often long and unbearably hot, and where water could be found at ever turn.

She followed along more slowly, keenly aware of her lack of dress, of the way her cotton undergarment clung to her wet skin when she rose from the water. But he was paying her no heed. He had risen, water sluicing from him, and she found to her distress that she was watching the way his cotton long johns clung to his muscles, his thighs, and his buttocks.

They were worn long johns. Threadbare in places.

She didn't have much time to watch. As quickly as he was out of the water, he was stepping into his trousers, slipping his shirt over his shoulders. Still barefoot, he turned back at last, reaching a hand to her to help her from the water. "I'm all right," she protested, arms hugging her chest, but he emitted a sound of impatience and she knew that he wasn't looking at her at all.

"I can manage—"

"Get out. You haven't a thing to hide with which I'm not familiar."

"You're not at all a Southern gentleman—"

"Want to see me get worse?"

Gritting her teeth, she accepted his hand, and he drew her from the water to the shore. He plucked her black mourning gown from the ground and handed it to her. She shivered, dressing with her undergarment soaking still, then trying to draw her hose and shoes over her wet feet and legs. A soft, clean towel would have been a sweet luxury, she thought. But it wasn't to be.

"Let's go," he said impatiently.

"Go where? Aren't we at the river—"

Yes, they were, but apparently, not exactly where she had thought they were. He didn't like giving her any more information than he had to, but since he was so anxious, he decided to explain their position. "The brook curls around this little spit of peninsular hammock. The deep water comes in around the other way."

He caught her hand and drew her along purposefully. They came back to the area where the camp tents were pitched and passed it by. As they followed another trail, she could see sails rising high out of the water. In another few steps she saw that a ship was anchored in the river, and small boats were coming into the shore.

Julian turned to her. "You were right. He *is* here."

Tia McKenzie stood anxiously by the water, waiting, surrounded by a number of the Florida militia men.

"You should go on alone. Your sister won't want me assisting when you tend to your own flesh and blood," Rhiannon protested.

He didn't let go of her hand. "Yes, she will. She wants him to stay alive. So do I."

As they came to the shoreline, he at last released her and stepped out to the water to help drag in a small boat. There were three men aboard. One rowed and one held the head of the third man who was wrapped in a blanket.

One of the men stood nimbly and jumped into the few feet of water at the embankment, dragging the boat on in.

Jerome, an arm then cast around one of the men, scrambled from the small boat and came toward them. Rhiannon saw his face, and though he was a stranger, she knew how he felt, and felt a strange trembling sensation fill her. She had thought that it was Julian at first in her dreams, because he looked so much like Julian. Or Ian. Except that he had higher cheekbones and a touch of auburn to his hair. And Indian blood.

Jerome McKenzie saw her watching him anxiously. He was obviously fairly gone in whiskey or rum, because he was singing with drunken cheer. "A-sail, a-sail, and up the canvas, pirates on the shore, and there they be, Lord, they be me, a pirate, fare me well!"

"Let's get him into the surgical tent, quickly," Julian ordered.

Rhiannon paused by the shore, but once again Julian turned back for her, catching her hand. They hurried to a tent where Jerome was situated on a makeshift hospital bed.

"David, sweet Jesus . . ." Julian murmured, talking to the man who had half carried, half dragged his cousin from the small boat.

"He's been fevered," the ship's doctor replied. "The bullet is close to the shoulder bone."

"Julian, Julian, dear boy, this man gave me complete hell. He kept insisting my chances of living were so much better if he lopped off my arm right away!"

"Jerome, immediate surgery does save a man's life much of the time—"

"But you can keep my arm."

"David is as good as I am, and you know that, and that's why he's your ship's surgeon!"

"I had to come here," Jerome insisted. He smiled drunkenly again and, despite his disheveled appearance, his grin was charming. In that, Rhiannon saw again the similarities between the McKenzies; when Julian chose to offer that smile, he was equally compelling.

Jerome abruptly tried to sit up. "You!" He wobbled his good hand in an effort to point at Rhiannon. She stiffened instantly.

"I know you," he said, frowning with some confusion. "You were in my dreams."

"Your wife will enjoy such knowledge," Tia, anxious at his other side, chastised.

Jerome gazed her way indignantly. "There aren't many women in this, but I've seen a good one here and there. She's a doctor, right?"

Rhiannon shook her head strenuously. "No, no, I—"

"A healer," Jerome said. The way that he looked at her, she thought that he was feigning some of his drunkenness, and that he had known someone very like her, or with her strange talents. Amazingly, he seemed to feel a bond with her—and to trust her.

Rhiannon saw Tia staring at her. She'd thought at first that the young Miss McKenzie hated her, but she realized now that Tia was waiting—reserving judgment.

Rhiannon looked from Tia to Jerome. "I'm the local witch," she told him, smiling ruefully.

"A Yankee witch, I take it."

"I'm afraid so. How did you know?"

Jerome didn't answer that. "And my nasty cousin dragged you here, did he?"

"Something like that," Julian said. "Jerome, lie back. You may be the scourge of the seven seas, but we're trying to keep you in business here!"

He did as he was told, but his eyes were on Rhiannon again.

"Don't let my cousin take my arm to save my life because he's afraid. He won't lose me, and he won't lose my arm. But we're close, you know. He loves me. He might decide to start cutting just because he's afraid to trust himself with his own flesh and blood. I have a wife, a babe, he may feel he owes them, but I'm not going to die."

"The arm should have gone right away," Julian said. "David was right about that."

"You haven't seen where the bullet is," David told him. "I haven't been able to get at it, and he was so insistent about coming here that it seemed better to do as he wanted." He hesitated. "Risa is near here, at the least."

Julian nodded, turning toward a private who had lingered at the entrance to the tent. "We need someone sent."

"Liam can slip in and out like a shadow," the man said.

Julian nodded, looking back at his patient.

"Don't take my arm, I am going to make it. Right, Yankee witch?" Jerome asked Rhiannon.

She nodded. She was startled when his fingers, on the hand with the good arm, curled around hers.

Then his eyes closed.

"Oh, Lord," Tia whispered. "Jerome, Jerome . . . Julian, he's not responding," she said worriedly, smoothing her cousin's dark auburn hair from his forehead.

"He's been fevered, slipping in and out of consciousness," David Stewart said.

"Oh, God . . ." Tia breathed.

"Let's get started," Julian said.

"Are you sure you want me here?" Rhiannon asked. "You've enough hands—"

"I want yours," he said harshly.

Was he testing her somehow? No, she thought. He wouldn't risk his cousin's life on such a trial. He believed she had a power. She shivered suddenly. *She didn't have any special powers. She wasn't a witch. She had just learned a great deal about poppies, and she was cursed sometimes with the ability to dream things that were real . . .*

"Mrs. Tremaine?" Tia said, black eyes hard. She was pleading. The injured man meant a tremendous amount to everyone here, Rhiannon realized.

Yes, he was their blood kin. And he also provided supplies to the Confederacy. He kept soldiers in ammunition, he kept food coming through, medicines.

"Mrs. Tremaine, my cousin knew that you were here. He wants you here now. God knows why, but . . ."

Rhiannon's palms felt damp. "I'm here. I can't assist, but I can try . . . but I'm not magic, you know. I'm not really a witch with any powers."

"Medicine is magic, isn't it? Help my brother save my cousin. Too many people seem to believe that you have a special talent or power for there not to be some truth to it all. Jerome is a good man. He has brought us the means to save children as well as the injured time and time again. He has been our life's blood."

Rhiannon lowered her eyes, thinking that she could remind Tia McKenzie that Jerome's services had aided and abetted the Southern cause—one totally opposed to her own. But when she lifted her eyes, she saw that Tia knew that. She was praying that Rhiannon could help save her cousin's life and his arm.

She glanced up, aware that Julian was watching her, too. "Obviously, I want to help save lives, any man's life," she murmured.

David Stewart and another Reb—a huge fellow Julian surely used to hold his patients down—remained in the tent. In the short time they'd been there, Julian had been preparing; Tia, despite being so upset, had helped as well. Julian's instruments were neatly laid out—and clean, Rhiannon noted.

"Tia, bandages," Julian said as he and David began unrolling those tied around his cousin's arm.

Tia nodded but didn't obey the order. Stunned, she simply stared at her cousin.

Rhiannon stepped forward, looking at the wound as it was revealed.

"Minié ball," she said. The Reb named David cast her a quick, appraising glance. She ignored him. The wound was a dangerous one. The minié ball was conoidal in shape, of a lead that moved at a relatively slow velocity, changing shape and brutally ripping and tearing flesh, blood, and bone. If a man was lucky, the bullet went right on through. This bullet hadn't. It had lodged against a throbbing blood vessel.

"You can see my dilemma," David said. "He could bleed to death if the bullet isn't dislodged just so."

"Take the arm. You have to take the arm to save his life," Tia said.

"Tia, he could still bleed to death," Julian remarked. Rhiannon saw that because of the way the bullet had struck and settled, Julian would have to take much of the shoulder as well as the arm. Dangerous indeed.

Rhiannon hadn't been asked, but she moved closer, standing by Jerome McKenzie's head and taking an even closer look at the wound. The arm had been kept clean, and infection had been kept at bay by the use of compresses.

Just then she realized that Jerome had come to again. He was staring up at her. He was very handsome, striking, different. He wasn't used to being down on an operating table. His eyes, very much like Julian's, were on her. "You can do it, you're the witch. Save my arm," he told her.

She set her hands gently on his head. "Julian is the surgeon. And you have to remember, your life is most important."

"Julian, you can do it. You can save my arm. I know. I need it. I need to keep sailing. Trust the witch. She can feel what to do. You wouldn't hurt me, would you, Yankee witch?"

She bit her lip, thinking that the Union effort would be in better shape if this man were to die.

They were all looking at her now. Her gaze turned to Julian.

"What do you think?" he asked politely.

"I don't know what you mean—"

"Yes, you do. I can't get a ligature in there, nor do I dare trust one. Think you can hold the blood vessel for me, keep him from hemorrhaging?"

She sucked in her breath, amazed at what he was asking her. And the trust he was putting in her.

She swallowed, then shrugged. "If the ship's surgeon here and your man can keep him steady, my fingers are long and thin and agile enough to keep the blood vessel steady while you go for the bullet."

If she slipped, if she lost her hold, if Julian faltered with his forceps, Jerome would probably bleed to death. They'd be taking a chance. But the bullet had to come out—or the arm had to go. Given much more time, the bullet would wedge into the artery, and it would kill him.

"Oh, God," Tia breathed.

"Bandages!" Julian said to her. "Tia, bandages!"

Tia moved as commanded.

"All right," he said. He looked at David, and at his man at the foot of the bed. "Jerome?"

"Yes?"

"Good, you can hear me. I'm going for the bullet, and it's going to hurt like hell. I'm going to give you some ether. You just have to breathe slowly when I have the bag over your mouth—"

"No ether!" Jerome McKenzie managed to get out. "Save it for men who will need it. There's . . . enough whiskey in me . . . do it."

Tia was still preparing the bandages, her back to the operating table. Rhiannon instinctively reached for the scalpel Julian would need first, and the bullet extractor he would need after clearing his position. She handed him the instrument he needed, meeting his eyes again. "Tia, you've got to come back over here. I need David to steady Jerome, Malcolm to keep him from jumping, and Rhiannon on the artery. When I've cleared the way, soak up the blood and then take the scalpel and hand me the forceps as quickly as you can. Understood?"

"Yes, Julian."

He turned away for a moment. Rhiannon saw that Jerome McKenzie was looking up at her again. His handsome, bronzed face was sleek with sweat from his fever, tense with pain, but he remained conscious and aware. He gave her a rueful smile. Then words formed on his lips.

"If anything should go badly . . . please, tell my wife I love her."

She found herself nodding, fighting the tears that formed in her eyes.

"Now," Julian said.

She reached into the wound and felt the man's flesh, his blood, his life.

They were in her hands.

Chapter 10

Corporal Anderson could never have known just how much Rhiannon would love the brook.

She sat there by twilight, watching as the sun set. She thought that nowhere in the world could the sky put on such a show of God's artwork. The sun was a huge orb glowing red and orange, and as the afternoon waned, it slid with startling speed down the blue backdrop of the heavens. As it did so, it brought a rainbow of pastels along with it—pinks, purples, blues, yellows, golds. Rays of heat seemed to streak in tremulous waves, and if she lifted her chin, she could feel the wonder of the warmth, the soft touch, and it was like nature's caress.

If only that were enough . . .

She was suddenly aware that she wasn't alone. Turning, she saw that Julian stood by one of the moss-laden oaks. He was watching her.

"How is he?"

"Tough as an old 'gator—so far."

"He survived the surgery."

"As I said, tough as a 'gator."

He left the oak and walked over to her, taking a seat by her side on the fallen log she had found. She felt his eyes upon her and wished that she did not feel his presence so keenly. She looked at the water, not wanting to meet his eyes. Yet she had a strange feeling that there was already no escaping this man, and for the life of her, she did not understand why.

"You are extraordinary," he told her.

She lifted her hands. "You're the surgeon."

"Yes, and I'm good," he said dryly. "But I couldn't have

done what I did without you. You have incredibly steady hands. It's as if you were trained. You can feel where you need your fingers to be even when you can't see what you're doing."

"Perhaps I'm lucky."

"Gifted," he said, still watching her. "As many doctors are not."

"But they have knowledge—"

"Umm. My brother Ian wanted to play the piano once. He had good teachers, he acquired a great deal of knowledge—and he was always a horrible player. Music is something in the soul, and you're blessed with it or not. Medicine is much the same. You have a gift, a talent, and all the schools in the world couldn't teach it."

"If I do have a talent to heal, then I'm glad. If only—"

"If only what?"

She shook her head. "If only it didn't come with the dreams."

"The dreams?"

She stared at the water. "You won't believe me, but I see things in dreams, people, places, things that have happened, things that will happen."

He was silent, staring at the water as well.

"You don't believe me. Well, many people don't."

"I don't know what I believe. You saw Jerome." He glanced at her. "Tell me, do you see an end to this war?"

She shook her head. "I don't choose what I see. Sometimes I just have visions."

"Have you always had them?"

She smiled, folding her hands over her knees and resting her chin on them. "Always . . . I'm not certain. Before the war I used to think that they were good. A little girl was lost in St. Augustine once . . . she had gotten tangled in some old fishing line by the beach. Her parents were frantic. I was there with my father. Her mother had heard about some work I'd done with a doctor there and was somehow certain that I could find her child. And I did. And it was wonderful. But since the war has come . . . All that I see is death and destruction."

"Not always. You saw my cousin coming."

She shrugged uneasily.

"You knew him, knew his face, the moment you saw him."

"He looks just like you."

"Not just like me."

She couldn't help smiling. "No, your brother looks just like you."

"Except stronger."

She flushed. Had she ever said such a thing? Julian was all lean muscle, sinewy, taut, sleek. His features were gaunt and hard, sharply, handsomely molded. His eyes were direct, cobalt, demanding at all times. Not a movement was ever wasted. His hand were fascinating, lean and hard and as cleanly sculpted as his face, with long, dexterous fingers. Strong. So capable in surgery.

So evocative when they touched . . .

"Rachel has gotten quite fond of your man Paddy. She's decided that he needs to be entertained while he's convalescing, and so she'd reading him Chaucer's *Canterbury Tales*."

Julian smiled. "I saw. She's a wonderful little nurse. A wonderful human being," he added. "Loyal to her cause, but far too full of compassion to neglect those she can help, no matter what their beliefs—or what deceit we played upon you."

She looked at the water. "You lied; I called the Yanks. And leave it to my luck, Colonel. Your brother showed up."

He grinned wickedly. "And you passed out."

"I was exhausted."

"Was that it?"

"Don't torture me right now, I'm far too weary."

"One day you'll have to admit—"

"I'll admit nothing, ever, Colonel McKenzie."

"Yes, you will."

"Never."

"Maybe I'll just keep you imprisoned until you do."

She was alarmed by the way his husky words made her feel. Her husband hadn't been dead that long . . .

But, oh, God, it had been a long, long time since she had seen him, touched . . . other than in her dreams. And McKenzie, for all his faults, perhaps because of them, was compelling. Rugged, no-nonsense. Far too masculine. Just the raspy tone of his voice was like feeling a brush of fingers against her flesh.

"Stop it."

"Stop what?"

"Watching me that way."

"Do you want me to go away?"

"Yes. No. Of course not, you must be worn from the strain of the operation. I . . . tell me about your family." She found herself returning his stare with honest curiosity. They were all so striking, the McKenzies. So much alike, and yet so unique. "He's Indian, right? Jerome is, I mean," she said.

Julian grinned. "Seminole."

"So your uncle—or aunt—is Seminole?"

He was still smiling. "Teela, I believe, is Irish, like my mother. She has the red hair to prove it. My grandfather was married twice, to my grandmother and Jerome's grandmother, who was part Indian. The bloodlines have made a deep impression on us all." He plucked a blade of grass from the ground and chewed it thoughtfully. "Your General Sherman had some of his first lessons in real warfare down here. The Union army chased the Seminoles right into the ground, slaughtered them, chased them some more. But they could never fight long enough or hard enough to really win, though they did all but annihilate a people."

She watched him for a long moment, hearing the bitterness in his voice. She didn't speak, and after a moment he continued. "That's one of the reasons," he said lightly, "that my uncle and cousin will never bow down to a Union uniform."

"But, Julian," she protested, "there are men and women on both sides who fear and hate the Indians. Some of those same men who pursued the Seminole are wearing Confederate gray—"

"Some. Maybe a lot," he admitted after a moment. "But show Union blue down in the Everglades, and I promise, you've got some hatred on your hands."

"Is that why you swim so well, make your way through the trails so well—"

"It's why we're all so familiar with the different aspects of the Florida terrain," he said. He smiled at her wryly. "Ian was oldest, Jerome and I are the same age. I have another cousin, Brent, just a little younger than I am, there's Tia, and Sydney, Jerome's little sister. Well, of course, when we were little, we played white men and Indians. We were always trying to prove we could be as silent, as brave, as stalwart and noble as our Indian kin. Aunt Teela and Mother yelled a lot, and we fought now and then, but the whole lot of us were like one tribe, ready to take offense and go to battle for the other, whether brother, sister, or cousin. We were very close. And then the war came."

She smiled slightly. "The war. It hasn't stopped you."

"It's changed things," he assured her.

"Ah, but you and your brother managed to conspire against me!" she told him.

"My brother is a Yank. Why would he conspire against you?"

"Because blood is thicker than war."

"If that were the case, there would be no war," he murmured.

Again, he sounded bitter. Tired and bitter. And she was tempted to reach out and touch him. A mistake. She shouldn't. She couldn't.

She clenched her jaw tightly, staring at the water where the sun cascaded beneath the surface. Before she could do something she would regret, she rose. "I should find Rachel—" she began, but as she did so, Julian rose, turning back toward the trail as she had done. There was a blond woman hurrying toward them.

"Julian!"

She was petite, golden, an entrancing ray of sunshine, and she came running along, then hurtled herself into his arms. He held her tightly, hugging her. Embarrassed, feeling like an outsider, Rhiannon stepped back. There were an awful lot of women in his life. And she'd already met his sister. And this was no cousin, for this beautiful blond didn't have a drop of Indian blood.

"Julian, it's amazing. He looks well. He's going to make it, isn't he?"

"Time will tell."

"He won't die, he won't let himself die, especially now. Risa is here. Julian, thank God he had you—"

"He wouldn't have made it without Dr. Stewart. Alaina,

it's wonderful to see you, but how did you come so quickly—"

"We knew he'd been injured," she said softly.

"Ian told you what he'd heard?"

"Yes, of course. Risa was beside herself to reach this camp, knowing that Jerome would come here. And now Ian is worried sick, but he was sent back north today. Not even he could talk his way into another reprieve. There's sure to be an awful battle somewhere soon, I think—"

She broke off, seeing Rhiannon standing back against the oak, silent in the darkening twilight.

"Oh! I'm so sorry." she exclaimed.

"Indeed, I'm sorry as well," Julian murmured, stepping back. "Alaina, Mrs. Rhiannon Tremaine. Rhiannon, my sister-in-law, Alaina."

"Rhiannon! The Yankee wit—" Alaina began, then blanched, remembering her manners. "Oh, I am really sorry. We've just all heard about how wonderful you were with Jerome, and of course, I heard about you from my husband. In fact, I heard quite a bit about you from my husband. It's a pleasure to meet you."

"Mrs. McKenzie," Rhiannon acknowledged, wondering just what Ian McKenzie might have said about her.

"Risa is here?" Julian asked.

"Of course. She's with Jerome now. She's anxious to meet you, Mrs. Tremaine. To thank you."

"She needn't," Rhiannon murmured.

"Oh, but she feels she must. Her father is a Union general, and she realizes this must be very difficult for you. I am, naturally, grateful for Jerome's life, though I'm afraid that Unionist my husband might be, I was born and bred a Rebel and find it anguish on a daily basis to pray that my husband lives while hoping that his cause perishes."

She might have kept silent, should have kept silent—but she couldn't. "The Union will not perish, Mrs. McKenzie."

Ian's petite blond wife smiled, a brow slightly hiked with amusement. "You're very assured, Mrs. Tremaine. Though you're the enemy, such unquestioning loyalty is certainly commendable."

"My loyalty is unquestioning," Rhiannon said softly, "But not without strong logic." She shrugged, then looked at Julian, her chin raised, and only a bit of mischief in her voice. "Take a look at present evidence, Mrs. McKenzie. Your husband, your brother-in-law. One is ragged, the other is not."

"Thank God," Julian warned, crossing his arms over his chest, "that you didn't suggest again that my brother is stronger. He is simply a bit heavier due to that portion of an inch I have over his height. Ragged. Now, that I can live with."

He was amused. Alaina managed a small smile, but then turned to Rhiannon.

"There was a time, Mrs. Tremaine, when I might have taken great offense from your words, but they're honest, and frankly, I just wish that it would end, but it doesn't seem that it will do so soon enough."

"Julian! Julian!"

A second woman came tearing down the trail to the brook, disturbing the quiet with her cries. She burst upon them, a study in speed and motion, throwing herself against Julian.

He caught her, whirled her around. She hugged him tightly, crying and laughing. She was taller than the petite Alaina, with auburn hair, aqua blue eyes, and stunning face structure.

"Oh, Julian!" she cried again, holding tight against him. "He is going to make it. Please, God, tell me, he is going to make it—"

"He came through the surgery just fine, Risa," Julian assured her.

"I couldn't bear it, Julian. I couldn't bear it if I were to lose him. I've never been so afraid, Julian, if he were to die . . ."

Her voice trailed away as she realized that she was staring at Rhiannon. And as Risa McKenzie stared at her, Rhiannon could see in the woman's eyes that she knew all about Rhiannon, certainly including the fact that Rhiannon's husband had been killed.

She went white as a sheet.

"Oh, Lord," she murmured. She stepped away from Julian, glanced at Alaina, looked at Rhiannon, and apologized. "I am so, so sorry. What a terrible thing for me to have said when I can't begin to tell you just how grateful I am."

"It's all right," Rhiannon murmured. She felt Julian watching her. "Really," she said, her teeth grating. "I-I've gotten past thinking that other men should be dead because my husband died. I'm delighted that your husband is doing so well."

The woman's smile was warm and unreserved. The first such Rhiannon felt she had received from any of these McKenzie women. Then Risa quickly stepped forward, and took her hand, gripping it warmly and shaking it with fervent energy.

"Thank you . . . thank you. He's sleeping now . . . and I understand that the laudanum that's helping him rest is thanks to you as well. This must be agony for you, I can understand, honestly, because—"

"She's a Yank," Julian said.

"Her father is General Magee," Alaina explained.

"*The* General Magee?" Rhiannon inquired.

"*The* General Magee," Risa agreed. "It does make war hell, doesn't it?" She stared down, realized she was still pumping Rhiannon's hand. "Or sadder than you can imagine. We had to slip Julian into St. Augustine not too long ago to repair my father's foot—and my father is quite fond of both Julian and my husband and of course, we all just pray that not only do our family members not get killed, but that they not kill each other. Of course, it's still war. And these Rebs are so suspicious! It's terrible, just terrible, not a one of them had a decent word for me until I'd borne a McKenzie child—and that's a rather drastic measure, of course, we're not expecting you to take it—"

"Oh, Risa, what an awful thing to say to her. And it's a lie, we were friends before that child of yours was so much as a frisky feeling!" Alaina protested in a long, wicked drawl. "We're not nearly so bad, Mrs. Tremaine. We've been horrible tonight, but then we're so afraid for Jerome . . . which I know you understand."

"Of course. I do understand," Rhiannon said. She understood, but it all seemed rather too much. The relationship between the women and Julian . . . they were all so close. They had created an intimate circle, and she wasn't a part of it. "If you'll excuse me, I'll let you talk with Julian. I know you have a dozen questions for him. It's been a pleasure to meet you both—"

"No, please, don't go," Risa said. "We interrupted you."

"It's all right. Your husband has just gone through a terrible operation, and you'll want time alone—"

"Not at all," Alaina said. "We brought a substantial quantity of fresh fish, which young Private Llewellyn has nearly served up."

"Stay with us, please. We'll have a certain privacy in Julian's quarters, and we want you to be a part of that privacy," Risa said.

Rhiannon felt trapped. Julian was watching her, the women were watching her. She had felt like an outsider; now they were dragging her in, and she wasn't sure that the feeling was any more comfortable.

"Thank you, but I have to see to my ward—"

"Rachel? That darling girl!" Risa said. "She's sitting with Jerome for me now while he sleeps. Do come and join us. Julian, convince her. Alaina, come on, let's find Tia and set up some dinner—I haven't eaten since I heard Jerome was injured! Julian, make her join us."

Slipping an arm through her cousin-in-law's, Risa led Alaina back along the trail.

Julian's lips were quirking with amusement. "Do join us," he said. "It's not entirely a Rebel family reunion, as you can see, so no one is going to be sharing military secrets."

"I really don't wish to interrupt. You seem very close, exceptionally close—"

"I knew Alaina from the time she was a little girl, and both she and Risa have worked with me often. They are both good friends."

She found herself wondering what would happen if Ian or Jerome were to fall in the war. Would one of their wives turn to Julian for solace?"

"How nice to have such good friends."

He shrugged. "And enemies, of course. They hated one another at first, or something very close to it. Risa had nearly been engaged to Ian, you see. A long story, and it's not my place to tell it."

"Then there's your sister—"

"Ah, yes, now . . ." he murmured as he set a booted foot upon a fallen log and leaned an elbow upon his knee. "There beats the true heart of the Confederacy. It's true.

She didn't trust Risa in the least until Jamie was born. So there you have it. She did have to bear a McKenzie child to be granted admission to the family circle! It's easier for Rebs, of course. We all loved Alaina right away. Well, the Yanks were naturally wary of her . . ."

"Since I'm a Yank, I should leave you all in peace," she said, and turned about, starting along the trail leading back to the camp from the brook.

"A Yank, but then . . ."

She had been expecting the words. *If only she knew the truth of just exactly what she had done, what had been real, what had been dreams . . .*

She halted, and stood dead still, then spun around.

"A Yank, but . . . Colonel?" she queried coldly.

He smiled. Relaxed, casual, amused, his gaze just ever so slightly disdainful. "Perhaps you will bear a McKenzie child," he said with a shrug.

She returned his stare, wishing suddenly that she dared run to him, laugh and cry, beat against him, demand to know the exact truth. She could not, of course. She already felt too great a dependency on him, too great a fascination for him. His voice alone could create a quickening within, when she watched him, touched him, felt him near . . . she felt far too great a draw. It was frightening. She could not care for a man again the way she had, could not betray Richard.

"Colonel, my name is Tremaine. It would be quite impossible for me to bear a McKenzie child."

He left the log, apparently unaffected by her words. He strode to her, a slight mocking smile remaining upon his face.

He stopped by her side. "You said you hadn't really seen Richard for almost a year. No dead man comes back in dreams to create living flesh, Mrs. Tremaine. They teach you that in medical school. Excuse me, if you don't care to join us, my ragged, skinny, pathetic body and I are quite famished, and since a wonderful meal is promised, I'll leave you to your brooding sorrow."

With a very correct bow he walked on by her.

Chapter 11

~

Rhiannon returned to her field tent and stayed there.

To her surprise, she found that she couldn't rest. She tried to get ready for bed, telling herself over and over again that she was tired. And though she felt moments of deep unease and discomfort, the anguish of withdrawing from the drugs she had abused did not keep her from resting either.

It was curiosity. She longed to join the McKenzies and find out what was going on.

Rachel had done so. Her ward didn't come to bed until late at night, and then she said that she was exhausted, that she had spent the time watching Captain Jerome McKenzie as he slept. Then she had dined in Colonel McKenzie's tent. The McKenzies were all charming, so warm, and they had all been kind and polite to her and grateful for all her help.

"Well, of course, they are Rebs," Rachel said with a sad sigh, "but so many people in this state were your father's old friends, so we know that they were decent, good, people."

"Yes, we know that. But we are at war. Rachel, I never, ever said that all Rebs were bad people. But we don't have to become the best of friends with the enemy."

"I was having dinner," Rachel said indignantly. She turned her back on Rhiannon then, bidding her good night.

Rhiannon lay there then in misery, wondering how the world could be so torn.

No one came near her during the night.

Jerome was not a model patient. Despite the fact that he knew full well—without both David and Julian reminding him—that he still ran the risk of infection and death, he wanted to be up and about not two days after his surgery.

Rhiannon had kept her distance from Jerome's sick bed and the family McKenzie. Young Liam had brought her meals. She'd kept Paddy's bandages changed and looked in on the few other fellows in sick bay. But she hadn't joined the McKenzies for any family tête-à-têtes; she had, indeed, stayed as invisible as possible.

Admittedly, she had assumed that somewhere along the line Julian would have come to her, insisting she be more social, join them whether she was a Yankee or not. But he didn't come near her.

On the afternoon of the second day, she sat in her tent, repairing a pile of clothing. It was well washed in the brook, but like everything else here, all but threadbare. She didn't want to aid and abet the enemy, but seeing the fellows so shockingly attired—their privates could surely pop out of some of these worn trousers. And so she was sewing.

Rachel found her there. "My Lord, but that man is a demon! He's trying to get out of bed, saying that he can heal just fine on his ship, and poor Risa is declaring that he hasn't got a right to go kill himself when he has a baby boy, not to mention her. Julian is threatening to waste what drugs they have in their Confederate stores to knock him silly so that he'll quit being such a—" She broke off, giggling. "Well, he said it, he did."

"Said what?"

"Pain in the ass!"

"Rachel!"

Rachel sobered. "I guess he does have to settle down, doesn't he?"

"Yes, he does. And you're learning atrocious language from these Rebs."

"Umm. Yanks don't know atrocious language?"

"Don't be cheeky," Rhiannon said sternly, setting her sewing aside and rising.

"Where are you going?" Rachel called.

"To see the patient."

She walked across the camp. Soldiers, busy at various tasks, stopped in their whittling or gun cleaning to glance up at her. All nodded in polite acknowledgment, and she bowed her head in turn as she moved quickly among them.

Coming to the tent where Jerome McKenzie lay, she paused briefly. Julian was angrily telling him that he had to stay down at least another few days; Risa was furious and then in tears. David was trying to be a voice of reason, explaining the risk they ran of infection if they moved him and he started hemorrhaging.

She stepped into the tent. Jerome, who looked a little feverish, which she thought he must be to be so cantankerous to people who loved him so much, had been in the middle of a tirade. Seeing her, he fell silent.

The others, who had been facing him where he lay on his cot, turned to her. "Ah, well, here we have the black widow," Julian said irritably.

She ignored him as she walked past him to Jerome. She shook her head, looking him right in the eye. "Don't you even think about leaving."

Somewhat to her surprise, he hesitated. "Why?"

"You've heard that I can see . . . things. I'm just telling you—don't go now."

"If I do?"

"If you do . . ." She broke off with a shrug. "All right, you want the entire picture? There's a storm due. You'll get caught in it—"

"I'm an excellent sailor," he challenged.

"So you are. But this time a wave is going to hit your ship."

"What is my ship's name? Can you see that?"

"The *Lady Varina.*"

Julian let out a sniff. "All of Florida knows the name of your ship, James."

"Hush up, Julian, please, she's telling him not to go!" Risa pointed out.

"Indeed. Pray, do go on, Mrs. Tremaine."

Rhiannon gritted her teeth. "A wave will hit your ship. You'll be unbalanced; you'll fall. The fall will tear your stitches, you'll bleed profusely, and lose consciousness."

"And I'll die?"

"Without you at the helm, your ship will go down, and your entire crew will die."

"I'm very young, Jerome," David Stewart said. "I don't want to die. Especially not for a bloody storm!"

Jerome smiled slightly, glanced at David, then back at Rhiannon. "And if I don't sail?"

Rhiannon found herself glancing up at Jerome's beautiful wife. The woman watched her so eagerly, and with such hope. A fellow Yank. Married to this fellow here. The scourge of the seas. She should let him die. But she felt the warmth of Risa's gaze, the gratitude in it, and she felt that she wasn't being a traitor to anyone to help this woman—she was, after all, the daughter of a Union general.

"You'll have another child next year."

"Oh!" Risa said, flushing as she found everyone staring at her. Her husband grinned broadly. "Boy or girl?" he asked, amused.

"Another boy."

He looked at Rhiannon again. "I'll survive to see it?"

"You'll live," she said softly.

He watched her, his lip curling slightly. "Through the whole war?"

"I believe so."

Still watching her, he lay back in his bed. His large hand covered his wife's where it lay upon his shoulder.

He shrugged. "Well, then, I guess I'm bedridden a few more days."

"Great. We tell you all about the risks of blood and death, and a Yankee comes in and beats us all," Julian murmured. "Risa, he needs—"

"I know, Julian. Cold cloths; I can feel that he's a bit warm."

"Damn, Julian, don't go getting offended. I mean, I could lie here and die worthlessly, or move and die doing some good, that's the way I was seeing it until . . ." he broke off, watching Rhiannon again. He pulled Rhiannon closer to him. "I've heard an awful lot about you, Mrs. Tremaine. From before the war." He glanced at his cousin. "Remember Rede Corley?"

"Yeah. He was in a group of boys commissioned into the artillery right when the first fighting started," Julian said.

"She kept him from heading out in a worm-eaten old dinghy one day when he had a hankering to go fishing. Worked for her father back then."

She looked at Julian. "I saved him before the war, of course. He wasn't the enemy at the time."

"But I'm the enemy right now," Jerome said. "Maybe you're plotting to keep me from a strategic Rebel sweep."

She hesitated. "Maybe I'm trying to keep you alive because your wife might one day talk some sense into you, sir. Excuse me, please, will you."

She spun around and exited the tent. She was shaking as she did so.

She headed back for her own tent, afraid she was going to fall. To her dismay, Risa McKenzie came running behind her.

"Once again, thank you so much!" She paused, hands on her hips, shaking her head. "You're amazing," she whispered. "And you really see so clearly."

Rhiannon hesitated, then opted to tell the truth. "Mrs. McKenzie, honestly, I didn't see a blessed thing. But I thought that if other people believed what I said . . ."

Risa McKenzie started to laugh. She reached out, ignoring Rhiannon's stiffness, and hugged her fiercely. "Thank you, thank you, so much! If there is ever anything I can do for you . . ."

Unnerved, Rhiannon eased herself from Risa's hold. "Just don't let on that I'm a liar, please?"

"Never, never!" Risa promised. "Again, if there's anything—"

"Perhaps there will be. When you go back to St. Augustine, I believe I'll be coming with you."

"Yes, that's what I've heard."

"I'd like to work with the wounded in the north. On the battlefield. Perhaps you can arrange it for me. With your father."

Risa smiled. "My father will be very glad to have you assisting with his injured. He'll think that God has granted him an angel."

"Or a witch."

"Women sometimes have to be a little bit of both, don't they?" Risa asked softly.

"Perhaps. And oh!"

"What?"

"Please, don't mention to Dr. McKenzie what I plan to do."

"Why ever not?" Risa asked, surprised.

"Men being men, I believe he'll think I'm risking the dangers of the damned if I head off for a battlefield."

"Ah . . . yes, I know, they go off and fight, and we wait in anguish, and we are to take no risks! I promise, I'll keep your secret," she swore. Then she left Rhiannon, spinning around to head back to her husband.

There was always general excitement with any arrival at the Florida base camp along the St. Johns.

Miles before reaching the camp, riders and those on the river could be observed by pickets. It was the only way to keep the camp safe. It was in an accessible area; the Yanks at St. Augustine knew that it existed. But until some general came in determined to throw away an unacceptable number of Union lives, there would be no attempt to clean out the camp. There was a strange acknowledgment of one another along the river. Prisoners were exchanged; messages came and went. Tobacco, coffee, salt, and more were often swapped.

Soon after Julian's argument with Jerome, riders were seen on the trail approaching the camp. The Yankees were not in Jacksonville at the moment, and as Julian watched them approach—Paddy, on crutches, by his side—he commented that they might have headed south from Jacksonville. There were three riders, and they were moving cautiously. They were regular army boys, information quickly sent back by the first lookout, and they appeared to be from a Georgia unit, though it was getting harder and harder to tell. Julian ordered two men out to meet them and escort them the rest of the way.

He stood in the trail beneath the pines, waiting, as the men rode their sorry-looking nags into the camp. He saluted the officer, a slender old man with thick gray hair and a thick beard to match. The fellow saluted in return, dismounting from his horse, and removed worn mustard gloves to shake Julian's hand. "Captain Christopher Rogers, Georgia regulars, Doctor. Private Justin Ewell and Corporal Evan Haines, accompanying me. Official business from the front line of the Confederacy, I'm afraid."

Julian shook the man's hand, amazed that his Yankee brother could be so accurately aware of what was going on in the enemy's camp. "We're to be ordered out?" Julian asked politely.

Captain Rogers arched his brow, surprised. "I'd meant to bring this up a mite more delicately, since the powers that be are aware of the problems here in your home state."

"Naturally," Julian murmured. "And we are fighting for states' rights, aren't we?"

Rogers arched his brow a bit higher at the bitterness in Julian's tone. Julian shook his head. "Sorry, Captain, excuse my manners. Will you join me in my tent? I do happen to have some brandy not immediately required for medicinal purposes."

"Thank you, Dr. McKenzie."

Julian stretched out an arm, indicating his canvas quarters. "Paddy, you'll see to the men?"

"Aye, sir."

Once seated behind his camp desk, Julian poured brandy. Rogers sipped it, and the expression on his face as he savored the brew was such that Julian felt a moment's guilt; Rogers obviously hadn't had brandy in a long time. He was an old-timer and still willingly accepted the hardships of war, taking whatever assignments were given him.

He'd been damned lucky himself. Yes, the state was stripped, and he got no help from the central Confederate government. But he'd had Jerome to see to it that his Florida boys did have what medicines could be procured. Often, though his father remained loyal to the Union, his mother managed to send him smoked hams and dried beef from their plantation in Tampa, just as he'd received supplies from his Uncle James down the peninsula.

That, he realized, was about to change.

Captain Rogers sighed with pure pleasure. "Thank you, Dr. McKenzie."

"I'm delighted to see you enjoy it so. I think we can spare a bit more."

Rogers smiled, accepting another portion of brandy. "I've heard your cousin was shot up, and that his ship is in. The Yanks know it, you can be sure. You'll have to take care."

"Yes, the Yanks know it," Julian agreed, waiting for Rogers to go on.

"Well, down to it, then, I'm here to tell you to report just outside of Jacksonville in five days' time. You're to be commissioned to the regular army and sent north to help with the surgical needs of the Army of Northern Virginia."

"My entire company?"

"Oh, no, sir, they'll be sending another young surgeon here. And you may choose your assistants, of course."

"Why me?"

Rogers shrugged. "You've managed to keep people alive. You've written letters on the subject of sanitary conditions—"

"I wrote personal letters to my cousin," he said, eyes narrowing.

"Yes, and your cousin, Captain McKenzie, used paragraphs from those letters when writing entreaties for supplies that could improve conditions when operating on the battlefield. The major medical officers of the Confederacy have asked for assistance, Doctor."

Julian drummed his fingers on his desk. "Will I be working with my cousin?" Naturally, he would be glad to be with Brent, though at the moment he'd like to strangle him. How could Brent have shown others their private correspondence? But he knew that they were both aware that filthy conditions and unsanitary water caused more deaths than bullets and sabers combined. Brent had done what he felt he had to do. He couldn't have know the consequences.

"I'm afraid Brent McKenzie is being sent on to a grave task indeed."

"Oh?"

To his amazement, old Rogers blushed. He leaned forward, as if there were others in the tent who might overhear their conversation. "Prostitutes!"

"I beg your pardon?"

"Why, sir, it is an epidemic. Where men will fight, women will go. We have so many men downed by diseases of the . . . well, you know, sir, diseases of the flesh—"

"A problem with crabs?" Julian couldn't help but ask bluntly.

Rogers became pathetically pink. Julian decided a little kindness would be in order. "Sorry, sir."

"Much more than that. There are women . . . so many women. Well, Dr. Brent McKenzie is being put on special assignment to try to contain some of these awful diseases and get our men back in the field."

Julian lowered his head, a small smile curling his lips. Well, it was war. Here he had been, sick at heart at leaving his state. He sure as hell couldn't be angry with Brent anymore. Brent had been passionately dedicated to the men on the field. And now he was being sent off to deal with prostitutes! He was surely fit to be tied.

"I'm sure my cousin will rise nobly to the task ahead," Julian said.

Rogers nodded somberly. "You've been noted by the important men in medicine, sir, and they are pleased with your records of success."

"I've not had to work under the same conditions as many of the men in the midst of the major battles."

"You've treated men in the field."

"We've had skirmishes here. I've worked with the same illnesses and the same injuries, but never under some of the truly horrifying circumstances about which I've read. From the major battles, sir, the numbers of wounded, missing, and killed are staggering."

"Staggering," Rogers agreed. "That's why you're in such high demand. Don't be too dismayed, Doctor. Your Governor Milton spends hours writing to the Confederate government, decrying the way his state has been stripped and left to fend for itself with so little defense. The Confederacy has deep sympathy for your plight here. When the summer campaigns are over, there's a good chance you'll be relieved of national duty and allowed to come back home. That's not a promise or a guarantee, sir. You know that I can't give that. We all go where we're ordered to go."

"For the cause," Julian murmured, lifting his brandy glass to Rogers.

"For the cause!" Rogers repeated passionately.

"Tell me, sir, how did you draw this assignment, finding me here in this Godforsaken little hammock?"

"Why, I'm in the process of being reassigned as well, sir. And I'm from Georgia, familiar with north Florida here."

"Why are you being reassigned?"

Rogers rimmed his brandy glass with a finger and then smiled ruefully at Julian. "Well, the boys and I are all that's left. We started out with a company near fifty men back at the beginning of the war. My company. I financed them, you see, and I was elected captain—we were militia to begin with as well, you see. We fought at Chancellorsville. By then, we were already down to about twenty-five men. And after Chancellorsville . . . well, we're all that's left. So we'll be seeing you outside of Jacksonville as well, sir."

Julian nodded slowly. "I'm very sorry, sir."

"So am I, Doctor. So am I."

"It seems to me you've fought a hard war. Perhaps you should be seeing out the rest of it back home in Georgia."

"That sounds like a right fine proposition. But it's strange, Colonel. Once you're in this thing, seems like you're in it to the end."

"I suppose you're right," Julian agreed.

"You keep your head down, working out on the battle-fields, Doctor."

"I will. And you, Captain, you take care of yourself, too."

"I'll drink to that, sir! That is, if you can spare me a touch more of that brandy.

Julian poured them both another drink.

It was late the following afternoon when Rhiannon ventured out to the brook. She was feeling hot, sticky, and restless. Corporal Lyle stood guard at the passage to the water and assured her that he was on duty for several hours to come and would let no one disturb her. Of course, she had heard that story before, but she was beginning to feel a strange sense of fatality, and of recklessness, and she realized that she missed sparring with Julian, and that he had carefully kept his distance from her since his cousin's surgery.

At the brook she hesitated, then stripped her shoes, stockings, petticoat, pantalettes and mourning gown. In her thin linen shift she stepped into the water, delighted by its cool caress. She moved into the deep area, floating on her back, looking at the canopy of trees above. The cool water trickled through her hair, seemed to massage her scalp, to wash away the heat of the daytime sun and all the dust of the earth and air that had surrounded her during the day. The water was lulling, cleansing, crisp, and sweet. She delighted in it.

She didn't know when he came; she just knew suddenly that he was there, by the brook, leaning against an old oak, watching her. She straightened, treading the water to keep her toes from touching the muddy bottom. "Were you waiting for me?" he inquired.

"Certainly not. Corporal Lyle swore to me that he'd guard the pathway."

"Oh, I see. And it never occurred to you that for those of us who know these woods so well, there might not be another path?"

"I was told there was but one."

He pushed away from the tree and came toward her. On the shore line, he hunkered down, trailing his fingers on the surface of the water. "As far as Corporal Lyle knows, there is but one way here." His touch remained on the water. "So cool . . ." he murmured. "Touched by the sun, and still so pleasantly cool. In summer, of course, when the water level lowers . . . it's like bath water. But not today."

His eyes met hers. He straightened. She realized that he was already barefoot; he stripped off his cotton shirt and stepped into the water in his trousers. "You don't mind if I join you, do you?"

"Well, yes, actually—" she began, but he had walked straight to the deeper section, very near her, and plowed in. She continued to tread water nervously, looking around. He didn't surface. He remained below far too long.

Then his head shot smoothly from the water. He was some distance away from her, in the deepest section of the brook leading toward the river.

"I do mind, but, please! Hop right in," she called to him dryly.

He started swimming toward her. Strong, sure strokes. She started to back away, but it was too late. He was suddenly before her, capturing her hands.

"You don't mind. If you did, you wouldn't be here."

"Don't be absurd. I was assured that—"

"That what? I came here and found you before."

"I came to swim, McKenzie. The coolness, the cleanness—"

"Wash away the feel of all those Rebels you've been touching, eh?" he queried.

She jerked her hands free, and turned, ready to swim

toward the shore. She got nowhere. His hands settled on her hips as she tried to flee, and he turned her back to face him. The material of her shift had never felt so thin. His hands all but burned against the coolness of the water and that of her flesh. His eyes were steadily on hers. She set her hands on his, trying to free herself. "Mrs. Tremaine, you are the most atrocious liar I have ever met."

"I don't know what you're talking about!" she snapped, working at his fingers where they lay against her waist. "Let me go—"

"You came here to wait for me. You knew that I would come."

"Now there is the lie, Colonel—"

"Have you been drinking, Mrs. Tremaine?"

"Drinking? While working with your injured soldiers?"

"Have you?"

"Of course not!"

"Any laudanum in your system?"

"No!"

"You're sure, absolutely sure?"

"Yes, of course, I'm sure—"

"Good!"

He drew her hard against him, caught her chin between his fingers and thumb, and kissed her. Very hard, open-mouthed, with a startling, searing passion. Instinctively she struggled. Set her hands against him. His chest. Bare. Sleek. Furred with dark hair, tautly muscled, alive with a searing heat that seemed to explode from the water. She couldn't breathe . . . that was it, of course. The lack of air. She couldn't breathe, she was losing consciousness, sanity, reason, her touch with reality. She felt the wet heat of his tongue and lips, so seductive, ravaging her mouth. Felt his hands, as if they touched her bare flesh, moving over her body creating an erotic friction through the sheer linen that only seemed to enhance his slightest touch . . .

She made a sound in her throat . . . pressed against him again, pushing him, trying to free herself, and yet . . . her strength was fading, along with her desire to be free. She'd never felt anything so evocative, the liquid heat of his touch, the fire of his body. The coolness of the water causing her to burn and shiver in one. Her fingertips remained against his naked chest. Her lips parted freely to the sweet, raw, raking of his tongue, the touch of searing wet fire that seemed to sluice all around her. He tilted her head, tasted her more fully. His fingers moved over her breast, the tips brushing her nipple beneath the linen, hot and cold, sluicing seductive fire everywhere . . .

Then his head lifted. His lips hovered just above her.

"Not drunk, eh?"

"What? No . . ."

"And no drugs?"

"No."

"Good. Then you'll remember me this time."

He released her, inclining his head politely.

She stared at him blankly for a moment, still feeling the pressure of his lips, but now the coolness of the water around her felt like a cold wake-up slap.

"Why, you Rebel bastard."

Naturally, she tried to strike him. But naturally, he was prepared, capturing her wrist and then drawing her against him one more time. "If you ever want the truth, Mrs. Tremaine, look me up. This time, at the very least, you'll remember my name. And my face. Call on me, if you ever decide that you need me."

"Need you!" she gasped furiously.

"You never know, do you, Mrs. Tremaine?"

"I will never need you—"

"You may."

His eyes were deep blue and steady on hers, intense, and yet touched with just the slightest amusement. Maybe more. Maybe something deeper. She was held so closely against him that she felt the muscle and sinew of his body again, felt the strength. She couldn't see Richard's face anymore, just his. His face. He had wanted her to know it, to remember it.

She railed inwardly against her own weaknesses, the darkness in her heart that allowed desire when love was dead, slain on the battlefield.

"Do you know what I need, Colonel?"

"What?"

"Trust me, I know your face and I need just one chance to lay a right jab against your smug cheek!"

He released her, stood back. Smiled, eyes alive and dancing. "One chance. Go for it," he said.

She swung. Hard, with all her strength. She thought that her blow would land. He spun like an acrobat at the last second, and she careened into his arms, pinned hard against him once again. "As I said—"

"You're a rude oaf!"

"But an honest one."

"Honesty and honor are slain on the field like all else, Colonel."

"Life itself has a way of going on, madam, in defiance of all else. Life will always find a way."

"I will never need you!" she whispered again.

"Regardless of that, my dear, I would move heaven and earth to come to your assistance if ever you should beckon. The name is McKenzie. Julian. Remember that."

"Let me go this instant, Julian McKenzie—"

"There you go, you've got it!"

"Julian—"

"Remember me."

He still held her so tightly. His lips touched hers once again. Now the touch was light and swift, like the whisper of a flame against her soul.

When he released her, she was scarcely aware. She lowered her head, suddenly bereft of strength.

And when she lifted her eyes again . . .

He was gone.

She wasn't to see him again until he touched her in her dreams.

Chapter 12

"Why, Miss Sydney, welcome, how are you this evening?"

"Fine, Sergeant Granger, just fine, thank you, sir," Sydney McKenzie replied to the man on duty at Capitol Prison, Washington, D.C. She offered him a pleasant smile. She smoothed back a straying lock of rich dark hair that glittered with a touch of auburn in the lamplight. "Come to see my boys, of course."

"Yes, Miss Sydney, don't worry none. We might sit here and wish you were coming to pay a visit to us Yank fellows, but we sure do know better." Sergeant Granger was an old enlisted man. A bit grizzled, a bit worn, but a pleasant family man; the kind who made her realize at times that the war was all about fighting their own ex-fellow countrymen. But though she'd acquired a fondness for him along with some of the other Yanks she encountered in the Federal capital, her fondness didn't go so far as to cause her to feel any guilt for what she was doing: anything she could to get the Southern boys out and back home.

Or anything she could to carry important messages where and when they needed to go.

She'd first come north to help free her brother Jerome when he'd been a prisoner here. He was to have been exchanged for Captain Jesse Halston, a dashing young cavalryman wounded and imprisoned in the South. But the exchange had been halted, mainly because of Jerome's father-in-law. Union General Magee had thought that his son-in-law would better survive the war in prison. He hadn't known Jerome well enough; Jerome had been determined to leave one way or the other.

Sydney had been Jesse Halston's nurse at Chimbarizo

Hospital in Richmond. He'd been an important prisoner, one for whom the South had known they could exchange an officer dear to their own cause. He'd been a model patient, and he was a handsome, reckless, daring young man. They'd formed a friendship.

Destroyed completely, of course, once he'd stopped her from leaving with Jerome. Oh, he'd done it well. Though the North had refused to exchange Jerome, Jesse had been exchanged for a Confederate general. Jerome had been determined to leave, and one of the other prisoners' old Irish grandmother had brought some friends—Southern sympathizers—and so a number of the men had escaped dressed as part of the Irish ladies' singing group. Jesse, however, had caught on to their plan, and in the middle of the Confederate flight he'd caught up with her—threatening to alert the authorities about the prison break if she attempted to leave the city with her brother. He'd been adamant, and she'd had to put on one of the performances of her life to convince Jerome she had meant all along to stay in Washington. Of course, Jerome had been very aware of the danger she would have been in traveling with him, and since she had been the one to introduce Jerome to Jesse back in Richmond, her brother had trusted her. He had even been relieved that she would be out of danger.

Jesse had forced her to stay behind, detained in the parlor of the handsome town house he had inherited from his father. For hours she eyed him with barely controllable rage. "I'm making you stay for your own good," he had told her, "so you can't go chasing after your brother and wind up with a bullet in your head."

She'd finally fallen asleep on his sofa, and she'd slept there ten hours after all that. When she'd awakened, however, he was watching her. She'd told him, "You can deliver me to President Lincoln, for all I care. Jerome is gone. And now I'm going. You can arrest me, or shoot me—I'm not staying in this parlor any longer." He had turned his back on her and told her to leave.

At Old Capitol, the Irish ladies were no longer admitted, but Sydney, who hadn't been blamed for the escape, was allowed to come to see the prisoners, to bring them food and clothing and other donations. Her brothers were Rebels, but her cousin Ian was a Northern cavalry hero—

very much like Jesse Halston himself—and so she was often granted special privileges. People seemed to trust her.

Jesse had been sent back to war.

Since then, she'd twice been able to relay information from prisoners. She knew it was a dangerous game—other family members had played it. But she was careful, and she was charming and good at her game, and she never trusted anything to paper. The messages she carried were by voice alone, her own or that of Marla Kelly, a young Irish girl she'd met during her brother's escape. Marla's brother, with whom she'd come to America, had been killed at Sharpsburg. The young husband she'd married just before the war had perished protecting Richmond during McClellan's Peninsula campaign. Left so alone and bereft and far from home, Marla wanted revenge. She was acquainted with Rose Greenhow, the bewitching Washington widow who had charmed the capital society while informing Southern generals of Federal military movements. Rose had been caught, sent to Old Capitol herself, and finally brought South—where she still worked for the Confederacy. Many women were managing to help the Confederacy. Her cousin-in-law Alaina—wed to Ian, that most ardent of Yanks!—had become a Confederate spy, working with Rose. In the end she had been caught, but by Ian, and so, on her honor, she was done with spying. Sydney's older half-sister, Jennifer, had also turned to espionage after her husband's death—the pain and bitterness had made her reckless as well. Jennifer had actually been hanged, but Ian had found her before the rope had strangled her, and she had ceased her far too dangerous activities.

Sydney never felt that she was in danger. Nothing could be proven against her. She was different from Jennifer—she wasn't in pain and she wasn't bitter—she was just angry. Therefore, she wasn't reckless. And she knew so much. About both sides. She had lived in both Richmond and Washington, D.C., and knew the hearts of both countries. She was loyal to her cause, knowing the terrible weakness of the South—and the strengths. The South, despite her fabulous generals, excellent cavalry, and the fact that her young men were defending their homeland and their way of life, couldn't win a war waged on manpower and technology alone. The North did have the factories, and the capabilities of drawing from far greater resources of manpower. Dead Northern soldiers could be replaced. Some died without ever speaking the English language.

The South, however, could win on morale. The Northern people had to tire and sicken of the war. They had to want to let their Southern sister go, say good riddance to the bloodshed. The South could win if politics swung to the Southern favor, and every time the South won a battle, every time lists of the Union dead were read, the people came a little bit closer to wanting it all to be over.

She knew how that felt herself. She wanted it over. She was sick to death of worrying about her brothers, her cousins, her friends. She wanted to be able to go home, and find her family there, and she wanted to see her mother and her new baby sister. She had been with her brother Brent in Richmond for a long time, and now she missed him as well. She was living among the enemy. She needed to go home, except that she was useful here. Please, God, she'd heard it here, among the whispering Yank soldiers and from the prisoners of the South—Lee wanted to take the war to the North. If he could only win his great battle on Northern soil, strip the North as the North had stripped the South. Lay so much waste . . . like so much of her homeland. Not the far south of the state, where she had been born. But the more northern cities. Jacksonville. The Yanks had been in and out, burning, looting, destroying. St. Augustine, taken over. And so many of the people so fickle! The city just couldn't make it, it seemed, without her Yankee tourist dollars! Inlets and coves, shelled and lambasted. Salt and cattle scavenged, when every little bit of supplies was so desperately needed by an army growing evermore ragged and malnourished, day by day.

It was high time for the South to scavenge cattle from the Northern states, trample the crops, steal the corn.

"You're a bit late tonight, aren't you?" Granger asked.

"I guess I am. May I still come in?"

"The boys are in the public room having just finished their suppers, so I suppose I can let you in. But I'm going to have to see your basket, Miss Sydney, you know," Granger told her.

"Why, of course."

She handed him the basket she had brought. There was

no danger in it. She carried nothing but food—meat pies, sweetments, fresh breads, apples, and cherry marmalade.

Granger carefully looked through all that she had brought.

"It just confounds me," he said, shaking his head, "that we have so many women living here—in our own capital, no less!—who are so willing to feed the boys killing their own sons and husbands!"

"Why, Sergeant, you just don't understand the cause of the Ladies of the Convention," she said, explaining the group of women who helped her. "They do believe in the Union, and I swear to you, sir, they do love their sons and husbands just the same as all women, but they want them home. They want the war over, and they just can't see forcing the Southern states to remain in the Union if they want to go."

"Hmmph," Granger murmured. He'd placed all the food on the desk in front of him and went on to carefully inspect the basket itself. Sydney made a mental note never to underestimate Granger for being a suspicious old coot—if a good enough fellow.

"Admit it—you like some of the prisoners kept here," she challenged him flirtatiously.

"I like some of them well enough. Young lady, I find a man in here now and then who used to be an old friend or acquaintance. Before the war, you know, I sold carriages. Only the best. Sold plenty of them to folks down in the South."

She smiled. "May I see the boys now? As you can see, I came in carrying no rifles, knives, cannons, or the like."

"Fine, you go see the boys, Miss Sydney." Granger nodded to one of the guards who had waited to escort her to a courtyard where the Rebel men were sometimes allowed to gather. As she started from the outer office, he called her back. "Miss Sydney."

"Why, yes, Sergeant?"

"You watch your step, young lady. You're a might too charming for your own good."

"Why, thank you, Sergeant, I am always careful."

"That's what scares me," he muttered.

The guard let her through the building and to the back. It was a strange prison. Called Old Capitol because for a time it had served the government, it had also been a boarding house before taking in its current inhabitants. There were worse places to be, Sydney had heard, including Southern prisons.

The Federalists were outraged by the conditions at Southern prisons, but what they didn't seem to understand was that, in most cases, the authorities weren't cruel on purpose—they offered their prisoners the same pitiful and rotten rations that went to the boys in the field. As far as supplies went, the blockade against the South was ever tightening, and the boys in the field were often starving just the same as the men in the prisons.

The men were in a crude hall with long tables and simple chairs. In winter, it was their exercise room, in summer, it was a common room. As she came in with her basket, she saw that there were about twenty-five men in attendance there that night. They spilled forward, polite, eager to see her. Treated well enough in this prison, they were still all far too thin and tattered looking. They were the proud boys who had started off so dashingly just a few years ago. Their pride remained, but their weariness was visible as well.

"Miss McKenzie, dear Miss McKenzie!" Lieutenant Aaron Anderson, an artillery man from Alabama, strode through the crowd of men, taking her hands. "Miss McKenzie, you are a sight for sore eyes. The boys and I are so grateful to you for these visits! What have you brought us tonight?"

"Treats, gentlemen, do take the basket and dig in!"

"Why, my mouth is watering already!" said Private Thompson of Mississippi.

"Thompson, take over and distribute, will you please?" Anderson said.

It was a way to keep the two of them in the center of the floor with the men milling all around them. Although guards remained in the room, they couldn't hear the exchange between Anderson and Sydney while the commotion went on.

"Listen carefully," Anderson said, his smile and his leisurely manner gone. "A Union General Pratt is in the process of bringing a supply train down the small pike just off the Harpers Ferry Road in what used to be Virginia." Even among the noise, he said those words with deep contempt.

At the end of 1862, Virginia had been split into Virginia and West Virginia. Southerners were convinced that the vote to secede from the state by the West Virginians had been forced at gunpoint. Now, West Virginia was about to be admitted to the Union, and there were two separate and distinct Virginias, the old Virginia, and West Virginia, and a sad affair it was.

"Pratt," Sydney said.

"You know the road?"

"I do, sir."

"Get the information to Jeffrey Watts at the Watts Mercantile down by the bridge, and he'll see to it that it's brought on over where it's needed. There's only a small party of men escorting the train, because it's mainly medical supplies. Not so important to the Yanks—just ether, bandages, morphine, quinine—but it could keep some of our boys alive. There won't be more than fifteen men on it, three drivers, an escort of ten to twelve. Oh, and I hear there's a shipment of shoes packed in with the medical supplies, something we need in a dire way, as I'm sure you've heard. I can't tell you just how desperate the Army of Northern Virginia is getting for something so simple as shoes! Half our boys are wearing Northern boots, stolen off the dead with honest apologies. The old pike just south of the Harpers Ferry Road. Both armies are moving already, and the South sure could use those supplies. Have you got it straight, Sydney?"

"Yes, of course."

Anderson raised his voice. "Miss Sydney, I declare, you do bring us the finest, tastiest creations I do remember. Bless you, child."

"Bless you, Miss Sydney!" the group around her chorused.

It was a good feeling.

"My pleasure, Lieutenant Anderson, fellows. How are you all doing now?"

"Foot's a bit bad, Miss Sydney," Private Lawton said. Sydney frowned, looking downward. Lawton's foot was bandaged. The bandaging was filthy—bloodied and blackened. He had been thumping around on rough wood crutches far too short for his lanky height.

"Let me see that foot," Sydney told him.

"Why, no, ma'am," he said, blushing. "I ain't having no lady look at this foot!"

"This lady has worked the hospitals in Richmond, Private. Let me see that foot."

"I was just complaining, Miss Sydney, hearing myself talk," Lawton said, offering a shy, boyish smile. "I'm going to be all right. I promise that if it ain't better when I see you again, I'll let you take a look."

Sydney gazed unhappily at Lieutenant Anderson.

Anderson shrugged. "I'm hoping to see you tomorrow, Miss McKenzie. We'll take a good hard look at Lawton's foot then."

"All right then, that's a promise you're making me, Private," Sydney said sternly.

He smiled. "Right, I am duly honored," he said, bowing. "I have not ever had a lady make me promise to show her my bare foot before."

Soft laughter rose. Sydney smiled a little unhappily. She didn't like the way Lawton looked.

"Well, boys, I will be going." She kept her voice high and light, her eyes on Anderson's. "And I will be back tomorrow."

Granger himself came to escort her from the common room. Sydney looked at him. "Sergeant Granger, if I were to need a surgeon hereabouts, would you know where I might find one?"

"The army is full of surgeons, Miss Sydney."

She shook her head. "I mean a good surgeon."

He hesitated. "Interesting, I heard tell . . ."

"What?"

"Well, there's a widow in town . . ."

"I don't need a widow, sir. The man isn't dying for feminine companionship, he needs a surgeon!"

Granger looked at her, shocked, thinking that Sydney had assumed that he was offering the widow as a prostitute. "Miss Sydney! Why this war is doing things to men and women alike, I swear it! I'm telling you about this woman because she's the buzz of Washington at the moment. She's known to have a magic touch." He frowned suddenly "Come to think of it, there's a McKenzie connection in her being here."

"Pardon? What do you mean?"

"She's to be riding out to join the surgeons with General Magee's boys. She's a Florida Yank."

"Imagine that!" Sydney murmured with only a trace of sarcasm. She really did like Granger.

"Why, come to think of it, Miss Sydney, it isn't just a McKenzie connection, it was your sister-in-law who sent her up there. I can send for Mrs. Tremaine if you like. If you want to tell me what's wrong with which soldier in there."

Sydney still hesitated. She needed to see the man's foot herself. If the poor private was in bad shape, he was going to need surgery, not just magic. And often, soldiers would rather die than face the surgeons from the enemy camp.

"If I need help, Sergeant, I'll let you know tomorrow."

"Fair enough. We're not all monsters, though. You know that, Miss Sydney."

"Yes, of course, I know that, Sergeant Granger."

"We'll see you tomorrow, then?"

"Yes, Sergeant, you will. I try to keep the boys here in good spirits."

"That's why you don't go back to Richmond and help out in the hospital there?"

"Of course," Sydney said. "Why else?"

"You wouldn't be spying would you, sending messages back and forth?"

"From imprisoned men? What could they know of any worth, Sergeant?"

"Take care, Miss Sydney."

"Oh, I shall, Sergeant."

Sweat dripped into Julian's eyes.

Inside the tent the heat seemed to shimmer around him with a brutality that intensified that of the wounds inflicted during battle. He'd been told that Florida was a hot, mosquito-infested state, but he'd never been as hot in his native land as he was here in Virginia.

Not a full week ago, he'd been at his base camp, and God help him, but he'd liked it when he'd been the ranking militia officer, giving the orders. Now he was a captain in the Army of Northern Virginia. He was respected, given command of his field hospital. The officers around him were willing to oblige him, but there were so many areas in which he was now out of control.

He'd joined the regular army by way of the railroads, arriving at this camp outside Brandy Station. Just two days ago, the great Confederate General Jeb Stuart—dubbed "Beauty" by his West Point classmates for his homely face now made more dashing by a full, thick beard—had held a review of his troops to the entertainment and pleasure of the local ladies. But Stuart had been caught by surprise by Federal cavalry looking for Lee's troop movements, and what was ensuing was a battle with twenty thousand horsemen, almost evenly divided.

Brent had been with these troops until just before the battle, and Julian had arrived only in time to be told his cousin had anxiously waited to see him, but then been sent on to take control of the hospital facility outside Richmond.

Sweat dripped into his eyes again. His orderly saw that he was nearly blinded and wiped his brow. He was a good solid fellow, but not one of his own men. They were busy trying to pull more wounded from the field, bring them in, give them a chance . . .

He could have wept. There was no time, no time . . .

"Sir, look, the bullet," Thomas, his young orderly, commented.

A broken leg, but the bullet had gone almost cleanly through. "I see, Thomas. Give me the bullet extractor."

"Do you have time?"

"Yes, give me the extractor."

Time . . .

Was he risking another man's life while he took the precious time to operate so this man could walk again? God, he had to work so fast.

He felt a strange tremor seize him. In the midst of this madness, an irritating sense of longing crept into his soul.

If only she were here with him. Strange, she said she despised him, but when her eyes touched his, he never doubted himself. Perhaps he saw in her the same. Maybe it was all belief. She believed that he could work miracles. He believed that she could heal.

If only she could believe in the truth . . .

"Sir, it's clear. We'll get him off the table and get him splinted."

"You're a good man, Thomas."

"No, sir. You're a good doctor."

Thomas shouted for help, and the man was moved from Julian's operating table. As soon as he was gone, another was brought.

"Gut shot, sir!" the assistant surgeon cried.

So why bring him to me? He almost shouted aloud. Gut-shot. The man on his table was clutching organs that were destroyed, tossing and moaning in agony.

"I'm going to die, I'm going to go, God-a-mercy, I'm going to die!" the boy on the table cried. He was young, maybe eighteen. And he was right.

"Just hold on, lad, and we'll see what we—"

"Doctor, don't—"

He had sandy hair, both pimples and whiskers on his chin, and maple brown eyes. Those eyes widened suddenly on Julian. The boy fell back to the table. Dead.

"Sorry, sir, we didn't see how bad—"

"Bring them even if they're bad!" he cried hoarsely. "Maybe I can't do anything, but I won't know if I don't see them."

The day went on and on. He saved a few lives—for the time being, at least. He lost a few. He never knew their names. He could barely remember their faces. And when he fell exhausted into his cot that night, all he could really remember was the feel of the sweat dripping into his eyes . . .

He knew his business, but, strangely, he felt different. She'd been with him, and now she was gone. He could remember her eyes, silently sharing his knowledge. Remember her fingers, helping, her touch, delicate; she had anticipated his needs.

She had somehow . . . entered his blood. His soul. He wished that she were with him. She was a witch, a beautiful witch of the earth or sea, and she infuriated him, and . . .

He wanted her with him, even in the midst of the tense, agonizing tumult of the battlefield surgery.

"Perhaps I should go," Marla mused, watching Sydney change to a skirt and shirt to ride down to the mercantile by the river. She seemed uneasy. She was a very pretty girl, petite with ebony dark hair and brilliant blue eyes. She could flutter her lashes in a way that had gotten her past many a confused young sentry.

Sydney looked at her. "Why on earth should you?"

"You've had a long day—"

"No, no, I've got to go. I told Anderson that I would, and I'm ready to go."

"I'm a widow. It's more proper for me to be riding out this late."

"It isn't proper for either of us." Sydney said, then hesitated. It wasn't proper. "I won't ride alone. I'll take Sissy with me."

Sissy was their young black maid. She had come looking for work soon after Sydney and Marla had taken the rooms together. She was quiet and efficient and managed to be discreet in all that she did. She was so quiet and efficient, as a matter of fact, that both Sydney and Marla forgot she was around at times. Even as Sydney decided that she had best take Sissy with her on the ride, she made a mental note to be more careful of what she said and did around the girl.

Marla nodded, but she still looked unhappy.

"What's the matter?"

"Nothing," Marla said. Then she shrugged. "I don't know. Irish intuition. My grandmother used to tell me that such a feeling meant the banshees were flying about, looking. Meant a man or woman had best take care."

Sydney smiled. She had Irish in her blood, and she even felt a little unnerved by Marla's uneasiness, but there was nothing she could do. She had to get her message delivered.

"I've got to go," she said simply. "I may fail . . . but if I don't try, well, then, we haven't got a chance at all, right?"

Marla shrugged.

"Sissy!" Sydney called.

The young black woman appeared in the doorway. She was of medium height and had a tendency to keep her eyes downcast. But she looked straight at Sydney now, and Sydney realized that the girl was very beautiful. Her flesh was as black and velvety as the night sky; her eyes were very large, as ebony as her flesh. She was slim and quick, and had a wonderful smile. She was a free woman living in Washington, but Sydney thought she might have been a slave at one time, the way she was so quick to look down.

She wondered if she'd had a vicious master, or one who had used and abused her. Neither she nor anyone in her family had ever owned slaves; her grandfather had not believed in slavery, and he had instilled his beliefs in both his sons.

"Sissy, I need to ride out to a mercantile on the river. I know it's late, but I've this desire to see some stock . . . and quite frankly I'm bored and restless."

"Yes, ma'am?" Sissy looked surprised. Sydney remembered that she didn't need to give a servant an explanation for what she was doing.

"You'll accompany me."

"Yes, ma'am, of course."

"We have to ride there." She hesitated, realizing the matter had never come up before. "You do ride?"

"Yes, ma'am."

"You may change if you wish. I'll see you outside in ten minutes."

"Yes, ma'am."

"Be careful out there," Marla warned when Sissy had gone. "Give me a hug."

Sydney did so.

"I wish you wouldn't go tonight."

"I have to go tonight," she said.

She turned and went outside, calling to Tim, the lad who cared for the horses, to bring them out. She waited at the white picket fence that surrounded the small yard of the town house where she and Marla had taken their rooms. It was a beautiful night; the temperature had cooled. It was a good night for a ride.

Thankfully, she had good animals for her journeys. The South had been known for breeding horses, but the war had brought their beautiful stock low. She had been able to buy better horses in Washington, D.C., than she'd been able to get in Virginia.

Her father, Confederate that he was, sent her the money that she needed. But then, of course, her father thought that she wrote letters, read books, baked pies, and tended to the needy. James respected his children and expected them to be opinionated individuals. But he was also a strict parent, more so with his daughters than his sons, as fathers tended to be. So if he knew what she was really about . . .

especially after what had happened to Jennifer, he would be up here himself, brandishing a sword at her to get her home.

She paused for a moment with a smile on her face. She wondered what would be worse if she was caught, facing her father—or the Yanks.

She couldn't dwell on such worries. Tim brought the horses around, two healthy bays, a good sixteen hands each, sleek and fast. Sissy would be with her. They would be just fine.

She was simply riding to a Watts Mercantile to make a few purchases and nothing more. She carried nothing written whatsoever.

What could possibly happen? What could go wrong?
Nothing, nothing, nothing! She told herself.

Marla had unnerved her with her superstitious talk. And yet . . .

She should have been forewarned.

Chapter 13

◡

It was dark, and Corporal Rugby lit the way with an oil lamp as they came to the last of the rooms. The existence of the special hospital outside of Richmond wasn't a military secret, and he'd heard mention of what the soldiers termed the "All Saints Place." Now he was here—put in charge. Throughout the day he had seen dozens of patients. Often, it was better to see a man maimed and bleeding than one entering the final stages of syphilis. The wounded man had the chance. The man dying of syphilis did not.

"He's the worst of them, sir. A Captain Henderson, artillery, old fellow, shouldn't have been in the service, you know, but . . . well, he was a good, loyal Southerner and so he upped into the army."

The man lying on the bed had obviously suffered from the disease for many years. In the first stages, ulcers appeared; they might then go dormant, and a man might think himself cured. But the disease didn't go away; it just waited. Then it ate at the body and the mind, and eventually . . .

He lay on the bed, groaning. He looked at Brent with pleading eyes. Not for help. He knew that he couldn't be helped. He wanted to be shot, put out of his misery.

"This man was let into the army?" Brent said with quiet incredulity.

"Well, you know, sir, doctors examine the men, but quite frankly, we can't be too darned picky anymore. We're taking boys and old folks these days—"

"But this man must have come into the army at the start of the war for this disease to have so ravaged him by now!"

"Yes, sir. He was head of a Virginia militia unit from way back before the war. He financed his company, bought horses, equipment, uniforms . . . and when his troops were commissioned into the regular army, he didn't seem to mind one bit. He just came right along. He fought bravely, gave his all . . . and came here. Some time ago now."

Yes, obviously, this man had been dying for some time. There were treatments that could control the symptoms of syphilis, and men and women could go for years bearing—and spreading—the disease before it began to wreak the final havoc upon the human mind and body.

"There's nothing I can do for this man—except help him die with less pain."

"That's what we all thought here, sir. But then, they said that you were awful good with diseases."

"I'm not a miracle worker, I'm afraid. This poor fellow needs strong doses of morphine. We'll do everything we can to make him comfortable. I can prescribe some herbal baths that will be soothing for the sores. We're limited here, of course. I've only two assistant surgeons to help with all the patient care so we'll need a dedicated orderly or nurse with a strong stomach—"

"Oh, he has the most dedicated nurse in the world. Miss Mary is here with him," Corporal Rugby said.

"Miss Mary?" Brent inquired.

"Ah, and here she is!" Rugby said cheerfully.

Brent turned as Rugby smiled over his shoulder. A woman was coming toward them. *One of the whores,* Brent thought. *The place was crawling with them. Old, young. Pretty, worn, sweet, nasty, and sour as turned wine.*

This one was beautiful. She was small, slim, with generous breasts and a minuscule waist, exquisitely proportioned. Her hair was a golden blond, her face was a classical oval with just a touch of a heart shape, and her eyes were large and gray. Her hair was tied back simply with a ribbon, and she was dressed in a plain gray cotton day gown with no corseting beneath. The dress was chastely buttoned to her throat, with a white collar that had somehow stayed white and added a look of prim innocence to her gown. She flashed a quick smile to Corporal Rugby before turning her gaze on Brent.

She was straightforward, offering him her hand. "I'd heard you were coming. My name is—"

"Mary, yes, and you look after the captain here."

"Yes. Can you do anything for him?"

The girl was young, perhaps eighteen. In a society where many young women became wives at fifteen and sixteen, she wasn't so terribly young, but as a consort to the man on the bed, she was a babe. She apparently cared something for him as well, because her eyes and tone were anxious as she spoke.

"I can help him die," Brent said quietly but bluntly.

He thought for a moment that her eyes would well with tears. She looked away. "We thought perhaps that you knew . . ."

Magic. They all thought he had some kind of damned magic. He felt weary, beaten—and angry. He wondered if this girl knew that syphilis was contracted through sexual activity. A lot of them didn't. These foolish girls! She didn't look as if she had come from desperate poverty. She spoke well, as if she had been educated. Whatever made these young girls turn to such a life?

"I can help him die," Brent said. "and that is all. I'm sorry."

Her jaw tightened as she blinked back tears. "I work very hard here, helping out," she said. "Long hours. I work with all the men, I don't shrink from any task. All I ask is morphine for him in return—"

"He'll be given all that I can give him."

"If we need money—"

"No!" he snapped. "We don't need money." Money! She was plying her trade here, where they were busy fighting the spread of venereal disease throughout the army. "Money can't buy what can't be obtained at any price. What we have, we will use. I will see that he lives in the least pain possible and dies with the most dignity we can give him. I have just told Corporal Rugby that I'll be prescribing baths to soothe his sores. Tomorrow morning, you may follow me through rounds and I'll show you how I want him treated. You may help out with treatments, but you may not . . . fraternize with the men. Am I clear?"

She pursed her lips, and her eyes flashed with anger. "Perfectly, sir," she told him.

"Good."

Bone tired, sick at heart, Brent turned away. He'd been harsh with her, but he had dozens of prostitutes on his hands, and they were all going to be given a few brutal lessons. Tomorrow afternoon, he thought with a wince, he'd call the female inhabitants and patients of the hospital to a meeting. The topic was condoms. English hats, as the French called them. French coats, as the English and Americans termed them. Not an easy topic, no matter what term was used.

As he walked away, he could hear Mary talking quietly with Corporal Rugby. He again felt an almost overwhelming anger. How could such a perfect young beauty turned to such a trade? Was she destined to die like her captain, bleeding, ulcerated, devastated, barely human, much less left with even the remnants of a faded beauty?

If they had contracted syphilis, most of the prostitutes would die so. It was his task to see that they didn't bring more and more men with them to the grave . . .

"Nasty bastard!" Mary said angrily. She knew that Corporal Rugby was looking at her sympathetically, and she was about to burst into tears. Of course, it had been foolish to hope for a miracle.

Rugby cleared his throat. "Not so bad, really. I think he's overwhelmed. So many prostitutes here needing help, and then the men, the dying men, those he can help, those he'll send back to war. Others he'll have to furlough home . . . it's a big responsibility."

"He's angry that he's been sent here," Mary said. "He's young and handsome and thinks he should be on a battle-field or in Richmond, dancing with the debutantes! Well, it won't matter any. I'll be the best nurse he's ever had."

"It will be all right, Miss Mary," Rugby said somewhat helplessly.

"Yes, of course . . ." Mary said. She forced herself to smile. "I'm fine here, you go on. He'll realize you aren't with him in a minute and bite your head off."

"But you seem so down—"

"I'm fine. Get going."

He nodded, hesitated, left her.

Mary watched him go. Then she turned to the captain, bent over him tenderly, touched his cheek. "My poor, poor captain!" she said, and an unbidden tear fell down her cheek, and dropped upon his. He opened his eyes. For a moment he saw her, and the ghost of a smile touched his lips, and then was gone.

General Angus Magee stared across the table at his beautiful, refined young guest.

She was slim, regal, seemed to float across the floor as she walked. She was quiet, she listened—an amazing virtue in the young, these days, he thought. There was a distance to her as well, an untouchable quality. Well, she was supposed to be a witch in a way. He knew he couldn't take his eyes off of her.

She'd lost a husband to the war, he knew. Risa had made that all very clear in her letters. And she wanted to work with the injured. She would be a welcome addition. He'd been ordered into the Capitol for meetings on the field hospital procedures, and it had seemed an excellent time to come and escort the lady back to camp himself.

They sat at a nice restaurant quite near the White House. White linens covered the tables; the silver was polished to a high gleam. A violinist played. Waiters in white gloves poured their wine. Yes, she looked good here. Even in her simple black, she was elegant.

He leaned slightly across the table as she sipped her wine. "Are you sure you want to join me? The South thinks that the political climate in the North will eventually force the Union to let the Confederacy go, but it isn't going to happen. I know Mr. Lincoln. I have never seen a man so singularly dedicated to a cause in all my life. This war isn't going to be over soon."

"I know that, sir," she said with one of her pretty smiles. "Sir, if there was to be no fighting, you wouldn't need me."

"Oh, so you're saying that I need you—*you in particular*?"

Her smile filled her face, touching the radiance of her eyes. "Yes, sir, you need me. I'm excellent with sick and injured men. As you know, I just came from assisting with a Southern surgery. I helped with your son-in-law."

Magee sat back with a huff. "That boy will be the death of me!"

She lowered her lashes, still smiling. "General Magee, I can imagine how hard it is to have your daughter married to a Rebel, but . . . well, sir, it's quite obvious that the two love each other very much. I hope that is some solace."

"It is some solace. He's a fine man. But it's a thorn in my side as well! So you assisted Julian McKenzie, eh?"

"Yes."

"When the war is over, I owe that young man. If he makes it through it. He's a damned reckless fellow—it seems to run in the family."

"You owe Julian?" she inquired, surprised.

"I'm walking today because of Julian," he informed her. "Risa insisted I see him. She married his Rebel cousin, you must remember. Julian had been keeping a surgery in St. Augustine until the city was taken over by the Yanks. He was slipped back in to operate on my foot. Such comings and goings are not so strange in this war as they should be, perhaps."

He was startled by the strange play of emotions that swept over her usually so serene features.

"What's the matter?" he asked her.

"Nothing . . . I, umm. I suppose I owe Julian as well." She smiled suddenly. "Just what I owe him, I'm not sure."

Magee leaned back. "Were you injured in some way? Ill?"

She hesitated, then her beautiful eyes locked steadily with his. "I was addicted," she said. "To laudanum. After my husband's death . . ." Her voice trailed, and she shrugged. "I was taking more and more. Julian pointed out the error of my ways."

Magee lowered his head, smiling. He wasn't sure if Mrs. Rhiannon Tremaine hated Julian McKenzie or . . . felt something else. There was only one thing about which he could be completely certain. She loved him or loathed him—but whichever it was, she did so with intensity and passion.

He lifted his wineglass to her, glad that she was accompanying him. "Welcome to the Army of the Potomac, Mrs. Tremaine. Did you know, by the way, that Julian McKenzie has been moved into the regular army? He's been seeing the action south in Virginia already."

"Yes, I'd heard he was being sent to the regular army."

He leaned toward her. "You know, Mrs. Tremaine, when

you accompany me, we might wind up facing his troops in action one day."

She nodded, swallowing her wine. "He's a doctor. He'll be with the hospital staff."

"Field hospital, remember, the same position where you've asked to be on the opposite side."

"But it's not like infantry facing infantry—" she protested, and he saw that she was concerned. Was she afraid of seeing Julian? Or of seeing him stretched out on an operating table?

He thought she shivered slightly. And he wondered just what she saw.

Sissy seemed nervous when she joined Sydney in front of the house and mounted one of the bays.

"It's all right, Sissy. We'll be fine on the streets, if you're afraid," Sydney assured her.

"I'm fine, Miss Sydney."

"You look as if you'd just seen a ghost."

"No, ma'am, I'm just fine."

"If you're really afraid—"

"No, no, Miss Sydney, I wouldn't have you out alone on a night like this. Wouldn't be fittin' for a young lady."

Sydney wasn't sure that she'd actually ever been a young lady. The McKenzies had held a definite social status in the state of Florida before the war, but there were those to whom her Indian blood would always make her an outcast.

"Fine, Sissy, mount up," Sydney said.

She rode slightly ahead. Though it was night, the capital city of the Union remained alive and bustling. Couriers came and went. Soldiers marched by. Carriages clattered along the streets. It was a hot summer, and so men and women dallied on their porches, seeking whatever breezes they might find. Sydney heard snatches of conversation as they rode along, their gait slow and steady as they headed for the river.

"They should quit the fighting!" one old-timer bellowed, slamming a fist on his balustrade. "I heard tell there's trouble in the Confederacy between Jeff Davis and his people. All those Rebs thought they were fighting for 'States' Rights.' Now the Confederacy is taking more of those individual rights than the North ever did!"

"We've got our own problems, Father," a woman answered him wearily. "Draft riots, generals who won't fight."

"We need a victory, a real victory," a younger man said.

"There was Antietam Creek," the old-timer protested.

"Oh, yeah, Sharpsburg. Well, both armies claimed that one."

"All that both armies can claim with truth is that they've achieved incredible fratricide!" the woman said.

And Sydney thought that she was most probably right.

"Miss Sydney, do you know where you're going?" Sissy, riding behind her, called out to her.

"Yes, of course."

Sissy fell silent, and Sydney knew why. They were leaving the area of handsome homes for warehouses, factories, and shanty towns. But she knew about Watts Mercantile, Jeff Watts had been a spy for a long time, using his position on the river to carry information swiftly south.

"We're nearly there."

"If'n we make it!" Sissy grumbled.

Sydney remained silent for a moment. "Fine, we'll hurry then." She spurred herself. As they loped along, she was suddenly certain that she heard horses coming from behind them. She reined in, spun her mount around. The dark streets appeared empty.

"What is it?" Sissy asked, reining in behind her.

"I heard horses."

"I don't see anything."

"Let's hurry."

"Yes, good."

They raced onward, breaking into a full gallop since they were so close. Sydney was relieved when they reached the mercantile. She flashed Sissy a smile as she dismounted from her horse, tethered her bay in front of the large dock-side store.

"Made it."

"Yes. Just what was it we came for?" Sissy asked.

"Shopping, of course. I'll speak with Mr. Watts while you gather a few of the general groceries. We need salt, sugar, flour, coffee, tea, and some meat. A good ham if he has one."

"Yes'm," Sissy said.

There was something about her tone . . . but she lowered

her head, walking in ahead of Sydney. Sydney followed, heading straight for the counter.

There was a man there in a flannel shirt and denim overalls. He had a thick middle and the hairiest face Sydney had ever seen. Thick red brows, a thick beard, a long mustache. His eyes and nose were barely visible in all that hair.

"Mr. Watts?"

"I am," he said and smiled. "Young lady, just what is it that I can do for you? It isn't often that I get such a lovely young miss in here at this time of night!"

She moved closer to the counter. "I've come from Old Capitol," she whispered. "Union General Pratt is taking the road just south of the Old Harpers Ferry Pike with a supply train."

"Is that all?" he asked thickly.

"The Union knows that Lee's army is on the move north and west, that the fellows are moving up the Shenandoah Valley. Those supplies . . ."

She broke off, hearing movement behind her. As she spun around, she saw two men in plain black jackets aligned on either side of her. Sissy was standing just to the rear of one of them. She turned back to Watts.

"I'm sorry, Sydney," he said softly.

Then she recognized the voice and realized what a fool she had been.

Jesse Halston. Her dashing young cavalry officer. The man she had nursed back to health. The wretch who had kept her from joining Jerome when he had escaped Old Capitol and gone south . . .

"You bastard!" she cried. She flew at him, fists flying. He captured her wrists, struggling to hold her steady.

The plainclothes men behind her stepped forward immediately.

"No!" Jesse said, breathing heavily as he secured her wrists at last. "Sydney—"

She freed a hand and struck him hard across the face. One of the men came forward again, but Jesse stopped him once more. "No!" He caught her wrist again. "Dammit, Sydney, am I going to have to tie you up?"

She pretended to go limp in his grasp, and he released her.

She hit him again.

He swore, and this time when he spun her around, he slipped iron shackles around her wrists. Tears stung her eyes. She blinked them back furiously. She faced him with her chin high, her eyes blazing.

"Get into the carriage," Jesse said, wincing as he ripped off his fake beard, mustache, hair, and eyebrows. He reached into his overalls, slid out the huge pillow that had given him the appearance of a gut. And there was the Jesse she had known, should have known, with his lean, agile physique and rich dark hair.

She should have recognized his eyes. Hazel, direct. Sensual at times. The eyes with which she had once been fool enough to fall in love.

"Where am I going?" Sydney asked him.

"Old Capitol," he said softly. "Where else?"

She spun around, looking at Sissy, her eyes narrowing. "You were in on this."

Sissy didn't deny it. "I was," she said quietly.

"You worked for me; I trusted you."

"I was just another darkee to you, Miss McKenzie."

Sydney shook her head. "We never owned slaves, Sissy."

"No?" Sissy smiled, lifting her chin. "But you're fighting for people who do."

"I'm fighting for the rights—"

"The right the Southern states want is the right to own slaves. And it's wrong."

"You're wrong! Men like General Lee have outlined plans to free their slaves in a way they aren't left penniless and destitute and wandering the streets—"

"Miss McKenzie, it's wrong to own another human being. I know. I was born free, but seized by bounty hunters as a slave and brought back to a man in North Carolina who beat me with a whip—"

"Not all men are so cruel!"

"But many are," Sissy said. "And I have the scars on my back to prove it. So if I've disappointed you, I'm sorry. I don't want the Southern states to have the right to own men and women."

"Shall we go, Sydney?" Jesse suggested.

Sydney started out of the mercantile. She hesitated, spinning back to Jesse. "Where's the real Jeff Watts?"

"He escaped," Jesse told her. "Come on, Sydney."

Sydney walked on past. A wagon waited for her just outside. She felt Jesse behind her, felt his hand on her elbow. She shook off his touch.

"Dammit, Sydney, I—"

She spun on him furiously. "No! Damn you!" she told him, and she made it into the carriage on her own.

Chapter 14

After Brandy Station, Julian found himself on the move. The Army of Northern Virginia was heading north. That was no great surprise. Everyone knew that Lee wanted to fight on Northern soil. If he could bring the war to them, maybe he could sap their will to keep on fighting.

In the western theater of the war, the Mississippi River was being choked off. Vicksburg was under siege. Word came to the troops in the east that the residents were eating rats, that there wasn't a pigeon to be found anywhere near the city. They hid in caves in the cliffs in the nearby hills while the bombs exploded around them. The South was hurting. They needed a victory in the north against the North.

He was with his troops in the Shenandoah Valley near Harpers Ferry, waiting for some of the supplies he had requisitioned, when one of his new assistants approached him with Corporal Lyle, who had accompanied him north along with Liam Murphy. His new assistant, Surgeon Dan LeBlanc, fresh out of medical school, was a bright young man. Julian was pleased with him because he had an open mind and a belief that they had a lot more to learn about medicine than what anyone knew.

He had been in his tent—a canvas tent with a folding desk, chairs, and camp bed, much like he'd had in Florida—when the men came in.

"What is it?" he asked, seeing the unhappy look on Dan's young face.

Dan produced Julian's requisition list.

"They can supply us with about half of what you've asked for."

Julian sat back, swearing.

"Well, you have asked for a lot—" Dan began.

"Yes, I have. I am a doctor, not a butcher."

"Captain, there's no help for it—" Dan began.

"But this time there might be," Henry Lyle interrupted.

"You're going to get us all court-marshaled" Dan put in quickly.

"Whoa, whoa, what's going on?" Julian demanded.

"Well, a fellow got some information off a captured Yank. There's supposed to be a Union supply train headed this way to meet up with Yank troops. It's coming along just south of the old Harpers Ferry pike—"

"Then surely," Julian interrupted, "someone in this army is going for it?"

"No," Dan said.

"What?"

"Because we don't have any reliable information. The whole thing could be pure rumor, really," Dan explained. "Maybe a trap. And the troops have been commanded to move north toward the west of this rumored supply train—"

Julian rose, pulling out a map of the area. "Show me!" he told Dan.

"Sir—"

"Show me!"

Dan pointed to where the pike lay just beneath the Harpers Ferry road. Julian stared at the point. He might be medical staff, new to the job here. There were surgeons who outranked him, but he had been brought in by request, and, at the end of the day, he was answerable directly to Longstreet, and then Lee. If he asked for permission to explore the situation himself, he'd be turned down. But by tomorrow night, the way they were riding, he'd be in a position to intercept the supposed supply train. He looked at Henry Lyle.

"Guards, troops?"

"No more than a small company of men is what I heard."

"Well, what do you think?"

"I'm with you, sir."

Dan groaned. "What are you talking about? Is this some kind of a Florida code? No, no, Dr. McKenzie, sir, you don't understand the workings of the regular army. I don't mean to be offensive, but you've been militia, taking things into your own hands way too often. There is structure here—"

"You're not going to be a part of any wrongdoing, Surgeon LeBlanc, so don't you worry. And if anything comes up, I'll deny to my dying breath that you knew a thing about this."

"But, sir, you need troops to take a supply train—"

"Not always, Dan. Not always."

Julian looked at Henry Lyle. They needed Liam, just Liam. And three good horses.

"You're being reckless. You're a doctor, sir. You're taking a horrible risk—"

"Yes, I am," Julian admitted. "But you see, the prize is worth the risk."

Sydney had her own room, and the Yanks guarding her were quick to let her know that it had once been occupied by the spy Rose Greenhow. It was little comfort. She was miserable, embarrassed she'd been caught, and worried sick about what would happen when her family discovered what she had done. And Jesse! He had accompanied her to the prison, signed for her arrest, and left her. He'd been as unyielding as rock, cold as ice. She wanted to rip his eyes out. She wondered if she was destined to rot here throughout the rest of the war. Then she worried again that her father and her brothers would never let it happen; they would somehow kill themselves to get her out. Unless, of course, Ian could intervene, but Ian, she knew, was out on the front now.

Her only comfort was the soldiers in the Old Capitol, though she had to admit that it was the captivity that was galling, and not her circumstances. Sergeant Granger saw that she was given clean bedding and decent food.

She was in solitary through the night, but in the afternoons she was allowed to fraternize with the captured soldiers. Anderson apologized to her a thousand times over. He suggested that she turn him in as the man who had given her the information—perhaps she could bargain to be sent south for such information. But she knew that she would never turn him in, and she knew as well that as much as she had to worry about with her family, not even her father would suggest that she trade such information for her own freedom. She finally managed to make Anderson quit talking about it.

On her second afternoon in the prison, she was sitting at a table in the outside exercise yard, when she remembered Lawton's foot.

"Young man, you're limping. And I've nowhere to go today," she said, smiling ruefully. "Show me that foot."

"Oh, no, ma'am—"

"Not this again!" Sydney protested.

"But—"

"Your foot, Private Lawton, please!"

"You heard her, young man," Lieutenant Anderson ordered.

Unhappily, Private Lawton limped over to the table. He set his injured foot up on a chair, wincing. One of his friends reached over and undid the bandaging.

Sydney almost retched. One look at the foot, and she doubted if even her brother or her cousin, Julian, could save it. The bullet had cleared the foot, but debris in some form had entered the wound, and the injury was now rank and putrid.

"Doesn't hurt near as bad as it used to. It's going to be all right," Lawton said.

Sydney shook her head. "Private Lawton, do you have a wife?"

"Why, yes, Miss Sydney, I do, sweetest little girl you'd ever want to meet."

"Do you want to see her ever again?"

He reddened. "I love her, Miss Sydney. Of course I want to see her."

"That foot's probably got to go."

He shook his head. "No, ma'am—"

"Why? I'll go to the right people; I'll be with you when they amputate."

Lawton shook his head strenuously again. "Why, Miss Sydney, I'm not a rich man. Got me a little spit of land, and a little farmhouse—it's right down from my ma and pa. I work my land myself, and I need my foot."

"Your wife needs you home. You keep that foot much longer the way that it is, and you're going to die."

He hesitated a long time, then looked at her. "What if my wife don't want me no more with just one foot?"

"Private Lawton, I've got two brothers and two cousins in this war, and I just want them back. I love them for being the men that they are, and so help me, I'd take my loved one without an arm rather than a corpse. You understand?"

He glanced down, ashamed. His voice was a whisper. "I'm just scared, Miss Sydney. No man likes to admit that. I'm just scared."

She came to him, reached for his face, took it between her hands. "But, Private Lawton, what a fine man you are. Why, I know that your wife wants you back in the very worst way! We'll see to it that you're taken care of by the best man possible." She wasn't sure who that might be, but she trusted Sergeant Granger.

She rose suddenly, calling to one of the guards. "Please, I need to see Sergeant Granger."

"Now, Miss McKenzie, you're not a guest here any-more—"

"I need to see Granger," she repeated, eyes narrowing. "And he'll be very angry if he hears that I needed him and you didn't tell him!"

"All right, all right!"

The surly guard unlocked the door to the office, indicating with his chin that she should get up and go in. She glanced at Lawton encouragingly, then hurried into the main office.

Granger smiled ruefully when he saw her coming to him. "Can't tell you how it hurts me to have you here this way, a prisoner behind bars, Miss Sydney."

Yes, it changed things, she realized. She used to come here frequently. She had never felt as if the walls were closing on her before. But that was because she had been free to come and go as she chose.

She lowered her head, thinking of Sissy. *Freedom. Good God yes, but freedom was a precious right to have . . .*

"Sergeant, do you remember—"

"Medical help, of course," he said softly.

"You won't betray me, will you?" she asked.

He frowned. She had, in a way, betrayed him. She sighed.

"Private Lawton is a good man, surely you've seen that. He's terrified about losing his foot—"

Granger lowered his voice. "I can bring you the widow, but it will have to be soon. She's leaving for the army with General Magee in less than two days."

Sydney sat back, hesitating. The Yankee witch widow. Not a surgeon. Yet then again, her mother was a healer, known as a woman with a special touch. If there was a way to cure Lawton's foot . . .

"Well, Miss Sydney?"

She paused, thinking it over. Risa would never have sent this woman north to work with her own father if she wasn't a decent, capable human being.

"When can you get her here?" she asked Granger.

"Right away."

Rhiannon was startled by the arrival of the soldier who said he had come to escort her to Old Capitol, but glad of it as well. She had packed, she was ready. She had seen something of Washington, and she didn't like it.

War was ugly, she knew. But, being here in Washington, she knew that politics could be uglier. She was ready to go to the front, to be useful and busy—and she'd had to wait. She had nothing to do but sit or pace until it was time to go.

Or dwell on her own thoughts.

And she was afraid, uneasy. She knew what had happened. And yet, what she thought she knew was so incredible that she wouldn't allow herself to believe . . .

And so she'd counted. Days. Not that many, really, not that many.

Yes . . .

And at certain times during those days she felt just as sick as a dog . . .

So when the soldier came for her, telling her she was needed at Old Capitol, she was intrigued and ready to go.

A carriage brought her to the prison. She was escorted into the outer office, where she was greeted by a grizzled older man. "Sergeant Granger, how are you?" she said politely.

"Grateful that you've agreed to come," he told her.

"Why am I here? Has the Union run out of surgeons?" she asked lightly.

Granger grinned and shook his head. "I've a special prisoner who has asked a special favor."

"Who?"

"Come with me, will you?"

They walked through a room where she saw many ragged Confederate prisoners sitting around a table. They all watched her as she passed, every man nodding politely. Granger pushed open another door that led to a stuffy little room. A man was lying on a cot, and by his side, a woman. The woman turned to her, and she was startled at the resemblance she saw to the McKenzies.

The man on the cot groaned. Rhiannon turned quickly from the young woman to the man. His shoe was off, his pants had been ripped so that his foot was bared from the upper ankle down.

It was horrible. Swollen to twice its size, pussy, infected. Rhiannon came to the man. He was a Rebel. He might have killed her husband. But he was young. His eyes were green, earnest, pained. He was so anxious. She realized that holding on to her resentment was a lost cause. She had been among Rebels already. She had learned that they were men who fought and died and worshipped their God and loved their wives and children just the same as Yanks. She had always known it, of course. Most of her neighbors had been Rebels. The people with whom she had grown up, her father's friends, business associates . . .

She'd just had to remember.

She sat by the Rebel private, offered him a smile, and gently took the foot into her hands, setting it on her lap to study the wound.

"Oh, ma'am, you mustn't touch it—" the soldier on the cot protested.

"Sir, I must touch it if I'm to heal it."

"They say it's got to be chopped off. That I'll die." He was afraid, and he tried so valiantly to hide it.

"Maybe," she admitted. She studied his foot, looking up his ankle. Though the foot was horrible, it didn't seem that the infection was spreading. Perhaps . . .

She looked up at Granger. "Sergeant, I need some clean, very salty water."

"Salt! Ma'am, are you trying to torture me?" the wounded Rebel said.

"No, I'm not, young man, honestly," she told him, a rueful grin on her face. She felt the woman in the room watching her, and she turned, assessing her in turn. "You're Julian McKenzie's cousin?" she asked.

The young woman was surprised by the question. "Yes, I'm Sydney McKenzie." She looked at the boy on the cot. "No, she's really not trying to torture you. I should have thought of this myself—salt water is one of nature's finest cleansers."

Men came with a big bucket of salt water, just as Rhiannon had asked. "Can you ease up, soldier?" she asked the injured Reb.

"Yes, ma'am."

Sydney supported him. Rhiannon had him set his foot in the water. It must have stung like crazy, but he bit his lower lip, holding back any cry of pain.

Rhiannon rose. "Soldier, you have to stay there with your foot in that water. I've got to go out and make an ointment for you. You have to soak the foot for a full hour, at least three times every day, then bandage it with the poultice thickly spread on it." She looked at Sydney, knowing that she would be the one caring for the man.

Sydney nodded, understanding that they were going to try to clean out the infection.

"Will I keep my foot?" he asked anxiously.

Rhiannon smiled, lessening the blow, she hoped. "I don't know. Maybe not. But the poison from the infection hasn't spread. You've had this injury some time, and it doesn't appear to have affected the rest of your leg. We can *try* for a cure. No guarantees, but we can try."

He grabbed her hand. "Thank you. Thank you."

"Don't thank me yet, we haven't saved the foot. I have to go, but I'll be back."

In the early evening she returned. Just one thorough soaking had made a difference. She might have imagined it, but it seemed the swelling was down some. She spread the poultice she had prepared over the foot, then bandaged it. Sydney stood at her side helping. To her surprise, the other girl didn't blink when she had told her she had made the poultice out of moldy bread, among other ingredients. "It's been known to work," Rhiannon said. "Although . . ."

"Although?" Sydney asked her.

"Well, to guarantee that he'll have a chance to live, he should have the foot amputated right away."

Sydney studied her seriously. "You're not trying to kill him, right? Make sure that it goes so long he won't have a chance?"

Rhiannon stared back at her. Sydney was hostile toward her—but carefully so.

"No, I'm not trying to kill him. Excuse me, but didn't you ask that I be brought here?"

"Yes, I did—at Sergeant Granger's suggestion. He heard that you were a witch—please don't take offense."

"I'm not offended. And I wish I did have magical powers. All I have is what I've learned through observation, mainly. And, of course, I read. And . . ."

"And?"

"I've worked with your cousin Julian."

"Ah," Sydney said with a strange note.

"And what does that mean?" Rhiannon asked.

"Well, you are quite a curiosity, you know. I was told that you are connected with General Magee through my sister-in-law, Risa. Yet you came here and noted immediately that I was Julian's cousin—rather than Ian's cousin, or Jerome's sister, or Risa's in-law."

Rhiannon wondered if her cheeks flooded red with the sudden heat she was feeling. Sydney had a point.

"I met Julian first," she murmured vaguely.

"But you're a Florida Unionist."

"Yes."

"Then how did you meet Julian?"

"You know, really, you do ask a lot of questions for a proper young woman."

"I'm not proper, and I never claimed to be. How did you meet my cousin Julian?"

"He came to my house looking for shelter."

"And you let him in."

"Not by choice. One of his men claimed that they were Yanks."

"But you knew better."

"Yes, frankly, I did."

"But you let them in."

"They came in. I didn't have the power to see them out."

"Ah. Then how did you meet Jerome?"

Rhiannon narrowed her eyes at Miss Sydney McKenzie. "I was brought back to Julian's camp." She hesitated, realizing that Sydney probably hadn't heard what had happened. "Your brother was wounded—"

"What?"

Sydney had been cool, aloof; now she was tense, her fingers clutched into fists, her eyes frightened. Despite the hostility she had shown her, Rhiannon couldn't help but feel a moment's empathy.

"He's going to be fine. He had a bullet stuck in his shoulder. Julian took it out."

"Infection?"

"He was doing well when I left."

"What did you have to do with his injury?"

Rhiannon smiled wryly. "I didn't shoot him, if that's what you're asking. I assisted in the surgery."

"His wife, my cousin Tia, Alaina were all near—"

"Tia was there, Alaina and Risa hadn't been able to reach the camp. They arrived after the surgery. And excuse me, but you've no right to demand answers from me on anything or make the least accusation. I don't owe you any explanations. I—" Rhiannon broke off. "Why are you here, at this prison?"

Sydney's rich, dark lashes fluttered. "I—I'm a prisoner."

"What?"

Sydney stared at her, hard. "Don't you dare say anything to anyone!"

"I beg your pardon—"

"Please! Don't you understand? I'm hoping my family doesn't discover my situation until . . . well, until I'm out of it. Someone might get killed."

Rhiannon watched her a long moment. "All right. I won't say anything. Who would I say anything to? But, Sydney . . . surely, the information that you're here is bound to get out. Your family is certain to hear what has happened sooner or later."

"Perhaps, but in this instance, later is better. I could be released, deported back to Virginia. Something could happen before . . . something *good* could happen before something *bad* happens."

"It could. Well," she murmured brusquely, "I'll be back

to see Private Lawton in the morning, and then he'll be your patient and the foot will be your call. I leave tomorrow."

"To travel with the Army of the Potomac!" Sydney mocked.

"Yes."

"Well, don't worry too much. The Yank generals spend more time avoiding Lee than they do going after him. You may have a nice quiet summer."

"I may," Rhiannon said, turning to leave.

"Watch out for Julian!" Sydney called after her.

She spun around, meeting the other girl's enigmatic gaze.

Sydney said, "If the Yanks do find Lee, you will find my cousin. His will be the field tent closest to the fighting."

Rhiannon felt a strange chill, like cold fingers, curling around her heart. "I'll watch out for him," she murmured coolly. "You watch out for yourself."

"They've yet to hang a woman here."

"There's always a first time," Rhiannon warned her.

"You could try to get me out of here."

"Why would I want to do that?"

Sydney shrugged. "For Jerome's sake, perhaps. His wife did get you here, right? And then . . . if not for her . . . well, then, for Julian."

"For Julian!"

Sydney shrugged. "Help me."

"I haven't the power."

"Maybe you underestimate your power."

Rhiannon hesitated. "If you were to be free, would you go home and . . ."

"Behave?" Sydney suggested, arching a brow.

It was Rhiannon's turn to shrug.

"I would leave here, never to return," Sydney vowed.

"If there's anything I can do, I will do it," Rhiannon said.

"You're a witch. You'll find the power," Sydney said.

Rhiannon stared at the other woman, wondering if Sydney desperately needed her help, or if she simply enjoyed mocking her. She didn't owe Sydney McKenzie a thing. Or did she?

She felt a sudden trembling sensation, a deep unease, and with it, the knowledge that blood would be spilled if Sydney weren't released. She didn't see pictures of mayhem

and death in her mind's eye, as sometimes had happened.
She just felt that terrible sense of unease. Someone would
die. And she didn't know who.

"I'll see what I can do," she said.

Chapter 15

~~~

Near midnight, the camp was quiet. Thankfully, the medical tents were to the rear and off to the side of the camp, a better way to keep infection from spreading. In the midst of moving north, twenty boys had come down with the measles. Farm boys from South Carolina, they'd never been out of their own country until the war, and thus they had avoided many of the childhood diseases that many of the soldiers from areas of greater population had already survived. Julian had gotten the sick soldiers isolated, treated them, and left them in the care of an assistant surgeon.

The day was over; and they were in position.

Dan LeBlanc paced his tent. Young Liam arrived, and behind him Henry Lyle. Both of Julian's Florida boys waited his instructions.

"It's time," Julian said, reaching for his hat.

"I can't let you go," Dan said.

Julian paused, staring at him. "How do you intend to stop us?"

Dan hesitated. He started to lift his hands in defeat, then paused, staring at the entry to the tent. Hearing a whisper of movement himself, Julian spun around.

A young man with a bearded face and long blond hair stood there, a plumed cavalry cap in his hand.

"You're Colonel McKenzie."

"Captain, regular army," Julian said.

The cavalryman smiled. "Colonel, we let our fellows keep their highest ranking, brevet or militia. When it comes down to who outranks who, we argue a point then."

"What can I do for you?" Julian asked.

"There's a whisper out you're interested in seeing some of the countryside."

Julian crossed his arms over his chest and leaned back against his camp desk. "Oh?"

"I'm Captain Elijah Henley. Know the area well. A night ride isn't any good with too many people, but then, there might be a Yank or two out yonder. Three isn't so fine a number. Six could be just about right."

Julian hesitated. "What makes you think I'm going for a night ride?"

Henley smiled. "Because I rode with your brother once before the war. If it's out there, you're going to get it." Henley's smile faded. "I was at Sharpsburg, sir, in a far field, when the surgeon ran out of anesthesia first, and then whiskey. A friend of mine was on the table. He died. I think it was the shock of the pain on top of being half blown to bits. If you're going for ether and morphine, I'd be mighty pleased to show you the way."

"You're taking a risk."

"Not much of one, sir. I'm officially assigned to General Stuart, who is off on other business now, as you know. I'm to scout around and keep my eye on the enemy. What better way?"

Henley, Julian realized, was on the level. "Let's go," he said simply.

"I've taken the liberty of having horses ready," Henley told him.

Julian nodded to Liam and Henry Lyle, who both followed him out. Two men waited with six mounts—decent-looking horseflesh for the Reb army. Henley introduced his men as Abe Jansen and Alistair Adair. They all nodded quick acknowledgments, mounted, and rode hard from the camp.

Thirty minutes out of the camp, they slowed their gait. Elijah Henley moved his horse next to Julian's. "You're the spittin' image of your brother."

"So I've been told."

"Too bad he decided to stay a Yank," Henley said without rancor. "We sure could have used him."

"Well, the war has been hell for him. He feels he's fighting for what he thinks is right, but he's fighting his own family."

"Sure is a shame. All way around. Why, I heard one of Mrs. Lincoln's brothers was killed fighting for the South. And all she could say was that he shouldn't have been a-fightin'. The Yanks just jump down her throat if she so much as sheds a tear for her own kin! My General Jeb likes to find ways to sneak notes under his father-in-law's plate when he's eating in the capital with other Yanks, just to pull the old fellow's cord and prove the Southern cavalry is fast enough to do anything. Well, I sure hope so. Jeb is off sniffing around the Yanks right now, trying to figure out just where the Union army is. Hell, good thing the Billy Yanks are slow. Else they would have had us a half dozen times by now!"

"So we're heading for a major battle."

"Well, we know the big Yank army is near, they know we're near. Hell, yes, we're going to clash in a major way." He went silent suddenly. "There's your road, Dr. McKenzie. Straight ahead. Did you have a plan?"

"Yes, as a matter of fact, I did. Dismount, hide the horses, into the trees."

The men hurried to do his bidding, Elijah Henley's boys as quick, agile, and quiet as Lyle Henry and Liam Murphy. Julian found himself taking up the last position; the wagons would have to be directly beneath them all, then they'd have to leap down and catch the guards, using speed and surprise to suppress resistance before it could turn into a skirmish.

Time began to tick by . . .

The night was warm. An occasional breeze stirred. When it did, it felt like a slice of heaven. Julian scratched an itch on his knee, hoping that the trees weren't full of ticks. It was the right time of year for them.

He heard Liam, just down from him, swearing.

"Liam?"

"Sorry, sir. Varmint of some kind, don't rightly know what."

"We've got to keep quiet. You know that."

"Hell, yes, sir."

More time passed. Julian began to wonder if it had been a rumor. Then he heard Lyle, first man out, give a soft bird call. Meant a lone man was coming. Lone man . . . a point rider, watching for guerilla Rebs?

He waited, tensing, He heard a horse, then saw a rider. Nice blue uniform, new and unsoiled. His horse looked as if it had just come off the farm, fat and sleek.

The boy was whistling as he rode—whistling, Julian thought, because he was afraid.

The rider kept coming, unmolested. They wanted him deep into the trap before they sprang . . .

When he was beneath Julian, Julian hesitated, then leapt. He fell silently, knocking the boy from his horse and to the ground in a matter of split seconds.

The boy struggled and Julian whispered to him. "Hush, now—"

"Rebs, Rebs, Rebels, oh-my-God-Rebels-oh-my-God-Rebels—"

"Shut him up!" Henley called. "The wagons are coming."

"Son, shut up," Julian warned.

But the kid was scared to his brand-spanking new boots. "Rebs, Help. Oh, help, help, Jesus above us, help—"

"McKenzie! The others are coming round. Kill him!" Henley shouted.

"What?" Julian called.

"We need you! They outnumber us, remember? It's a war, Julian, kill the little momma's boy. We can't jeopardize the whole action."

Julian stared down at the boy. Kill him. Easy. Take the knife, slide it into the heart. He knew all about death.

Kill him.

Couldn't do it. If he did, it made everything to which he had dedicated his life to a lie. It was one thing shooting bullets when he was escaping Yanks in Florida. He was being shot at, he shot back. But this would be murder.

The Yank beneath him, young, mute with fear, was staring at him. Eyes as wide as that of a buck.

"McKenzie, get it over with!" Henley hissed.

If he killed the boy, he'd have no chance of getting out of the war with even the remnants of his sanity left.

"Julian, they're coming—"

"Sorry, kid," Julian said softly.

Rhiannon had tried every move she could think of. General Magee had sent word that he'd try to get Sydney out; of course, he'd have to go through the proper channels and authorities and it might take time. She'd appealed to Granger, she'd tried to find out where Ian McKenzie was, but he'd left for the battlefront. It would take time to find him, too.

It was Granger, however, who told her about Jesse Halston.

Jesse was still in town, for another week. A second injury on the field and he'd been sent back to the capital from his company to work with the Pinkerton men trying to guard the security of military information here.

Jesse Halston had been involved somehow when Jerome had escaped, and he'd been instrumental in getting Sydney arrested later. With little choice, Rhiannon sent word to him with her name and a message that she urgently needed to see him. She received a message back from a young soldier inviting her to Halston's office across from the White House. She arrived at dusk.

He was a handsome young fellow with level hazel eyes and a quick smile.

"Sir, I need your help."

"Why, Mrs. Tremaine, I would just be willing to help you in any way that I possibly could," he told her.

"Sydney McKenzie. You arrested her. Perhaps you could free her."

"Ma'am, if I wanted her free, why would I have arrested her in the first place?" he asked, his eyes suddenly guarded.

"She's a McKenzie, and I know that family," Rhiannon said firmly.

Halston sat back on his desk, arms crossed over his chest. "She can't be trusted."

"I think she can be. She could swear that she wouldn't cause any more trouble. I know that people have been freed by signing vows of allegiance—"

"Do you think that Sydney McKenzie is going to sign a vow of allegiance to the United States of America?" he asked her.

Rhiannon looked down, smoothing out a pleat in her skirt. "No, but I believe that she will swear to leave Washington, to cease her spying activities."

"And then you want me to trust her?"

"Yes."

Halston watched her, shaking his head. "If you're worried about Jerome coming after her, I understand. But if you're in love with him—"

"I'm not!" she snapped indignantly.

Halston grinned. "Good, because he's got a wife, though when I saw you—"

"When you saw me, what?" she demanded, eyes narrowed, jaw locking.

"My apologies, nothing intended, Mrs. Tremaine. It's just that you're a very beautiful woman, and you seem so passionately and sincerely worried about the McKenzies."

"Captain Halston, I'm becoming passionate about human life—and it not being stupidly wasted when there is so much carnage to begin with!"

"I am sorry, Mrs. Tremaine. But what makes you think that Sydney will let me help her? Especially since I did put her in there."

"She said that she'd do almost anything to get out. I believe she's really afraid of someone in her family becoming too reckless in their efforts to save her."

He smiled, watching her curiously. "They say you're a witch."

She groaned. "Dear God, not that again—"

"Yes, that. Are you a witch?"

"It's all in the eyes of the beholder, isn't it?"

"Well, I guess we can thank God that you seem to have such unusual powers. You've convinced me to do your will, and I didn't believe that you could do so. I will get Sydney out, Mrs. Tremaine."

Rhiannon was so startled by his agreement that for a moment she didn't respond. "Thank you. Thank you!" she said, flushing and rising.

"It's my pleasure to help you in any way, ma'am."

"But how will you manage this, and when—"

"I'll get her out tomorrow," Halston promised.

"But you haven't told me how—"

"You want me to trust you, right? Well, you'll have to trust me on this one, Mrs. Tremaine. You'll just have to trust me."

Julian leaned back, clenched his fist, and cracked the boy in the jaw. As he had hoped, the boy's eyes closed, a whoosh of air escaped his lips, and he was out cold.

Julian leapt to his feet, then dragged the boy out of the road, and swatted the horse hard on the haunches. The horse obediently ran into the night.

Hurrying back along the trail, Julian saw Elijah Henley's position and scurried up the tree opposite from him. Just in time. The first of the wagons, with two men on the seat, two men riding guard, reached the point directly beneath them.

He looked at Henley, then let out a sharp bird call. He and Henley leapt together, taking two of the Yanks entirely off guard. The man on the left of the wagon was so stunned he dropped his rifle. Julian bellowed out an order that the Yanks were surrounded; they had only one choice, and that was to surrender.

"Lord, yes! Surrender, Captain!" one man cried.

"I surrender," another called out down the road, throwing down a Spencer repeating rifle. Henley looked at Julian, tipped his hat to him. "Hell, damned good rifle you got me there, Doc."

Julian frowned, warning him that they had yet to have the Yanks all corraled as captives. He aimed his newly taken rifle and his own Colt at the disorganized Yanks while Liam, Henry, and Elijah and his cavalry boys herded the fellows forward. "Liam, Henry, get their weapons," Julian ordered hoarsely.

There were fifteen men total, including the boy who remained oblivious to the world in the bushes. They milled in the center of the moonlit road as their weapons were taken. "Gentlemen, now, if you'll get into the rear wagon . . ." Julian said.

"Where we headed?" one of the Yanks asked.

"South," Julian said. "You can walk or ride. It's a fair long piece, though, fellows."

Grumbling, they crawled into the rear wagon.

"Watch them," Julian commanded, taking a brief look at the contents of the rear wagon, then searching through the first. He folded his hands together prayer fashion and looked up to the sky.

"Thank you, Lord!" he breathed.

Ether, lots of it. Morphine. Bandages. Quinine. Root and herbal mixtures, sulphur, mercury, iodine . . .

It was better than a diamond mine.

He realized that Henley was standing behind him. He turned. The cavalryman saluted him, grinning. "The Yanks have just now realized that they're not surrounded, Doctor," he said.

Julian nodded. "Well, they were bound to find out."

"But they haven't got so much as a butter knife left among the lot of them."

"Good. They won't be getting too feisty back there then."

"You're something, sir. I wouldn't have thought to knock that boy out, and I wouldn't have thought to demand a surrender. I'd have killed half of them, and probably lost one of two of us in the process."

"Let's get this stuff back, shall we?"

Once again Henley saluted him.

By late morning, Rhiannon was leaving Washington behind.

She had naturally been invited to ride in one of the ambulance wagons, but after a day of riding she was rocked and tortured and miserable. The next day she asked permission to ride with the general, was invited to do so, and found herself much happier mounted on a black gelding with a beautifully tended coat and pleasing gait.

Magee was charming and personable during the ride, telling her anecdotes about the military and about his daughter.

"I miss her. Miss her badly, I do. I've got to admit, I was happiest myself when they had Jerome McKenzie in that prison and my daughter was here with me." He sighed after a moment. "No, that's not true. She wasn't happy, he wasn't happy . . . but it was good to have my grandson here with me. Handsome babe, ma'am."

"Yes sir, he's a very handsome child."

"You saw young Jamie?" he asked, his tone gentle for a man used to thundering out orders.

"In St. Augustine, sir. When I arrived there with your daughter and Alaina McKenzie."

"And her babes?"

"Healthy and fine, sir."

"Ah, good, good. I'm always glad when a man has had a chance to have his children before the war. It's a sad thing when a fellow dies and his grieving widow is left without even a babe to love. And for a man, well, it's an important thing, to leave an heir behind."

Rhiannon lowered her head and her lashes, feeling a wave of unease wash over her. An important thing, yes. She wished that she and Richard . . . She bit her lower lip, then raised her head. Well, she and Richard hadn't had children. But now . . .

"Are you all right, Mrs. Tremaine?" the general asked worriedly. "You're quite pale."

"Fine," she said, flashing him a smile.

"If there's ever anything wrong, you will come and tell me? I'll try to help in any way that I can."

"Thank you."

"Ah, there!" the general said, reining in.

She looked ahead, and gasped. There, before her, was the Army of the Potomac. Men, tents, weapons, cook fires, more men, fires, horses, tents . . . The waves of men and tents and horses and guns seemed to stretch forever.

A massive battle was eminent. The promise of gunfire and blood seemed rich, a whisper that grew louder and louder on the wind even as dusk fell to darkness and a cold moon rose high above them.

Chapter 16

❧

"Sir . . ."

"What is it, Mrs. Tremaine?"

In the great Yankee movement, with the cavalry trying to ascertain Lee's movements, General Magee's troops were moving into Maryland. Magee had taken a small force along an old mountain trail, looking for the enemy.

They had camped for the night on a stream. Riding with the army was proving a difficult experience. There was a lot of sickness in the camp; even in the north the summer was becoming wickedly hot. They had yet to fight, but everyone knew that the enemy was out there.

That morning she had wakened with a strange premonition. Not a vision, just a premonition. And she leapt up, hurriedly washed and dressed, and made her way to Magee's tent. She was almost stopped several times by his aides. "Mrs. Tremaine, the general is busy now, you can't interrupt him—" Lieutenant Garby, his personal assistant, told her, trying to stop her.

"I have to see him."

Another of his aides stepped in front of the command tent, rifle in hand. "Mrs. Tremaine! This is a war, you can't just—"

"What are you going to do, shoot me, sir?" she demanded.

"No, ma'am, but I'll . . ."

"You'll what?"

"All right, now, Mrs. Tremaine, I just can't let you by—"

"I have to get by!"

She pushed through the middle of the two men, trusting that neither of them would really dare physically accost her. They trailed after instead as she burst into the general's tent. She found him talking to Colonels Wheaton and Willoughby, both of them scouts.

"Sir! We tried to stop her," Garby said.

"Yes, yes, it's all right, men, back to your posts," Magee said, frowning. "So, Mrs. Tremaine, what is the problem?"

She walked straight to the map spread out on the table. She pointed to the trail Magee had circled. "You mustn't go that way."

He arched a brow. "That's exactly the way we're going, young woman."

She shook her head emphatically. "We're moving with what's here, sir? A few hundred men. Don't go that way. There are Reb troops foraging there—"

"Mrs. Tremaine, we are looking for the Rebel troops," Colonel Wheaton told her politely.

"You don't want to find this many. If we go blithely riding in that southeastern direction, sir, I swear, you will lose more than half this company. The Confederates have the superior forces this time. Please, General, send one of these men and see if I'm not right."

"We'd be wasting time," Willoughby warned.

"Please, I beg of you!" Rhiannon entreated.

"How do you know this?" Wheaton asked.

"Instinct," she murmured.

"We're going to change our plans because of a woman's instincts?" Willoughby asked incredulously.

Magee gazed at Rhiannon. She stared back at him.

"It will cost you a few hours my way," she told him softly. "General, you have scouting forces; the bulk of the army is too far behind now to come quickly. If I'm right, it could cost a great deal more than a few hours!"

Magee nodded after a moment. "Gentlemen, you'll both ride ahead. And keep low. If you find as many forces as Mrs. Tremaine believes you will, Willoughby will return to camp, and Wheaton, you will ride as quickly as you can back to the main body of troops with the information."

Wheaton and Willoughby saluted, accepting the general's command without argument, but the looks they gave her as they exited the command tent made her wonder just who the enemy might be in the future.

"Thank you. You won't regret trusting me."

"How do you know these things? How can you be sure?" he asked, curious.

She shook her head. "Trust me, sir. I don't want to know these things."

She left him.

The camp waited. The day was hot, and the soldiers grew restless. Those men who were fevered and sick were plaintive and irritable. She and the other three nurses with the scouting troops moved briskly, bringing water, applying cool rags, rebandaging old injuries.

Finally, hours later, when she had returned to her own small tent to wash her face and smooth back her hair, she was startled to hear her name called by Magee. She hurried from the tent. He was mounted on his big dappled gray mare.

"You were right. The estimated Reb forces would have outnumbered us three to one. We would have faced a slaughter."

She lowered her head, exhaling softly.

"You think that it's a curse, my dear," Magee said. "These visions?"

"Yes, sir, I do."

"Well, your curse might have just saved hundreds of lives. I, for one, am grateful. Don't ever hesitate to come to me."

She came forward, patting the gray's neck as she looked up at Magee. "No, sir, I won't."

Sydney paced her small, solitary room. Another long night stretched before her. If she could only sleep . . .

More prisoners had come in today. They were weary and depressed; they had come from the siege at Vicksburg. The situation grew worse daily. Lee was trying to force Union soldiers back to the Eastern front by threatening the Yankee capital, but nothing seemed to be of any avail.

Her only solace was that a soldier came in who had seen her brother Brent. Working at a hospital outside of Richmond for "special" diseases, he hadn't heard about her predicament. The soldier had heard that Jerome was back at sea, doing well. Julian was moving with the Army of Northern Virginia. Ian was moving with the Army of the

Potomac. Any day now, Julian could be sorting through the fallen, looking for the dead, and find his own brother.

A tap on her door startled her. It was late; she was always left alone at this hour.

She walked to the door. She was a prisoner here. Jailers were not required to knock.

"Yes?"

"You decent, Miss Sydney?"

She smiled. "Yes, Sergeant Granger, I'm fully clothed."

The door opened. "You've a visitor, ma'am," Granger said.

She arched a brow, hopeful and worried. Then, as Jesse Halston, back in full blue cavalry uniform, entered her room, she stepped back, wary and unnerved.

She couldn't help but be distressed; she felt as if the prison stink and maisma had settled over her. As if she were worn, ragged, and dirty. And there was Jesse, dashing, handsome.

"What on earth do you want?" she demanded harshly.

"I'll just let you two talk," Granger said, stepping back.

"No!" Sydney cried. "Don't you leave me in here with him."

But even as she raced toward the door, it closed.

She turned back to Jesse. He was leaning against the wall by the window that looked out over the streets of Washington. A small window, but a window nevertheless. Rose Greenhow had used a similar window to continue relaying messages to cohorts on the streets while she had been imprisoned here. It might have been much worse.

"Sydney," Jesse said impatiently, "just what are you afraid of? What have I ever done to you? I'm not here to molest you in any way."

She spun back to him, leaning against the door. "You bastard, you're the reason I'm in here."

"No, Sydney, you're the reason you're in here."

"When the war is over, the winner will write the history of it, and victory will prove who was right, and who was wrong."

"Certain things are morally right and wrong, Sydney, and not even history can change that fact."

"Why are you here? I'm weary of debates about the war.

If you've come to torture me with conversation, you can just get out."

"I haven't come to torture you with conversation."

"Well, it's torture simply having you here. If you haven't come to get me out, then please, for the love of God, go away."

"Hmm. Well, actually, I did come to get you out."

"What?" Sydney gasped, her breath catching in her throat.

"I said that I've come to get you out."

Her heart slammed against her chest. She'd been so afraid. When one of the boys wound up in prison, it was one thing. But she was a woman, and the good Southern men in her family would feel honor bound to risk their lives for her honor. She had desperately wanted out, and yes, she'd been willing to do almost anything to get out . . .

"Why?" she whispered. "You got me in here!"

"A friend of yours came to see me and pointed out the danger of you being here."

She frowned. "Rhiannon Tremaine?" The witch—she almost said it out loud. And not with rancor. Private Larson's foot was miraculously well on the mend.

"Yes."

She nodded, moistening her lips. "How?"

"I have a way."

"Oh?"

He shrugged. "You're not going to like it. But Mrs. Tremaine told me that you said you were willing to do almost anything to get out."

"Almost anything," Sydney agreed. Then her eyes narrowed. "All right, Captain Halston, just exactly what is it that you have in mind?"

"I'll lay it out for you, Sydney, and you'll have about five minutes to decide."

"Why five minutes?"

"I've been reassigned once again, back to my troops. The need for cavalry scouts has just grown quite great, and I'm reputed to be an excellent officer."

He said the last dryly. She almost—almost—felt a shred of sympathy.

Fool. Never, she promised herself.

"So what, sir, is your plan?"

He told her.

"No!" she cried, her back against the wall.

He lifted his hands. "It was the only chance I had of getting you out," he said with a shrug. "Suit yourself." He started to walk from the room. She found strength and pushed away from the wall. If he left, if he went to the war . . .

She would be alone. A prisoner here until she rotted. Or until her father determined to pull a desperate mission and break her free.

"Wait!" she told Jesse.

He paused, his hazel eyes sparkling with golden amusement. "Change of heart?" he inquired.

"You're a horrible Yankee piece of cow dung!" she told him regally.

"Dear Lord, with such a gentle proclamation ringing in my ears, I will march off to war with warmth in my heart!"

"When do we do this thing?" she demanded impatiently.

"Now," he said.

"Now?"

"Right now."

Strangely, what was to prove to be the most terrible battle of the war was not supposed to take place where it did.

Since June, after his spectacular victory at Chancellorsville against far superior forces, Lee had been moving north, determined to take the war to the Yanks. His objective, however, had not been the sleepy little town where the massive armies met.

It was called Gettysburg.

While Lee moved north, Union General Hooker had been riding parallel with his troops, determined to protect Washington, D.C., and Baltimore, Maryland, from a possible Confederate attack. Harrisburg, Pennsylvania, had been Lee's actual objective, but events in the Union army changed things. Hooker resigned as commander of the Army of the Potomac, and Lincoln replaced him with General George G. Meade. Lee's army had almost reached the Susquehanna River when he ordered it to move back toward Cashtown. By chance units of the two armies met at Gettysburg. Naturally, both troops sent back for reinforcements as skirmishes escalated.

The chance meeting took place on June 30. The next day, the Confederates moved into position. They drove the Federals back through Gettysburg and occupied the town. The Union troops, forced back against the hills, formed a line south of the town along places called Culp's Hill, Cemetery Ridge, and Little Round Top. Lee placed his troops in a north-south arc along Seminary Ridge. The ranks began to swell. Lee wanted to turn the Yankee tide before all of Meade's forces could arrive.

On July 2, troops were still coming on to the field. Julian had his field hospital established to the south of the arc. Longstreet was to take the flank, but he was late. His cannons didn't roar until four in the afternoon.

And so the fighting went late. What had been a steady trickle of wounded became a deluge of the maimed and dying. Cannon fire obliterated the sky. The sound of guns went on and on. Julian's hands grew red with the blood of the injured; soon, he was bathed in blood, as if dropped into a crimson sea.

They kept coming.

A cannon exploded overhead. "Sweet Jesus!" a man shouted.

Ten minutes later, one of his orderlies burst into the tent. "Captain! Just on the next hill . . . they were mown down. There's a company of men out there, caught in the fire . . . oh, Lord above us, but they're not dead, not all of them, they're alive . . . and screaming."

"Well get them in here!" Julian said.

"There's no troops, no troops . . . they've already moved on."

Julian hesitated just briefly. He looked over at Dan LeBlanc. "Take charge here."

"McKenzie, what are you doing? We've already got enough injured men here—"

"If we can help it, sir, we do not leave our injured abandoned on the field!" Julian argued.

He headed out. His orderly followed.

Outside the tent there were men sprawled around—some waiting their turn with a doctor, some waiting for an ambulance to come and convey them from the front. But some of the men weren't injured so badly that they couldn't be of some use. Julian paused in front of the men. They were from mixed units, he knew. Virginians, Georgians, North and South Carolinians, Texans . . . even Floridians. All fighting a war far, far from home.

"We've injured on the field. I'm going for the men we can bring back. Any volunteers?"

He was met with silence. Then one man with a sling around his shoulder rose. "Bullet's in my left arm, Doc—sir! Guess I can drag my countrymen out with my right arm!"

"Good, good, anyone else?"

A dozen men had stood by now.

"If I could walk, Doc, I'd be with you," a man offered. Julian looked down. Two hours ago, he'd taken the man's left leg. Luckily, the fellow hadn't lost his knee, which always made the use of an artificial leg better. Julian smiled. "You've done your duty, soldier."

"I'm alive!" the man said softly.

Julian nodded. "You stay that way. Come on," he told the others. "You!" he said, calling back to the orderly who had come for him. "What's your name?"

"Evans, sir."

"Evans, get me an ambulance. Bring it as close to the field as you can without getting it blown up. The rest of you, grab what mounts you can and follow me."

They followed him to what had been peaceful farm land, where wheat had grown, golden in the sun. The sun was obliterated from the sky by the black powder around them. The wheat was mown down by shrapnel and bullets. Gold was gone, and the color of the day was red, for dead and dying men lay everywhere, Rebs and Yanks.

Cannons continued to explode and bullets whistled by, since the fighting had moved just slightly south. But Julian and his volunteers moved quickly and efficiently. Injured men saw them and cried out for help. They went to those who called for them first, then tried to find the unconscious living, testing pulses. Julian was bent over a Rebel soldier when fingers curled around his leg. He looked down. A Yank soldier. His heart catapulted. This hadn't even been a cavalry engagement, but every time he saw a blue uniform, he was afraid. So afraid that he'd find his brother.

The man wasn't Ian. But he was injured, badly.

"Help me," the fellow whispered.

"Help me with this man!" he shouted.

The volunteer by him spat. "There may be more Rebels out here. I ain't pausing here for no Billy Yank."

"Yes, you are, and that's a god-damned order!" Julian shouted.

Together, they dragged the man to the ambulance.

Evans stopped Julian then. "Sir, no disrespect intended, but you're needed badly now back in the surgery. We won't leave the men."

The soldier with the sling around his arm stood next to Evans. "I'm Captain Bentley, artillery, sir. I'll see to it that we find all the living we can—Rebs and Yanks, sir." Bentley's eyes met his steadily. "My pa's fighting over with the Yanks," he said quietly.

Julian nodded. "Fine, thank you, Captain. I will go back then."

He returned to the surgery. More and more men appeared before him. And then the Yank he had saved. The fellow looked up at him and smiled. "Lord, A-mighty! Why, you must be Colonel McKenzie's brother."

"Yeah, I'm Ian's brother."

The man kept smiling, despite the fact that he was shot in three places. "You're his spittin' image, Doc, sir, you ever hear that?"

"All the time. Have you seen my brother? Is he—"

"Yes, sir, he was right as rain when I saw him, just a few days ago. Guess I'm glad to be here, with you, even if it makes me a prisoner. Your brother sure does brag on you, sir. Says you're the best there is."

"I do my best, Yank."

The Yank's, Walter Smith, left knee was shattered. It was bad. He was going to lose it.

"Wish I could tell you something better, but I've got to take the leg. No choice."

The man stared at him, nodding, accepting his fate. "I know you'd save it if you could. I heard that you saved limbs better than anybody."

"My brother told you?"

"Naw . . . the angel."

"An angel?"

"No, sir, I said *the* angel. Mrs. Tremaine. She's from Florida, sir. Just like you are. You know her, sir?"

"Oh, yes. I know her."

Sound seemed to dim behind Julian. He felt cold in the midst of an awful heat. *He felt afraid, very afraid. The field hospitals were far too close to deadly action, to fighting, to cannon fire, to bullets . . . Cannonballs didn't know good men from bad men. They didn't recognize hospital tents and avoid them. They didn't know not to kill women . . .*

He wondered how many nights, when he should have been exhausted and sound asleep, that he had lain awake, worrying about her. Damn her, why couldn't she have been happy working in St. Augustine?

"She's here at Gettysburg?" he asked quietly.

"Yes, sir."

"With what troops?"

"With Magee's forces, sir."

Magee. He mentally damned himself. Well, he had introduced her to Risa, and it was surely through Risa that she had come to be with Magee.

"Ah, we're grateful to have her. She made Surgeon Grimley leave a young boy's leg be the other day when Grimley wanted to hack it off. Said you'd saved dozens of limbs, she'd seen you in action, and she'd look after the boy herself. She's strange, so beautiful, so ladylike, and so *determined*! So I know, sir, that if you could, you'd save my leg. Frankly, I'll be mightly grateful just for my life."

"I'll do my best, soldier," Julian promised him.

The man closed his eyes as Julian nodded to an orderly to administer ether with the bag and nose cone they'd been using.

"If the angel were just here too . . ."

Well, she wasn't here, but damn her, she was with Magee's troops. Why the hell did Magee have her so close to the action?

Angel . . .

She'd kept men alive. Kept them whole.

Witch.

Had Magee come to trust her strange instincts?

He couldn't think about her now, didn't dare think about her. There were too many wounded still coming. But tonight, when finally the guns fell silent . . .

Chapter 17

~~~

July 2 had been a brutal day. Rhiannon had never seen fields of such death and devastation. Perhaps it was natural that she later dreamed.

The day had begun early, with troops arriving throughout as both sides began to realize the enormity of the battle that would ensue. General George Meade, replacing "Fighting Joe" Hooker, fought a defensive battle and held his own. From the start to finish, the day was filled with wounded. Working nonstop in a field hospital east of the action, Rhiannon heard bits and pieces of news. Union soldiers had been beset by the Rebs at places with such poetic names as Devil's Den and the Peach Orchard. At Little Roundtop, a Colonel Joshua Chamberlain from Maine had performed a feat of pure bravado, charging back against the assaulting Confederates, his troops armed with only their bayonets when they ran out of ammunition. The desperate charge so unnerved the Rebs that they broke and fled.

The fighting ended late. A charge by the Confederates against the Yanks up Cemetery Hill did not even begin until dusk, and then lasted through the evening until ten, and even after that, the occasional crack of a bullet could be heard. Campfires burned across a landscape rich in the blood of the fallen. Confederates and Unionists finished the day with no clear victor in sight.

Stories of courage and cowardice, success and failure, cheer and despair, all came into the surgery. And so it was that Rhiannon heard firsthand accounts of a Reb surgeon who had defied guns and cannon fire to come for his wounded. McKenzie. By all accounts, he had come for men in blue and men in gray, and men so covered in blood and

mud that the colors of their uniforms were barely
discernible.

Perhaps, it was natural that she dreamed. And so, when
she slept at last . . .

It came.

The dream.

At first she relived the dream in which she had seen
Richard die. She knew she was seeing it again, but she
couldn't stop it from coming. She could hear the cries of
the men, the shouts of command, just as she had seen it
all today, except that this was a different battle, a different
time. There had been cornfields. Great waves of green and
gold, bending and bowing to a summer's day. Now those
stalks were shorn, stripped down by thousands of
bullets . . .

She struggled; she tried to cry out. She wanted to turn
away, and yet she could not. She wanted to call to the men,
to stop them from dying, and yet she could not.

Then she saw Richard . . .

Leading the men.

Oh, God, she had dreamed this dream before.

Bullets began to fly in a terrible hail and men began to
fall. She tried to cry out; she tried to stop Richard.

The bullet struck him, a mortal hit.

For a moment he was frozen in time, *life* caught within
his eyes. Regret, pain, the things that he would never see,
never touch again. He mouthed her name . . . But as life
faded from his eyes, so light faded from the sky, only to
come again.

A different hill. And in her dream she was here, in the
little Pennsylvania town called Gettysburg.

They came in great sweeping waves, more and more of
them. The field was alive with smoke, with powder, with
the thunder of cannon, the screeching of the cannonballs,
the screams of dying horses—and men. And still they came,
marching across fields, up hillsides . . .

Yet among the other sounds there was a strange, challenging ripple on the air, and despite the terror she realized
that she was hearing a Rebel yell. It was the South dying
here, attacking the North—bold, brave, desperate, and
dying.

Her dreams were suddenly patterned in a wild array of

pictures. The old dream mingled with the new. Richard was dying, staring . . . then Richard rolled and turned over, and it wasn't Richard anymore.

Julian.

He lay upon the ground, unhorsed by cannon fire, thrown far from his mount. The animal was down, whinnying in pain. But the soldier didn't stay down. He rose, calling out to those who had followed him, ordering help for the dead and dying men. He raced through the barrage of fire all around him. He tied a tourniquet on one man, ordered another dragged back—announced another dead.

He was too close, far too close to the battle lines. The clash of steel could be heard as foot soldiers charging enemy lines met in hand-to-hand combat with their foes. Julian was in the midst of it.

She saw the bullet strike, saw the look in his eyes. Mortality registered instantly, for he was a physician, and he knew . . .

And he started to fall . . .

The field was suddenly alight with a burst of color against the black powder of cannon and rifle fire. Streaks of sunlight, gold and hazy, mauve, crimson, colors like that of a setting sun, a dying day . . . life perhaps was like a day, sunset bursting like a last glory, fading to black . . .

She awoke with a start. The sun was no longer setting upon rolling hills and fields bathed in blood; it was just rising in the eastern sky, yet its gentle morning streaks touched the white sheets of her camp bed, nightdress, and canvas tent with a haunting shade of the palest red . . .

Like an echo of blood.

She sat up, breathing deeply, looking around. She was not at the scene of battle, yet she knew . . .

The first battle had taken place.

It had occurred some time ago, just as she'd first dreamed. And she'd awakened then, crying out, keening with agony. She had given way to desolation, sobbing in great, violent spasms.

For she'd seen the captain's face, seen his eyes. She had seen the light of courage, honor, and compassion within them.

She had seen that light diminish as he had fallen forward, his blood then a part of the crimson drenching the field.

She had known, and a part of her had perished that night as well.

But now a new dream had come. And she'd seen *him*. And she knew what would come . . .

Her stomach churned, and she bit into her lower lip, placing a hand upon her abdomen.

If she didn't stop it.

How? How could she stop this great, deadly tide of war? She couldn't, she didn't have the power. But perhaps . . .

Perhaps she could stop him. Warn him. Stop him? With his fierce pride, loyalty, determination—sheer pigheadedness?

She had to stop him. She would not bear this agony again.

She rose quickly, washed, dressed, and emerged from her tent in the medical sector of the Yankee camp. Corporal Watkins, the orderly standing guard duty, was just pouring coffee. "Why, Miz Rhiannon, you're up way too early. It will still be several hours before the firing commences again, I'll wager." He handed her the coffee he had poured, shaking his head. "This must be mighty hard for you, and other folk, I imagine. I mean, to some Northern boys, the only good Reb is a dead Reb, but then you folks from the South who were against secession, why you know there're some good folks in Rebel butternut and gray. And cannon-balls, ma'am, they just don't know the difference between a good man and a bad, now, do they?"

She took the coffee he had offered her. Her fingers were shaking, she knew that she was pale. "I have to see General Magee, Corporal Watkins."

"Why, he'll be busy, ma'am, planning strategy—"

"Now, Corporal. Tell him I have to see him. And he'll see me. I know that he will." Yes, he would see her. She'd already been able to tell him several times when he needed to take certain evasive measures.

Yes, he would see her. What then? Once she'd baited, tricked, and betrayed Julian McKenzie, what then . . .

He'd loathe her. But he'd still be alive.

And one day perhaps, far in the future, a child would have a father.

Julian had been lying awake a long time.

He hadn't gone to bed until he'd been ready to drop. So many injured.

But then he'd awakened as the very first rays of dawn were beginning to touch the heavens. Awake, he came to sit out in the open, aware that he had to rest, if not sleep, before entering into surgery again. He was glad of the night's touch of coolness against the summer's heat, even here, far from home. The air was clean tonight, good, so delicious to him. Sometimes, he didn't think that he'd ever be able to breathe without feeling that the air around him was not redolent with the smell of blood, the smell of death.

He had feared he would dream about *her*. Witch, they called her, and indeed, it seemed she had cast a spell upon him, for damn her, but he could not forget her. From the moment when he had first seen her, standing upon the stairway, she had somehow slipped beneath his skin and into his soul. At each turn she had been there, even when he had turned away. And all that had happened between them she denied. She had teetered above an abyss, loath to accept the hand of the enemy. And even when he forced his way through the steel shell of will with which she wrapped herself, he could never take the place of another man, nor would he ever willingly allow her to pretend, to use him . . .

Sweet Jesus! In the midst of death and mayhem, he was thinking about her. She was a witch. Haughty, stubborn, far too proud, ridiculously argumentative, annoying, totally pigheaded, foolish, dangerous.

And yet . . .

God, how he wished that she were with him.

No one had such a touch. When she walked into a room, she was magic. There was no one with whom he'd worked who could save more lives. She healed others. She haunted him. And he was afraid, because she was with the Yanks now, as she wanted to be. Not in safety but on this battlefield. At dawn the guns would roar again, raining death even on those who were trying to save lives . . .

"Captain! Captain McKenzie!"

Startled by the urgent call, he rose quickly to his feet. Dabney Crane, one of the civilian scouts, rode toward him. He dismounted in haste, looking around anxiously, and Julian knew then that Dabney had a message for him. Fear seared his heart—too many of his kin were embroiled in this conflict.

"What is it, Dabney?"

"A message from the Yankee lines, sir. I was approached by one of their riders."

This war was a sad, strange jumble of loyalties. By day, the battle raged in a deadly hail of cannon fire, bullets, and bloodied swords. But when the fighting fell silent, messages often passed between battle lines, and those who should have stopped them coming looked aside, aware that the day might come when their own kin tried to reach them.

"My brother—" Julian began, a terrible lump in his throat. Was Ian across those lines? He never knew where his brother was fighting.

"No, sir, there's no bad news about your Yankee soldier kin. This has to do with a lady."

"My sister, my cousin—"

"No, sir, a different lady. A Mrs. Tremaine. She's serving with their medical corps, sir. The rider, a man I've met with now and then regarding other personal exchanges between troops, gave me an envelope, and I was to give it to you and no one else, and that I keep this all in strictest confidence. But I'm to summon you now, quick, before the day's fighting can commence. She has to see you, sir, at the old Episcopal church down the pike."

"She has to see me?" he inquired, his stomach tightening. She had some warning for him. Or some trick. He started to hand the envelope back, unopened.

"Tell her I can't come."

"She says the matter is urgent, you must come, sir."

"Why would this lady think I would be willing to see her when I am so sorely needed elsewhere?"

"Sir, I can't say. Perhaps you should open the envelope."

He didn't want to do so. His hands clenched as he looked down at the cream parchment. He couldn't help himself. He opened the envelope, and read the words.

Colonel McKenzie, I know how unwilling you must be to answer any missive of mine, but I must see you. I am relying upon the fact that you were raised a gentlemen, and as such, with death on every horizon, you would not leave me to lead a life of shame, nor cast an innocent into the ignomy of a tainted future. Therefore, sir, I beg of you, meet me. There is a small

Episcopal church down on the pike. I'll not keep you
from your war long.

Dabney Crane didn't say anything. He studied Julian
with intense curiosity.

Julian stared back at Dabney, determined to betray nothing but disinterest. Yet his heart was suddenly hammering
with a fierce beat as he wondered just what was truth here.
Had she finally ceased to deny—since truth had born fruit?
He didn't know what he felt. A strange stirring warmth and
pleasure at what just might be the truth—despite her feelings toward him, and his turmoil that she could create such
rage and anger within him . . . and that he could want
her still.

"Captain?" Dabney said anxiously.

"I can spare but a few minutes. Men are dying."

Dabney shook his head sadly. "That they are, sir. But I
do suggest, sir, that if you have a mind to see this lady at
all, you take your few spare minutes now. Colonel Joe Clinton from Georgia had agreed to meet his nephew, Captain
Zach Clinton of Maine, at the river last night. Captain Zach
showed, but Colonel Joe had been killed."

*Every muscle in him seemed to tighten. What if he refused
to meet her, and he died? And what if she was expecting his
child? Would she raise it with another man's heritage, another man's name?*

"Sir?"

"I need my horse—"

"Take old Ben, sir. He's a healthy mount, and as fast
as the wind. You must go now. Before the troops begin
to waken."

And before it's determined I'm a deserter, he thought.

"Sir," Dabney reminded him, "time is of the essence."

Julian hesitated. He didn't trust Rhiannon. With good
cause. What if all that she had written was lies, meant to
lure him to her and nothing more? It could all be a ruse.

Well, he determined, she would pay a price. She would
get what she had asked for, one way or another.

"I'm going immediately. Go quickly now and waken Father Vickory. Send him behind me, quickly."

"Yessir." Dabney smiled, delighted that he had brought
off what seemed like an intimate liaison.

Julian accepted Dabney Crane's offer of the use of his horse, and leapt atop the messenger's dappled gray gelding. Riding past Rebel pickets, he identified himself, and crossed the Rebel line into the no-man's-land between the Rebs and the Yanks. Approaching the church, he slowed his mount and waited on a slight ridge where trees still stood, remnants of a copse all but destroyed by cannon fire. He watched, carefully surveying the area.

The church itself was on a spit of open ground with much of the foliage and many of the fields around it mown down by yesterday's fighting. If there were yanks surrounding the church, he would have seen them.

Dismounting by the trees, he nonetheless watched cautiously a moment longer, then hunched low to the ground, inching his way across the open expanse before the small church. Reaching the doorway, he pressed it partially open, and entered low against the ground as well, waiting still.

She was there.

She stood before the altar, her back to him, her head bowed. She still wore black. Black was the color typically worn for a full year of mourning—and God knew, she mourned her Richard!—but for her wedding to another man? he mused. Yet even if she was sincere in this endeavor, it still meant nothing more than words—and respectability. She wore black inside, around her heart, and he hadn't the power to lighten that shade.

Still, it appeared that she had come alone, and he felt his heart quicken. He again took his time, rising from his wary crouch in silence. Wanting to appear casual, he leaned back comfortably against the doorway, arms crossed over his chest.

"You summoned me?" he said at last, and she spun around, startled, her hand flying to her throat.

For a moment, in the soft, flickering candlelight of the small church, he thought he saw a flash of emotion in the depths of her bewitching green eyes. Then she regained control, hiding whatever feelings had plagued her.

"You've come!" she said.

He shrugged, keeping his distance from her. It was amazing, but nothing seemed to mar her. Her mourning clothing was simple, as befitted her work in the Union field hospitals. She was slim, worn, weary, and still regal, stately, and very beautiful. Her hair was neatly pulled back, netted into a bun at her nape, yet its dark richness seemed to shimmer blue-black with the slightest touch of the candlelight. Her throat was long and elegant; her fingers cast against it were the same.

"I repeat, you've summoned me."

She nodded, looking down then. "I didn't hear you come," she murmured. "Have you been there long?"

"Long enough. Are you communing with God? Or with Richard?"

She raised her head; her eyes caught his. There was fire in them at his caustic tone.

"This is extremely awkward for me," she told him, her voice pained.

"I can imagine. You have gone from thinking you could convince me that nothing had happened to demanding that I do the gentlemanly thing."

"I believe . . . that it's necessary!" she whispered.

"And Richard has been dead just a little too long?"

"How dare you mock him!"

"I'm not mocking the dead, Rhiannon, just calculating the facts."

"How rude!"

"This is war, Rhiannon. I'm afraid some of the niceties of life have slipped away. You summoned me because you want something out of me. So please, talk to me."

"What do you want out of me?" she demanded fiercely.

"Well, an admission that something happened."

She appeared as white as parchment, and for a moment her eyes touching his appeared to carry an honest glitter. "Oh, my God, don't you understand? I didn't want anything to happen, I still can't believe that I . . . that I . . ."

"Mistook a flesh-and-blood man for Richard's ghost."

They still stood the length of the aisle apart. He thought that she would have slapped him had they not. Perhaps he deserved it. Maybe he was being cutting and cruel. It was simply hard to have been used as a substitute, then summoned as a social convenience.

But if there was a child . . .

He waved a hand in the air. "Never mind. As you pointed out in your letter, it's a deadly war. I want my child born with my name—it is my child, right?"

She stared at him with regal disdain, fury evident in her every breath. Then she started down the aisle, determined to walk out. "Never you mind," she said heatedly.

He didn't allow her past him. He caught her arm and forced her eyes to his.

"Where's the priest, Rhiannon?"

"What?"

"You summoned me to marry you. Where's the priest?"

Her eyes widened. "He's—he's on his way. I—I needed time to talk with you, to ask you first, naturally, to—"

"To set me up?" he accused softly.

"No! I—I—" she stuttered. Her lashes fell again. "Damn you! I need you to marry me." She stared at him again, fire in her gaze once again. "Do you wish to do it or not?"

He hesitated, smiling slowly.

"If you've just come to torment me, let go—"

"Marry you? Of course, with the greatest pleasure. How could I possibly refuse such a heartfelt request?"

A sound at the door sent him spinning around. Damn her! She so easily taunted him from the care he usually took with every move. But it was Father Vickery who had come, a young Georgian Episcopal priest.

"I'm sorry I've taken so long," he apologized, nervously stroking back his long straw-colored hair as he hurried in. "I wanted to make sure that I properly record the marriage, assure that it's legal."

"Of course!" Rhiannon said softly. "You were sent here, to help us, of course?" she queried.

Julian watched her. Had she been expecting a priest? Or was she assuming Vickery had been sent by her Yankee cohorts?

Vickery cleared his throat. "We needed witnesses as well," he said, opening the door a few inches farther. "I really moved as quickly as I could, recruiting these ladies!" Two young women had accompanied them. They both smiled.

"This is so romantic!" said the rounder of the pair. "I'm Emma Darrow, this is my sister, Lucy."

"Lovely, just lovely!" Lucy agreed.

"Thank you," Rhiannon murmured.

"Charmed!" Emma supplied, and giggled.

"So lovely!" Lucy said again.

"We must hurry and get back. The dawn is beginning to break in earnest," Father Vickery said. He caught Rhiannon's hand, hurrying down the aisle with her. "You stand there. I'll give you into marriage myself—you are the lady in question, right?"

"Yes, she is, Father," Julian supplied dryly, since she was the only other female present. If the whole thing wasn't so sad, it would be amusing.

But Father Vickery, though nervous, suddenly seemed to gather his wits about him. He began the rite of marriage, speaking very quickly. When it came time for Rhiannon to give her vows, she stared at Julian in silence.

Of course. She had done this before. The memory must be quite painful at this time. And it seemed possible she hadn't really intended on doing it again.

He squeezed her hand so tightly she cried out, but then, choking over the words, she spoke them. Clearly. Loudly.

Keeping her hand tightly in his, Julian gave his promise to love, honor, and cherish her, as long as they both should live, with grave solemnity. Julian used his family signet ring for a wedding band.

"I now pronounce you man and wife. Kiss your bride," Father Vickery said.

He hurriedly started down the aisle to exit the church, anxious to be on his way. "Emma, Lucy, come along, come along. Julian, you must hurry! Kiss the lady, be done with it!" It was a final warning. Father Vickery fled on out of the church.

Julian didn't touch his bride. "This is what you wanted, isn't it?" he asked. She looked as if she were about to expire.

"Well, one way or the other, it is done," he said briefly. "But you'll forgive me; I really can't linger. Yet, I warn you. I pray to God you'll have the sense to keep safe."

He turned away from her. "Wait!" she cried.

He turned back.

"Stay, just a minute . . ." she whispered.

He shook his head. "I can't stay."

Suddenly, she threw herself at him. She came into his arms, smelling subtly, seductively like roses. Her fingers twined into the hair at his nape, she came upon her toes, and found his lips. She pressed her lips to his. Her tongue teased for entry. Stunned, he found himself enfolding her to him, weeks of abstinence suddenly tearing at him, giving him a hunger for her that stole away his heart and mind. He kissed her passionately in return, holding her close, tasting, savoring, lips crushing, tongue sweeping, hands upon her, memorizing . . . remembering that one shining time denied until this night . . .

Vaguely, he became aware of the sounds beyond the church. She broke away from him at last.

Her words were whispered with lips not an inch from his own, still damp from the passion of their kiss.

"I'm sorry, Julian. But, you see, you would have died."

Passion?

Or trickery.

He'd been right all along. He'd been the biggest fool in the world.

She had lured him here, careful of the timing, keeping the Yankees away at first, knowing full well he would be watching for a trap. But now they had arrived. They were outside the church, ready to break in, to seize him.

He wore a Colt in a holster at his side, and at times he wore a utilarian dress sword as well. Not this morning, and not that it mattered. He was a surgeon, a medical man, not a soldier, not the usual Yankee prey.

Bitterness swept through him. He wasn't going to pull the Colt, kill the men sent to seize him, and go down in a blaze of glory himself.

He intended to live. The child was his too.

He pulled away from her, staring into her eyes. The truth was there. Every bit of it. She had planned this so that he might be captured. She had embraced him so that he would not leave too quickly.

"You bitch!" he accused her.

"I had a dream. You died in it!"

He caught her about the waist once again, jaw taut, ice seeming to fill his veins. He held her with such force that she was crushed against him, her back arched, her chin high. "Dear wife," he promised her, "trust me, I will see to it that you are very, very sorry, indeed."

She shook her head, angry at the way he held her—and that she hadn't the power to escape his arms. "You persist in being a foolish Rebel. I'm not your wife, and you will not make me sorry! That priest was no more real than my story."

So she had lied. But she was mistaken.

He laughed softly. "I beg to differ, my dear. That was Father Vickery, out of Atlanta, devoted to his Georgian boys. Georgians, being Florida's neighbors, try to help us out, and the good Father Vickery just happened to be the closest clergyman when I was getting ready to ride out. You may not be expecting my child. But I'm afraid that you are my wife."

Disbelief touched her eyes.

The door to the church burst open. "Captain McKenzie! Julian!"

He knew the voice, and he wasn't surprised, other than the fact that a general could be spared at this hour to take part in a capture. He had saved General Angus Magee's foot when only amputation would have saved his life.

"General Magee, sir!" he returned pleasantly, still looking at Rhiannon.

"Julian, step away from Mrs. Tremaine and drop your weapon, sir!"

He stepped away, his eyes pinned upon hers. He smiled slowly, reached for the Colt, tossed it down. His stare didn't alter as he heard the men rushing into the room to take him. Yet as they reached him, they didn't touch him; they hovered awkwardly around him.

At last he drew his gaze from her stricken green eyes. "Good evening, gentlemen. No, I'm afraid it's morning. Where does the time go? It seems to fly when so many are about to die, doesn't it?"

One of the men cleared his throat and started toward him. Julian shook his head, smiling. "There's no need for force, my good fellow. Point me where I am to go, and I shall proceed."

"Just come along, Julian," General Magee said. His still striking—if aging—face, lined with pride and character, seemed to sag. He stood just in the entry of the small church. He was bone tired.

"Aye, sir, as you wish," Julian said politely. "Tell me, since we have this happenstance to meet, sir, do you know if my brother is well?"

"Yes, Julian. Ian is well. But he isn't a part of this; he knows nothing about it—"

"No, sir. My brother wouldn't be a part of such naked treachery."

"You died in the dream!"

Magee stiffened. "Mrs. Tremaine?" he said softly.

Julian had reached the general at the door, but he knew she came behind him. He stepped past Magee, into the clearing before the church. Yankee horsemen were aligned thirty feet from him. He turned back. Magee had exited the church, Rhiannon close behind him.

He smiled, addressing them both. "By the way, your pardon, General Magee, but she is Mrs. McKenzie now. I'm afraid you and your men were a little late," he said, his tone apologetic.

Magee stared at Rhiannon.

"My dear girl, is it true?"

"No!" she said, her whispered word alarmed.

"General, I swear to you that it is. Father Vickery will tell you so, before God. The lady is over twenty-one. So am I. The marriage is legal and binding. With witnesses. Ah! And in private, sir!" he said, lowering his voice so that only the general and Rhiannon could hear his words. "As I did the right, proper, and most gentlemanly thing, coming here at the lady's summons—and since I have become your prisoner—I ask you to do me a service. As an officer, and a gentleman. Rhiannon is in your medical service," he said softly, "be kind enough to keep an eye on her. She has a tendency to believe herself dreaming of her dear departed Richard—then turning to the nearest living, breathing body—"

She stepped forward and slapped him. It was a hard, stinging strike. Hard enough to make him feel the blow straight to his jaw.

He lifted his hand to his face, then bowed deeply to her. He turned around and started for the horse that the Yankees apparently held for his use. He swung atop the animal. It was sleek, well fed. He mounted the horse, then saw the opportunity he'd been waiting for. A gap in the Yankee line before him. Lying flat against the horse's neck, he moved his heels against its flanks, and the sleek bay leapt to life, bolting straight for the gap.

"Stop him!" Magee commanded.

Two cavalrymen managed to fill the gap, but it didn't matter. Julian needed only spin his mount and ride hard straight back, and to the left.

But when he swung his mount around and started pell-mell back, *she* was there.

She stood in his path, eyes on his. Tall, straight, as still as a statue, challenging him . . .

Not much of a challenge. She knew he would stop.

He reined in his mount. Instantly, the soldiers were on him, dragging him from the horse. He struggled to free himself, but the Yanks were having none of it. One of the men swung at him with the butt of his rifle. A good, solid blow. Julian's head clamored and rung. The whack had been strong enough to cause a fracture, pray God no . . .

He started to fall, the world going black. But he saw her. Saw her beautiful green eyes upon his.

He reached out. She screamed, but he had caught her hand. And with what strength he had left, he pulled her to him.

And she came down with him. The world was fading. No matter. He smiled at her. Tried to mouth words. "I swear, dear *wife,* you will be sorry."

Indeed. Brave, bold words, especially when the world was fading to a total black.

"He's unconscious ma'am, if you'll take my hand . . ." one of the young horsemen offered.

Rhiannon nodded. Then she looked down at Julian again, eyes closed, a long lock of dark hair fallen over his forehead. She wanted to trace the lines of his face. Touch him, stay with him until he had come to, make sure that he was all right. She bit into her lip, dismayed by the admission she was making then, if only to herself.

"You'll just never know, never believe, that I did this . . . because I love you," she whispered, knowing that neither he, nor anyone else, could hear her.

Cannon fire suddenly exploded, far too close to them. "Get the prisoner up and to the field hospital!" Magee commanded. "The day's work has commenced, and gentlemen, may I remind you! The fate of the nation rests on your shoulders today!"

The fate of the nation. The fate of thousands of men

who would die. She couldn't stop the death and destruction, no one could stop it. Yet she wondered . . .

Had she *changed* fate, did she have that power? She'd been willing to risk anything to change her dream. But just what had she done? She had deceived Julian, betrayed him. She'd wanted to save him, as he'd saved her, then run . . .

She'd tricked him.

He'd tricked her. And now, if he'd told the truth, they were evermore entangled in a hopeless tempest.

Especially because there was one truth she had told.

Fate. Had it all been fated, from that first night when he had ridden through the foliage to the isolation of her house, and into her life?

Chapter 18

~

There was nothing as awful as the sound of battle.

Kept with other prisoners, mostly infantry and artillery men taken during the fighting, Julian sat tensely on a log behind one of the Yankee field hospitals, listening to the thunder of cannon fire that seemed to boom forever, coming first from one direction, then the other.

The first day's fighting had left the Confederates at an advantage, taking the town, forcing the Yanks back. The second day had brought savage fighting, leaving no clear victory. July the third, the armies battled again, despite the fact that the dead lay everywhere, that the number of wounded was staggering, that blood drenched the field.

He was tired, but more than tired, he was wretched. He couldn't endure feeling so useless when he knew how many were being injured, how many would die for lack of attention. Listening to the sounds of gunfire, the screams of men and horses, he damned himself a thousand times over. Not so much for himself. But for what he had done to the men. Every surgeon was needed. And here he was . . . listening.

The battlefield was enormous, stretching across hills, fields, orchards, roads, a cemetery. He didn't know where his own troops were, and worse, he didn't know where Rhiannon was. In the midst of the action somewhere. And he was powerless. He felt a certain victory in having tricked her in what might be a more binding way than she had him, but it was a hollow triumph. She was legally married. Little good it did him. He was a prisoner, under guard.

Screams, closer at hand, caught his attention. He rose, seeing that an ambulance was coming in. The conveyance stopped just outside the Yankee tents. The man at the driver's side hopped down, shouting. "Help, we need help out here, Dr. McManus—"

A doctor, clad in a blood-soaked uniform, stepped from the canvas field hospital. "They'll have to take their turns."

The doctor disappeared. The soldier looked over the twenty or so Reb prisoners and the two men guarding them. "G'd Amighty, I've got fellows dying here . . . some fellows may not make it for as much as a drop of water . . . Sweet Jesus, someone help me!"

Prisoners and guards alike stared at the soldier for a moment.

"We've got the Rebs to watch," one of the guards said awkwardly.

"Damn it!" Julian swore, striding over to the conveyance with impatience. "We may be Rebs, but by God, we're all human beings! Someone give me a hand, let's get these out of the ambulance, see what we can do . . ."

"I'm with you, Doc!" one of the Rebs said, jumping down to join him.

A big fellow in a fraying infantry uniform stood up to block Julian's way. "If they live, they'll come back and kill us!"

"Maybe. And maybe not," Julian said, hands on his hips, staring at the fellow. "Let me tell you the way things work. I'm a Reb, because I'm a Floridian first. And before that, soldier, I'm a God-fearing human being, not to mention the fact that I'm a doctor who swore an oath to preserve life! So you can either try to stop me or you can get out of my way!"

The fellow frowned, then stepped back. "Ah, hell!" he swore. "I can't just sit here with them Yanks screamin' either. Tell me what you want me to do, Doc."

Julian looked at the Yankee soldier who had brought the wounded in. "May we, son?"

"Doc, please!"

Julian began giving orders, carefully pulling the men from the ambulance wagon. He found three dead men in with the wounded, along with three Rebs. He did his best to get the twenty odd men shaded from the merciless summer sun beneath a patch of oaks. The field hospital had been set up by a small creek, so there was no problem getting them water. Julian had nothing with which to operate, but with even the Yanks listening to directions, he managed several splints, stanched wounds that were hemorrhaging, and made comfortable those who were going to die.

He was involved in tying off a makeshift tourniquet when the Yankee doctor, McManus, came out of the tent. He viewed the scene before him with a moment's surprise, then seemed to take it all in his stride.

"You're a doctor—" he began, eyeing Julian. Then he broke off, frowning. "You're a McKenzie. Damned if you don't look like Colonel Ian. You his twin?"

"Younger brother," Julian said.

"The surgeon . . . yes." He studied him for a moment. "Well, I can't say as how we couldn't use your help. Would you work a Yank field hospital, sir?"

Julian didn't hesitate. "I would." He looked around him at the Rebs who had helped him with the Yanks. "No man here is a monster. We're just fighting opposite sides."

Dr. McManus looked around at the Rebs. "Thank you, boys. I'm grateful for your help. Dr. McKenzie, follow me."

Julian did so. In the tent there were five tables. Each held a man and awaited another. Three doctors were moving from table to table.

A man on the one nearest their point of entry began to stir. "Jesus, Doc, you're bringing the Rebs in here on us?"

"Another surgeon, soldier—"

"Ain't no enemy operating on me!" the man protested.

"He'd like to kill us all!" another man agreed.

"Yeah, Doc, get him out of here!" one of the orderlies protested.

"Julian!"

Startled to hear his name called, Julian walked to the far table. He frowned at first, then recognized a Yankee cavalryman who had been in St. Augustine at the time he'd been brought in to operate on Magee's foot. He'd assisted, getting Julian from and back to the river.

"George Hill?"

"Julian . . . it's my leg. Shot through the calf. Can't feel anything, but I don't think the bone is shattered. Can you . . ."

"I don't know. I've got to see the wound."

"You letting him operate on you, Captain Hill?" Another man called.

"Damned right," Hill said, leaning back with a subtle smile. "Hell, this man operated on General Magee!"

Julian lifted his hands. "I have no instruments."

One of the orderlies came over to him with a black bag. "Belonged to Captain Naismith, Forty-fourth Maine. He died yesterday morning."

Julian looked at the bag for a moment. "Dr. Naismith wouldn't begrudge you using his things, sir. He never did cotton to this war. He said time and again, all we were doing was killing out a whole generation of Americans, the flower of our youth. You use these, sir. He'd be mighty proud you were saving men."

Julian nodded and accepted the medical bag. The orderly's name was Robert Roser. He appointed himself Julian's assistant.

To his vast relief, Julian discovered that he could save Captain Hill's leg. The bullet had gone clean through. Next, however, was a shattered elbow, and the arm had to come off. He removed a bullet from the next man's lower abdomen, then it was a foot wound, a bayonet wound to a shoulder, a bullet in the back, shrapnel, broken jaw . . .

The day began to pass.

He moved with all the speed that he could manage. Later, he began to discover that more and more Rebs were brought to his table. He was startled when he came across a lieutenant with Pickett's troops; Pickett rode with Longstreet, and he had just treated the lieutenant recently for a case of chicken pox.

"Why, Captain McKenzie, sir. What are you doing here?"

"I was captured. But I'm still a doctor," Julian said, frowning as he studied the man's wounds. A bullet in the arm, one in the leg . . .

No hope.

His intestines were slipping from his stomach, he'd been hit so many times at close range.

"Let's just give you something for the pain—"

But the lieutenant grabbed his hand, smiling. A little trickle of blood came from his lips. "Sir, I'm no fool. You're a mighty fine surgeon, but you ever hear that kid's poem? All the kings horses and all the kings men couldn't put me back together again. I don't know what I'm doing on this table. Wasting time for some fellow with a chance. Can't believe I can even talk, 'cause I can feel it going, sir, you know, I can feel it! Life slipped away, like a coldness coming. I ain't afraid, sir. Weren't no saint, but I always did what I knew to be right. It's just a shame. I just heard my cousin Joe was fighting right where I went in, fighting with Hancock's boys. They're the ones that caught us when we came in . . . yessir, we went charging right for the line in the middle of Hancock's men. If you see him, sir, Joe O'Riley, Captain Joe O'Riley, you tell him that his cousin Adam says good-bye. Will you do that for me, sir?"

"Of course, Lieutenant, but—"

"Don't bullshit me—whoa, sorry, sir!"

"It's all right. No bullshit."

"It's cold as hell. Hold my hand."

He curled his hand around O'Riley's. Like O'Riley had said, you could feel death coming. A cold, cold stiffening . . .

He inhaled on a deep breath. Unwound his fingers from the dead soldier's. He hadn't cried in a long, long time. He felt like sobbing.

"That one dead, Dr. Reb?" Robert Roser asked, then saw his face. "Sorry, sir, but there's more men out here . . . hundreds of them." Julian stared at him blankly. "There was a charge against the Union line. One of those damned fool valiant charges . . . but it went bad for the Rebs. They were just . . ." He broke off.

"Go on," Julian said.

"It was a slaughter, sir."

Julian closed his eyes.

"Maybe you need some rest, sir. Even Dr. McManus has taken a break."

"No, no, I'm fine. Bring them on in."

News from the battle came with the injured men. As Roser had said, it had been a slaughter. Pickett's men had sought the honor of charging against the Union line. Time and time again, pure Rebel bravado had taken the South to victory over far superior forces. The swell of a Rebel yell on a battlefield could be bone-chilling, and it was true that raw courage and gall had given the Confederates many an advantage.

But today Pickett's men had charged the line. Cannon fire had spewed at them again and again. Men had dropped step by step.

They had kept coming.

Coming and coming . . .

They had reached the line. The few who had made it through the hail of cannon fire and bullets. But at the Union line they had been stopped. Those who had not fallen were met by the waiting Yanks with their bayonets and close-range gun fire.

The Yanks were jubilant, with just cause. They had stopped the Rebs. Southern daring had failed.

Yet as night fell, there were few could feel the victory without a sense of pain. The dead lay everywhere. Both sides attempted to retrieve their wounded. Rain began to fall.

Somewhere around midnight, Julian began to waver. He could no longer work without endangering the wounded by his own exhaustion. As one man was moved, he leaned his head upon his arms. He closed his eyes and saw no more.

Bathed in blood, he slept where he stood.

By morning the Confederates had begun a slow, steady retreat south.

Julian was surprised that General Meade, who had stood firm against the Rebs and claimed the field here at Gettysburg, did not attempt to pursue. Not only had Pickett's charge been stopped, but Julian had been hearing more and more about the events to follow. Lee, the great commander hailed by North and South alike, had openly wept. He had claimed to everyone that it had been "All my fault, all my fault." For once the army had been utterly demoralized.

It was a great day of triumph for the Federals. They had won the field at Gettysburg. And word had come that Vicksburg, besieged by Grant for months, had finally fallen as well. It had come to a matter of surrender, or total starvation for those in the city—the last rat, one man said, had been eaten. Not a pigeon dared fly in the sky.

And it was the Fourth of July. Independence Day.

If only . . .

There weren't the problem of the dead and wounded.

Retreating, the Southerners hadn't been able to find all their wounded among the dead; as it was, Lee was lucky that Meade, like so many of his predecessors, had neglected to come after him. His ambulance vehicles would slow him down; hundreds, perhaps thousands would die along the way, and be buried in unmarked graves. At least, since the Union army stalled, he would have a chance for some of his wounded.

Some Union soldiers grumbled. They could finish it! They could go after Lee, attack while his army was so crippled. They could end it, perhaps, oh, God, end it!

But Meade didn't choose to follow.

Julian thought that he might have been glad himself if Meade had done so. It was a traitorous feeling but he had never felt such a sense of loss. Men had been dying for two full years. Too many lay dead.

Standing on the soaked earth, looking across the fields where bodies already began to rot, where carrion birds began to fly, where it was almost impossible to tell the quick from the dead.

July the Fourth . . .

It was a strange day. High excitement, a sense of triumph that went beyond the battles won, but came with the fact that Lee's troops could be bested, beaten, worn down, stopped. It combined with the date—surely an omen. And yet, as the gunshots fired represented celebration, death still surrounded them in a serious manner. The injured had to be found quickly. The dead had to be interred. The number of bodies could well cause a quick influx of deadly diseases.

Julian ignored the celebrations going on around him and concentrated on the injured that were still coming before him, one after another, almost as quickly as they had come during battle. There was a difference today; most of the men who had come before could be saved. Those with mortal wounds had perished on the fields. He wondered how many had died who might have been saved if only they'd been found and brought from the scene of battle quickly enough.

That afternoon, while he paused between the wounded, McManus offered him coffee. He accepted it gladly. "Have you heard anything about General Magee's troops?" he asked.

"Magee came through fine."

"My brother?"

"He was circling around after Jeb Stuart's troops through the first part of the battle. He's been sent on to Washington." McManus paused for a moment. "He was never told that you had been taken prisoner."

Julian nodded, relieved. In the back of his mind, he'd been afraid that Ian had been killed or wounded. If not, his brother would have been to see him.

"You're sure he's alive and well?"

"Yes, he left early with dispatches."

"My wife?" Julian asked.

McManus frowned. "Wife?"

Julian smiled dryly. "Yes. It was a shotgun wedding, sir, in a strange sense. Rhiannon Tremaine is a nurse. I understand that she is a godsend to the Union troops."

"None of our nurses was injured, Dr. McKenzie, as far as I've heard." He paused, studying Julian curiously. "She is a godsend to the troops. I asked to have her assigned to me, but I'm not on General Magee's staff, and so she works with his surgeons."

"Can you find out for me if she is really well? I'd be grateful, sir."

McManus, watching him, nodded. "I am the one grateful, sir. You've proven yourself a true man of your oath. I'll make sure that the lady is well. Did you wish to see her?"

Did he want to see her? No. He was unshaven, sweaty, wearing the grime of the muddied battlefield. "No, sir. I just want to make sure that she is well."

McManus nodded. "It will be done. Is there anything else? It seems that you're to be in my keeping for the next few days."

"If we've got a river or a stream anywhere, I'd take most kindly to a bath."

"I think we can arrange that as well."

An hour later, McManus came by to tell him that a messenger had gone between the field hospitals, and Rhiannon was well. She had been kept far to the southeast of the action, bandaging men as they came from surgery to be sent back to the hospitals in Washington.

It was almost dusk, and they were also preparing wounded soldiers for the long, rough ride back to D.C. when a man on horseback arrived, anxious for a word with McManus. There had been riders coming and going all day. Julian ignored the man, since he knew he would hear whatever information had come eventually.

But McManus came to him and addressed him with the rider at his heels. "Captain McKenzie, you're needed at Magee's surgery. Seems there's a patient there with a wound in the shoulder that could prove quite treacherous."

"And he wants a Rebel surgeon?" Julian asked skeptically.

"Apparently, he's a relative."

Julian eyebrows shot up. "You told me my brother—"

"It's not your brother. It's a fellow named Jesse Halston. Captain Jesse Halston, U.S. Cavalry."

"I don't have a relative named Halston—"

"Yes, apparently you do. Your wife wrote his request. She knows the fellow, if you don't. Says he recently married a cousin of yours, Sydney."

"Sydney married a Union cavalry officer?" Julian said incredulously.

"Recently. You McKenzies are prone to hasty marriages, so it seems, sir."

Julian felt a strange sensation of his blood boiling. Sydney had married a Union cavalry officer. When? Why?

"Well?"

He lifted his hands, feeling a strange bitterness. The world had gone soaring completely out of control. All of their lives, they had all watched out for one another—all McKenzie males protective of the girls, Jennifer, Tia, the new baby—Sydney. And now . . .

He lowered his head. There was a story that went around that General Robert E. Lee, who had sons fighting as well, had not recognized one of his boys while reviewing troops in the middle of an action. He was never able to see his own family.

He lifted his hands. "Of course."

"I'll accompany you. I want to see this procedure."

The ride from field hospital to field hospital was grim. All across the hills and valleys, men were sorting through the fallen. The rain had turned much of the battlefield to filthy mush. Soldiers had handkerchiefs tied over their mouths. Between the rain and the sun and natural decomposition, the ground was beginning to smell of rot. God, how he pitied the living! In the midst of the dead, wondering if help would ever come.

Magee's field hospital was set up far from the scenes of the worst fighting, just as McManus had told Julian. His surgery was in an old farmhouse, and Julian was glad to see it. The rain didn't seep into the ground underfoot here, and when he was brought in, he found that his patient was in a real bed in a real bedroom.

Surgeon Reginald Flowers was in command of the hospital, and he greeted Julian politely, telling him that he'd planned to take the arm from the shoulder, since the bullet was wedged against blood vessels, but that his civilian nurse, whom he had come to trust, had insisted that Julian McKenzie could operate without taking the arm.

"It's a risk . . ." Flowers said, then hesitated. "But she's been right about many things many times . . . and she says that Captain Halston is a relative now, your cousin-in-law, and that you can do this. Frankly, if it weren't for the fact that Captain Halston is one of our heroes . . . And then there's also the fact that Rhiannon claims she has done similar surgery with you before."

"She has."

"And the man is married to your cousin?"

"So I've been told."

Flowers lifted his hand. "Your patient, Doctor, if you wish to examine him and tell me if you think you can save the limb. Dr. McManus, if you would join me for a moment for a look at a few other patients . . ."

The two left him.

Julian approached the bed. The man who lay there was a young, handsome fellow with curling dark hair and strong features. Now he was pale, his skin grayish white. He'd lost a great deal of blood already. His eyes were open, though. They were hazel, steady on his. He even offered up a half smile that must have pained him. "So you're the younger brother, the doctor. If they'd given me a drink, I'd think you were Ian playing at a hospital game."

"I'm not Ian, I am Julian, and I am a doctor. Hurt much?" he asked. Halston was shirtless, but there was a bandage on his shoulder and arm that was already becoming bloodied. Julian gently removed the cotton wadding.

The bullet had smashed against bone and wedged next to a blood vessel. The arm was broken, but the break was clean. The injury was almost exactly the same as that which Jerome had received. Rhiannon did know what she was talking about. The location of the wound made amputation dangerous, just as the position of the bullet made its removal dangerous as well.

"Hurt? Hell, yes. Like a son of a gun," Halston said, wincing.

"You married my cousin?" Julian asked as he studied the texture of the skin around the wound.

"Yes."

"How did that come about?" Julian asked.

Halston was staring at him steadily. "Should I answer you now, or after that bullet comes out?"

Julian smiled grimly. "Now."

Halston shrugged. "She was carrying military information. She was picked up and put in Old Capitol. She was afraid that one of you reckless McKenzies would risk life and limb to come and get her out. Maybe she was afraid of her father's reaction, I'm not sure. But she wanted out."

Julian was impressed by the man's honesty. "So she married you?" he queried.

Halston inclined his head slightly. "Rhiannon came to me. She'd promised Sydney that she would help her. She couldn't find Ian—he was already out with the army. Magee couldn't do anything under the circumstances . . . I had been with Pinkerton in the city for a while, and I admit, I was instrumental in Sydney being where she was."

"My *wife* was involved?"

"Well, she wasn't your wife then, was she? She came to Old Capitol to see a man with an infected foot."

"But Sydney married you—and she was set free?"

"She also swore to cease her activities."

"And you intend to keep my cousin in Washington?"

Halston smiled slowly. "Doc, I think I'm bleeding enough without that pressure."

"Sorry." Julian said, lifting his fingers from the wound.

"I hope to keep her in Washington," Halston told him. "Well, I hope to survive to be able to be with her anywhere. But you should know this. I love her. I think she loves me. She's just so tied up in being a Rebel that she won't admit it."

"But you really married her."

"Yes." Halston was staring at him steadily. He asked softly, "So you tell me—what are you planning to do?"

Julian smiled ruefully, carefully removing all the bandages. "I'm going to try to save your arm, and your life."

"I'm counting on it," Halston said.

Julian looked up as he saw a shadow come across the door.

Rhiannon. Tired, drawn, and still straight and tall and regal and ever-beautiful in her widow's black. But she was no longer a widow. She was his wife.

His heart started beating too hard; he couldn't allow his hands to tremble. He wanted to grab her, shake her, demand to know why she betrayed him.

He straightened. "What are you doing here?" he demanded sharply.

Her shoulders squared. "This is where I've been working. Thankfully, since Jesse came in here. I'm going to assist you—"

"No."

She seemed puzzled. "But, Julian—"

"I don't want to work with you."

"A marital spat already!" Jesse said from his bed. "If the two of you don't mind . . . Doc, this really hurts. I mean, it really hurts."

"Get out, I mean it," Julian told Rhiannon.

"Julian, dammit it—"

"Yes, dammit, I'm a prisoner of war. But that doesn't mean I have to work with you."

"Julian, I'm not going anywhere, I—"

"Well, I'm not working with you."

"Julian, you don't understand—"

"Yes, I do. You're a treacherous witch. I was warned about you the first time I laid eyes on you."

"Julian, please!"

Julian gritted his teeth. Halston needed help—now. He had already lost too much blood. And dammit, but it was true. He needed Rhiannon for this. No one else had her touch.

"Get two orderlies. Ether. I'm assuming the Union army has ether here?"

"Everything is ready; the men are just outside," Rhiannon said. "There are surgical instruments laid out on the table there."

"Fine."

"I don't need anesthesia—" Jesse Halston began.

"Trust me, sir, you do," Julian told him.

Rhiannon was quick and efficient. There were bandages, his neatly laid out instruments. Two burly orderlies came in to brace the patient. Both Doctors McManus and Flowers came in to watch the proceedings; McManus administered the ether with a skin bag. Julian asked Rhiannon for the instruments he needed, telling her where and when to apply pressure, when to use her delicate touch to hold blood vessels. It wasn't a lengthy procedure; the minié ball came out of Halston's arm in so smashed a state that Julian was amazed more damage hadn't been done to the bone.

All through the surgery, she anticipated his every need. It felt far too comfortable to be working with her again. His fingers brushed hers; he breathed her scent. The bleeding was stopped, the wound was sewn, the broken bone was splinted. With the delicate surgery nearly completed, he felt his own shabbiness. His uniform was threadbare. His hair was overgrown, his cheeks remained unshaven. He didn't want these other people around. He wanted to be alone with her, make her realize that she might have tricked him, but that, by God, she had married him, and it wasn't a trick she could get out of . . .

But he couldn't be alone with his wife. He was surrounded by Yanks.

When it was over, Jesse still slept. He'd been given an ample dosage of ether.

"Interesting procedure, but it can't be done unless the blood vessels are properly held and tied," McManus said to Julian.

"That's true," Julian said, his eyes on Rhiannon.

"You asked for a new sponge."

"I'm convinced that infections travel with the supplies we use."

"But you manage to keep enough fresh supplies—"

"I really believe that it saves lives."

"Will you have a drink, sir?" Flowers asked, indicating the hallway beyond the bedroom.

He shook his head, his eyes on Rhiannon. "No, I'd like to leave Dr. Flowers to his surgery and return to Dr. Mac-Manus's field hospital. I'd like to keep working there. There are still wounded on the fields. And I can hardly blame the Yanks if they choose to bring in the Rebels last."

Flowers nodded. "As you wish, sir. I understand your concern."

Julian met his wife's eyes. He turned to exit the room.

"Julian!"

She called him, following him to the door, her voice very tight.

He paused, willing himself to exercise every bit of self-control he could manage. The temptation to reach out and grab her, shake her, hold her, scream, yell, make love right there on the floor, seemed so strong that it was like a current of lightning ripping through him.

"Julian, you're being extremely pigheaded, even for a pigheaded person—"

"Pigheaded prisoner of war, if you don't mind."

"Damn you, Julian. I had to do it!" God, she was something. So vibrantly alive. Her eyes were like an emerald fire. He wanted just to touch the contours of her face. There was so much passion in her words, so much grace in her most subtle movement. If he stepped closer, he could breathe in the scent of her flesh.

Not here, not here, not now. Both Flowers and McManus were giving them a moment's privacy. But they were there.

"Julian, I had no choice!"

"So you say. Well, do you intend to share my prison?"

"I have work to do here."

"What were the words? Love, honor, and obey? I forbid you to remain here. Do you intend to obey?"

"I have work here. But you could remain with Dr. Flowers—"

"And we could work together. And at night they could drag me back off in chains. Or were you intending on setting up housekeeping? Maybe a little cannon-shelled farmhouse on the outskirts of town. The doctor and his loving wife could retire together every evening?"

"Julian, this is a war—"

"Yes, I've noticed that." He studied her for a long moment, then asked, "So is there, or isn't there, a child?"

She stiffened, rich lashes falling over her ever so green eyes. "I'm well aware, sir, that I'm not your image of the ideal wife. I said what I knew would appeal to your sense of Southern honor."

"Ah. What a pity, you've trapped yourself for nothing."

"I'm not trapped—"

"But you are. I'm a prisoner. So are you."

"Julian, this is a ridiculous argument. You are a doctor. You save lives. And we do work exceptionally well together, which has—"

"No."

"Julian—"

"I don't claim to be able to see the future, but I can see nothing good in it. So . . . if you don't mind . . ."

He turned away from her, wondering if he had done the sensible thing, or if he would damn himself a thousand times over for not taking any possible chance to be with her.

No. He couldn't work with her. Not here.

He left the farmhouse. She didn't try to stop him again.

For the next two days, he—along with Yank soldiers busy at the same task—walked through the battlefield. At first they found a number of men living. They were treated as best as Julian could treat them at the scene, then brought to field hospitals. Toward the end of the second day of searching, they began to find nothing but dead men. While they picked their way through the bodies, ascertaining death for a certainty, Julian saw the men with the cameras.

"What's going on?" he asked Robert Roser, who had been assigned to watch him. Roser was a good man, and Julian couldn't help but like him. He was also well over six feet tall and big as a grizzly.

"Oh. Those men are from *Harpers*. You know, the paper."

Julian stopped, watching. They were taking pictures of the dead. Mostly Rebel dead.

"Doc," Roser said behind him. "It's a victory. We haven't had that many. Folks back home are going to want to see it."

Yes, the Northern papers would want pictures of Gettysburg. But did they really want women and children seeing scenes that were so horrible?

He started to turn away, then halted. The photographer was telling an assistant to move the bodies. To put them in more grotesque positions.

He stopped, turning as the man began to drag the dead around.

"They should be stopped," Julian said.

One of the men with them, a New Englander named Jim Brandt, spit into the dirt. "They should be stopped. But hell, they're from *Harpers,* we're just supposed to let them go."

"They're desecrating the dead."

Suddenly, they heard a groan.

"Dammit, someone is alive there!" Julian snapped. Followed closely by Roser, he strode over to where the photographers were working. The photographer, a man of perhaps thirty with muttonchops and a sleazy smile, ignored the groaning. He lifted the drape and looked through his lens, giving his assistant directions to move one of the men a little farther right.

"No, no, no!" the photographer snapped, coming around his camera. "I can't see his eyes, I can't catch the expression."

The dead couldn't defend themselves. Neither, at this point, could the injured man—wherever he might be. The photographer didn't seem to hear the groaning.

Julian placed himself directly in front of the man and his camera.

The photographer arched a brow, looking at Julian, his gaze sweeping over his worn and muddied Rebel uniform. "Get out of the way," he told Julian.

"There's an injured man in here somewhere. You get the hell out of the way."

The photographer laughed, looking at the men surrounding Julian. "You letting Rebs give the orders here, fellows?"

"Get out of the way. There's a living man here somewhere, and we're going to find him."

The groan came again. Julian spun around, realizing it was coming from one of the "dead" men that the photographer and his assistant were moving around for their perfect shot.

"There, that man's alive," Julian said, looking at Robert Roser.

"Leave him be. He's the enemy, and he'll be dead in another hour!"

Julian felt a torrent of pure anger, as red as the blood that stained the fields where so many had died. He strode forward with a menace that turned the photographer white, back-stepping quickly.

Not quickly enough.

Julian was before him, tight as a drum. The photographer took a wild swing at Julian. Julian ducked and came up swinging himself, catching the man hard in the jaw. The photographer's assistant came running, throwing himself on Julian. While Julian grappled with him, the photographer rose and once again tried to land a punch. Julian swung around—the photographer slugged his own assistant.

He swung around again, dropping the assistant on the muddy ground. The photographer took another swing at him. Julian retaliated, and the man went down. Once again, the assistant came up. They both tried to jump him, like children, attacking from both sides. A balled fist caught Julian's face, but he barely noticed it. He hooked the photographer's assistant with another right that made him squeal.

"I'm going to make you eat dirt!" the photographer shouted, hopping on Julian's back.

Julian fell to the ground with him and rolled. He pinned him with a wrestling hold that could have cut the air from the man's windpipe. He'd never felt such a tremendous temptation to kill in raw fury. It was as if a blanket of rage had fallen over him.

"Julian, Julian . . . Doc!"

It was Robert Roser. He was by him, helping him to his feet—and then pulling him back.

The photographer rose slowly, shouting at the Yanks. "What the hell is the matter with you boys? You a bunch of sissy cowards, you let this barbarian Reb attack me like that?"

"There's no cowards here," Jim Brandt told the man.

"We fought here. We died here. And you leave the dead the hell alone, do you hear?"

"I wasn't messing with the Yanks—"

"Don't mess with the Rebels, either!" Brandt said. "They weren't vultures, like you."

The photographer turned around to his assistant, who was dusting the dirt from his clothing. "Let's go, we'll find a better picture." He spun on Brandt, wagging a finger at him. "I'll report this. You can mark my word!"

As he stamped away, Brandt swore—and spat in the dirt again. "Bastard. Still, there's going to be hell to pay for this one."

Julian looked at him, and at Roser and the other Yanks lined up behind the two. The death detail. Maybe they'd all seen too much. "Thanks," Julian said quietly.

Brandt grinned. "I sure as hell would have loved to have gotten one of those punches in!"

"There will be hell to pay, you know. He'll go to the officers, he'll write up the way we cotton to our Reb prisoners," Roser said.

"McKenzie, honest to God, we're not all like that," Brandt told him.

"I know that. Hey, there are Southern monsters, too," Julian said wearily.

"He needed to be hit," Roser declared angrily.

Julian heard another groan. "Roser. Brandt . . . here. Come on, help me."

Julian walked back to the arranged pile of men. Their uniforms were covered in mud. He found the man, found him breathing, found a pulse.

"He's still alive, I don't know how!" Julian said.

Roser, Brandt, and some of the other men were at his side. "We'll get the stretcher," two privates, Lem Grady and Ash Yeagher, offered. It was hard moving across the fields. Although burial details were out, there were still bodies everywhere. The Feds wanted to know the identities of the men they were burying. Some of the fallen, if important enough in the military, might make it home to be buried among their own kin.

Some would lie in the earth, their names forever unknown.

So few remained alive. . . .

Like this poor fellow.

Julian tried to ascertain the injuries.

Unless he were missing something, the soldier wasn't so badly injured—a blow from a rifle butt when the enemy had run out of bullets had apparently been the cause of the wound. The wretched conditions on the field had brought on a fever. The soldier was barely conscious.

Roser stood next to him. "What is it, sir? Why, he ain't a Reb, is he?"

Julian looked up at him. "No, not a Reb. Not what he seems at all."

"What do you mean? We should get that *Harpers* fellow back."

"Yes, we should. He missed the real story here."

"What—"

"He's not a Reb, and he's not a 'he.' It's a woman."

Chapter 19

~~~

She had taken five bullets.

Amazingly, not one of them had punctured a vital organ, and although she was unconscious when they brought her into the hospital, she awoke soon after he had fished the last bullet out of her lower leg. She hadn't even broken a bone. Icy compresses had brought down her fever; he'd dosed her with quinine. After surgery, one of the plump, kindly women who followed along as a nurse had bathed her, dressed her in a clean white gown, and washed her hair. She was very young and very pretty, and when Julian came to see her, she was very grateful.

"They left me! Everybody just left me. But you . . . you're a Rebel, aren't you?" she asked.

He smiled, feeling her forehead for fever. She was so much cooler. Sometimes youth and a will to live were more important than any other factor.

"I'm a Rebel," he told her. "And you're a lucky young lady. Lucky to be alive. What were you doing in uniform."

"Fighting."

"You hate the Rebels so much?" he asked her.

She shook her head. Her eyes were big and blue, and her smile was sweet. "I had nothing left, that's all. My mother died when I was about three. My father was killed in the war, my brother was with the army . . . we couldn't pay our bills. Lost the farm. I came with Hank—that's my brother—into the army. Hank got killed in Virginia. I don't even remember what they called the battle. By then the men had accepted me . . . some knew, but they watched out for me 'cause I had been Hank's sister, and he was a right fine fellow."

"No more fighting," he told her.

"So what do I do?" she asked, her eyes round. "Want a nurse? I'd work with you, sir."

"I'm a prisoner here, like you said, a Rebel. But you can work as a nurse. I'll tell Dr. McManus to put you to work when you're well enough."

"Where will you be?"

"In prison."

She grinned. "My name is Sam Miller. Samantha, that is. I suppose I might as well be Samantha now."

"And I'm—"

"Dr. Julian McKenzie. I know. I asked. And you're all that anyone is talking about now."

"I have to go, Samantha."

"I know. They don't want that *Harpers* fellow getting any civilian authorities on you. They're afraid you'll wind up hanging yourself in some jail cell. But, sir, you saved my life. I will find you."

"Sam, it's not necessary—"

"I think it is." Her eyes were wide and very grave. "I love you, you see."

He hesitated. "Sam, that's wonderful. If any soldier was going to fall in love with me, I'm awfully glad it was you," he teased. "But . . . I have a wife."

Sam sniffed. "So I heard! She tricked you. She doesn't deserve you. I would do anything for you!"

"If you would do anything for me," he said sternly, "survive. Just survive the war, all right? And when you do, look us all up. We have a big plantation down outside of Tampa, in Florida."

She smiled. "I'll find you, sir."

"Take care of yourself."

He squeezed her hand and left her bedside. He passed by some of his other patients, amazed to feel a certain sorrow that he was leaving.

Robert Roser came up to him. "Sir, you're welcome to wash up a bit by the creek. Brandt and I will be escorting you to another facility soon."

"Thank you, Roser."

"We're sorry to see you go, sir."

"Believe it or not, I'm sorry to be going."

* * *

"Well, hell, who in God's name was going to stop him? They say that the fellow was arranging the dead, trying to make the battlefield look more gruesome. As if it weren't bloody enough! They say the Reb doctor nearly broke his jaw."

"Yeah, and what happened to the Reb doctor?"

At the mention of "Reb doctor," Rhiannon straightened from her task of checking the bandage on the arm of a soldier with a saber wound. The soldier looked up at her, aware that the gossip had caught her interest. "Don't pay no mind, ma'am, there was nothing bad happened."

The soldier's name was Axel Smith. He was young, with the 20th Maine. "What did happen?" Rhiannon asked him.

"Well, I don't know for certain." He grinned. "I've been here, you know."

"Corporal Smith—"

"Seems they were out hunting for wounded among the dead. Some photographers were on the field, and they were moving bodies around." He paused, watching for her reaction. Stories traveled like lightning in the aftermath of battle. The men she had treated knew who she was, and knew that she had lured the Rebel doctor into captivity, and that she had married him in the process. That they had known one another before, that they were both from Florida, enhanced the story.

"Please, go on."

"McKenzie stepped between the man and his business, so they say. I heard tell that the photographer started swinging first. But they say that your husband flattened him, ma'am, and that there wasn't a Yank soldier out there who was sorry to see it happen. One of the bodies they were trying to move around for their picture turned out to be a live Yank. Young girl at that."

"Girl!" Rhiannon said.

"Won't be the first time, ma'am, a woman's been found out to dress up to be in this war. Wives have put on uniforms to be with their husbands, sisters have come with their brothers, even sweethearts, and just a tart miss here or there who wanted to whip the opposing side. Just like, sometimes you see young fellows you know couldn't be over eighteen, like they say they have to be when they're enlisting forces. Fellows just write the number eighteen on a little piece of paper, stick it in their shoe, and say they're 'over' eighteen. Lots of folks have gone through great lengths to be in this war, ma'am. They just want to help in some way. Why . . . look at yourself."

"I just couldn't—" Rhiannon began, then broke off.

"You couldn't shoot a Southerner. 'Cause you are one," Axel Smith told her with simple logic.

"Maybe."

"They'll be taking Dr. McKenzie out of here, you know. There's going to be a big stink about a Rebel prisoner belting a fellow from *Harpers*."

"What do you mean? What will they do to him?"

"He can't stay here anymore, that's for sure."

Leave it to Julian, Rhiannon thought. She busied herself for a moment, pretending to adjust the bandaging, which was just fine. But tremors of fear were shooting through her. Just what had he done, how bad was it, what would they do to him? Why should she care? Whether he had gone through great extremes to marry her or not, his rejection of her had been blunt, determined—and painful. He'd wanted no part of her. He'd wanted to get away from her as fast as humanly possible.

But he claimed that they were legally married. And it was still true that . . .

"Mrs. McKenzie," Axel Smith said to her, studying her eyes with a kind light in his own, "if you want to see him before he's taken out of here, you'd best hurry up."

She nodded, straightening. She hurried down the hallway and down the stairs. At the door, she slipped out of the hospital smock she'd been wearing, smoothed back her hair, and hurried outside. As always, the trampled lawn outside the house was littered with soldiers, those who had been injured, awaiting transportation, or further orders. Cooking fires burned; soldiers played instruments. Orderlies and nurses brought water, coffee, and moved among the multitude of men. She was glad to see that Captain Jesse Halston was among the men outside. His arm bandaged and in a sling, he leaned against a tall oak.

"Jesse!"

She hurried out to him. "Jesse, I heard that—"

"Julian leveled that bastard from *Harpers*."

She paused. His hazel eyes were alight with amusement. "Jesse—"

"Don't worry so much, Rhiannon," he said, smiling with reassurance. "Our own men wanted to rip into the fellow. Don't you think the generals feel the same way? They're not going to let Julian be hanged or shot—"

"Hanged! Shot!"

"They'll be getting him out of harm's way," Jesse said softly.

"Where?"

"Where else? They'll take him back to Old Capitol. If you want to see him, you'd better hurry. You ride, right? Take Talisman over there. The bay. He's my own mount, a fine fellow. He'll take you to Julian—if he's not gone already."

"Thank you."

She spun around and tried to walk with dignity to the horse, yet she was running long before she reached him.

"You had to hit him. You just had to hit him!" an amused, deeply masculine voice accused.

Julian stood by a tall oak that grew by the little creek outside the field hospital. He'd stripped down completely to rinse in the shallow water, and now, in his breeches alone, he felt the coolness of the night coming to sweep away some of the summer's heat.

He knew the voice well, and turning, he grinned.

Ian had come.

He strode to his brother and embraced him. They held together for a long moment, then Ian drew away.

"It's pretty damned good if we're both here, still alive," Ian said.

"You were in the fighting."

"Tail end of it. We'd been routed around to find Jeb Stuart."

Julian looked out over the water. "I'm hearing bits and pieces of things. They say that Jeb failed Lee."

"Well, he didn't get his communications the way he usually did. And this was Lee's first major encounter without Stonewall Jackson."

"But Meade didn't pursue Lee," Julian said.

"I know." Ian sounded disgusted. And standing there,

Julian knew that they all just wanted it over. Ian touched his face. "Nice bruise."

"You should see the other guy."

"I heard." Ian exhaled on a long breath. "We can arrange an exchange, since you are medical, but it will take a little time."

"Ian, you don't have to—"

"Yes, I do. We share a father and mother, remember? They'll come north and whomp the daylights out of me—"

"Ian, they never whomped the daylights out of us."

"Yes, but they'll start now if they find out I didn't do my best to get my little brother freed—even if your new wife did get you here."

"So you heard."

"Yeah."

"Tricked . . . by a woman. Pretty humiliating, huh?"

"Julian—" Ian said, then paused. He shrugged. "She probably really did save your life. Magee told me about a couple of instances on the way here that were uncanny. It's not like she can read the future, but sometimes she has a flash of insight. If she was that determined . . ."

"Doesn't matter. It happened."

Ian nodded after a moment. "McManus is sorry to be losing you."

"He was a good man with whom to work."

"They're taking you to a farmhouse tonight. Tomorrow, on to Washington. They want the *Harpers* fellow to think you're already gone."

"I know."

Ian grinned. "Brought you a new shirt."

"Ian, I'm a Reb prisoner. You're not supposed—"

"Julian, swallow some pride. It's a plain white cotton shirt from home. You can wear your worn gray frock coat over it."

Julian nodded and reached for the shirt, slipping it over his head. "Thanks," he told Ian huskily. "I kept trying to wash that one, but some of the blood just wouldn't come out. So much blood, so many dead men. Sweet Jesus, Ian, I wish it would have ended here."

"Yeah," Ian said. "So do we all."

They heard a clip-clop of horses' hooves. Robert Roser

and Jim Brandt had come for him. "Colonel, sir!" they said, saluting Ian.

He saluted in return, then told Julian, "I'll see you again in the morning, right before you head out for D.C. Get some sleep. Apparently, the politicians may be outraged, but the soldiers on the field think you're a hero. You're getting a nice soft bed for the night."

"Good then, brother. In the morning," Julian said, heading for the horse Jim Brandt led for him to take. But he turned back. Hell, he might be seeing Ian in the morning, but the damned war just went on and on. He embraced his brother once again, then mounted at last. It was time to ride out.

Rhiannon reached McManus's field hospital quickly, dismounted, and hurried into the tented enclosure. Weaving her way through the injured, she tried to find Julian. She felt dismay curl around her heart as she failed to spot him. To the far side was a curtained enclosure. She lifted the canvas to slip inside.

There was a single bed there, a real camp cot, and not just a makeshift table, the type on which so many of the soldiers received surgery.

The occupant was female. A pretty girl, such a contrast to all around her! She was virginal in a white gown, with fresh-scrubbed cheeks, cropped rich sable hair, and blue eyes that seemed the color of the sky. To Rhiannon's surprise, she stared at her as if she were a loathsome enemy, and she was quite certain that they had never met before. She knew, of course, though, that this was the "soldier" Julian had found on the field.

"Hello, you seem to be doing well. Have you seen Dr. McKenzie?"

"You're his wife?"

"I—yes. Do you know where he is?"

"If I did, I wouldn't tell you."

"Oh?"

"You tried to get him killed."

"What?"

"When I'm well enough, I'm going to find him. He should be with someone who cares about him." The girl smoothed back her hair. "I'll live with him, and I won't care if you never give him a divorce. He hates you. He said so."

Rhiannon stared at the girl, amazed. She was a child and acting childishly. Julian would never share such information with a stranger. She didn't think. And yet she felt a strange fear in her heart, because whether Julian had said these things or not, they were true.

"Excuse me," she told the girl.

She closed the canvas curtain and hurried along the rows of wounded until she found Dr. McManus.

"Rhiannon, ah, child! I'm afraid he's gone—except that he might still be by the creek. He was bathing before the boys took him out."

"He's all right—" she began worriedly.

"Yes, Rhiannon. He's fine. They'll let no harm come to him."

She nodded, hurried outside, and looked anxiously around for the creek. One of the men—a bandaged stump for an arm—pointed the way for her. She ran down the trampled trail that led toward the water. Then she paused, inhaling, grateful. He stood there, alone. Someone had given him a new frock coat and plumed hat, and his head was bowed. He was watching the water.

Her heart slammed up to her throat. "Julian!"

She raced toward him. He could push her away, but . . . "Julian!"

She threw her arms around him as he turned. Then she gasped, deeply embarrassed, her fingers curling into the material of his frock coat.

"Ian!" she breathed.

"Rhiannon!"

"Oh, I'm sorry, so sorry!" she murmured, easing back from her toes to her heels, letting him go. But his hands were on her shoulders; his eyes were warm with light. "That felt good, actually. I miss my wife, and I know that she wouldn't begrudge me a hug from my new sister-in-law."

She felt her cheeks flood with color. "I didn't do it to hurt him."

"I know. I've seen General Magee."

"Ian, is he—"

"He's my brother. Do you think I'd let anything happen

to him for what he did—something that every man out there wanted to do? He didn't need my help or protection. All the Yanks were on his side. But don't worry. He's been taken away. The photographer can rant and rave, but he won't get near Julian. He'll be all right. They'll take him back to Washington."

"And you'll get him exchanged, won't you?"

"I'll do my best, yes."

She lowered her head. He lifted her chin. "If he knows that I'm getting him out, he'll bide his time. Left on his own, he might pull some fool stunt to escape."

"I know." She squared her shoulders. "I suppose I'll be back in Washington soon enough myself. I'll try to see him there."

Ian was studying her. "He is pretty angry with you," he admitted.

She shrugged. "I had to do it."

"Umm. General Magee told me you were frantic. But I'm curious. How on earth did you manage to trap Julian? I hadn't thought that you'd gotten on especially well—I mean, when we met, you did pass out because you thought that I was him returning. That hardly seems a case of undying devotion. What did you say to him to convince him to come and meet you—to *marry* you?"

She hesitated, started to lower her head, then shrugged. "I told him I was expecting his child."

Ian's expression was very much like one his brother might wear. "And it was a lie?"

Again, she hesitated. "No. I—I told him that I lied. He was pretty hateful. But . . . it's the truth." She winced, and spoke very softly. "I—I was addicted to opiates . . . I . . . well, you see, he was there. And I suppose I tried to make the night what I wanted it to be, with Richard, and oh, God, I can't believe that I—"

"It's all right, you don't have to explain anything to me," Ian said. "Come here."

He put an arm around her, pulled her against him, and smoothed back her hair. To her horror, she burst into tears.

She cried, and he soothed her. Finally, the overwhelming currents ended, and she was flooded with embarrassment once again. "I'm all right, really. I'm sorry. It's just . . ."

He lifted her chin. "If you could endure all those injured

men without crying, I'd be very sorry indeed that you had
married my brother."

She smiled. "Thanks. But I am all right. I'll be all right.
I know that you're looking after his welfare, and that's all
that really matters. I—"

"But you married him."

"But of course, it's not a real marriage, I'd never hold
him to it. I have to get back to Dr. Flowers now."

"That's who you're working with?"

"Yes, of course, you know that he's General Magee's
chief surgeon."

"And where are you staying? You're not still on the field,
are you?"

"No, no, I now have a little room with some of the other
nurses in the attic of an old farmhouse, the old MacIntosh
place. I'm fine, I'm in good hands. Thank you, Ian." On
her toes, she kissed his cheek, and then she turned around
and fled.

He had just put his head down on a pillow in the little
farmhouse that was his way station on the trip to Old Capitol when he heard a tapping at his door. "Julian!"

It was his brother's voice. He rose, frowning, and came
to the door. "Ian?"

"You were sleeping?"

Julian arched a brow. "Of course. Ian, I work from dawn
to dusk—"

"Yes, but you can sleep later. We have to take a ride."

Julian inhaled. "You're helping me to escape?"

"Sorry, I can't do that. But . . . the fellows and I . . ."
He paused, and turned, indicating that Jim Brandt and
Robert Roser were behind him. "We think that you should
have a wedding night."

His brow shot up higher. "Ian, the war may make a man
pretty desperate, but I'd prefer my own company to an
audience of the enemy, especially under the circumstances
of my marriage."

Ian sighed. "My boy, I can't help you if you won't help
yourself. No audience. Your wife is alone."

Julian frowned. "Alone? How? She knows about this?"

"Not exactly. So many nurses have been moved out that
she wasn't terribly surprised, so I heard, when General

Magee assigned her to private quarters—a little caretaker's house to the rear of the farm he took over as his hospital building."

His heart quickened. No . . . the whole of his body quickened. He could feel his own pulse, pounding in his ears. He looked beyond Ian, to Roser and Brandt. "You two are all right with this?"

"I said that you'd give them your word you wouldn't use the night for a chance to escape. And that McKenzies keep their word."

Julian nodded. "What about—"

"The Yanks whose lives you saved? I think they'll be all right with it," Ian said.

"But Rhiannon—"

"Well, that's up to you. No, she doesn't know you're coming. Well, of course, if you don't want to take this opportunity . . ."

"Let's go," Julian said.

They had a good mount for him to ride. They escorted him through a glade, across a field, and along a rear trail that circled the back of an old farmhouse. "That's it," Ian said, indicating one of the outbuildings far back. His horse pranced nervously. "Don't fall asleep. You have to be out before dawn."

"I wasn't planning on sleeping."

"There's one thing you should know."

"And what's that?"

"She is expecting a child."

Julian nodded. "Thanks." He dismounted from his horse and walked swiftly toward the small cottage.

She awoke swiftly with a sense of panic.

She'd heard . . . something.

It was a small cottage, two rooms, a bedroom, and a parlor and kitchen area with a big fireplace for heat and cooking. The fire had ebbed, and the light in the cottage was dim and misty. The windows were open to the cool night breeze, so something might have been knocked over.

She halfway rose, clutching the covers to her chest. Had she imagined that there was movement in the parlor area? General Magee had commandeered the farmhouse and all the outbuildings, and she wondered if the owners, put out of their own home, had come back.

Or maybe it was a deserter, someone out to harm her. She was always in Magee's protection, and the officers were so respectful of her and so careful, she had forgotten to be afraid. But now she was alone.

She picked up a heavy brass candlestick by the bedside and crawled out of the bed. Carefully, on her toes, she made her way across the room. She tiptoed into the parlor, toward the door.

Then she heard a sound behind her. She spun around, her candlestick swinging.

"No, ma'am, I don't think so!"

The harsh voice terrified her. She opened her mouth to scream as the candlestick was wrenched out of her hands. The candlestick clattered to the floor, and she was lifted, a hand clamped firmly over her mouth. She kicked wildly, struggling. She tried to bite the fingers that crushed her mouth.

"Rhiannon, you are a damned witch!"

Rhiannon . . . He'd used her name.

Her panic subsided; her anger rose. He was walking through the doorway to the bedroom with her, and she was shaking so badly she couldn't have hit him if she'd tried. How in God's name had he come here? Why hadn't he said something? Why had he scared her to death?

She felt herself flung back on the bed with him atop her. She came back to life again, struggling to push him off, to sit up. She had wanted to see him so desperately, wanted to touch him, to know that he was all right.

"Stop it, damn you!" he swore. "I've borne enough indignity, and I'll be damned if I'm going to let you kick me and cripple my intentions!"

"Your intentions?"

"You married me, remember?"

"Julian, we're on a battlefield."

"No, we're in a cottage. On a bed. Damned good place, the way I see it."

She couldn't breathe. She wanted him. Wanted him more than she had that night that seemed so long ago now, when she had been so lonely and drugged. She couldn't remember Richard's face tonight, and it didn't even matter; Richard would have understood. She craved Julian, even the harsh feel of his hands, his scent, the lean hardness of his body, the feel of his lips, the touch of his eyes . . .

And yet he was so angry. There were women who did not madden him, women who fell passionately beneath his spell, like the young soldier girl with the huge blue eyes he had taken from the field, from death . . .

"Julian, no, this isn't right!" she stated firmly.

"Oh?" He rolled from her, a brow arched. Propped on an elbow, he gazed down at her. She steeled herself to keep from reaching out to stroke his jawline.

"No."

She rose, wishing she had a robe. She was clad in a bleached muslin nightdress that kept falling from her shoulders, leaving her no dignity. She walked to the foot of the bed, staring back at him. "You're a prisoner, Julian. They'll come hunting you down. You've got to get back."

"Oh?"

He rose as well, walking toward her. She backed away from him. "Yes. You're in danger."

"Am I really? In danger, from more than you?"

"Julian, if they catch you—"

"Yes?"

"You're an escaped prisoner. They might kill you."

"What if I were to say that a night with you was worth it?"

"I'd call you a liar."

"I'm not leaving."

"You know, I could scream, I could summon the Yanks."

"Yes, you've done so before."

"Yes."

"But I eluded them."

"Not here."

"I'll take my chances."

"Julian, I know what you feel. In fact, I was told in no uncertain terms today by the girl you plucked from the battlefield that you hated me."

He paused, a smile curling his lip. "She told you that?"

She lowered her eyes, irritated that her voice became so low. "It wasn't necessary for you to tell people—"

"I told her I had a wife."

"You have to get out of here, Julian. You don't have a real wife."

"What I don't have," he stated, "is a great deal of time!"

With that, he reached for her, so suddenly and with such fierce determination that a soft cry left her lips. She was swept up, and before she could move, his mouth came crashing down on hers. Hard, demanding, his kiss ravaged with passion and ardor. She tried to twist, and could not, and though she felt his anger, she couldn't fight, didn't want to resist. Her lips parted to his savage assault. The sweep of his tongue ignited fires deep within her. She pressed her hands against his shoulders, then just her fingertips. He walked with her, and again she felt the softness of the mattress against her back. And he was above her, straddling her. His fingers fell on the buttons of the simple muslin gown.

His mouth was on hers again, savage, demanding, fierce. His hands tugged at the buttons of the gown, then gave up, and with an impatient oath he ripped it apart. The surgeon who could perform the most delicate of operations could not deal with the tiny buttons. And it didn't matter, because his hands, his talented, supple hands were on her bare flesh, thumbs teasing her nipples, palms caressing . . .

The sensations burned like molten silver straight to a center between her thighs. She gasped as his lips trailed the touch of his hands, as his tongue curved around her breasts, as his fingers lowered in a long stroke down her side. Her fingers curled into his hair, tugging at his head.

Then his hands were on her thighs. His touch was between them. His lips were on hers again, and she was returning his kiss with a fierce explosion of hunger all her own. Her fingertips fell on his throat, his shoulders. He moved long enough to strip away his shirt, shed his boots and breeches. The remnants of her nightgown touched the floor, and the searing fullness of his body brought its heat against her. His limbs entwined with hers. She felt the hardness of his erection against her flesh, and the longing and excitement she felt brought a flush to her cheeks, even in the darkness, even though they lay alone together.

His fingers entwined with hers. His mouth covered hers, then moved to her throat, to her breasts. His body shimmied against the length of hers, until he lay between her thighs. She closed her eyes, fingers tautly vised with his. She gasped, embarrassed again at the wave of windswept pleasure that engulfed her with the intimate stroke of his touch and tongue. She writhed, twisting, squirming, rocking, wanting more, fighting the unbearable waves of ecstasy that threatened to spill and splash and engulf her . . .

And suddenly he was with her. Moving, thrusting, rocking, soaring. Her arms locked around him, released. Her fingers danced over his shoulders, kneaded, clung, embraced. His lips found hers again as his body drove and retreated and brought her even higher. The world erased, pain faded, and for brief shining moments all she knew was the splendor of being in his arms, of the ecstasy that shot through her like fireworks against a velvet heaven. She held fast to him, trembling, shaking, jerking, holding closer and closer and burying her face against the sleekness of his shoulder. And finally she lay against him, silent in the night.

After a few minutes, she felt his knuckles brushing lightly over her cheek. "Well worth any risk," he whispered. Then he shifted slightly, pulling the drapery behind the bed, looking out at the night, or the coming dawn—she didn't know which, she had no idea of the time. Then she felt his eyes on her.

"Is the child mine?" he asked her.

"The child . . ." she murmured. She didn't know why his question put such unease into her. "I . . . but I told you—"

"The child, Rhiannon. It must be mine."

"Yes—" she began, and broke off. Of course. He had seen Ian. Ian had arranged her housing. Ian was outside somewhere now. They might be at war, but Julian was his brother.

"I didn't think that your brother would see you again for some time," she said tautly. She gazed back at him, her anger growing. "Worth any risk, sir? Is your brother waiting at the door?"

"He would never be so rude."

"But he's near?"

"Yes."

She tried to twist away from him. "Julian, damn you—"

He straddled her, catching her wrists. "Ah, music to my ears! Say it again."

"Damn you, Julian, let me up—"

"No." His eyes seemed to invade her very soul again. "Not yet."

"Julian . . ."

This time his kiss was slow. As if he tasted every fragment of her being. And when he had finished with her lips, she was filled with slow, sweet-burning fire again, and with a hunger that grew more voracious again with each passing second. She needed to touch him, kiss him, feel him. Her lips found his shoulders, his chest. Her fingers caressed the muscle that jerked and trembled beneath them. She moved against him, the length of her hair winding around the sleek dampness of his flesh. She grew desperate, suddenly more aware than he that time was slipping away.

She touched him, caressed him, made love to him. Most intimately took him into her mouth. The world seemed to spin to an ever more blissful rhythm as his hoarse whispers filled her ears, as passion seized him and he swept her hard beneath him, into his heated embrace. They seemed to dance. She felt his every movement, the searing warmth of his sleek, damp body, the force of his rhythm . . . and she felt she touched the sky, and she wished that she could stay in his arms.

She felt the massive tension in his body, the shuddering that swept him as he climaxed, and then the simple wonder of being in his arms as they drifted down.

Yet not sweet. For he was instantly up, and looking out the curtains once again.

She reached for the sheets, hugging them. "You're—you're not going to try to escape?" she asked.

He looked at her, shook his head as he stumbled into his clothing. "I gave my word," he said simply. Then dressed, he came back to her side.

"You are going to have a child—and it is mine?" he asked, gently lifting her chin.

"Yes."

"Take care of the babe, and yourself. Get off the battlefield."

"But—"

"Work in Washington if you must. But get off the battlefield."

"Julian—"

He kissed her lips lightly. "Until we meet again."

"You're a prisoner, Julian—"

"In more ways than you know, my love. But I will not remain so long. That I promise you."

His lips touched hers briefly once again.

Then he was gone.

Chapter 20

❧

As the news came in about the terrible clash of arms at Gettysburg, Brent couldn't help but feel the weight of resentment. Men were dying. Men had been left behind. The injured died on the field for lack of help, they died in the ambulances on the march home, they suffered in anguish, and they died.

But here he was . . . With the ladies.

He sat at his desk, late, reading the dispatches that had come in from the front. With every word, he felt more powerless, more pained. So many dead. But the war would go on. The Union general, Meade, had not pursued Lee. Lee was deeply distraught, ready to resign his position. He accepted the blame for what had happened, yet he had once again made good an escape with the bulk of his army. Lee was revered; he had held together an army and found victories where few men could. Brent was certain that they would not let Lee go until the bitter end.

"Doctor!"

He looked up. Letty Canby, a pretty young woman of about twenty, stood in the doorway. Letty had come here suffering from something as simple as crabs. She was round, cheerful, and big breasted. She was very popular with the men, even those who were already suffering from their affairs with the ladies of the night.

"Hello, Letty, what is it? It's very late."

"I know that, and I see you in here working, and so very sad!"

She walked into his hospital office and perched on the corner of his desk. She never bothered with a corset or petticoats, or any piece of feminine apparel that might detract from her natural assets. She had a tiny waist and flaring hips.

"Now, you're almost smiling!" she told him happily.

"Letty, I have to admit, I was thinking that you've the perfect personality for your chosen profession."

She pouted, looking at him. "What does that mean?"

He shook his head. "No insult intended, Letty. You're a sweet girl, full of fun and life. I'm just sorry that your chosen vocation is eventually going to hurt you."

Letty tossed her head. "Dr. McKenzie, I was making a fortune in this war. Working for the Union soldiers first." She grinned. "They have this general, General Hooker. And he was so fond of procuring female entertainment for himself and his men that they began to call us 'Hooker's girls.' He had good wine, champagne, silk stockings from Paris! I was doing well . . ."

"And then?"

She frowned. "Well, I had this ridiculous rush of patriotism sweep through me! I had to come home."

"Where was home?"

"Richmond. Before the war it was a decent place for a young woman to work. A good clientele, men into Virginia politics, you know. Rich fellows with big plantations, lots of slaves—and sometimes, fat, sassy wives who didn't know how to lose their pantalettes! I do declare, the things they will teach women . . . anyway, it makes for good business for an enterprising soul such as myself."

Brent leaned back, lacing his fingers behind his head, smiling. "So you decided to ply your trade patriotically."

She nodded. "It was wonderful for a while. I have this special for Southern soldiers. I call it the Rebel Yell."

"Clever."

"Want to find out how clever?" she asked coyly.

"Thanks, Letty, but—"

"For free, of course, Dr. McKenzie. You've done so much for all of us here . . . oh, and I admit, it's not all that often we get a chance at a fellow like you these days . . ."

"Thank you, Letty. That's quite a compliment. But you're my patient."

"I can be much more."

"Letty—"

She giggled. "You won't catch anything. I'm clean now.

And besides, you've taught us all about those little French hat things." Letty made a face. "We can use a condom."

"Letty, you're my patient, I'm your doctor."

"And you really want to go back to the war, right?" she asked sadly.

He nodded. "Yeah, I guess I do, Letty. So many men were wounded at Gettysburg."

"Dr. McKenzie!"

As his name was called from the doorway, Brent looked up. Mary stood there. It amazed him that she could always appear so fresh, young, and both competent and innocent.

Since he had come, she had been his mainstay, more than the orderlies, more than any of the other religious and moralistic matrons who had come here to help these misbegotten creatures who were still God's children. She was an excellent nurse, careful of her patients and herself. When he was working with patients, she followed him, anticipating his needs, keeping records for him, excellent records. "Oh, yes, some of us do read and write!" she had told him when she had first offered him her assistance. His temptation had been to turn her down. But she lived at the hospital because of Captain Henderson. She was there, she was convenient. And the more she worked with him, the more he came to depend on her. He was too harsh with her, he knew.

But he felt that she was throwing away her life, that she had already thrown away her life. And it was just such a terrible waste. She was so young, startlingly beautiful, intelligent, compassionate . . . and of course, totally foolish.

"What is it, Mary?"

"If you could come with me . . . I think it's the end."

He stood quickly. Her devotion to Captain Henderson had been perplexing, but he had grudgingly begun to understand it. Henderson had been a good man, a hero to his men. He had never asked a soldier to charge into battle before him; when danger threatened, he had been at the lead. He had known every man by name, written every widow personally, supplied every need he could from his personal fortune. Men had followed him out of respect, not out of fear. He had heard more and more about the fellow daily from others being treated here, but no one ever mentioned his relationship with Mary.

He rose. "Excuse me, Letty."

"Sure. Mary, I'm so so sorry," Letty said. "Hey, Dr. Mc-Kenzie, you keep thinking about my offer."

"All right, Letty."

He felt Mary's gray eyes touch on him briefly, and he thought he heard a little sniff of disdain. "Offer, sir?" she murmured as they walked along the hall.

He glanced at Mary, surprised at her interest. She had helped him, but she had kept a rigid distance from him. She had refused to become his patient, even when he had explained her chances of having contacted disease. "Letty can't imagine that any red-blooded male could refuse her, no matter what the risks."

"Ah, and yet . . . you can refuse her?"

He glanced at her. "She's my patient."

"But I'm not. Could you refuse me?" she inquired.

Brent hesitated, staring at her, surprised at the way his body constricted, at the sudden thickness in his throat. "I intend to survive the war," he told her.

She smiled. "Don't worry. You won't hurt my feelings. I wasn't offering. I just wondered if you were really righteous enough to turn down all offers."

He stopped dead in the hallway, spinning her around so that she was forced to face him. "I don't understand you, Mary. You have everything. Beauty, youth, and intelligence. And you've thrown away your life. No, I wouldn't accept your offer. Don't you understand, unless you can change your way of life, there isn't going to be a good offer out there. There won't be marriage, there won't be a family, a home—"

"I don't think you understand," Mary interrupted furiously. "There won't be any of the usual things out there after this war! Haven't you heard? The South is losing. Gettysburg was a disaster for us. Men are dead, and we can't get them back. I've read the news accounts. There were fields of dead men. If some of those young fellows died after a taste of a whore like Letty, then by God, at least they got to live before they died! Who do you think you are? What right have you got to condemn others?"

He shook his head, startled, and somewhat shamed. But he wasn't about to tell her that.

"Captain Henderson," he said softly, for they had come

to the door. "Captain Henderson. Look at him, and tell me that I don't have a right to hate this disease."

The wind seemed ripped from her sails. Her eyes were brilliant as silver stars as tears threatened to spill from them. They entered the room.

Henderson couldn't breathe, he was gasping for every breath. Along with that, a low keening sound was coming from him, as if he were being pierced by thousands of knifes. He wasn't really conscious, but tears appeared in his half-closed eyes and ran down his cheeks. The sound of his anguish was terrible. Brent walked to the bed and sat beside the man.

"Can you do anything?"

"I can give him more morphine."

"Can you spare it?" she asked worriedly.

He spun on her suddenly. "No, we can never spare it," he said bitterly. "But we will. God help us all, we'll have to get more from somewhere."

He rose to get the morphine. She touched his arm, looking up into his eyes. "For this I have to thank you . . . I owe you."

He gritted his teeth. "You owe me?"

She stepped back. "Yes, you self-righteous bastard, I do owe you."

He didn't know what demon seized him then, but he reached for her hand, drawing her close to him. "Fine, Miss Mary. You owe me. Maybe I am as red-blooded as every other damned male in this war. Ready to take a few chances with a French hat! You owe me, fine. I won't expect anything right away. Because you know that we're going to bury your captain after tonight. But after that, hell yes, lady, you can pay up. Is that a promise?"

Her eyes were wide with disbelief.

"Is that a promise?"

"Yes!" she hissed, amazed.

He strode out of the room to get the morphine.

At midnight that night, Captain Henderson died. Mary tenderly touched his ravaged face, then pulled the sheet over him.

Watching her, Brent couldn't help but feel pain and empathy. "I'm sorry, truly sorry."

She looked up at him, tears glazing her eyes, but a

strange strength in them as well. "I'm grateful that his suffering is over."

"There was nothing . . ."

"I know."

"I'll leave you with him for a while."

He exited the room, leaning back against the door as he closed it. Henderson had died an awful death. Life was fickle and could be cruel. Such a man had not deserved such a fate.

He listened to the woman inside as she sobbed, taut with empathy for the pain she was feeling. He wished that he could comfort her. He walked slowly down the hall, summoning an orderly and telling him that they would need a coffin for Captain Henderson.

He went back to his paperwork. The hospital was quiet. He finished a report, then rose again, returning to Henderson's room. She still sat by his side, but her tears were over.

"I am sorry."

"I'm glad that he's passed on," she said. She looked at him and managed a smile. "I've known it, he hasn't been himself, he's been dying . . . it's a relief. He suffered so horribly, and now the suffering is over. I will miss him. But I'm glad that he's passed away, that it is over."

He nodded, leaned against the door. She rose, coming toward the door. She arched a brow to him. "May I get by you, Dr. McKenzie?"

"Yes, of course. Mary, I've asked for a coffin. We'll have him laid out so that mourners can pay their respects, but we'll keep it a closed coffin. We'll have a service for him tomorrow."

"Thank you."

"The men here admired him. I heard nothing but good things about him."

"He was a good man. A wonderful man. Kind and giving. Loyal, generous, dependable. His sin was loneliness."

"That's not a sin, Mary."

He moved, opening the door for her. She started out, then turned back to him. "By the way, Dr. McKenzie, I never slept with Captain Henderson."

She smiled, and began to leave again, intending, he realized, to leave him doubtful and puzzled. But she was the one who had brought it up. He caught her arm, pulling her back. "What?"

"I never slept with him," she said, and he was surprised by her sudden anger as she added sharply, "You ass! He was my father."

He gritted his teeth and forced a smile. She had set out to make a fool of him. She had carefully kept that information from him for weeks. She had allowed him to spout off time and time again.

She had just lost a man she had loved, he reminded himself. Ah, but she had started this! He could feel entirely justified in responding. "All the better, my dear. I won't feel half so tainted when you pay your debts."

She went white, staring at him. Then she turned and started running down the hall.

"Mary!" he called after her.

But too late.

She was gone.

And he was left alone with the dead man she had rightly loved.

"It seems that we're insistent on having someone here by the name of McKenzie."

Julian stood by the window in his small room, and looked out on the late afternoon where the citizens of Washington moved along the sidewalks and streets as they went about their daily business. It was an interesting prison. From here, he knew, the Confederate spy Rose Greenhow had received messages and sent them along.

He turned, smiling at the sound of his cousin's voice. Sydney moved across the room, coming into his arms for a long, tight hug. At last he released her. Sydney was still stunning, perhaps more so with the maturity gained through years of the war. Her Indian heritage gave her a slightly exotic appearance that was mysterious and compelling. Her eyes were her mother's green; her hair was incredibly rich, thick, heavy, and dark, her father's gift from his Seminole blood.

"I understand I have your room," he told her.

"Yes, same room. They must reserve it for McKenzies. We're privileged, you know. Not everyone is deserving of such private space."

"Umm." He crossed his arms over his chest. "And I understand that you managed your release by marrying a Yankee?"

She looked right back at him. "Well, at least I managed my *release*. It's my understanding that you managed your *capture* by marrying a Yankee."

"Touché, cousin," he murmured.

But the smile she had given him quickly faded. "I heard that Jesse was injured again. That it was a serious injury. And that you operated on him."

"He's going to be all right, I believe."

"So you did do the surgery?"

"Yes." He hesitated a moment. "Sydney, you didn't want him to die, did you?"

"God, no!" she gasped. Then her cheeks flooded with color and she shook her head. "He was a friend . . . more than a friend. He was injured before. I was his nurse when he was brought to Richmond. He's known Ian."

"Yes, they're both regular cavalry."

"It was an important prisoner for the Rebs, so he was to be exchanged for Jerome when the Federals were holding him here. Only someone changed things at the last minute, and Jesse was exchanged for someone else. But Jerome had no intention of staying, as you know, and during the escape, Jesse caught hold of me and warned that if I tried to leave with Jerome, he'd call out an alarm. Because . . . because he thought I'd be in danger running with Jerome. But I was furious, he went back to war. And then . . . well, I had gotten familiar with the prison here, and they'd brought in some new people—much more decent than some of the wretches holding Jerome! So I started coming to see to the Reb prisoners. And naturally, I began to find out all kinds of information regarding the war . . ."

"And passed it on?" Julian asked.

"It seemed the right thing to do with information," Sydney said.

"After Jennifer was nearly hanged? After everything that went wrong with Alaina?"

She stared at him. "Well, men are shot daily, and still more and more of them go to war!"

"There's not a lot of choice for a man," he told her.

"Not true. There's not a lot of choice for a woman."

"Sydney—"

"Well, there's the whole point. You, Ian, Jerome, Brent, my father, your father—well, you would all think it your sacred duty to protect me from the trouble I had gotten myself into. I told Rhiannon that when she was here. And I asked for her help."

"So she went to Captain Jesse Halston."

Sydney nodded. "Well, it seems that General Magee still believes that we're all better off being in prison. But, though I hate to admit it, since Jesse is the one who escorted me here as a prisoner, he was decent about getting me out. He didn't have much choice. He came here, we were married, he warned me not to become involved in espionage in any way, and then he rode off to join the army. And he did so in time to reach the fighting at Gettysburg." Her voice, at the last, was bitter. "Julian, I heard that he was hit in the shoulder, that it was a serious wound."

"He came through the surgery fine."

Sydney bit her lower lip. "Was Rhiannon with you when you operated on him?"

"Yes."

"Well, then, maybe he does have a chance."

Julian lowered his eyes, wondering whether or not to be resentful that his own flesh and blood could find faith in his ability only once she had learned that his wife had been with him.

"Well, I'm curious. How did you come to meet Rhiannon and discover her special talents?"

"She didn't tell you?" Sydney asked.

"We really never had much time to talk."

"Well, of course not, knowing the male McKenzie temper—"

"Excuse me. The *male* McKenzie temper?"

"I didn't sock a photographer from *Harpers*."

"You weren't there. You would have torn his hair until he was bald if you had been," Julian assured her.

Sydney smiled. "There's a young private here who had a serious foot injury. I thought that he would have to have it amputated. But Sergeant Granger, the fellow on the desk, suggested that we see her . . . and she was like magic. She has an ability, a talent . . . her hands heal."

"Umm, she has talents, all right," Julian murmured.

"Risa had sent her up here. If my sister-in-law thought enough of her to send her to work with her father . . . well, she worked magic on Private Lawton. I know your abilities. So I know that if Jesse had any chance at all . . . well, he had that chance with the two of you. Now, as to getting you out of here—"

"Sydney, wait!" he said softly.

"What?" she asked, beautiful eyes wide.

"Sydney, you can't be involved in getting me out of here."

"But—"

"You swore to this man that you wouldn't become involved in espionage."

"Well, of course, but this is different."

He took both her hands. "No, Sydney. It's not." He shook his head. "Sydney, they won't keep me that long. I'll be exchanged."

Sydney looked at him, frowning, then shook her head. "Julian. They've lots of injured Rebel prisoners. They're on a high! They believe that the battle so recently fought at Gettysburg was the turning point of the war, that they've found out how to beat us, that the Rebs haven't the strength to be a real threat to the North. And Vicksburg has fallen. The Yanks can choke us freely now on the Mississippi. Julian–"

"Sydney, I will not have you involved."

"If Jesse becomes angry–" she began with a toss of her head.

"It has little to do with his anger," Julian warned her. "He is probably responsible for you. And if you betray him, he is probably the one who will pay the price."

"He shouldn't have arrested me."

"What choice did he have? He's a Yankee. You were exchanging information that was hurting the Northern war effort."

"But if he had lo—"

"If he had what?"

She flushed. "If he had cared for me, he wouldn't have arrested me."

Julian threw up his hands. "Sydney! It's a war. He is a Northerner." He shook his head. "You've seen what war does to families. You can't expect a man to go against his beliefs."

"I want to go home, Julian."

"But you married him."

"I said that I wouldn't spy. I never said that I wouldn't go home. And if I helped you escape, I could go home with you—"

"Sydney, that would be the same as when Jerome escaped."

She shook her head stubbornly. "Jerome is a blockade runner. The Yanks hate him; he's made a fool of them time and time again. The Yanks don't hate you—you've saved body parts for far too many of them!"

"I assure you, there are Yanks who hate me. But Sydney, Ian knows I'm here."

"Oh? And what is Ian going to do? Say, 'My brother is with the medical department, you should let him go'?"

Julian shrugged. "Maybe. You never know."

"Well, I do have a plan, you know."

"Oh?"

"One that has worked before."

"You want me to dress up like one of the singing Irish ladies as Jerome did?"

Sydney arched a brow indignantly. "Don't be silly, they would recognize that ruse immediately."

"Then—"

"A coffin," she said somberly.

"A coffin?"

"When the dead are being brought out . . . you crawl in with them. It's worked well on many occasions. And God knows, there will be plenty of dead men with all the injured from the battle at Gettysburg."

He opened his mouth to protest.

But he paused.

Sydney had a point. There were so many men who were dead . . . and dying.

Coffins were abundant. Ian would do what he could, yes. But how long would it take?

As they stared at one another, church bells began to toll. They had been tolling frequently since he had arrived for all the prominent Yankee officers who had made it from the battlefield only to die in the hospitals.

Here, in the Yankee capital, the Rebs were not so mourned. All that awaited them was . . .

Coffins.

And transport home.

South.

In the days that followed the great clash at Gettysburg, the Union army began making some movements toward stopping the Southerners. Rhiannon knew what went on—and what didn't go on—because of General Magee.

The long, exhausting, endless hours—in which day turned into night turned into day again—immediately after the battle at last began to come under control; injured men were treated, then sent on to hospitals or sent home for convalescence.

The Rebs were treated, and sent on to hospitals, or prisons.

Many were buried in hastily dug graves not far from the field hospitals where they had perished from their wounds.

But finally, many of those who could be moved were moved. The numbers of men to care for became manageable as the injured were dispersed. Some would stay on at Gettysburg for a long time, under the care of patriotic Yanks. Some went on to Harrisburg. And like the Rebs, some of them died, and were hastily buried. Organized graves would have to come later. At times, Yanks embraced their Rebel brothers in death and into the ground, for the numbers were so terrible to deal with, and the threat of disease from the tens of thousands of bodies was so great to the living that such small indignities had to be done to the dead.

The hospital at the farmstead where she worked began to function under more normal hours. General Magee began to return for set meals and to have a few precious hours at night where he could put his feet up, rest, correspond—or talk to her. And since he had very firm opinions about what was going on, he kept her well informed. They should have moved—immediately. Lee must be shaking his head over the Union army. No wonder the Rebs were convinced they could win the war despite the numerical and technical superiority of the North. The Yanks couldn't get a single man in charge with the capacity to fight.

Lincoln was delighted with the victory—and beside himself with frustration over what had happened since. The Rebs were slipping away. Meade believed that his troops were just too exhausted to risk another encounter with Lee.

But then, Meade planned an attack and took it to a "council" of generals. A few of the generals vetoed his plan.

Lincoln's response was swift and angry. Meade wasn't to have a council with his generals, he was to give orders, and they were to go after the defeated and retreating Confederates. There had been some fighting, at Boonsborough, Maryland, at Williamsport, Maryland, but Meade never gave the order that would send the army in force after the Rebs.

By mid-July, Meade finally moved large forces after Lee. Word had come by then of draft riots in New York. At least a hundred people had been killed or wounded. Churches had been burned, there had been massive destruction. Despite the success of Gettysburg and what might be a real turning point, there were those Northerners who wanted nothing more of war.

Toward the end of July, Rhiannon found herself on the move again with General Magee's forces. They moved southward into Virginia. Magee's cavalry became involved with skirmishes as bands of Union and Confederate soldiers met, clashed, and withdrew.

Most often at night, she lay awake, afraid to sleep—afraid to dream.

She had parted ways with Jesse Halston at Gettysburg. He would be convalescing at Harrisburg before returning to a quieter duty in Washington or to his cavalry troops. She had written to Sydney, though, of his condition, and asked about Julian. There had been no reply. To the best of her knowledge, Julian remained at Old Capitol, safe. There were many prisoners for him to treat. Ian had come to see her, telling her that it would be late summer or early fall before he could arrange for an official transfer. She needn't worry; Julian knew he was only biding his time. He wouldn't do anything reckless.

Meade camped near Warrenton, Virginia. September began with hot weather that turned chill at night. Rhiannon found herself busy enough, because Meade, though he wouldn't actually move his army further at the moment, found his troops engaged whether he liked it or not— Southern guerillas came to him and his supplies. The days simply seemed long, sometimes busy, sometimes dull, and still, far too often, tragic. Helplessly holding a gut-shot boy while he died one afternoon after a skirmish that involved no more than two companies, she wondered what difference it made when a man died in a great battle or because a single shot was fired.

In mid-September, she found herself haunted by snatches of a nightmare that involved a child. He was little more than a toddler, a handsome boy, but she could never really see his face. He seemed to walk a fence, teetering along it. Behind him, she heard the explosions of cannon fire. All around her, the landscape seemed cast in shades of darkening yellow as the sun fell, and sunset was like the drenching of an artist's pallet in red. Men shouted, horses screamed, and she saw Julian running again, across the terrain where the dead and dying lay . . .

She woke one night from the dream in a deep sweat. She was glad to have awakened. She didn't understand the dream. It wasn't telling her anything that she could comprehend, that she could use to help anyone.

Julian remained in Old Capitol.

Then she started, feeling a subtle fluttering in her abdomen. She didn't know what it was at first, then realized that it was her child. She gasped, rising in wonder, thinking she had imagined it. But then it came again, and she found herself laughing, and then silent tears eased down her cheeks. Death surrounded her, she didn't know what the future would bring, but life was so wonderful.

Julian had been furious with her for tricking him into captivity, but he was alive. So no matter what his feelings toward her, this child had a father. She wanted him in prison. It was safe in prison.

Yet, the next morning, she couldn't help but find herself disturbed when she listened to some of the soldiers talking over coffee.

"We sit here and sit. And Lee regroups," complained a sergeant bitterly.

"If the generals would let the enlisted men fight this thing, we might have won by now," replied a worn private.

"Gettysburg, Vicksburg . . . hey, and did you hear? They've got that Belle Boyd locked up in Old Capitol again."

"Ah, she won't stay long! Have you ever seen the woman? Now, there's some Southern hospitality for you! She's flirted her way out of captivity before, she'll do it again!"

"Well, they're certainly entertaining the Washington press."

"They?"

"The Rebel doctor, McKenzie. She came in with a fever, and he treated her."

The men started laughing.

Rhiannon retired to her camp tent, sat on the bed, and started shaking. She clenched her hands into fists, jealousy washing over her. She'd never seen Belle Boyd, but the Southern spy was supposed to be a rare beauty. And now Belle Boyd was locked up with Julian. Who had married her, but loathed her.

It didn't matter, as long as he stayed alive! she told herself. But it hurt. Oh, Lord, did it hurt. With Richard, she had known peace in her marriage. But she hadn't wanted to love Julian. But he had come to her . . . She had touched him, known him.

Death would be an agony she didn't know if she could bear again. But there was no way out of a simple truth either—love was anguish all in itself.

He was a captive; he was safe, she tried to tell herself. But the next night, she began to dream again. And she dreamed of him in a coffin . . .

Chapter 21

〜

Sydney started for the door, stopped, and spun around. As she had suspected, Sissy was behind her. Sissy watching over her had been part of her deal for freedom.

She and Marla still shared an apartment—with Sissy. She hadn't moved into her new husband's quarters because her new husband wasn't there. He had, in fact, rather dispassionately told her that she could obtain an annulment easily if he was to fall in battle. If she hadn't felt so terribly resentful and off guard that night, she would have told him that he couldn't fall, that she couldn't believe that God would be so cruel as to allow the death of such a fine man. But she was still bitter and afraid of what was happening— and God had allowed the deaths of far too many fine men already. He had been hurt again, her cousin had probably saved his arm and his life, and she could only pray that wherever he was, he was recuperating.

Marla, she thought, had been glad to end their spying days. She had been passionate and reckless at first, but then more uneasy. And since the night when Sydney had been taken—and she had claimed she'd heard the howling of the banshees, she had been afraid.

Jesse had gone to see Marla before coming to Old Capitol the night he had married and freed Sydney. He had explained that they had been caught, that there was to be no more activity, that Sissy would remain with them until he could return to Washington, D.C., and make new arrangements for his wife.

Marla readily accepted the situation. Naturally, they had both been cold and rude to Sissy, but the beautiful young black woman hadn't noticed. She followed Sydney everywhere. At the prison, oddly enough, she didn't insist on sitting in on Sydney's conversations with her brother, but she waited outside, ready to follow Sydney once again after she left the prison.

"Well, are you ready?"

"Of course, Mrs. Halston."

Sydney lowered her lashes, thinking that Sissy had a way of being polite while mocking her at the same time.

"We're going to Old Capitol—"

"I know."

Sydney studied the black woman pointedly. "You've nothing to say? No lectures, no warnings? Don't go helping any Rebs escape, ma'am, you'll hang, and I'll see to it that the noose is properly tied?"

Sissy returned her gaze steadily. "Miss Sydney, your brother is a surgeon. He has plenty to keep him busy. And when he isn't busy . . . well, his brother will see that he's exchanged. Dr. McKenzie was taken, so I understand, because he'd saved General Magee's foot once, and because—"

"He was betrayed by a woman," Sydney said flatly.

"Who only wanted to keep him alive."

"Well, haven't you heard, Sissy? There are things worse than death. That's what the abolitionists say, you know. Slavery is worse than death."

"Do you doubt that?"

Sydney hesitated, remembering what it felt like to be a prisoner—to have lost her freedom. "My family never owned slaves, Sissy. In fact, my grandmother's people, the Seminoles, helped runaway slaves all the time."

"Well, I commend your grandmother's people, Mrs. Halston."

"You weren't a slave," Sydney said.

"Not born a slave, no," Sissy said, suddenly angry. To Sydney's surprise, she spun around, unbuttoning her bodice, slipping her dress down so that Sydney could see her back. Sydney swallowed back a gasp of horror at the scars there. "I wasn't born a slave, but I was seized by some men to be returned to my supposed 'master,' a man who owned a plantation in Alabama. Papers were forged, and there I was, a slave. Who listens to a darkee over a rich white man? You know that's the truth. When I wasn't agreeable to anything he wanted, he beat me."

"Sissy, most masters aren't like that. Their slaves are valuable, they're often loved—"

"That is so ridiculous, don't you understand? Some men are good. Yes, I've known many really fine white men, in the North and in the South. But there are evil men who beat their slaves, who are careless with their 'valuable' property. A slave doesn't have freedom, don't you understand that? Slavery allows for men to have the legal right to whip and beat and torture other men. Slavery allows men to rape women, to sell their children."

"Maybe, but—"

"For the love of God, I've seen how you care for other people. I know that you can't just accept this because you're Southern. You—"

"It's a matter of states' rights, Sissy!"

"But the important 'right' to the South is the right to hold slaves."

Sydney sighed softly. "Slavery is wrong. But, Sissy, what will happen if thousands of slaves are suddenly free? Many will starve, they'll have no homes, they'll suffer terribly. Slavery should be abolished with a plan, with education, with—"

"Yes, it should. But men never will release that 'valuable' property so generously without force. John Brown said it. Our land could not be purged without blood."

"John Brown was a murderer," Sydney said.

"Yes, he was. He thought he was God, judge, and jury. But the land is bathed in blood, and it's a terrible thing."

Sydney walked over to Sissy. She touched her shoulder, near a scar. "I'm sorry. So sorry."

Sissy smiled. "I know that you are. And I'm sorry that I betrayed you. Do you understand why?"

Sydney put her arms around her and hugged her. Sissy hugged her back. They were both lost, and both found.

"Are you still a Rebel?" Sissy asked.

"I'm still a Southerner," Sydney said slowly, meeting Sissy's eyes. "But you sure have made me think."

"Let's go see your cousin," Sissy suggested.

"It may be dangerous for me to go to him—with you

behind me. My cousin longs to escape. He can't help but want to save his own countrymen."

"I heard he saved Captain Halston."

Sydney paused. "You're good friends with Jesse?"

"Yes. I admire him very much," Sissy said solemnly.

"Well, then," Sydney murmured. "It's good to know that you'll be here to watch over him if—"

"If?"

Sydney lowered her eyes and shook her head. "If I don't happen to be here when he comes back."

Sissy hesitated a moment as if wondering if she should or shouldn't take the impropriety of a personal observation. "He loves you, you know."

Sydney felt the world twist and roll. There had been a time when his smile had made her feel a trembling deep inside. A time . . .

That time still existed. The touch of his eyes still made her quicken. She had been falling in love with him since she had first met him. Feeling the sweet excitement of learning more about him every time she saw him. But then . . .

"He captured me and put me in a prison camp."

"You were spying."

"That's the point, it's all wrong, he's North, I'm South, he's from the snow, and I need the sun to survive, it's just all—all wrong!"

"Slavery is wrong."

"Oh, Lord, Sissy, do you know how many Southerners believe that it's wrong? Many, and many were against secession, and against war. The division remains. And Jesse is a Yank, and I'm a Rebel."

"You married him."

"Yes, I did. And you may be right about everything, but . . ."

"But what?"

"We are still at war. That's the crux of everything. *We're still at war.*"

More injured came into the hospitals in Washington—and to Old Capitol. Julian realized that he was being given more supplies to work with—medicines, sutures, opiates, and more—than he would have had he were free. It wasn't a miserable existence. Sydney came to see him fairly frequently. She often helped him with the injured men, but as time went by, she seemed to grow more somber. Every time he saw her, he asked about his wife, and then about Jesse Halston.

Both of them remained at the front.

"What were you expecting?" Sydney asked him one day. "That Rhiannon would immediately return here to Washington because you were a prisoner here?" She smiled with a trace of bitter amusement. "All right, her prisoner at that."

He scowled at his cousin. "I told her to get away from the field! Who knows when she'll put herself in danger again?"

Sydney hesitated. "She might know when she's going to be in danger."

He shook his head. "You don't understand. She doesn't close her eyes and see the future. She has dreams, moments of intuition. She can't protect herself from all harm."

"She's a grown woman."

"Carrying my child."

"Ohhh . . ." Sydney breathed, her mouth forming a circle. "I see." She was watching him with a greater amusement. Who was he trying to fool?

"No, you don't see," he said irritably. "She belongs at home."

"But you're a prisoner."

"Not for long."

"Julian, you mustn't do anything too reckless. I know that Ian is surely talking to the right people."

"I'm sure he is as well, Sydney."

"Don't put yourself into danger. Heed the advice you gave me!"

"I intend to be very careful."

His chance came unexpectedly that very night when his last patient of the day died in the courtyard before Julian even had a chance to see him.

Few of the other prisoners were around; the guards were equally as busy. The sick and injured who had died that day were lined up against the wall. Guards and government-contracted coffin makers were busy bringing in simple, poorly made boxes for the Rebel dead.

As he stared down at the boy who had died before he'd even had a chance to find out what his injury had been, he felt a touch on his shoulder.

"So many are dead, Julian. You can't take each death to heart, as if you somehow failed the man."

"I know," Julian said softly. "It's just that now . . ."

"You have to realize that you have done good work here. That you've saved lives." Belle was a pretty woman, sweet, but with a wild heart. They had quickly become friends. No more, no matter what the Northern papers would like.

"Yes . . . but . . ."

There was so little else he could do. His eyes touched on one of the coffins. He stared into Belle's pretty eyes. She smiled slowly. "Want a little free time, Colonel McKenzie?"

"Captain, ma'am."

"You're deserving of all the rank you've ever held, sir!" she said, and bowed gracefully to him.

"You know, Belle, you should be on stage."

"One day perhaps I shall be. Trust me, Colonel, and I'll put on a fabulous performance for your benefit!"

She walked away. As he watched, she entered the main building, taking a seat at a table in the common room. She was quickly surrounded.

Julian looked around himself. A few fellows were moving coffins, lifting the dead into them, like so much refuse.

Inside, Belle Boyd was holding court, flirting almost wantonly with prisoners and guards alike. He could hear her voice rising dramatically, she was telling them all about some of her wild night rides and how she wouldn't be anyone's prisoner long. With her bobbing brown curls and lust for life, she was charming and captivating, adept at keeping attention focused upon herself.

He looked at the dead man so recently lost. The sun was falling. A bored guard dropped a coffin by the table. "One more in the wagon, we've plenty of places for the dead, it seems. I'll see that you're finished for the last Reb, Doctor," the guard said, and ambled off.

That had been the last dead man . . .

Coffin . . . there was an extra one. Sydney herself had suggested it. The dead were being placed. Soon the guards would realize that there was an extra pine box. He had to move fast.

He looked around. The last of the guards stood near the doorway, or hauled coffins, already occupied, to the wagons. The extra coffin lay before him, next to his impromptu diagnosing table. The lid was ajar . . .

He looked around hastily. No one was watching. Those who should have been were occupied, listening to Belle. He crawled in. He didn't even have to share his space with a dead man. The guard had counted the dead and dying with one too many.

He had just pulled a poor pine lid over himself when he heard voices again. The men coming back for the last of the coffins. Coming to take them to the wagons.

To go . . . somewhere.

He didn't know where he was going. It didn't matter. He felt his box lifted on the shoulders of two men. Heard them complaining that he was one heavy dead Reb. He was jostled, nearly dropped, finally slid upon a wagon bed.

It was dark. So dark in the coffin, darker than the night. Stifling. The night might be cool, but the box, in the dead heat of summer, was suffocating. He nearly panicked, nearly beat against the wood with his bare hands. Better to be a live prisoner than a dead Reb in a coffin . . .

No . . . endure the ride.

He fought for control. Gained it.

And rode on through the night in his stifling dark pit of hell . . .

The dream about the coffin continued to plague her. It was dark, it was night. She was walking, and there it lay, in a copse in the trees, a forest copse. She didn't want to walk to it, but she did, and she didn't want to see inside, but she couldn't help herself. She reached out and touched the lid. It was nailed down, and she couldn't move it, but then the nails gave, and she was terrified and wanted to look away.

Alone at night, she sat by a stream in northern Virginia wishing that she were home. She held a note in her hand, written to her by Sissy Walden, the girl who worked with Jesse Halston. It was a quick note, a kindness on Sissy's part, and a kindness on the part of the soldier who had ridden out with what personal mail he could bring from Washington.

"Both McKenzies doing fine; like Sydney more every day. Julian works hard at Old Capitol; seems adjusted to his stay. My best to you and hoping to see you when, as they say, 'this cruel war is over.' "

She hugged her knees to her chest. *There was no coffin.* Julian was fine. Her dreams had simply come to torment her.

She was seated so when she heard movement behind her. Turning, she was startled to see that General Magee, his head bowed, stood behind her. She leapt up, swinging around to stare at him. "General, sir."

"My dear child, come here." He stretched out his arms to her.

She had been afraid that something had happened to Risa in Florida, that Jerome had been killed, that there might be some terrible news that would concern them both. Perhaps Ian McKenzie had been injured.

But no. The way he looked at her, held out his arms. She shook her head, moistening her lips. "Julian . . . ?" she whispered.

"Rhiannon, please come here. There's a vague rumor that he . . ."

"That he what?"

"He's gone. Missing."

"Missing? From Old Capitol?" She felt her heart thundering. "Then he's escaped," she said.

General Magee shook his head slowly. "They took wagons of the dead from the prison, and it was after the dead Rebels were taken that they realized he was gone. I'm afraid that . . ."

She remembered her dream about the coffins.

And she passed out cold.

They were there again in her dreams . . .

Coffins . . .

A parade of them. They marched by, one after another, again, again, again. No soldiers carried them, just cloaked figures, a score of grim reapers, all come for the dead. Pine boxes held by the bony spectral hands of the figures who cast out maniacal laughter, for it was Death that fed off the war, Death claimed the only true victory.

They marched and marched, a parade of coffins, and she was in the middle of them, running, running. She couldn't run to the end of the parade, couldn't look for the living among the dead, for the fingers reached out and touched her.

She awoke with a start. It was dark; she was in her canvas field tent. From somewhere she could hear the chirping of crickets. The night had cooled. The days had been blistering. A Virginia summer, with temperatures rising far above those of her native peninsula.

There was someone beside her, fingers did touch her hair. Blue eyes touched hers. A handsome, well-known face hovered above her own. Her heart started to jump with joy, then careened. Not Julian, it was not Julian.

"Rhiannon, I'll find him."

"Ian?" She was glad, of course. She hadn't seen him, nor heard from him, since the battle at Gettysburg. She hadn't known where he'd been sent. And it was good to see anyone alive these days. But he was the wrong brother. And she was so afraid.

"I'm going to find him, don't worry. I'll catch up with the wagon of dead heading down to meet up with the company of Rebs sent out to retrieve their own. We'll know one way or the other just what has happened to my brother. But I know him, Rhiannon. I don't have your abilities, but my brother . . . I'd know if he were dead. I would know it."

"Ian . . ."

His lips touched her forehead. He rose from the folding chair at her side and started from the tent. Stunned, she watched him go.

Then she leapt up, suddenly ashamed. She'd heard frightening news—and fainted.

She slipped out of the tent and saw Ian disappearing toward a line of tethered horses. He spoke to one of the soldiers there, reaching for the reins to a handsome, healthy bay. She started to race after him, then paused. He wouldn't let her come, he'd try to protect her.

She slowed her gait, smoothed back her hair, and started along the trail toward the line of horses. She waited until Ian was mounted, until he'd called out to the sentry. When he had disappeared down the path, she started walking again, hurrying toward the cavalry mounts.

"Whoa, there, Miz Rhiannon!" the sentry called to her. He was a middle-aged farmer, laconic, slow, firm. "Where are you off to in the middle of the night?" He spoke gently; she was certain that most of Magee's men were aware that her very newly acquired Rebel husband might be as dead as her original spouse. Magee had been Ian's commanding officer for years before the war.

"I have to catch up with Ian."

"Miz Rhiannon, you mustn't just go running off."

"Sir, I must reach my brother-in-law."

"No, I can't let you do that . . ." he protested, trying to figure out how to stop her as she untied the reins of a roan gelding, turned the horse around, and leapt up.

"Are you going to shoot me?" she asked him.

"Well, now, no, ma'am, you know I'm not going to shoot you—"

"Good. Because that's the only way you're going to stop me."

She nudged her mount with her heels, and the horse obediently swung around to follow after Ian. She raced hard past the lines, reining in when she was challenged once again by a voice that rang down to her from the branches of an old oak.

"Halt, or I'll shoot."

"Accompanying Colonel McKenzie!" she shouted back hoarsely.

"Hurry then, he's headed down the pike toward the Reb camps!"

"Aye, that I will!" She leaned against her horse and gave the animal free rein.

He must have dozed; he awoke again to stifling heat and a horrible sense of entrapment. *Still in the coffin, still moving. He could feel the endless jolting of the wagon, the sickening sensations . . .*

Then, suddenly, a rush of bullets. Shouts. Cries, screams. The motion of the wagon increased to a wild, reckless pace. He was thrown back and forth in the tiny space with such violence he was afraid he was going to be sick when he had the time to be afraid of anything. Suddenly, there was a huge jolt. A strange sound penetrated the coffin along with another flying sensation and slamming. Again, he heard the explosion of bullets, screams, cries. Then his box slammed against something with such force that his head struck the wood with savage force, splintering the top.

"Don't shoot, don't shoot. For the love of God, we're just returning the dead—"

A bullet whizzed. The pleading voice fell silent.

Stunned, Julian tried to gather his forces. He heard groaning, then more voices. "Virgil, move fast! Both damned armies are in this vicinity."

"Billy, shut up and give me time. The lids are nailed down!" the one named Virgil called back.

"Rip the damned lids off faster." Billy ordered.

"Nothing! This fellow has nothing in his pockets at all."

"Hell, this one has a pack of playing cards!" Billy snorted.

"What were you expecting? These are Reb prisoners. What did ya think, that they'd knocked off a bank in D.C. before expiring?"

"Shut up, shut up, get to work—there! Must be this here feller's old dead Pappy's watch, it's a fine piece, keep going—hey, this dead Reb has a fine gold wedding band, too!"

His head buzzing, Julian lay still in his coffin, listening. Whoever these men were, they had killed the Yankee drivers to steal whatever they could find off the wagon of dead men. They were robbing from those who had fallen, and it wouldn't have mattered if they were Rebels or Yankees. The men here had fought and died for something they believed in, and now, dead, they were being dumped and ravaged for precious mementoes from the lives they had lived.

Footsteps . . .

He heard a grind of steel against wood as a bar was set against the coffin lid that covered him. A ripping sound followed, and all of a sudden one of them was staring down at him. He was an ugly fellow with a mouthful of yellowed, broken teeth. He was wearing a frock coat, stolen from a Union calvary officer, with a Confederate sash. His hair was long and greasy, and his eyes were small, brown, and glittering with a light of greed.

Then, looking down as Julian's eyes opened, he suddenly shouted, "Hell, this one's back from the dead!"

He jerked a knife from his side and raised it above Julian. Julian caught his arm before the weapon could plunge. They struggled. Julian managed to turn the knife. When the man twisted to reach for the gun holstered at his side, Julian jerked forward. The knife plunged straight into the robber's heart.

"Virgil, Virgil?"

The second man came running over. He was carrying a Spencer repeating rifle, aimed at Julian.

Trapped in the pine coffin with Virgil's body over his own, Julian had no choice. He reached for the Colt in the holster at Virgil's side.

He hit Billy first. But Billy got off a shot. It careened just past Julian's forehead. The noise of the bullet whizzing by his temple and plowing into the pine was deafening. The bullet gave him a fierce sting.

He tried to rise. He fell back, the world going dark . . . again.

Dark . . . dark.

Darker than it had ever been before.

Chapter 22

~

Rhiannon thought that she had followed Ian for almost an hour when she was startled and unnerved to hear hoofbeats on the road behind her. She reined in, spinning her well-trained cavalry mount around. As she had expected, he had circled around and come behind her.

"What in God's name are you doing?" he demanded angrily.

"Coming with you."

"But it's dangerous."

"War is dangerous. In the midst of it, a cannon could explode at any time. If I were home, deserters could come and rob me and slit my throat."

"You should be in St. Augustine."

"Where the Rebs might decide to seize the city back and warfare could break out and anyone could be killed."

"Even at Gettysburg—" Ian began.

"Even at Gettysburg, a young girl was hit by a stray bullet. Ian, please, I have to come with you."

"All right. Then ride with me. Don't trail behind!"

She managed a weak smile, smoothing back a lock of hair. "I'll be delighted to ride with you, Colonel McKenzie."

They rode together. "I'd finally arranged an exchange for him," Ian said softly.

She glanced at him. "You said that he was all right, that you'd know, in your heart, if anything had happened."

"I lied," Ian admitted.

She knew that he was waiting for her to offer him a deeper insight. She shook her head. "I don't know. I've been dreaming about . . ."

"About?"

"Coffins."

Just as she said the word, Ian reined in sharply, putting out a hand to warn her to stop as well.

"What is it?"

"A wagon wheel. Get behind me. If anything happens, ride like hell, straight back to our camp, do you understand?"

"Yes, of course."

He started trotting forward. As ordered, she stayed behind him. There, strewn in the road, was the body of a man, next to him, a broken wheel. And as they rode farther . . .

They came to a copse. She had to gasp.

A wrecked wagon lay against the trees, upended and on its side. All around it lay . . .

Coffins. Some broken, with their sad inhabitants hanging halfway from them. Some had been split open, some were untouched, some men were nothing but bones, some wore bloodied clothes, some had begun to rot . . .

"Rhiannon, get away!" Ian warned.

But she was already off her horse. One man lay with fresh blood oozing from a wound in his chest. Near him lay a ripped coffin with a second man sprawled across it. While within it . . .

She started toward it on rubbery legs.

There he lay. Face white in the moonlight, hair impossibly dark against it. Frayed cotton shirt, gray frock coat . . .

"Julian!" she shrieked his name, racing toward him. "Julian!"

Her heart was in her throat. The wind seemed to rise and rush around her. She couldn't bear it. She would tear him from the coffin, shake him, force him to live . . .

Yet even as she raced forward, he began to rise, and she stopped, dead still.

Her voice.

He heard her voice from a tremendous distance. She was calling to him, and he had to answer. He opened his eyes. Had he been dead? Or dreaming. He blinked furiously, felt a searing pain at his temple, felt the weight of the man lying over him, the hardness of the wood beneath him. He strained and rose, sitting up, pushing the dead man from him.

He blinked again, because she was there before him. Rhiannon, with her ebony dark hair in curling disarray around her classically beautiful features, her eyes sizzling emerald in the moonlight, tall, elegant, an angel indeed, even in her endless black . . .

"Rhiannon . . ." he murmured her name, thinking it impossible that she could be there, and yet . . .

Her eyes. By God, in her eyes, he thought that he saw things. Such fear, such anxiety, care, concern.

Love?

He gripped the edges of the coffin, pushing the dead man from him, rising. And then he saw that Ian stood behind his wife. "Sweet Jesus, you're alive!" Ian breathed.

"Barely," he acknowledged, smiling awkwardly at his brother. He stepped from the coffin, shaking his head.

"What the hell happened?" Ian demanded.

"Grave robbers, not waiting for the coffins to hit the dirt. They apparently made a living attacking wagons of dead going South—or North."

Ian had stepped up, looking at Virgil, then at Billy. "Both dead."

"I know."

Ian touched his forehead, his concern in his eyes despite his words. "They nearly got you."

"It's a scratch."

"A damned close scratch."

"Well, the coffin wasn't great to begin with, and then things got worse." He was trying to speak lightly. He wanted to reach out for his wife, grab her, draw her to him, hold her. If he touched her now, though, he thought, she would self-combust, explode into a billion tiny pieces of pure fire around him.

"What are you doing here?" he asked her sharply.

"I thought that you were dead!" she said angrily.

"Oh? Were you celebrating?"

Wrong thing to say, he thought, wincing. But he'd just wanted to touch her so damned badly. And she was still in black. She was carrying his child, but she was mourning her husband.

She walked over to him at last and took a swing at him. Hard. She caught him in the jaw. His head started ringing again.

He did catch her wrist, pulling her against him. "I told you to get off the battlefield! What are you doing out here? Why didn't you come into Washington, go back to St. Augustine, go somewhere safe?"

"You let go of me, you son of a bitch. You scared us all to death!"

"Damn it, I asked you a question."

"You have no right to ask questions."

"I was a prisoner, thanks to you, I had every right to try to escape."

"Horses!" Ian interrupted suddenly. "Listen, naturally, anyone who heard any of what went on here would have notified authorities."

Julian pressed his wife behind him, pushing backward to the coffin to find the Colt he had used against Billy's attack. Ian stayed by his side and when the horses burst into the copse, they were together, Rhiannon forced behind them.

Rebs or Yanks? In this territory they had no idea which.

It was Magee himself, followed by two cavalry officers who burst into the copse. He looked at the situation and quickly ascertained what had happened. "If a war isn't enough," he said with soft disgust, "you have to have vultures to go along with it! Hello, Dr. McKenzie. Glad to see you out of that coffin rather than in it."

Julian felt Rhiannon's nails digging against his back. He gritted his teeth. She was afraid, of course, that he was going to pull the Colt, fight Magee, demand his freedom.

"Sir, the coffin wasn't particularly pleasant. It wasn't exactly my choice of conveyance as a way south, but . . ."

"We'll have to get a burial detail up here, take care of these dead," one of Magee's men said.

"We'll get the boys back in their boxes," Magee said, "then move out. This is Rebel territory, and we're too far from base camp." He leaned lower on his horse's saddle. "Longstreet's got a few companies just down the road a spell, Dr. McKenzie. Apparently, you were due for an exchange when you decided to jump into that pine box."

"I wish I'd known," Julian said, half smiling and shrugging to his brother. "Ian was kind of slow, you see."

"They didn't really want to let you go," Magee told him.

"I didn't know I was that dangerous."

"Horses!" Ian said.

"What?" Rhiannon murmured.

Julian heard the fear in her voice. She started to rush by him; he caught her by the arm. Rebs. The Rebs were coming now.

And they were. Julian knew that his brother tensed, and that he had taken a fighting stand.

But the captain who burst into the clearing on a skinny gray nag quickly raised a hand. His party was small as well. Julian realized he knew the man: Trenton Malden, out of Georgia.

He was among George Pickett's few survivors. Malden was young; not long ago, his shoulder-length curls had been gold. Now, already, they were touched with gray. He paused, his party of four behind him not drawing or seeking weapons as they surveyed the scene in the copse.

"Sir!" Malden said, looking at Magee. "I cannot believe you're responsible for this scene!"

"Of course not, Trent!" Magee replied impatiently. Seeing Julian staring at him, General Magee explained, "Trenton was in my service just before the war."

"Trent!" Ian suddenly exclaimed.

The Confederate captain smiled. "Ian. Good to see you alive and well."

"Same to you, Trent."

"What the hell happened here?"

"Grave robbers," Julian explained.

"These must be the fellows we were due to receive from Old Capitol?" Trent Malden asked.

"Yes," Julian said.

Trent arched a brow to him. "Dr. McKenzie, we all know that you do miracles, but have you managed to raise the dead?"

"Only myself."

"Ah . . ." Trenton murmured. He looked at Magee. "Well, sir, I surely don't want to shoot you or Ian or your boys, and I hope you don't want to shoot me. We should part ways."

"That we should, Captain," Magee agree. "If you need some help with the dead—"

"They're our boys," Malden said sadly. "We'll tend to them."

"As you say. Ian, Rhiannon—"

No. Julian had a firm grip on Rhiannon. "No, sir, my wife comes with me."

Magee hesitated, obviously in an awkward position. "But, sir, I have taken it upon myself to watch out for the lady—"

"Who is my wife, sir, through her own . . ." he paused, a brow arched, studying Rhiannon's eyes, alive with an angry wildfire as she found herself the one in a difficult position. "Through her own absolute determination."

"But . . . sir," Magee protested. "Her leanings are Union!"

"But, sir, her living husband is Confederate, and she is coming with me," he said firmly. "I will take my wife."

"Julian—" Ian began.

"Ian!" Julian returned, staring at his brother.

There could be no bloodshed here, he thought. But neither could he let her return to a Northern camp.

"Rhiannon," Magee said gently. "What would you have me do?"

And he saw it in her eyes.

She knew that life and death, and bloodshed, truly lay in her hands. She had no choice. She was a prisoner just as he had been.

"Apparently, I will go with . . . my husband."

"Are you certain?" Magee asked.

She hesitated, her lashes sweeping her cheeks. The tension in the copse could be felt on the air. Then she turned to Magee. "Of course, sir."

"God go with you, child. Ian, we will retire from this Rebel territory."

Julian felt his brother's embrace. He returned it quickly, but tightly. God only knew when they would meet again.

"We'll get you a horse, Dr. McKenzie," Trenton Malden began.

"Never mind. Mrs. McKenzie may take the animal she is riding. It is the least we can offer for her services," Magee said. "Trenton, keep your head down!" he called. He turned and started from the copse. Julian nodded to Ian, who turned, mounted his horse, and followed Magee.

"A healthy animal!" Trenton said, pleased. "Welcome, Mrs. McKenzie, we're delighted to have you."

She ignored him and walked to the horse she had ridden from the Yankee front. Julian followed her. She wasn't ready for him when he swung up behind her. When she would have spoken in protest, he slipped his arms tightly around her with a warning pressure, taking the reins.

"She's delighted to be with us as well, absolutely delighted," he said flatly.

And they rode to the Rebel front.

Rhiannon paced the tiny white tent where she had been given sleeping quarters.

Since her arrival at the Rebel camp, she hadn't seen Julian.

There were so many injured men! They were so sad as well, for the sheer volume of wounded men had overwhelmed the doctors and facilities of the South, and many who might have been helped were now dying. She knew that Julian was desperately needed, but she wished that she hadn't been left alone. She might have helped him. Instead, she had been escorted here, and Julian had been taken to the makeshift hospital.

Hours had passed. She should have slept; she could not. She lay upon the cot thinking how grateful she was that he was alive—and how furious she was with the situation she had brought upon herself. He was still so angry with her! It was possible to remember the night they had shared, but then she would feel again the way that she had when his eyes had touched hers in the copse, when she had struck him . . .

Perhaps not a loving and tender thing for a wife to do upon discovering that her husband was alive. But when she had first seen him, seen the blood, seen him lying there . . .

She rose from the camp cot and moved around the tiny tent. An officer's tent, with folding bed, chairs, desk, and shaving mirror. Amazing what they could do with so small a space! Outside, fires burned, the moon was high. Yet it was quiet at night. Pickets and sentries were up and about; soon it would be dawn, and the men would be about their war again. But now, right now, it was quiet.

Quiet . . .

She didn't hear him; she sensed him there, behind her. She spun around. He had bathed; he had been given new clothing, not much less tattered than that which he had worn before. He was shaven, lean, so taut, so hard, and so handsome. She lowered her eyes quickly, not wanting him to know that she had fallen in love with him.

"So things have changed!" she said softly. "You are free, and I am the prisoner."

He lifted his hands. "You're not a prisoner."

"You insisted I come here. That's the same, isn't it?"

He shook his head, smiling slightly. "No, you're my wife. My wife. Not Magee's, not Ian's. And Richard Tremaine is dead. You married me. Not your intent, I admit, but you did do the deed. Therefore, you are here."

"A prisoner," she repeated softly. "And if you touch me . . ."

She broke off. What was she doing? Pride was one thing. Foolishness was another. She was in love with him; she was here now. And they were both alive and well.

But it was too late. At her words he had risen. "If I touch you?" he demanded coldly. "Well, you know what, my love? I think that I will do so. I think I will be a savage Southerner and tear the very clothes from your back!"

"Julian!" she cried, startled, wrenching back and away from him as he suddenly seized her, pulling her against him. "I have had it with this black!" he swore, and he did shred her clothing, tearing a sleeve from her gown, then the skirt.

"Julian, stop it, stop it, I'll scream—"

"Fine! This is a Rebel camp, remember!"

"Yes! And the last of the cavaliers sleep here, isn't that true?" she demanded.

"Don't worry, I don't want anything from you tonight, my beloved witch, except that you cease with this black!" he told her, his eyes still molten blue as they bore into hers, his touch still as hot and angry and hard as steel. She slammed her fists against his chest, then stopped, gasping in a breath.

He too went dead still. The look in his eyes changed instantly. "Rhiannon, what is it? What's wrong? Did I hurt you? Rhiannon—"

"Julian . . ."

"What?" He swept her from her feet, lifting her, carrying her to the cot.

"Julian . . ."

Her fingers curled around his. She brought them down

to her abdomen. "You can feel him. It's so amazing, there's so much death . . ." She broke off, feeling a flush of color to her cheeks. "You've felt babies before," she murmured.

His large hands with their long fingers were covering her belly. The babe continued to move, kicking with a positive strength that she was certain he could feel almost as clearly as she did herself. "Never my own!" he said softly. "Never my own."

She lay back, glad of his touch, not willing to speak, to break the moment between them. His fingers moved in gentle patterns over her . . . so gentle.

She closed her eyes. It was good, so good.

There was a war on. She lay in a Rebel camp. And still, the night was so sweet . . .

And in time, she did sleep.

When she woke, Julian was gone. But a new gown, a simple cotton day dress in navy blue, lay at the foot of the bed. Maybe it was time she cast off the black.

She found that he had left her water with which to wash, and when she poked her head out of the tent, she found that a young drummer boy had been left to tend to her needs. The moment he saw her, he was at her side, offering her coffee.

"Where is my husband, do you know?"

"He's ridden out, ma'am," the boy said. He was perhaps twelve, with a thatch of straight wheat-colored hair, a quick smile, pert dimples. He was too skinny, but a precocious youth.

"Ridden out where?"

"There was some skirmishing. He went for the wounded. I'll get you some coffee and something to eat. I'm afraid that our food isn't very good, but we've a few fresh eggs left—I did that foraging myself—and I'm a very good cook."

"I'm sure you are . . . what's your name?"

"Josiah, ma'am. Josiah. Let me get your coffee."

He walked away from her to one of the cooking fires and returned with coffee for her. As she sipped it, he watched her anxiously. "Is it all right?"

"Delicious."

He shrugged. "We just traded for it. There's some Yanks

downriver. Corporal Reilly sent them some of his pa's best tobacco. I was hoping we'd made a good deal."

"It's wonderful coffee."

"I'll cook you some eggs."

"You needn't—"

"Dr. McKenzie says that you're going to have a baby, ma'am. We need to take care of the little ones. After all, your baby will be the future of our people, right?"

She hesitated, then smiled. "Yes, of course."

He walked off, and a while later, he returned with eggs and fresh bread—how he managed the bread, she didn't know. He sat with her while she ate, and she found out that his mother had died before the war and he thought his father was dead, because he'd been missing a long time. She asked him to take her to the wounded when she was done, and her heart went out to the row after row of wounded soldiers on camp beds, left here because they weren't in condition to go home, and yet there was no room for them as yet in the regular hospitals.

She brought water to the men, read, changed bandages. The day began to pass, same as any other. She was startled, however, when she came across Liam Murphy, one of the young men who had been with Julian when he had used her house as a refuge.

"Liam!"

"Mrs. Tremaine—McKenzie!" He smiled. "That's right, you married Colonel McKenzie. It's a wonderful story, you know. It's gone around."

"I'm sure it has," she murmured. "How are you, where are you wounded?"

He moved the sheet. She saw the empty place that had been his lower leg.

"Oh, Liam, I'm so sorry!"

"I'm alive."

"Thank God!"

"And I'm going home."

"That's even better."

"To fight again."

"No!"

"Yes. Why, the Yanks are having a renewed interest in Florida. They've had all kinds of meetings and the like over it. Seems Florida is feeding most of the Confederacy. The

Yanks think we're weak, that they can attack us. But the Reb commanders aren't fools. They're going to stop the Yanks," he said proudly. He lowered his voice. "Saw Julian this morning, Mrs. McKenzie. Sure was good to see him. He's anxious, too. He wants to go home. Says you're going to have a little one, and that he wants his child born in Florida. He's put in a request to be assigned back home, since they know now there will be more action there!"

"Well, we'll have to see, won't we?"

"Would you like that? Would you like to go home?"

She looked into his eyes for a long moment, then smiled. "Yes, I'd like to go home."

He touched her hand. "I called you a witch, you know. I'm mighty sorry."

"It's all right. I hope we all get to go home."

Liam suddenly groaned. "Watch out! He's coming."

"Who's coming?"

"The preacher man. Colonel Sheer."

She saw a tall, lean man with iron gray hair and a gray beard enter the hospital tent. She watched him with interest for a minute then realized that he had stopped to ask one of the orderlies a question—about her. He looked up, then came toward her. She instantly felt uneasy. His eyes were dark, small, piercing. The eyes of a zealot, she thought.

Followed by two aides, he walked through the rows of hospital beds until he reached her. "Mrs. McKenzie!" he stated.

She nodded, not replying to him.

"You will come with me."

"Where?" she inquired.

"To my command quarters."

"Why?"

"I have questions for you."

She shook her head. "But—"

"You were in the Yankee camp just yesterday, young woman!"

"Sir, I know nothing of Yankee military plans. I worked in the field hospital there."

"You will come with me."

"I'm not a prisoner here, sir."

"You will come with me, ma'am, or I will have you carried out of here!"

Furious, she started walking ahead of him.

She was startled when Josiah suddenly came before her, making a ruckus by dropping a bucket of water. When she bent to help him, he spoke to her quickly. "Don't worry, we'll get Dr. McKenzie!"

She nodded, but she wondered with a sinking heart just what was going on, and just what Julian could do. This man was a colonel—which Julian had been with the militia. But he was in the regular army now, and his rank wasn't as high as this man's.

Sheer was quickly at her side, taking her elbow. She jerked free from him, but he remained at her side, directing her. They came to a large tent, and he ushered her in. There was a chair beside a camp desk, and he indicated that she should sit. She did so.

"You may cease with the hostility, madam."

"What do you want? I'm not in the military."

"But your reputation precedes you."

"Reputation? Whatever you might have heard, I'm not a witch."

"I want to know the Yankee movements. What is Meade doing now? Where will he attack next?"

"I don't know!"

"I demand—"

"It seems that Meade is just sitting there, as he has been doing!"

She was stunned when the man slapped her across the face. Gasping, she leapt to her feet. He stood as well and pressed her back into the chair.

"How dare you!" she gasped.

"You will give me answers."

"I don't have answers, and I'm not your prisoner."

"You came with your husband, but you are a Yank, and for the safety of the South, I am now making you a prisoner."

"You cannot."

"I can, and I will. You will stay here until you answer my questions. You see the future. You know what is happening. Now, Mrs. McKenzie, you are my prisoner—a traitor to the South, to your own homeland."

He was a fanatic—a lunatic. "Sir, you don't understand," Rhiannon said, fighting for patience. "I do not read the future at will! I have dreams upon occasion, flashes of insight. I cannot foretell the future like a gypsy with a crystal ball. I—"

He was suddenly in front of her, hands on her shoulders. "Not a gypsy, a witch. You knew to tell Magee where to lead his troops. You caused the Yanks to win ground at Gettysburg."

"I knew nothing at Gettysburg, except fear and horror like everyone else!" she protested.

"I repeat this—you're a traitor to your birthright! You're a Floridian, fighting for the Yankees. And you've given them an unfair advantage. You should be shot like any traitor; no, burned at the stake like any witch."

This man could not possibly be serious. Bad things might happen at the hands of the enemy, yes. On both sides, women alone had been molested by enemy soldiers. Robbed, raped, perhaps left for dead. Spies had been arrested. They'd faced imprisonment. But no one had been burned at the stake. And this man was a colonel—directing troops on the field!

"Sir, I keep telling you that I couldn't help you now if I wanted to."

"You deny special powers."

She shook off his touch and stood suddenly, swiftly moving far enough away from him so that he could not easily touch her. "Yes, I deny special powers! I am cursed, plagued, sometimes with dreams! They are nightmares, and I do not seek them."

"Sit down!" He stepped forward, determined. She had nowhere to go. He set his hands on her shoulders, pressing her back into the chair.

Where was Julian? she wondered desperately. If he was still out in the field, he didn't know that Sheer had come to take her. And when he found out what had happened? What was he going to do? Sheer outranked him! Julian had no power over a colonel who was going over the edge of sanity.

"Let me tell you about Gettysburg, Mrs. McKenzie."

"You don't need to tell me anything. I was there!" she said furiously.

He didn't seem to hear her. "I had five sons when this war began. Proud, strapping boys. They went to war for their country, Mrs. McKenzie, this country. The Confederate States of America. Not one of them shirked his duty. I lost a boy at Sharpsburg, and then, Mrs. McKenzie, I lost four sons at Gettysburg. Four boys . . ."

"I'm sorry, sir. I cannot tell you how sorry I am. For everyone the losses have been unacceptable."

"The North should suffer! The Northern politicians started this war of pure aggression. We asked to be left alone to live our lives and nothing more. But my sons are not going to have died for nothing, Mrs. McKenzie. We will change the tide of this war again!"

She fought to remain calm and in control. "Perhaps you will."

"You will help us."

"You don't understand."

"No, Mrs. McKenzie. You don't understand. I will beat you if I have to. I will burn you, torture you, I—"

He broke off, staring into space. Then he stood. "Will you answer my questions?"

"I have no answers to give you."

He violently dragged her out of the chair. His hand went flying across her face again. "If you don't answer me, I will have you shot."

She tried to fight back, dodging his blows, returning them. His palm cracked against her face with such force that she came careening down to her knees in the center of the tent. He raised his fist to strike her again.

But his hand was stayed. He was swung around and cracked in the jaw. Dazed, tears stinging her eyes, she looked up to see that Julian had returned.

Sheer took a swing at Julian. He was a powerful man, and it was a hard blow. Julian staggered back. But then he came forward, jabbing quickly and with strength, catching Sheer on the right jaw, the left, the right. Sheer went to his knees.

"You'll be shot as well! Insubordination. Shot at dusk, shot with the bitch of Satan who helps the Yankees find our position even now."

Julian was staring down at the man incredulously. As he did so, Sheer went for the gun in the holster at his waist. Julian hit him again. Hard. Sheer went flat.

"Oh, my God!" she cried. "Julian, Julian . . ."

His arms were around her, blue eyes dark with concern. "Did he hurt you?"

She shook her head. "But he'll hurt you, Julian, he's a colonel."

"I'll manage. Let me get you out of here. The baby—?"

"I'm fine, I'm fine!" she whispered.

But he swept her up and carried her from the tent. Outside, the soldiers who had gathered at the sound of the disturbance parted ways, and he walked with her back to their own tent. He had barely laid her down before officers arrived for him. To take him under arrest.

"It will be all right," he told her.

But she was afraid.

"Julian—"

"It will be all right."

And he was gone.

Several hours later, she heard a man clearing his throat. "Mrs. McKenzie!" She hurried out of the tent. Two soldiers had come for her. "General Longstreet will see you now."

"General Longstreet . . . ?"

"If you will come with us. Please?"

She followed behind them. It was a long walk, but eventually they came to a small house. The soldiers opened the door, and she realized that they had come to the command quarters for Longstreet's division of the Army of Northern Virginia.

She followed behind the soldiers, looking anxiously for Julian. He wasn't to be seen. She was led into a dining room converted to an office. There were maps everywhere.

The tall, bearded man who had been sitting there rose. He did so slowly, as if it were an effort, as if he were very weary.

"General Longstreet, please, I know that you're a very busy man, and I know that I have made little secret of the fact that I am a Unionist, but . . . please, where is Julian? Don't let him suffer for this. You are supposed to be the last of the cavaliers, sir, and that man was beating me. He said that I should be shot. You've got to understand that Julian was only acting as a Southern gentleman, a cavalier of that lifestyle you are fighting to maintain, when he came to my defense—"

"Mrs. McKenzie, Mrs. McKenzie . . ." he murmured, taking her hands. He had a gentle touch and a kind smile for a man who had seen so much battle and loss. "Your husband is just fine."

"He's under arrest."

"He's receiving new orders, Mrs. McKenzie."

"What?"

"May I get you a brandy or the like?"

She shook her head. "Nothing, please, just—"

"I called you here to offer you my most heartfelt apologies. Colonel Sheer was once a good military man, a pious fellow." Longstreet spoke with a soft, slurring Southern accent that made his words seem all the more consoling. "Mrs. McKenzie, every man and woman has the right in a war to choose his or her side, and you are most honest in your belief in the Union. God knows, I spend many a day in sorrow regarding this great division! Colonel Sheer had no right to touch you, and your husband had every right to defend you. However, there are other fanatics among our numbers, so we're seeing to it that you and your husband are sent home as swiftly as possible."

"What?" she whispered. "Julian isn't under arrest?"

He smiled, and hiked his chin, indicating that she should look behind herself. She spun around. Julian stood there, papers in hand.

"Everything complete, Dr. McKenzie?"

"Yes, sir." Julian walked across the room. Longstreet stretched out a hand to him. "Good luck, Dr. McKenzie."

"And to you, sir. God keep you. It has been an honor to serve under you, sir."

"Well, now, you're still Confederate military, Julian. Just militia once again." He saluted. "Colonel McKenzie!"

Julian saluted in return. "General Longstreet, sir!"

"Take your wife. Go home," Longstreet told him.

"Aye, sir!"

They turned, and Julian led her from the house. A carriage awaited them, ready to take them down to the railroad.

She realized that they were, in truth, going home.

Chapter 23

∽

Reaching Florida was not easy.

They started out by train, but in some places the rails had been destroyed, the enemy was in close proximity, or they had to be rerouted because the enemy was literally holding the depot. They were constantly surrounded by other travelers, refugees from cities lost to the North at times, soldiers on leave, prisoners who had been paroled, orphans. It was a strange time for them; they'd both been so furious with one another, and yet things had changed after their awful experience with Colonel Sheer. There was little chance to really talk. They were so seldom alone.

At last they reached Jacksonville. They did so by wagon; the rails there had not been taken by the enemy, but they had been taken by the Confederacy since they were desperately needed elsewhere. The city was like a ghost town. It had been invaded and abandoned so many times that most of the families had fled.

Rhiannon was bone weary when they arrived. She'd had no sleep the night before, since they had not known they wouldn't have transport until the last minute. They rented a room, and they should have been alone. She had been anxiously looking forward to the opportunity, but they had done no more than come into the dining room for a meal when Julian was approached by a cavalryman in a worn, muddied uniform.

"Sir! Colonel McKenzie, sir! We're delighted to have you back!" He offered Julian a salute and continued, "There's news that the Yanks are planning to start a new offensive against us. They're making their plans now. Well, of course, the skirmishing never ends, the attacks on the coast go on

and on . . . but now they think that we're important—that
we're supplying just about the whole of the Confederacy
with the food that's keeping the army going. Don't that
beat all, sir—we're in the war."

"We've been in the war, sir. Look around you," Julian
responded dryly.

"Yes, of course, but . . . there could be a really major
battle here. Like the battles in Virginia and Tennessee!"

"Half the state could perish, I imagine," Julian murmured. "Sir, I don't mean to be rude, but we've traveled a
long way, my wife is tired—"

"Of course, my apologies. But, sir, you're needed immediately. There was some fighting today between here and
St. Augustine, on the old Indian road. I do welcome you
back, sir, but I'm afraid I'm also here to remind you that
you're a colonel in the Florida militia—and that duty, sir,
calls. I must have you accompany me."

"I am always glad to help when needed, but I've just
arrived. My wife—"

"We'll arrange an escort to have her taken back to
camp, sir."

Julian looked at Rhiannon. "You have to go," she told
him. "I will be at the camp when you reach it."

So he traveled on alone that night. She thought that she
would never sleep, but that night she did. Dreamlessly.
When she awoke in the morning, an escort awaited her that
included several of the men she had known at the Rebel
camp before. They greeted her warmly, and she was glad,
surprised at how much of a homecoming it seemed to be.

She was delighted to find that Rachel had heard she was
coming and had left St. Augustine to meet her in the camp
in the woods. Rachel was as boisterous as ever, talking a
mile a minute, describing the McKenzie children, and life
with Alaina and Risa in the Union-held city. "Such a place!
Some of the women are so funny. They're loyal Rebs to
the core, but when the Yank doling out the food comes
around, they're suddenly waving their Union colors!"

Rachel went on and on, but Rhiannon was glad to see
her. So many of the Rebels at the camp had been conscripted into the regular army that it was almost like Jacksonville, a ghost of the place it used to be.

She'd been back a week when she went to the little creek

off the river. Liam Murphy, his one leg gone, had returned two days after she'd arrived herself, and he'd set himself up as her guardian. She was grateful. At the water's edge, she stripped down to her shift, then plunged in. After the heat of the day, the water was amazing. She floated upon her back. Moss dripped from the trees. A crane flew overhead. A breeze picked up and rustled through the surrounding oaks. She closed her eyes. It was a scene of peace in the midst of chaos.

When she opened her eyes, he was there.

She sensed him, standing by the shore. Watching her. She came to her feet, ignoring the ooze of the creek bottom through her toes. She walked to a point several feet from where he stood. Dusk was coming, the sun falling. A rainbow of colors spilled across the sky, reflecting on the water. He stood tall, hard, lean, his frock coat dangling from a finger. She hesitated a minute, then walked the last few steps to him, slipping her arms around him.

He enwrapped her against him.

Together they came to their knees. Water soaked his uniform, but it didn't seem to matter; the soaked material was only something to be discarded. His hands were upon her shift, and it found its way to the embankment. His fingers entwined with hers, and she was stretched across the riverbank, and as his body came over hers, it was decked in the rainbow colors of the setting sun. She touched his face, wanting to talk, too full of the things she had to say to do so. He kissed her, lips lingering upon hers, then growing insistent. His tongue invaded her mouth, ravaged. His lips broke from hers, found them again. He seemed to taste forever and ever. Each kiss ignited a greater need in her, and she felt the length of him with a longing that surpassed need. His body was fire, and the river was ice. His kiss strayed from her lips. Her teeth and tongue grazed his shoulders. Hands caressed the fullness of her breasts, tender now, yet aching for his subtle stroke. The air around them swirled, caressed her naked flesh, followed the touch of his kiss, the liquid fire of his tongue as he drew patterns down her torso. His fingers moved over her hips, formed around her buttocks, drew her closer to the fullness of his erection. She thought that she would die, yet he did not cease to seduce. She murmured, writhed, undulated, pressed against him, seducing in turn. Kissed his shoulders, chest, stroked him, held him, cradled, whispered, and at last, when she was nearly mindless with longing, he came into her, a stroke that filled her, awakened her, excited her, erupted . . .

The sun continued to set. A bird cried overhead. The wind rustled the trees. Fire burned between them, explosive, consuming. Twilight became dusk, and the colors were gone, and the moon began to rise against the dying day. It seemed that all life exploded in a moment of fantastic beauty. That there could be such horror and destruction and in the midst of it such sweet beauty. She savored him, held his warmth as her body cooled and the night wrapped around her. She seemed to float upon a pinnacle of wonder for a very long time, but inevitably she drifted down, yet she didn't attempt to move. When he shifted, and his eyes met hers, she didn't flinch from them.

"I was afraid," he said huskily.

"You, afraid?" she whispered, smoothing back a dark lock of his hair.

He nodded, a crooked smile on his lips. "Afraid that I would come back tonight, and you wouldn't be here. You would have vanished, run to St. Augustine . . . somewhere. Or if you were here, I would arrive, and . . . we would be at war again."

"We are still at war," she said softly.

"Are we?" he murmured, and he leaned back upon an elbow, a frown touching his eyes as he gently drew his fingers over her arm, traced patterns against her hip. "I don't know that I'm at war. I'm not always sure what I'm fighting for anymore, sometimes things I don't think that I believe in. And yet . . ."

"And yet?"

"I just keep thinking now that this is home. That I'm back here."

"Because of me," she whispered apologetically.

He shook his head, his crooked smile in place. "You're not to blame because death sent a man over the edge." A hard core of anger touched his voice. "He was beating you!" he said hoarsely.

"They could have shot you for attacking an officer."

"Ah! A death I would have gallantly accepted, of course.

No man may touch my wife in violence. He had no right, even if he'd never touched you, he had no right. There are good things to our way of life. What he did went against everything that is what we call honor."

"The last of the great cavaliers!" she murmured.

"Yes, and no. I don't know of a Yank who would have behaved any differently," he admitted.

She smiled, reached out, and touched his cheek. He caught her hand, kissed the palm. "I wanted to come home," he said softly.

"So did I."

"You're not really home."

"We'll visit soon enough."

"You're back in a Rebel camp."

"I'm where I want to be."

"Oh?" He arched a brow, pulling her naked body closer to his. "Here, exactly here?"

She nodded solemnly, then looked steadily into his eyes. "Julian, I love you."

"My God, Rhiannon—"

"Wait . . . hear me out. There was a time when I wanted to die. When I hated the world, and I hated myself, and I couldn't bear the pain. Then you came riding in. And you made me see what I was doing, and . . . you gave me back love, Julian. Respect. For myself. You gave me love again, and more, you gave me life. And I do love you. Far more than any cause, than any war or battle. I look in your eyes and I see the pain there for others, and I love you more for it. We're not enemies. We both know that the war is wrong. You have given me back everything, even my belief in my fellow man, and wherever you are is where I want to be."

The moon shifted; the river seemed to glitter. The night was in his eyes, and he seemed to look at her forever, and then he pulled her to him, beneath him, and he was kissing her again and whispering against her lips. "I can't believe it. I never thought that I could dispel the ghost of Richard. It was torture, wanting you, being seduced, for you are a witch, my love, and from the moment I saw you, I was beneath your spell, and every minute away from you seemed to weave me more tightly into that spell until I wondered if I could survive, wanting you so much . . ."

She didn't respond with words. Her soul seemed alive with the moonlight that had come to glitter upon the water. She swept her arms around him, stroked the length of his back, felt the ripple of muscle beneath her lips as she kissed his shoulders, moved against him, kissed, touched, stroked, aroused . . .

His hands were upon her. The tip of his tongue was a sure stroke of fire against her flesh, teasing, intimate, seducing, demanding, finding every intimacy. And again he was in her. And the world was full of magic, and she was glad for this wild, wicked haven within the desperate storm of life around them, and she knew then that love and peace were in the soul, and though she couldn't change the world, she had changed herself.

They made love into the wee hours of the morning. And when they dressed and left the water at last, it was as if they had been baptized into a new life.

The days that followed were good. The camp was reestablished. Captain Dixie, or Jonathan Dickinson, the militia captain who almost single-handedly managed to keep much of Florida under Rebel control, came through with some of his wounded and reported on matters within the state. Yes, there were reports that the Yanks intended to make a major sweep into the state. They had to cut off the Confederacy. Florida was the breadbasket. The elusive coastline made it a maddening place to the Yanks.

Injured came in from the skirmishing. The days passed without incidence.

Then she was haunted by another dream.

There was shelling upon the water's edge. A ship had come into the river and was shelling salt works. There was an explosion, bodies flew everywhere, the dream seemed bathed in blood.

Julian was in her dream. Leading men to find the fallen. Then again . . .

There was an explosion. Sharp golden light burst across her vision in the dream, then faded, and she knew that . . .

Julian was dead.

She woke with a start. He wasn't beside her. She rose, threw on her dress, and came running out. To her horror she saw that he and a handful of men—all that manned the camp in the woods—were saddling their poor horses, ready to ride.

She ran to his side. "Julian, you can't go."

"Rhiannon!" he said, startled. The men were all staring at him. He dismounted from his horse, taking her hands. "I have to go. There's a report of a Yankee ship on the river."

"Don't go."

"I have to go."

"But you trust me. You can't go."

"I can't shirk my duty. I can't hide behind your skirts."

"I had a dream!"

He shook his head impatiently. "I won't be in the action, my love. But if there are injuries, this camp will be too far from the action."

"Julian!" she snapped, dismayed. He straightened, and she realized that, of course, she was making a scene in front of his men, that he had refused to see his own danger, even if he did trust in her visions. He was leaving. She hadn't the power to stop him. Or did she?

She stepped back. He shook his head, coming toward her again. Taking her by the arms, he kissed her. She kissed him back, suddenly passionate. He eased from her arms and mounted his horse.

When the men had ridden out, she went for her horse.

Liam watched her worriedly. "Rhiannon—"

"Don't ask, Liam."

"I can't let you go."

"I am already gone!"

But she had barely started down the trail when she realized that there was a horseman after her. She tried to race her nag; she was too easily run down. She turned, just before she was accosted, to realize that it was Julian. He had waited in the woods; he had come after her.

He caught her horse's reins, jerked the animal to a stop, dismounted from his own horse and jerked her from the saddle.

"So you would have me captured again!" he accused her furiously.

"I would have you alive!" she retorted.

"Well, you won't be going to the Yanks this time!" he told her angrily. She spun around. His men had ridden up behind them.

"Liam, take her back. Hog-tie her if you have to. Don't let her go to St. Augustine to report our movements!"

He thrust her toward Liam, who unhappily accepted his responsibility.

"Sir, she's hard to hold—"

"As I said," Julian stated determinedly, "tie her up if you have to!"

He spun around, mounting his horse again. And then . . . he was gone.

Liam would not let her leave, no matter how she begged and pleaded. She described her dream. And when she closed her eyes and it came again, she began to cry.

By the time night came the next day, she was certain that he was dead. She had never had such a dream that hadn't come true. She cried through the night.

At dawn she went to the creek. She watched the sunrise, and she thought of how they had been enemies, and then she thought of all that they had shared. They loved this place. The pine blanketed forests, the colors of the water, of the birds, of the day, the night, the sunrise, the sunset, the water . . .

The baby moved within her. Yet even that did not give her what she longed for, a passion to live. He had in truth given her the desire to love life itself again.

Without him . . .

She spun around suddenly, sensing warmth.

He was there. Leaning against a tree, arms crossed over his chest, watching her. He was an illusion, she thought. An image against the sunrise, life and day to her.

Yet he wasn't. He walked to her, calling her name. "Rhiannon!"

She turned, amazed that he was alive. She raced to him, and when she reached him, he swept her into his arms and then around and around in circles. She touched his face, his body, touched him again, assured herself that he was real, that he lived.

He touched her cheek.

"I saw the dream, saw the explosions . . . saw you die! Oh, God, Julian, I can't bear the dreams. Why do they torment me so?"

His palm caressed her cheek. "Maybe they aren't such torment. Maybe they are special warnings. You are gifted.

Rhiannon, what you saw might well have been. But I didn't exactly go, I never reached the point of the explosion. I realized how desperate you were," he told her, eyes dark upon hers. "I rode with the men, but as we neared the ship, I commanded them to hold back. The Yankees exploded a salt works. But not one man was killed, Rhiannon. My love, you saved all our lives." He tilted her chin and smiled. "My love, I promise that I will listen to you from here on out."

"Oh, Julian, but there's still a war!"

"My war will be here, Rhiannon. I know what I'm fighting for now. Life. For us, for our baby, for those around us. I will do my best never to doubt you again, and never, ever leave you."

"Julian . . ."

She slipped her arms around him. He kissed her, long, lingeringly. His lips broke from hers.

"There is still a war."

"But we will survive it."

The sun rose high above the water.

"I wonder what will happen," she murmured, feeling his arms around her.

"Can you tell me the future?" he asked.

She shook her head. "I wish that I could. I don't know the ending of this, when, how. I'm so afraid that it will go on . . . but I can't see the future. Honestly, I cannot."

"I can."

"Oh?" she said skeptically and turned in his arms.

"Certainly," he said, and he was smiling. "We're going to make love, tell each other how much we love one another."

"Ah!" she murmured.

"Well?"

"That is certainly future enough for me," she told him, and rising on her toes, she kissed his lips, prepared to meet his future.

Florida Chronology

～

(And Events That Influenced Her People)

1492	Christopher Columbus discovers the "New World."
1513	Florida discovered by Ponce de Leon. Juan Ponce de Leon sights Florida from his ship on March 27, steps on shore near present-day St. Augustine in early April.
1539	Hernando de Soto lands on west coast of the peninsula, near present-day Tampa.
1564	The French arrive and establish Fort Caroline on the St. Johns River. Immediately following the establishment of the French fort, Spain dispatches Pedro Menendez de Aviles to get rid of the French invaders, "pirates and perturbers of the public peace." De Aviles dutifully captures the French stronghold and slays or enslaves the inhabitants.
1565	Pedro Menendez de Aviles founds St. Augustine, the first permanent European settlement in what is now the United States.
1586	Sir Francis Drake attacks St. Augustine, burning and plundering the settlement.
1698	Pensacola is founded.
1740	British General James Oglethorpe invades Florida from Georgia.
1763	At the end of the Seven Years' War, or the French and Indian War, the Florida Territories are ceded to Britain.
1763–1783	British Rule in East and West Florida.

1774	The "shot heard round the world" is fired in Concord, Massachusetts Colony
1776	The War of Independence begins; many British Loyalists flee to Florida.
1783	By the Treaty of Paris, Florida is returned to the Spanish.
1812–1815	The War of 1812.
1813–1814	The Creek Wars. "Red-Stick" land is decimated. Numerous Indians seek new lands south with the "Seminoles."
1814	General Andrew Jackson captures Pensacola.
1815	The Battle of New Orleans.
1817–1818	The First Seminole War. Americans accuse the Spanish of aiding the Indians in their raids across the border. Hungry for more territory, settlers seek to force Spain into ceding the Floridas to the United States by their claims against the Spanish government for its inability to properly handle the situation within the territories.
1819	Don Luis de Onis, Spanish minister to the United States, and Secretary of State John Quincy Adams, sign a treaty by which the Floridas will become part of the United States
1821	The Onis–Adams Treaty is ratified. An act of congress makes the two Floridas one territory. Jackson becomes the military governor, but relinquishes the post after a few months.
1822	The first legislative council meets at Pensacola. Members from St. Augustine travel fifty-nine days by water to attend.
1823	The second legislative council meets at St. Augustine; the western delegates are shipwrecked and barely escape death.
1824	The third session meets at Tallahassee, a half-way point selected as a main order of buisness and approved at the second session. Tallahassee becomes the first territorial capital.
1825	The Treaty of Moultrie Creek is ratified by major Seminole chiefs and the Federal Government. The ink is barely dry before Indians are complaining that the lands are too small

and white settlers are petitioning the government for a policy of Indian removal.

1832   Payne's Landing: Numerous chiefs sign a treaty agreeing to move west to Arkansas as long as seven of their number are able to see and approve the lands. The treaty is ratified at Fort Gibson, Arkansas. Numerous chiefs also protest the agreement.

1835   Summer: Wiley Thompson claims that Seminole chief Osceola has repeatedly reviled him in his own office with foul language and orders his arrest. Osceola is handcuffed and incarcerated.

November: Charlie Emathla, after agreeing to removal to the west, is murdered. Most scholars agree Osceola led the party that carried out the execution. Some consider the murder a personal vengeance, others believe it was proscribed by numerous chiefs since an Indian who would leave his people to aid the whites should forfeit his own life.

December 28: Major Francis Dade and his troops are massacred as they travel from Fort Brooke to Fort King. Wiley Thompson and a companion are killed outside the walls of Fort King. The sutler Erastus Rogers and his two clerks are also murdered by members of the same raiding party, led by Osceola.

December 31: The First Battle of the Withlacoochee—Osceola leads the Seminoles.

1836   January: Major General Winfield Scott is ordered by the Secretary of War to take command in Florida.

February 4: Dade County established in South Florida in memory of Francis Langhorne Dade.

March 16: The Senate confirms Richard Keith Call governor of the Florida Territory.

June 21: Call, a civilian governor, is given command of the Florida forces after the failure of Scott's strategies and the military disputes between Scott and General Gaines.

Call attempts a "summer campaign," and is as frustrated in his efforts as his predecessor.

1837   June 2: Osceola and Sam Jones release, or "abduct" nearly seven hundred Indians awaiting deportation to the west from Tampa. October 27: Osceola is taken under a white flag of truce; Jesup is denounced by whites and Indians alike for the action.

November 29: Coacoochee, Cowaya, sixteen warriors, and two women escape Ft. Marion

Christmas Day: Jesup has the largest fighting force assembled in Florida during the conflict, nearly nine thousand men. Under his command, Colonel Zachary Taylor leads the Battle of Okeechobee. The Seminoles choose to stand their ground and fight, inflicting greater losses to whites despite the fact they are severely outnumbered.

1838   January 31: Osceola dies at Fort Marion, South Carolina. (A strange side note to a sad tale: Dr. Wheedon, presiding white physician for Osceola, cut off and preserved Osceola's head. Wheedon's heirs reported that the good doctor would hang the head on the bedstead of one of his three children should they misbehave. The head passed to his son-in-law, Dr. Daniel Whitehurst, who gave it to Dr. Valentine Mott. Dr. Mott had a medical and pathological museum, and it is believed that the head was lost when his museum burned in 1866.)

May: Zachary Taylor takes command when Jesup's plea to be relieved is answered at last on April 29.

The Florida legislature debates statehood.

1839   December: Because of his arguments with Federal authorities regarding the Seminole War, Richard Keith Call is removed as governor. Robert Raymond Reid is appointed in his stead.

1840   April 24: Zachary Taylor is given permission to leave command of what is considered to be the harshest military position in the country. Walker Keith Armistead takes command.

December 1840–January 1841: John T. MacLaughlin leads a flotilla of men in dugouts across the Everglades from east to west; his party becomes the first white men to do so.

September: William Henry Harrison is elected President of the United States; the Florida War is considered to have cost Martin Van Buren re-election.

John Bell replaces Joel Poinsett as Secretary of War. Robert Reid is ousted as territorial governor, and Richard Keith Call is re-instated.

1841 April 4: President William Henry Harrison dies in office: John Tyler becomes President of the United States.

May 1: Coacoochee determines to turn himself in. He is escorted by a man who will later become extremely well known— Lieutenant William Tecumseh Sherman. (Sherman writes to his future wife that the Florida war is a good one for a soldier; he will get to know the Indian who may become the "chief enemy" in time.)

May 31: Walker Keith Armistead is relieved. Colonel William Jenkins Worth takes command.

1842 May 10: Winfield Scott is informed that the administration has decided there must be an end to hostilities as soon as possible.

August 14: Aware that he cannot end hostilities and send all Indians west, Colonel Worth makes offers to the remaining Indians to leave or accept boundaries. The war, he declares, is over.

It has cost a fledgling nation thirty to forty million dollars and the lives of seventy-four commissioned officers. The Seminoles have been reduced from tens of thousands to hundreds scattered about in pockets. The Seminoles (inclusive here, as they were seen during the war, as all Florida Indians) have, however, kept their place in the peninsula; those remaining are the undefeated. The army, too, has learned new tactics, mostly regarding partisan and guerilla warfare. Men who will soon take part in the greatest conflict to tear apart the nation have practiced the art of battle here: William T. Sherman, Braxton Bragg, George Gordon Meade, Joseph E. Johnston, and more, as well as soon-to-be President Zachary Taylor.

1845   March 3: President John Tyler signs the bill that makes Florida the twenty-seventh state of the United States of America.

1855–58 The conflict known as the Third Seminole War takes place with a similiar outcome to the earlier confrontations—money spent, lives lost, and the Indians entrenched more deeply into the Everglades.

1859   Robert E. Lee is sent in to arrest John Brown after his attempt to innitiate a slave rebellion with an assault on Harpers Ferry, Virginia (later West Virginia). The incident escalates ill will between the North and South. Brown is executed December 2.

1860   The first Florida cross-state railroad goes into service.

        November 6: Abraham Lincoln is elected to the presidency and many Southern states begin to call for special legislative sessions. Although there are many passionate Unionists in the state, most Florida politicians are ardent in lobbying for secession. Towns, cities, and counties rush to form or enlarge militia companies. Even before the state is able to meet for its special session, civil and military leaders plan to demand the turnover of Federal military installations.

1861   January 10: Florida votes to secede from the Union, the third Southern state to do so.

        February: Florida joins the Confederate States of America.

        Through late winter and early spring, the Confederacy struggles to form a government and organize the armed forces while the states recruit fighting men. Jefferson Davis is president of the newly formed country. Stephen Mallory of Florida becomes C.S.A. Secretary of the Navy.

April 12–14: Confederate forces fire on Fort Sumter, South Carolina, and the first blood is shed when an accidental explosion kills Private Hough, who then has the distinction of being the first Federal soldier killed.

Federal forces fear a similiar action at Fort Pickens, Pensacola Bay, Florida. Three forts guarded the bay—McRee and Barrancas on the land side, and Pickens on the tip of forty-mile long Santa Rosa Island. Federal Lieutenant Adam J. Slemmer spiked the guns at Barrancas, blew up the ammunition at McRee, and moved his meager troops to Pickens, where he was eventually reinforced by five hundred men. Though Florida troops took the navy yard, retention of the fort by the Federals nullified the usefulness to the Rebs of what was considered the most important navy yard south of Norfolk.

July 21: First Manassas, or the First Battle of Bull Run, Virginia—both sides get their first real taste of battle. Southern troops are drawn from throughout the states, including Florida. Already, the state, which had been so eager to secede, sees her sons being shipped northward to fight and her coast being left to its own defenses by a government with different priorities.

November: Robert E. Lee inspects coastal defenses as far south as Fernandina and decides the major ports of Charleston, Savannah, and Brunswick are to be defended, adding later that the small force posted at St. Augustine was like an invitation to attack.

1862 February: Florida's Governor Milton publicly states his despair for Florida citizens as more of the state's troops are ordered north after Grant captures two major Confederate strongholds in Tennessee.

February 28: A fleet of twenty-six Federal ships sets sail to occupy Fernandina, Jacksonville, and St. Augustine.

March 8: St. Augustine surrenders, and though Jacksonville and other points north and south along the coast will change hands several times during the war, St. Augustine will remain in Union hands. The St. Johns River becomes a ribbon of guerilla troop movement for both sides. Many Floridians begin to despair of "East Florida," fearing that the fickle populace has all turned Unionist.

March 8: Under the command of Franklin Buchanan, the *CSS Virginia,* formerly the scuttled Union ship *Merrimac,* sailed into Hampton Roads to battle the Union ships blocading the channel. She devastates Federal ships until the arrival of the poorly prepared and leaking Federal entry into the "ironclad" fray, the *USS Monitor.* The historic battle of the ironclads ensues. Neither ship emerged a clear victor; the long-term advantage went to the Union since the Confederacy was then unable to break the blocade when it had appeared, at first, that the *Virginia* might have sailed all the way to devastate Washington, D.C.

April 2: Apalachicola is attacked by a Federal landing force. The town remains a no-man's-land throughout the war.

April 6–8: Union and Confederate forces engage in the battle of Shiloh. Both claim victories. Both suffer horrible losses with over twenty-thousand killed, wounded or missing.

April 25: New Orleans falls, and the Federal grip on the south becomes more of a vise.

Spring: The Federal blockade begins to tighten and much of the state becomes a no-man's-land. Despite its rugged terrain, the length of the peninsula, and the simple difficulty of logistics, blockade runners know that they can dare Florida waterways simply because the Union can't possibly guard the extensive coastline of the state. Florida's contribution becomes more and more that of a breadbasket as she strips herself and provides salt, beef, smuggled supplies, and manpower to the Confederacy.

May 9: Pensacola is evacuated by the Rebs and occupied by Federal forces.

May 20: Union landing party is successfully attacked by Confederates near St. Marks.

May 22: Union Flag Officer DuPont writes to his superiors with quotes that had the Union not abandoned Jacksonville, the state would have split and East Florida would have entered the war on the Union side.

Into summer: Fierce action continues in Virginia: Battle of Fair Oaks, or Seven Pines, May 31, the Seven Days Battles, May 25–June 7, the Battle of Mechanicsville, June 26, Gaines Mill, or Cold Harbor, June 27. More Florida troops leave the state to replace the men killed in action in these battles and in other engagements in Alabama, Louisiana, and along the Mississippi. Salt becomes evermore necessary: Florida has numerous salt works along the Gulf side of the state. Union ships try to find them, confiscate what they can, and destroy them.

August 30: Second Battle of Manassas, or Bull Run.

September 16–17: The Battle of Antietam, or Sharpsburg, takes place in Maryland where the "single bloodiest day of fighting" occurs.

September 23: The Preliminary text of the Emancipation Proclamation is published. It will take effect on January 1, 1863. Lincoln previously drafted the document, but waited for a Union victory to publish it; both sides claimed Antietam, but the Rebels were forced to withdraw back to Virginia.

October 5: Federals recapture Jacksonville.

December 11–15: The Battle of Fredericksburg.

December 31: The Battle of Murfreesborough, or Stones River, Tennessee.

1863   March 20: A Union landing party at St. Andrew's Bay, Florida, is attacked and most Federals are captured or killed.

March 31: Jacksonville is evacuated by the Union forces again.

May 1–4: The Battle of Chancellorsville. Lee soundly beats Hooker, but on May 2, General Stonewall Jackson is accidently shot and mortally wounded by his own men. He dies on the tenth.

June: Southern commanders determine anew to bring the war to the Northern front. A campaign begins, which will march the Army of Northern Virginia through Virginia, Maryland, and on to Pennsylvania. In the west, the campaign along the Mississippi continues with Vicksburg under seige. In Florida, there is little action other than skirmishing and harrying attacks along the coast. More Florida boys are conscripted into the regular army. The state continues to produce cattle and salt and provide for the Confederacy.

July 1: Confederates move toward Gettysburg along the Chambersburg Pike. Four miles west of town they meet John Buford's Union calvary.

July 2: At Gettysburg, places like the Peach Orchard and Devil's Den become names that live in history.

July 3: Pickett's disasterous charge.

July 4: Lee determines to retreat to Virginia.

July 4: Vicksburg surrenders.

July continues: The Union soldiers take a very long time to chase Lee. What might have been an opportunity to end the war is lost.

July 13: Draft riots in New York.

August 8: Lee attempts to resign. President Jefferson Davis rejects his resignation.

August continues into fall: Renewed Union interest in Florida begins to develop as assaults on Charleston and forts in South Carolina bring recognition by the North that Florida is a hotbed for blockade runners, salt, and cattle. Union commanders in the South begin to plan a Florida campaign.

SUSAN KING

☐LAIRD OF THE WIND   0-451-40768-7/$5.99

In medieval Scotland, the warrior known as Border Hawk setzes the castle belonging to the father of the beautiful Isabel Scott, famous throughout the Lowlands for her gift of prophecy. During the battle, Isabel is injured while fighting alongside her men and placed under Border Hawk's protection. As the border wars rage on, the warrior and prophetess engage in a more intimate conflict, discovering their love for the Scottish borderlands is surpassed only by their love for each other.

Also available:
☐THE ANGEL KNIGHT   0-451-40662-1/$5.50
☐LADY MIRACLE   0-451-40766-0/$5.99
☐THE RAVEN'S MOON   0-451-18868-3/$5.99
☐THE RAVEN'S WISH   0-451-40545-5/$4.99

Coming in April 1999 HEATHER MOON
☐0-451-40774-1/$6.99

Prices slightly higher in Canada

TOPAZ